Jame
Barty – A Tale

To my father Peter Braxton who sent me to school with a copy of
The Concise Oxford Dictionary inscribed

"To J.W.B.
Use daily.
Love Dad."

First published for the
Ceylon Literary & Art Festival 2024.

HSBC

Ceylon
LITERARY & ART FESTIVAL

Thanks to my first readers: Annabel Emslie, Carro Wolstenholme,
Paula Rehberg, Chas Parker and Richard Knight who corrected this reprint.
To my daughter Annie for the linocut front cover illustration and cover design.
To all my children Amelia, Charlie, Ned and Annie for their support and
just being delightful.
Finally, to my wife & editor Joanna, who was nicknamed Barty at school
and has been both my fiercest critic and loudest champion. Without her love
and support I would never have written this book.

First published in Great Britain, 2024 by James Braxton.
Reprinted 2024.

The moral right of the author has been asserted.
ISBN 978-1-0686480-0-7

Front cover linocut © Annie Braxton
Cover design & layout © Annie Braxton
@ @aobdesign
annieobraxton@gmail.com

Chapter 1

Hastings

Barty had always struggled with his weight. The elasticated waistband on his trunk-style underpants bore the horizontal crease associated with a love of good food and wine. He was too young to adopt the 'Willie Whitelaw', high waistband and braces combination. Instead, a navy-blue waistcoat had the same slimming effect. A fellow pedestrian might comment that Barty was neither fat nor thin, just well covered, in a sort of 'garden-toned' way. An observer might say, his step had a sense of purpose, as he walked down Queens Road.

Queens Road bisects the busy seaside town of Hastings, with West Hill and Old Town to his left and St Leonards to his right. Such is the spread of the town of Hastings, it has not one but three stations: West St Leonards, St Leonards Warrior Square and Hastings. It was towards the latter that Barty strode, not for a train but for the museum beyond. It was a June day just after 11am, the roads had quietened, with the public sector safely stationed in front of their computer screens. The steady incline from the station to museum grounds prompted tiny beads of sweat, quickly removed with a white and green spotted cotton handkerchief. Although he had no children and their associated sticky hands, there was always a spillage, and his cotton square was his first responder. The museum building was top-spec Edwardian: red brick and dressed stone, finished with a castellated parapet. A castle by the sea, below which were terrace upon terrace of houses marching gradually down to the shingle beach.

As Barty moved into a more dogged pace appropriate for a steepening incline, he lightly ran through the day's specials. Walled garden salad, with orange nasturtium flowers, purple peas, and plucked leaves. Momentarily checking the potential bitterness with a sweet lemon dressing, as he remembered the box of 50 lemons awaiting zesting and squeezing, his thoughts were interrupted.

"Watch yer guv'nor," came a young voice from an open window of a large white van, "could you tell me where I could find Norman Road?"

Flustered from the direct approach, yet retaining poise Barty replied: "Left at the next junction, follow gravity down the hill. When you see the sea, turn left, left at the lights and then next left, by the antiques centre with a blue mural." The young voice turned down his music, more Beyoncé than Marvin Gaye, and said, "sorry again, guv'nor?"

"All the lefts," came the reply.

The distillation of these directions confused the young voice, whose owner was a wiry youth, who suddenly started wrestling with his companion, a small dog anxious to meet the relayer of directions. Maybe the dog had a whiff of the next item on the specials board: ribeye steak.

"Sorry guv'nor, Clive here, is always keen to meet people," said the young voice, who had now stopped his van.

"I'm told Lionel, the antiques man in Norman Road, is halfway up on the left-hand side?"

The mention of Lionel had, for Barty, given this odd exchange some substance. Lionel, a ruddy faced gentleman, was a well-known antiques dealer in the town, plus a very dear friend, who normally wore linen in the summer and wool in the winter.

Barty looked at his watch. It was past noon. Lionel would no longer be on the left-hand side; his correct position after noon was straight ahead, in the Horse and Groom pub.

The young voice, who had now brought Clive under control, said

"Guv'nor, my name's Jack, and my mate, said Lionel is the man for bronzes."

Barty was now warming to this young man. There was a certain chutzpah about this wiry youth.

"Lionel is like the sun, rising in the east and setting in the west, but between the two he seeks shade," said Barty.

Chutzpah Jack looked puzzled and Clive became still.

"Lionel's shade is in the Horse and Groom pub, at the top of Norman Road."

Barty felt a sudden dryness in his mouth. Like young Jack, Barty had been up since six o'clock. It was summer after all. Winter is the time to linger in the basket but summer is the time for toning. The earlier you rise, the more calories you will inevitably burn.

"I will hop in, and take you there. Lionel will be amongst company by now, and a formal introduction may help your cause."

Barty was pleased for a lift. He rarely walked from the Imperial to the museum and he had forgotten how long it was. A 'hop', it wasn't. More a struggle up to the Mercedes Sprinter's footplate, but the seat and armrest were worth it. The latter providing a fragile barrier to the immediate attention from Clive. The dog was right, Barty had been trimming a rib of beef earlier.

The Horse and Groom is one of those pubs that doesn't shriek 'Open'. There are no signs announcing 'Home-cooked' food or 'Thursday's quiz night'. It's a pub that shields its merits from passers-by. Lionel was easily found, not by sight, but more by sound.

"I was telling Norman that the win of an old Austin Maxi car is stealth. Nobody thinks he has two pennies, but he took over £200 from me this morning, and I know I'm not his only buyer."

Lionel's companions nodded, as they knew when Lionel was talking, it was their role to be listening.

"Norman has enough for a Bentley..."

Clive let out an excited series of barks and heads turned. Lionel greeted Barty with a raised hand across a crowded front bar. Barty made a glass waving motion back towards Lionel, to which he mouthed, "Many thanks, just a white for me".

As he mimed this, he gave the landlord a nod, so that no party was in any doubt as to which white wine he wanted: a white Burgundy of course.

Barty had a Harvey's, East Sussex's finest best bitter, and Jack a Guinness. He needed a bit of 'food' as he hadn't had breakfast. Barty could smell the freshness of the beer. He had almost walked to the museum and certainly needed the restorative sugars.

"Lionel, this young man is Jack," said Barty.

"Marvellous," said Lionel, "but who's that chatty fellow?" looking down at the dog.

"That's Clive," Barty replied.

Clive remained very close to Barty; the smell of the rib of beef hadn't waned. Lionel would have stroked the dog, but there was little play in his suit and the dog was a little low. Clive knew he was being talked about, but he kept his eye on the prize, Barty.

"This young man has a bronze he wishes to sell you."

Lionel liked a heavy material and bronzes were among his favourites.

"What's the subject young man?"

"Horse and jockey," replied Jack

"Does the group have any age?"

"I'm not sure. It's been outside, so it's more green than brown."

"Ah, the verdigris."

At this point Lionel turned to his chums. They were waiting; Lionel was about to give a lesson and they were all ears.

"Verdigris is the name given to the oxidised copper which is the principal metal in bronze, with a little tin thrown in. Always remember, Mardi Gras is the carnival, and Verdigris is the oxide."

This was all meat and drink to Lionel, but Jack was more anxious about the amount of money he had peeled off for the bronze. Jack was new to the antiques trade. He liked getting up early, going to car boots and weekly markets, but he rarely paid more than £100 pounds for anything and he had paid £400 for the bronze. He thought it was large enough, certainly heavy enough, and he hoped, was of a commercial subject. Jack could see the party was settling in and he should bide his time. Who knows, Lionel might pay even more after a couple of drinks. Jack's eyes wandered around the front bar.

There were cartoons of the landlord and past regulars, some in pen and ink and some with a colour wash. They were the ephemera of a steady freehold pub whose interior had never been subjected to a 'group pub' refurbishment. There were ordinary solid oak tables, with scrubbed, not polished, tops and the seating was a mixture of chairs and settles. The bench-like settles were the best Jack had ever seen. Mostly they appeared to be made of walnut and oak. You could tell the walnut ones: they had a deep glossy polish, not from a weekly wax but from daily use. The backs of these settles had beautifully carved panels. One was of the Dutch style tavern interior, carousing men and wenches, and another of a harvest scene; not mechanical combine harvesters, but men, women and children with scythes and sickles. All the settles had lidded box seats, covered with flat squab cushions.

The sun was streaming in the back windows. Jack moved towards a glazed door and found a sheltered courtyard. He and Clive stepped outside and Jack rolled a cigarette. He preferred liquorice papers and Golden Virginia tobacco. There was an element of craft in rolling your own and hopefully less chemicals. Jack wanted around £800-£1,000 for the bronze, but he had never negotiated with Lionel before. With petrol and time, the bronze needed to be a least £600 to cover expenses. He knew, from watching others to get in early. Often the first number mentioned, became the benchmark figure around which parties haggled.

Jack returned to the bar and found Lionel and Barty were deep in conversation. "Hello young Jack," Barty said, "come on Lionel, isn't it time you looked at the young man's bronze?"

Lionel was reluctant to move. Drink and chatter was his preferred state, but the mention of the bronze earlier had been nagging him. It was only when they emerged into the daylight that Lionel's tweed suit came alive, with flecks of yellow, red, and blue, he glowed like a grouse against a Lancashire moor. Jack opened the split back doors of the van and removed a blanket revealing the bronze group.

"It's big," said Lionel.

"I was told by the seller that it's a quarter scale of a real race horse and jockey."

"It must weigh a ton," said Lionel. "It looks good raised on the van. Do you have a stand for it?"

"No."

Lionel was a master at quickly introducing a negative, before the bartering began. Barty could see Lionel was metaphorically slipping on the fez, the traditional headwear for a haggle. Jack knew he must get in early.

"I would like a thousand pounds for it."

"Wouldn't we all like a thousand pounds," replied Lionel, winking at Barty.

"Come, feel the weight of it."

"In this suit! I will take your word on the weight. Maybe, push it to the rear of the van, and I will give it a heave."

Lionel gripped the horse's back legs and heaved. It was reassuringly heavy, and he knew he could retail this for £2,000 to £3,000. It was of little age, possibly 1980s, from China or the Philippines, but well cast; impressively large and heavy too.

"£450, cash," Lionel said.

"He doesn't take cards," Clive would have barked, but he recognised his master needed no distractions.

"I could scrap it for that. £850."

Lionel liked this part. A couple of light blows exchanged; Lionel in the middle of the ring making the young man dance around him. Lionel was in control and the deal was coming to him.

"£600," he jabbed.

"I was told you're the man for bronzes and I was keen to start a relationship, as I'm more a runner than a retailer."

Barty, Jack and Clive looked at Lionel. It was now his turn to be wrong footed. Lionel paused. It now dawned on him that this could be the start of a new trading relationship.

"£750, on condition you bring the next one to me first?"

Jack jumped off the van and shook Lionel's hand.

"Thank you."

Chapter 2

Norfolk

Sir Roger Swotter liked the early mornings. He could pad about making tea without being Sir Roger. His cook, May, liked to take ownership of the kitchen at 8am. She lived with her border terrier, Punch, in a semi-detached cottage half way down the drive. As she walked towards the Towers she knew Sir Roger would be in her kitchen, making tea, and worst of all, in a mug!

May always walked to the Towers. She liked the coolness of her morning walk in the summer months, as the kitchen could sometimes attain Saudi-like temperatures thanks to the Aga range cooker. The gardens and parkland were maintained by Cecil the gardener, Lou the gamekeeper and a herd of fallow deer. Sir Roger had known both Cecil and Lou's fathers, and like them, they had all helped shape this beautiful piece of Norfolk. Skills handed down by each generation, and when concentrated in joint venture, produced an extraordinary landscape.

Sir Roger, as his father had, liked isolated oaks in the parkland, ash trees in the hedgerows and no sycamores anywhere. As he often said: "A sycamore is only good for a breadboard; all those antibacterial properties. One can't take a timber seriously without a grain." Oak, ash and elm have grains which record their stories: of dry summers, wet winters, and even nibbling squirrels.

The Swotters consisted of Sir Roger, his wife Lady Daphne, Sampson, the black Labrador, and numerous pugs, all with names but generally called 'darling' by Lady Daphne. Sir Roger, in spite of 30 years of marriage, was still to attain the same level of verbal intimacy.

The current baronet, Sir Roger, had inherited this perfect slice of Norfolk, north of Holt and west of Sherringham, from Sir Patrick Swotter, who had fought bravely in Burma during World War II and had had to fight even harder against Her Majesty's Revenue & Customs to retain his 2,000-acre estate of Kooling Towers. As Sir Roger knew, Kooling Towers lived up to its name in winter; a chilly east wind was a fearsome foe to both his household and the oil-fired central heating system. As Sir he said, "There is nothing like a drop in temperature to bring a family together."

It was in the library that the family gathered, with its magic combination of mid 17th century oak panelling and a good log fire. The fire was laid every morning by Cecil and consisted of a layered affair of newspaper, split pine kindling and ash logs, with a twisted newspaper tail, that required only one match from Sir Roger. Once struck, it wasn't long before the room boasted flushed humans and snoozing dogs.

To get to the kitchen door May walked down an avenue of pleached hornbeam. At the end of the avenue was a sarcophagus-shaped flint plinth with a racing bronze. Except this morning, there was no bronze. The bronze was modelled as a horse with jockey-up and at Kooling Towers it was known as Lester Piggott and Nijinsky, as every year Cecil drove Sir Roger and Lady

Daphne to Royal Ascot and May served the picnic. One year she and Cecil had placed £20 pounds on Lester Piggott to win The King George VI and Queen Elizabeth stakes, and had returned to Norfolk a little richer.

May walked up the avenue ignoring the morning dew. Something she normally avoided, as wet feet at the beginning of the day wasn't a great start. The bronze had definitely gone. Loose bricks had been hastily replaced after the heavy bronze was prized away from its plinth. May hurried back to the kitchen, and called Cecil. "Cecil, will you check Lester Piggott, I think the bronze has been taken."

Cecil lived in the other half of the semi-detached cottage. He and May were close, or as close as you can get with the ever-watchful Punch. He grabbed his bike and pedalled down the drive. As he rode he remembered hearing May's dog barking. He had dismissed it as Punch smelling a fox outside, but now he had a nagging feeling that it may have been a vehicle.

May was right, the bronze had gone. He could see lots of footprints highlighted in the morning dew. Cecil made for the kitchen. May was preparing Lady Daphne's breakfast tray: a silver shaped porcelain teapot, toast and home-made marmalade, delicious but runny. May never used pectin, just brown sugar. She used ingredients she knew, always chasing taste not appearance. May had reported the disappearance to Cecil and, for her, the problem was passed.

"It's definitely been taken," said Cecil.

"As soon as Lou arrives we will check the rest of the garden, before informing Sir Roger."

Cecil nodded. She knew Cecil had seized the baton. Lou entered the kitchen from his morning rounds.

"Some oik has clipped the verge, at the end of the drive."

"That figures, Lester Piggott has gone," replied Cecil.

"Lou, we must check the rest of the garden for any other missing items. Then we need to tell Sir Roger."

May poured mugs of tea. She knew the bronze or bronzes were long gone and there was always time for tea.

The garden was Cecil's turf and everything beyond was Lou's. Cecil checked the pair of bronze urns first; these were stationed either side of the front door. The urns, standing over a metre high, were much prized and believed to be extremely valuable. Lady Daphne's mother had bought them at the great Mentmore sale, conducted by Sotheby's in 1977. It was with some relief that Cecil directed Lou to check the rose garden as, amongst the geometric box hedging, there was a rather inappropriate statue of a nymph and satyr. Sir Roger had been after a couple of reconstituted stone statues of loosely draped Grecian maidens. The local sale room's estimate was tempting, but they had gone way beyond their estimates, unlike the group amongst the box hedging. The auctioneer had struggled below their lower estimate and who could resist a bargain? The gliding hand of the satyr had put off most, but not Sir Roger. In the morning sunshine, the satyr seemed to wink back at Lou as he moved on. Thankfully all was correct in the garden.

Cecil and Lou regrouped in the kitchen, where May was fussing around Sir Roger. "May has just informed me that Piggott and Nijinsky have been stolen."

"That's correct, Sir Roger," said Cecil.

"It will be Terry and his boys."

"Whoever stole it would have had to be strong, as it took four of us to mount it on the plinth. It might be the boys, Clem, Tom and Scan, but certainly not Terry. He's been confined to barracks since his latest heart attack."

"No wonder it's been quiet recently. I always felt that it wasn't the theft with Terry, more the challenge." Sir Roger picked up the kitchen telephone and dialled his local police station. A message was taken and a promise of a return call from CID was given.

Cecil and Lou looked at each other. Security was more Lou's field, he being the keeper. Lou had known Clem, Tom and Scan since they were boys, first with catapults and then with air rifles, but this theft was out of character.

"Cecil and I will go and repair the verge. I'm sure the police don't pursue garden thefts, but we will take photographs all the same. Is there anything else you would like us to do Sir Roger?"

"No, bar going to The Swotter Arms afterwards and spreading the word. It might jog some memories and the gossip might put Terry and the boys on notice."

It took Cecil and Lou almost all day, plus half a ton of sharp sand to repair the verge. Although fit, they were reminded how heavy a barrow full of sand could be. First job done, the second seemed more reward than task. They left the tractor and trailer at the end of the drive and walked to The Swotter Arms.

Kooling Towers lays to the west of the village; a former Swotter was obviously keen on sunsets. In the middle of Kooling village stood the half-timbered 16th century Inn. At its centre stood an opening, which led to a cobbled courtyard. Rather like a fireplace in a sitting room, the opening centred the building. The first floor retained its jettied overhang; its architectural integrity prompted visions of thrown chamber pots and buxom wenches. When built in the reign of Henry VIII, it was christened the Lamb Inn, because of its proximity to the adjacent parish church but a rather glamorous former Swotter, Sir Noel, Sir Roger's grandfather, had changed its name to The Swotter Arms.

They entered the Inn through the arch, left for the public bar and right for the saloon bar and dining room. The right-hand side was governed by Anita. Anita had run the Printmaker's Arms in Fleet Street, London, for 20 years, but when the newspaper industry was reorganised to Wapping, Anita decided to move nearer her childhood home of Beccles. Sir Roger had thought about placing an advert in the Innkeeper magazine, but the landlord for him would take either the Telegraph or Private Eye, preferably both. Anita was the first and only to apply. Sir Roger asked her for an interview and after a guided tour of The Swotter Arms, he knew that the Inn would be in safe hands. Anita, always in thick corduroy trousers and sensible shoes, only had eyes for the strong and sturdy. Members of the scrum held her attention, wingers and three quarters were fun, but where was the bulk?

The Swotter Arms was Cecil's second home. Lou, as gamekeeper, knew it would be foolish to establish a routine so, reluctantly, was a more infrequent customer. Cecil normally turned left into the public bar but he knew Anita would like to hear the news first. Anita smiled as Cecil and Lou walked through the door. Nothing passed Anita, seated on the first barstool between door and bar.

"Afternoon Anita, Sir Roger has asked us to call."

Cecil knew to pause, as news delivered in segments had more drama. Anita turned to her once younger self.

"Jess, would you please pull two pints of Camel for Cecil and Lou?"

Lou looked at Cecil, he might string out the news. Why blurt it out for a pint, as he knew that a more staggered approach might yield at least two!

"You both look like you have news. Thank you Jess."

Lou and Cecil lifted their straight glasses and gulped. Camel, Lou's favourite pint, was a craft ale brewed in one of Sir Roger's commercial units by men with better beards than Jesus. As Lou, a frequent visitor to their unit always said: "They have a magic touch with barley & hops."

"A large quarter scale bronze of a horse and jockey was stolen from the Towers last night."

"Oh," Anita lifted her glass of Sauvignon Blanc, "that sounds heavy, well at least the horse does, as a quarter sized jockey must be under two foot, but a two or three year old colt or filly with all those muscles must be big!" Anita, although not a subscriber to the Racing Post, always read the racing pages in the Telegraph.

"Any clues who may have taken it?"

Whilst listening, Lou and Cecil had been drinking and as Anita finished they both lowered empty glasses on the bar.

"Jess, another two pints for the boys."

Jess was close by as current news was rare in The Swotter Arms. Normally, the talk at the bar was of gentle ribbing and oft-told tales. Rarely did Anita offer a second pint, but it seemed wholly appropriate now.

Lou continued: "Sir Roger thought that Terry's boys might be involved, but I have known those boys since they were small and am sure they would think twice, being so close, and all."

"Unless they were really desperate," suggested Cecil.

"I wouldn't know, I don't think Terry or his boys have ever entered The Swotter Arms," Anita finished her glass and placed it in front of Jess. "I know the boys drink at the Squirrel, have you called in there?" Jess refilled Anita's glass and rather wickedly paused as both Anita and Jess knew Cecil and Lou had history with the Squirrel.

The Squirrel, or the 'other place,' as it was known at The Swotter Arms, was on the eastern end of the village. Using the phrase 'west is best' one would guess the Squirrel wasn't for the local gentry. Now a Pub Co. tenanted pub, it had once been part of Enifers Brewery, which had thrived during the 20s and 30s. Enifers had employed a local architect to build a number of pubs in the manner of the great Edwin Lutyens. All red bricks, end-tiles and, at lintel level, ran a strip of green tiles spelling 'Enifers Ales and Stouts'. Having been both well-built and always tenanted, the interiors had largely remained the same too.

Customers entered through a central door, well hinged with copper push plate, into a small hall with oak panelling to dado level and a bench seat and opaque glazed panels above. Left for the tap room, and right for the saloon bar. The whole was loosely governed by Mike, a man of pale complexion who carried a pained expression, and never moved without wincing. He rarely left the premises, bar his weekly trip to Bookers Cash and Carry, not to buy, more to check prices. As others use comparison websites, Mike used Bookers. There was no wi-fi at the Squirrel, as he had little tolerance for technology. He was keen on 'Best Price'. Cost was all, and there was certainly no adjustment for branded quality. He ran the pub with a young man from the village, Stringer, who looked after both bars from a horseshoe shaped central island. Mike sat where he could not see into the Tap room. This was deliberate. He would rather not know who was in and what they were up to. Much like a mid-17th century London coffeehouse, the Tap room was a marketplace: smuggled cigarettes, surplus building materials and much worse.

A couple of winters ago, Terry and seven friends had been drinking since lunchtime. After much excited chatter, they gave

Stringer £50 each, and left saying that they would be back by nine o'clock. Unbeknown to Stringer, they were heading for Kooling Towers. A roosting pheasant, especially in recently coppiced chestnut, is easy prey. Terry and his pals carried only torches and catapults. Two hours later they returned to the Squirrel's Tap room, and produced their grisly game: the severed heads of pheasants.

Roofer Robbie produced eight heads from his coat pockets, Iron Mike thirteen, swearing it should be fifteen, but Terry took the pot with twenty-two. Shortly before they had left the Squirrel, whilst the poaching party had been ironing out the rules, Terry had slipped into the gents to tell his boys to get busy. It wasn't the first time the family had pulled this stroke. Tom, Clem and Scan were so focused on their quarry, they failed to spot Lou. Often on moonlit nights, Lou did an evening round of the pheasant pens. He heard the boys long before he saw them but Lou didn't want to challenge them alone, as they were now grown men. He hurried from the pen wood to rally Cecil and some of the beaters. On returning, the poaching party had left so Lou, foolishly, decided to surprise them in the Squirrel. Lou, closely followed by Cecil and two other beaters, burst through the Tap room door and saw the severed heads of Sir Roger's pheasants beside crumpled banknotes on a fireside table. Lou lunged for the notes, but Terry sprung with such force crushing both Lou and Cecil against the door. They knew they were outnumbered, so Lou and his party scrambled out, leaving behind cheers and laughter in the Squirrel's Tap room.

Chapter 3

Hastings

Barty made his farewells to a happy Jack, an excited Clive and a rather smug Lionel. "Would you like a lift to the museum, Barty?" said Jack, as he opened the passenger door for his little companion.

"No, I'm fine, the walk will do me good, especially after those beers. Good luck Jack, and when you come to see Lionel again, call in at the Imperial in Queens Road. It's opposite the big Morrison's supermarket."

"I will, thank you once again Lionel. I'm just popping down to number 52 to deliver the bronze, and look at his stock, so I know what to look out for in future."

Barty gave Jack a knowing look, cheery wave and strode off towards the museum. He wanted to look at the Indian Room, the Durbar Hall, as it was named. Bought from the Colonial and Indian exhibition held in London in 1886, it was built on the exhibition site in just nine months by two woodcarvers brought from the Punjab. During the exhibition it was used by the then Prince of Wales, the late Edward VII, for official receptions, and a certain Lord Brassey bought the Durbar Hall at the end of the exhibition. Much like you might buy a plant at the end of the Chelsea flower show. Except in this case, Lord Brassey had had to build an extension to his London house in Park Lane. After his death, his son gave their seaside house, complete with Durbar Hall, to the town of Hastings, where it now serves as the town's museum.

Barty walked through the museum's sliding door, thinking: "Why are all automatic doors still magical, especially, in an internet age? How do they know when somebody is approaching?" These magical doors set the tone for the Durbar Hall. Once past the 'Tale of Hastings in 66 objects', Barty walked through a pair of metal studded doors and was amazed again. Two men surely can't have carved this in nine months. Every surface is not only panelled but carved too, with a repeat pattern of stylised flowers, typically Indian. When it comes to Eastern carving, Barty had developed a useful guide. If a surface is covered in flowers, it is probably Indian, but if there are more shapes and geometry, then it is probably Islamic, as a rule of thumb. But sometimes you need to think on your feet, and trust your instincts which are, after all, the product of seeing and feeling so many similar objects.

He stood in the middle of the hall and looked up. Light was coming from a rectangular gallery. Seeking the light, he climbed a small string of steps on the back wall. The ground floor had little natural light. Great if you're in the heat of India, but it doesn't really work in the duller climes of Hastings. The steep string of stairs had polished hardwood treads and risers, fine when ascending, but treacherous when descending. Each tread creaked, after all the stairs had been moved at least two times! As Barty emerged on to the upper floor he let out a "Wow," as this floor has all the light of India. He then walked to the galleried opening and looked up. Supported by columns, rose a panelled lantern. Each column had animal mask capitals of elephants, stylised foxes and even human faces, all carved in high relief with repeat floral patterns. There was little Damascus geometry here. The panelling was broken by a row of stepped arched windows glazed with both clear and citrine-coloured circular panes.

He walked around the gallery looking into the glazed cabinets. They housed a collection of Far Eastern curios, a set of the Japanese armour once worn by Samurai, Chinese blue and white porcelain vases, a pair of gilded lacquered stirrups, all bought for shillings and pence and now worth many thousands of pounds.

Barty checked himself, he had to get back to the Imperial for evening service and there was still some prep to do. He only opened for supper on Wednesdays, having been closed for Sunday, Monday and Tuesdays. Last Tuesday he had bought an Indian folding table, the fourfold hardwood base carved with a mixture of rather strange fruiting vines, lilies and orchids. The top was a circular brass tray, engraved with a series of concentric circles, all worked on the street by a man with a hammer and a punch. He had come to the Durbar Hall to see if there were any similar panels; grapes seemed a rather unusual subject for Indian woodwork, being less repeat and more realistic.

Barty generally used his three days off to scour the shops of Hastings and St Leonards, with Mondays often set aside for lunch or supper elsewhere, mainly in London. He followed the lovely Grace Dent's restaurant reviews in the Evening Standard, although he tended to avoid the clinical white-tiled restaurants, as they often came with hard single chairs. Barty was of an age that required chairs to have both upholstery and arms. In fact, he not only chose restaurants by their chairs, but also his holiday hotels. Numerous comfortable chairs and the sun loungers in the pictures were the hoardings of a luxurious hotel. If you can't get the chairs right, you are unlikely to get the beds or the food right.

Last Tuesday he had gone to a newly-opened restaurant on Hastings seafront, and enjoyed smoked haddock and lemongrass fishcakes, followed by confit of duck with puy lentils, washed down with two half carafes of wine, a fresh Viognier white wine with the fishcakes. It was, after all, the great chef Keith Floyd who is often credited with saying that, "Viognier is a poor man's Chablis". It's rich, buttery and dry, with a peachy aroma.

Although Barty wasn't an aroma sort of guy, more a quaffer than a taster; more interested in the finish than the entry. He figured if you spent your professional life tasting and spitting, you would be more interested in initial smells and tastes but if, like Barty, you actually swallowed the stuff, you might be more interested in the finish. A bit like a film; you can forgive a poor start, but not a poor finish. That aside it was £9.50 for a 375ml carafe, which was working well with the fishcakes. He was about to drift on to the lentils and a red Côte du Rhône when he remembered why he was in the Durbar Hall.

After lunch, he had walked up the High Street, and pottered into various antique shops.

He looked for items at odds with a shop's general stock: a piece of furniture amongst a sea of china and glass or a small cabinet of silver in a room of furniture. He was well-known in all the shops, but he particularly liked a junk shop where he rummaged for old bone handled steel knives. Thankfully, most people left them as they found the rust off putting, but Barty liked the softer steel, far better than the later stainless steel. He could get a razor edge on them which made them lovely to use in the kitchen.

Walking back down the High Street, he turned left into Courthouse Street, encouraged by dealers' vans blocking the road. "Fresh stock," Barty thought. Against the rear tyre of the first van he spotted a circular brass tray. He picked it up, which revealed the stand behind. Not the usual six-legged folding affair, with the turned and chip carved uprights. No, this stand was of four sections, shaped panels of solid wood, two of which folded to make the structural right-angled stand. What struck Barty as unusual was that each panel was well carved, as though the maker had had the time to make something special. The panels were carved with different flowers: orchids, lilies and rather strange stylised grapevines. The tray was heavy, and engraved in concentric rings with Indian deities, including the wonderful Ganesha with the elephant's head, revered as a 'Lord of Beginnings' and the 'Remover of obstacles', the significance of which was clearly lost on Huw, the owner of the illegally parked blue Renault van.

Barty was brought to the present by a hooting horn, which was casually ignored by Huw, a Welshman of devolved character. It had been £75. Barty had hoped it might be £40, but knew Huw only had one price, and that was his price! He didn't take kindly to offers, especially from Englishmen. Amongst the cash Barty produced a £50 note, he always liked to keep one in his wallet, to which Huw took great pleasure in scrutinising. Holding it up to the light, and examining both sides, whilst muttering about, "legal tender, and the privileged few."

Barty then scanned the room's panels for something similar. Amongst the many repeat carved mouldings and smaller panels, there were some similar larger panels, decorated with trailing flowers. Maybe his stand had come from Northern India like the two craftsmen from the Punjab. As he left, he spotted, in a niche above the door, a gilded figure Ganesha, the remover of obstacles. He smiled.

Once outside the museum it was downhill, luckily, as he had two bookings at 7pm, a table of two, and a table of six. It was sunny and the Queens Road was busy. There always seemed to be more people on the pavement than cars on the road. Barty had bought the Imperial five years ago as a pension fund. It was a classic Victorian corner pub with a dead-end road beside it. He let the ground floor and part of the cellar to two young brothers, who brewed beer and made pizza. To say 'made pizza' was an understatement. What came out of the wood fired oven was the best outside Italy.

"Afternoon team," Barty called, as he walked through the door. Three heads swivelled around: the brothers and the head brewer, Al.

"Hi, Barty, come and try this," said Al.

Barty squeezed through the opening in the bar, perfect if you were built like these three, but he had 30 years on them and probably the same in pounds. He took the extended glass. Good colour, good clarity, and the taste was spot on.

"That's good," Barty announced, "What's its name?"

"Charltons."

"It's as good as Kennedy's. What a great finish."

The brewers named all their beers after famous brothers, unsurprisingly as their company name was Brewing Brothers.

"Boys, I must leave you. I have bookings at 7pm. Would you kindly offer them drinks before sending them down?"

This arrangement worked well. Barty had only just enough room to squeeze in 22 covers, certainly no room for a bar, and most of his customers enjoyed drinks with the young first. It gave them courage to descend into Barty's vaulted cellar. An assortment of tables and mismatched open armchairs were squeezed amongst brick columns. With red candles in brass sticks, the space had a feel of an early 1980's wine bar. Behind the swing door Barty had the smallest of kitchens: a four-ring gas hob and oven, a couple of fridges, and a potwash area.

He had trimmed the ribeye fillet earlier in the morning, leaving just some green beans to cut, along with some new potatoes to par boil. Barty looked in the smaller service fridge to check he had some tomatoes and basil, then he quickly scribbled down the menu. Three starters: tomato and basil bruschetta, prawn cocktail, with his own homemade mayonnaise, ketchup and brandy sauce, and lobster bisque with sourdough bread. He was just about to start the mains when he heard a clattering of shoes, followed by the smiling face of Polly. She was one of two sisters, daughters of an old friend of his. He only needed one waitress, so Polly and her sister Pheonix shared the job, waiting tables and then, afterwards, helping him clean up.

"Polly, only two tables booked tonight. I've chalked up the starters, would you finish the board and light the candles, please?"

"Of course, what are the mains and puds?"

The latter Polly knew would be a thin affair.

"Main courses are: ribeye steak with green beans and pan-fried new potatoes, sea bass with a cream of mussel sauce, and a vegetarian Wellington stuffed with mushrooms and stilton, and for puddings..."

"I've got them," said Polly smiling. She knew it would be ice cream and cheeseboard, as it was still summer and it was only from the month of November to the end of February that Barty's favourite pudding made a glorious, and almost permanent entry: Sticky Toffee Pudding or STP.

Polly returned to the board and then lit the candles, whilst Barty boiled the new potatoes.

Shortly afterwards, Polly swung open the kitchen door, and said, "Who's in tonight?"

"A table of six, young I think, and the Chairman."

The Chairman and his wife Sunny, lived in splendour at the top of West Hill, they came often and, if the weather was fine, they walked down the hill and took a taxi home.

"Polly, remind me to mention a large bronze to the Chairman."

Chapter 4
Norfolk

Clem, being the eldest, spoke for both Tom and Scan. Stringer had been hunched over the newspaper with Derek, his boss. It was the two men's morning ritual: coffee and a moan, and their tabloid newspaper was the perfect catalyst. The door had rudely interrupted this ritual and the Squirrel's tap room was now filled with three large lads. They seemed to drain the space; even the kindling in the newly lit fire stuttered as the boys entered. Clem was large and ginger, Tom, black haired and muscular, and Scan was ginger with a wiry fox-like look. Around their feet was an ever swirling, turning mass of terrier dogs. Like a shoal of herring, they continually moved in rhythm with their masters.

"I hear you boys have been busy," said Stringer.

Derek at this point slipped from the bar; the less he knew about Terry and his boys the better he felt. As an older man he was keen to preserve his sleep.

"What do you mean, Stringer?" said Clem, moving closer and intimidatingly closing the space between him and the barman.

"Jess at The Swotter Arms was bursting with news."

"Jess, bursting with news, you don't say?" he turned to his brothers. "It's not the only thing that's bursting about Jess!"

At this the brothers laughed and the room relaxed.

"Come on Stringer, spill the beans. After all it's rare that we are the subject of gossip!"

"Cecil and Lou told Jess that a large bronze has been stolen from the Towers." Stringer had also relaxed; surely the days of shooting the messenger had passed.

"So what's that got to do with us?" Clem asked casually.

"Cecil told Jess that the bronze was at the end of an avenue and would have needed strong lads, as it was ripped from a plinth, and then carried a long way to a waiting van on the drive. They must've been in a hurry, as the thieves made a real mess of the entrance verge."

"Stop gabbling Stringer, it's got nothing to do with us. What would we want with a bronze?"

"Next time you see that Jess, you tell her from Clem to button it!"

Clem turned to his brothers, and they moved to the table next to the fire. They knew it wasn't them, as they would never take anything from Sir Roger, unlike their Pa. Since boys, they had used the woods at Kooling Towers like an adventure playground. They knew they shouldn't be there, Lou hoped they wouldn't be there, and somehow they rarely met. Clem had taught his younger brothers to use a catapult, first on sparrows and later on pheasants, and when Clem bought his first air rifle, the three quickly became crack shots. The woods of Kooling Towers had been their boyhood sanctuary away from their Ma and Pa.

"Let's go and tell Pa. Bye Stringer and you be sure to tell Jess."

Clem then pinched his lips together with his thumb and forefinger.

As the brothers and the swirling terriers left the tap room, Derek re-entered the bar.

"Did they pay?" Derek was keen on money, and it wasn't within Stringer's gift to give away free drinks.

"Of course they did," said Stringer. "You know they always pay, they need this place more than we need them. Lucky Slap has no pub and I'm pretty sure they're not welcome in Holt."

Lucky Slap was a small hamlet to the East of Kooling, which had sprung up during the 19th century. Having had a good deposit of clay, it had become a brick-works, manufacturing bricks for the expansion of neighbouring towns and villages. The houses in Lucky Slap had been built for the brick makers, whose current owners were not delighted when the county council designated the former brickyard as a travellers' site. The fact that the travellers stopped travelling seems ironic, but that's how it happens. After years of living on verges, then as the roads got busier, farmers' fields and recreation grounds, suddenly sites were made available. Although their Pa moaned, it wasn't the same. "Makes us soft," he often said.

The boys knew that their Pa couldn't travel any more. A life of fried breakfasts, meat pies and fish and chips had caught up with him. He rarely left the caravan now; under the watchful eye of Pearl, their Ma, Terry was on porridge oats. "Bit like prison," he always told his cousins at weddings.

The boys pulled into the site, their arrival heralded by a pack of barking dogs. Terry and Pearl's caravan was the largest. It needed to be with the three boys, but since they had grown up, the three brothers shared a smaller caravan neighbouring their parents. Clem entered first, followed by Tom and Scan. Somehow, the terriers stopped, as they knew Pearl and muddy paws didn't mix.

"Pa, a bronze has been nicked from Sir Roger's."

Clem sat down whilst his brothers stood. Terry turned and looked at Pearl, who was opening a tin of biscuits.

"Tea, boys?"

"No thanks Ma, just had some beers at the Squirrel."

"Come on Pearl, a beer for the boys and don't forget me."

Pearl opened the fridge, handed beers to the boys, and turned to Terry.

"It's tea for you."

As she turned to the kettle, Clem passed his opened can to his father and, after a good slurp, Terry spoke.

"Well, it's got nothing to do with me."

Chapter 5

Hastings

Barty was already flushed and hot and he was yet to turn the gas rings on. Whereas most chefs seemed to run permanently lit blue rings, Barty was more thrifty. It was 7pm and he could hear chatter above; Polly would be upstairs taking their orders. Unlike her sister, Phoenix, she was a self-starter who needed no prompting.

"Check on, four lobster bisque and two bruschetta to start, followed by four ribeyes and two sea bass. Barty, I have put them on table two, they wanted a round table."

"That's fine, I'll put six breadsticks in the oven now."

He had spotted the breadsticks or 'grissini' at the bakery in the High Street, when he had bought the Indian brass tray from Huw the Welshman.

"Polly, try and steer them on to the Côte du Rhone, Peter the German has given me a great price on the 2010 vintage, so I can sell them on to customers at £36 per bottle. They will notice a marked difference to the house Shiraz. Any sign of the Chairman yet?"

"Not yet, anyway his entry is normally heralded by Bertie badgering for a biscuit." Polly poured olive oil and balsamic vinegar in three shallow terracotta dishes in preparation for the breadsticks. As the oven door opened, the kitchen was filled with a lovely warm bready smell. Polly loaded her tray and left Barty with the starters. Four bowls in the bottom of the oven to warm, four portions of lobster bisque ladled in a saucepan. Next was the bruschetta: yesterday's bread brushed with olive oil and garlic in the top of the oven, then chopped tomatoes and basil. Starters done, next to cut and oil the ribeye steaks.

The swing door opened with Polly and a four-legged friend.

"There you go Bertie." Barty kept a jar of Donaldson's dog biscuits inside the swing door,

"The Chairman, Sunny and Bertie have arrived."

"I can see, and remember no dogs in the kitchen," Barty said looking straight at Bertie.

"Sunny is looking very glam: floaty dress and sandals to die for, very ancient Greece." Polly had a keen eye for clothes, something probably Sunny had taken note of.

"Barty, two bottles of Côte du Rhône sold, and a bottle of Chardonnay, Al upstairs is dealing with it."

"Well done Polly, my up-selling queen."

"Barty do you have the Chairman's handled beer jug? The knobbly one. Al has given him a pint of Charlton's in a straight glass, but he looks rather sweetly awkward with it."

"It's under the pass Polly, with the white enamelled chip jars. I forgot to take it upstairs from his last visit. How are the breadsticks being received?"

"They love them. One of the tall guys, he's mega fit Barty. He says it's like being at the Wolseley!"

"High praise indeed. Bruschetta are done, take them now, and the lobster bisque will be ready on your return."

A couple of swing doors later, and Polly brought in another check.

"The Chairman wants the bisque soup and Sunny a small, walled garden salad, followed by two sea bass, plus we have two walk-ins - a table of two, and another of four."

"Splendid," Barty said, but a sudden reddish flush and a wipe of the brow with a pink striped oven cloth told a different story. He knew once the starters were back from the six on table two, the checks would start coming in and it would be eyes down until 9.30pm.

"Polly, take the couple's order first, and then give me ten minutes before taking the table of four's order."

"Right-ho, will check all is happy upstairs."

Polly left a gently sweating Barty, who had rather hoped it would be a quiet night, especially after the beers with Lionel and Jack at lunchtime.

He put the breadsticks and soup bowls in the oven and then assembled the walled garden salad: lettuce, rocket, and red chicory for its contrasting colour, all tossed in a steel bowl with his sweet lemon dressing. Sunny kept badgering him for the recipe but Barty always politely changed the subject. Then linseed, and pine nuts, all decorated with three nasturtium flowers, both pretty and peppery.

Polly swung through the kitchen door and took the Chairman's starters, and returned with empty plates.

"Starters back on table two and they are loving the Côte du Rhône, and could 'Mega Fit' have another breadstick?"

"Of course he can. Is he single?"

"I'm not that fast Barty, but after a couple more glasses, I will no doubt find out." Polly smiled and winked, just like her mother used to do.

"That sauce looks good."

"It's the saffron in the cream. Polly, let me get the mains out to table two, and then take the table of four's order and here are two breadsticks for Mr Mega Fit."

When Polly was gone Barty turned back to his hot pans. He gently placed two steaks in each pan and then brushed sprigs of thyme and rosemary in pomace oil, before laying the herbs on top of the steaks. Luckily, all the steaks were medium rare; he would seal them and then rest them under the pass's heat lamps. He then turned his attention to warming the mussel, cream and saffron sauce, whilst pan frying crushed new potatoes and spinach in a little butter. In another hot, oiled, non-stick pan he laid the sea bass, skin side down, gently pushing the fillets down as they arched up with the heat. Then, when the pinky flesh started to turn opaque, he turned the two fillets at the halfway point. The trick was to get the longer jobs done first. Barty knew from experience never to put a dish on the menu that needed more than 15 minutes cooking time. He pressed the crushed new potatoes and spinach in three-inch aluminium ring moulds. He then placed the sea bass fillet on top, with the crispy skin uppermost, and finally spooned the mussel, cream and saffron sauce around the edge, so the dish looked like a floundering fish on seaweed-strewn rocks. Barty rang the bell.

"Polly, the sea bass can go, and the steaks will be ready on your return. What sauce did they want?"

"Three peppercorn, and one garlic butter," said Polly.

Barty muttered to himself, "Peppercorn sauce to warm, and garlic butter from the fridge, hope I have some?" With great relief he found a rolling pin-shaped, clingfilm-wrapped garlic butter. "Lucky it keeps," he muttered. In moments of stress, Barty found that he usually started talking to himself.

"Barty, Mega Fit has ordered two more bottles of Côte du Rhône, I hope he is trying to impress me. Starters are back from the Chairman plus the couple upstairs, now on table three, want bruschetta and salad to start, followed by ribeye steak, medium rare, with peppercorn sauce and a veggie Wellington, thanks."

Barty removed the pastry Wellington from the fridge. It looked like a small upturned pudding bowl, some two and half inches in diameter. He placed it on an oval metal shove dish and then covered it with a square of parchment paper to protect it from burning. He opened the oven doors and placed the dish on the top shelf. Barty kept his oven high at 220°C, with the doors opening the whole time, it was probably 180°C on the bottom shelf and hopefully at the right temperature on the top shelf.

Polly re-entered the kitchen looking a little flustered.

"I've got the order for the four, but have got another walk-in of four. The Brothers know them, a smart looking lot from Old Town."

Barty looked at the clock, 7:45pm, six mains out and only twelve to go!

"Polly, that's fine, can you cope? Or do you want to ring your sister?"

"No point, she's out tonight. I'm fine, and the tips will be all mine."

Polly left with the Chairman's and Sunny's sea basses, leaving the new check on the pass. Thankfully all mains and no starters for table five: two Wellingtons and two ribeye steaks, the 'Yin and Yang' of orders. Barty put six bread sticks in the bottom of the oven. They were eight inches long and about an inch in diameter, and only took a minute to warm. He placed the now warmed breadsticks on the pass, and rang the bell. Polly poured olive oil and balsamic vinegar into three shallow terracotta dishes and left with the warmed breadsticks. As every restaurateur will know, there is nothing like bread for buying time. Barty had always liked the 'conjuring up' of new dishes, plus the morning's prep with coffee and a radio as company. But service was a young chef's game. Luckily Barty and bruschetta were almost permanently coupled. As he popped them in the oven, he thanked the resourceful Italians: yesterday's bread with garlic, olive oil, tomatoes and basil from his green house, something from almost nothing. As starters went out, he put three Wellingtons in the oven. They took a good 10 minutes to warm through, with their pastry cases acting as firewalls to the mushrooms, spinach and blue cheese within. Then the two ribeye steaks. He would leave table three's ribeye until their starters came back. He took control of all the orders with his magic rail, moving every slip to the left until the mains were out, then onto the spike as they went out. A bit like counting the money when everybody had gone home, adding up the covers on the spike was of equal pleasure. A new check was used for puddings, and Polly used the Brewing Brothers's coffee machine upstairs. After cooking starters and mains, he had little to give, and that's why he kept puddings to a minimum. Polly popped back in to the kitchen. "Coffees on table two, and the Chairman wants a scoop of Bakewell ice cream."

"Have you the order for the last table of four?"

"No, back in a moment." Polly's concentration was being distracted by Mr Mega Fit, thought Barty.

"Three bruschettas and one lobster bisque, followed by four ribeye steaks, and Al has sold them a bottle of Côte du Rhône."

"Well done Polly, are starters back on table three yet?"

"No, I will clear them now."

Two minutes later the empty plates were back, plus the last check for the walk-in of four from Old Town: three bruschetta and one lobster bisque to start, and two sea bass and two ribeyes to follow.

"Polly, here is the ice cream, and would you ask Al to give the Chairman and Sunny one of those Somerset brandies? It's just like Calvados but British. I'll have the Wellingtons ready on your return." Barty had forgotten table three's ribeye, which he quickly put in in a hot and oiled pan. Polly took table five's mains out, and returned for two ramekins of mayonnaise. Then she took the three bruschetta and one lobster bisque for table four.

"Take table three's Wellington and ribeye out, and then it's only table four's mains. Polly, we have done it. On your way back, would you bring me a pint of Charlton's please?' Five minutes later Polly returned with Barty's pint, a £20 note and a check slip.

"Here is your beer, here is my tip, and here is my Saturday night! I swapped numbers with Mr Mega Fit."

Barty smiled and said, "are table four happy with their starters? I'm just going to have a quick chat with the Chairman."

Barty took off his apron, mopped his brow, and took his beer to table one. The Chairman and Sunny sat, not opposite each other, but in adjoining quarters. The Chairman had long legs which he crossed at his ankles showing sockless feet, lounging in a rather rakish pair of navy-blue suede loafers. His trim torso was covered in a pink gingham shirt, opened to the second button, beneath a cream linen suit. He was tall and slim enough to get away with cream. Barty would have looked like a pavlova, hence the navy blue, "So slimming!" Beside him sat Sunny who seemed to float in her chair, secured only to terra firma by her gladiator sandals, the straps like asps winding up to her knees. A sense of calm masked a determined course; as they say 'behind every successful man is a strong woman', often coupled with a surprised mother-in-law. Mercifully, there was none of the latter, just a non-judgemental, all-loving dog, Bertie, who was small, black and curly, a bit like a Russian astrakhan hat. A former Russian leader, Leonard Brezhnev, wore this traditional Russian hat. Imagine it with four legs and you have Bertie. Bertie hopped up as he approached, Barty had been trimming two ribeyes of beef earlier in the day! We humans may smell thyme and rosemary, but our canine cousins concentrate on the meat.

"Did you like the Somerset brandy?" asked Barty.

"A British Calvados, makes you feel proud?" said the Chairman.

"Only one cider maker in Somerset has a distilling license; not great odds against the hundreds of Normans over the water making Calvados, but it's a start." Barty continued; "I think it's delicious, and it courses through the tubes."

"Barty that was delicious," said Sunny.

"It's been a good service, six booked and 18 fed. Thank the lord for Polly. I was with Lionel today, who has just bought a lovely quarter-scale bronze of horse and jockey, no age but a great weight and of good definition. Just up your street, I thought. I would recommend you give Lionel a call before he starts ringing others."

Chapter 6

Hastings

The walk back to West Hill was taken slowly. There are steep flights of steps that cut a more direct course but the meandering road, with its wide pavements, was a far gentler option. The Chairman and Sunny decided to walk hand in hand, closely followed by Bertie, knowing never to be in front, as the Chairman had a certain authority over dogs. One of life's pleasures must surely be a walk after supper; the Italians even have a name for it, the 'passeggiata'.

"That lobster bisque was superb. Felt sorry for Barty tonight; just he and Polly looking after 20 people, but it's good to see the joint jumping, especially on a Wednesday Night."

"Pru's girls are lovely and so very different," said Sunny.

"How so?" said the Chairman, narrowly avoiding a potential threat to his navy blue suede loafers.

"Well, Polly just gets on with it. She's in control, whereas Phoenix needs direction, but will get away with it, as all pretty girls do."

"You should know,' said the Chairman, as he squeezed Sunny's hand.

"Do you want to have a look at this equestrian bronze Barty spoke of?"

"Of course," said Sunny, "it might work well at the end of the yew hedge against the boundary wall."

"I will give that terrible Lionel a call tomorrow."

The party of three entered the twitten between two terraced houses, then opened an arched door in a high brick wall into their secret part of Hastings.

Lionel had had a good morning. His day had started early. The life of a veteran antiques dealer was a charmed one: up at six o'clock, he had padded down the stairs, in his silk dressing gown, to his ground floor shop in order to peruse yesterday's purchases. A Victorian mahogany side table, four foot wide and shallow, a good reddish-brown mahogany with triangular backplate and ribbon turned legs, bought for £80 from Norman. He would sell it easily at £150, to somebody with a narrow hall corridor. Norman's trusty car, an early 1980's burgundy Austin Maxi, also yielded: an enamel sign, £45, saying 'GENTLEMEN', an oak snooker cue stand for £18, and two cardboard boxes packed with a suite of Edwardian drinking glasses: eight large lemonade glasses, perfect for beer, eight whisky tumblers and seven wineglasses, all cut with flame pattern to their lower section i.e. from feet to knees. The whisky tumblers would go quickly, but the wines would be harder to sell, being not a generous 175 millelitres, more like 125 millelitres. A sort of large sherry glass, not that anybody seemed to drink sherry any more. He would keep the seventh glass, and sell the six as a set. It would save an explanation of where the eighth glass was. Norman and Lionel had engaged in their normal too and fro: Norman wanting a fiver a glass and Lionel sticking firmly at £3. In the end they shook hands at £95 for the lot. Norman, over the years, had developed Lionel's eye. He knew that if an item would sit happily in a country house, Lionel would buy it. Their daily exchange was sealed with a cup of tea for Norman and coffee for Lionel. Lionel drank tea before 10 and coffee between 10 and noon, then stuck to something stronger, as water rarely passed his lips. He dressed in a three-piece tweed suit, open neck shirt and a blue silk scarf tied as a cravat. The scarf was heavy silk with a dotted pattern. He had five exactly the same that he rotated, not by day, but more by which he found first. After lacing calf high brown boots, he emerged from 52 Norman Road and walked down the hill to buy a newspaper. London Road had two newsagents, one run by a couple of Sikh brothers, both turbaned and very useful for Indian and Kufic script translations. The other was run by a couple, she Belgian and he English. She ran her shop with military precision; customers were vetted on their ability to walk in and out without leaving dirty footprints. Copious mats heralded forthcoming rain, way before any weather forecast. After buying a broadsheet, a litre of whole milk, an essential pork pie and almost vital tube of wine gums Lionel returned to his top floor kitchen and settled into his tub-shaped Lloyd Loom chair with the morning sun nicely on his back. The Telegraph newspaper was his daily companion: good photographs, a proper economist, fascinating obituaries and of a size that required craft, having had mastered its horizontal and vertical folds. He handled his paper with the same ability as a Japanese kabuki fan dancer. Life was so simple, when you only had to think of yourself. If he had had a wife, he knew he would 'like' green tea and eat granola with buffalo curd for breakfast. But, fortunately, Lionel was a stranger to all three. The Telegraph and wine gums, all before 9am, seemed such a delicious pleasure. He knew many a good man was envious, but sometimes he was lonely at the end of the working day, especially at around 6pm. He would have loved to have shared a drink and a natter with somebody he cared for.

"How was Ardingly or Ford?" or "What did Norman sell you today?" Then suddenly his mobile phone rang.

"Lionel, Chairman here. I understand you have just bought a large equestrian bronze. Sunny and I may have room for it. Would you bring it to The Crest after five today?"

"It's not cheap Chairman."

"Your cheap: may not be my cheap. See you at five."

With that the Chairman put the phone down. Best to stay in control from the outset, he thought.

It took Lionel a little time to settle. He knew the Chairman was direct: to be hauled away from the letters page before nine, seemed a little discourteous but on the other hand, he must be keen. How did the Chairman know? As Lionel mused upon this, his mobile rang again. 'Popular this morning,' he thought.

"Morning Lionel; it's Barty. Wanted to call to say: I tipped off the Chairman and Sunny regarding Jack's bronze."

"Thanks," said Lionel.

"They came to the Imperial for supper last night, and I thought that it might be right up their 'street', or more rightly up their 'garden'."

"Barty, you must have said the right thing. The Chairman has already called me and I'm taking the bronze up to his home today at 5pm. Do you want to join the party?"

"I would love to, but I have lunch and evening service today and I'm already behind on the prep: we had a busy night yesterday. Call in for a drink afterwards?"

"Will do. I'd better make sure Justin and Jamie are free for carriage. By the way, I will definitely pop in as I have some outside tables and chairs for you. Bye Barty; see you later."

Lionel's mornings weren't normally this frantic but if he didn't do it, list it or photograph it: it would be forgotten.

Next, he dialled Justin, the most careful carrier in the business.

"Justin, it's Lionel. I bought a large bronze yesterday and I've already got a buyer in West Hill.

It's a two man job, and they have asked to see it at five today, can you help?"

"At your service, will be with you at 4.30."

His morning work done, Lionel returned to the letters page. There was a charming letter about obesity and the increased portion size of porridge oats sachets. Everybody seemed to have a different threshold before they took pen to paper: porridge oats or politics – everything was soundly treated by the good people of Norfolk or Shropshire. Lionel thought, did they have an extra hour in the day or was a more isolated county, more conducive to comment on the day's affairs and irritations? Presumably, with less noise and bustle, issues of the day may seem clearer.

Lionel looked at his drop dial clock; the black enamelled hands read half past nine. Only two and half hours before he could respectfully enter the Horse and Groom. Norman was at Ford market, so no callers today. He would have arrived at Ford at seven before the vans. The organisers allowed the buyers to congregate with teas and bacon rolls: only on the dot of 7.30am were the vans ushered in, to be immediately picked and poured over by the now-refreshed buyers. Why should Lionel feel guilty while others fought over treasures? Surely enjoying a little sun on your back whilst devouring another editorial column was no crime.

Unlike Lionel, Barty had had a busy morning. Yesterday's evening service had diminished his stocks. He needed more breadsticks, another two ribeyes of beef, sea bass etc. Barty's fish was delivered; so too, his vegetables, but meat and bread were bought from the Old Town's High Street. Sensibly, Barty was in loose linens today, as the steep steps of Whistlers and Noonan twittens took it out of him. But once they were climbed, the descent over West Hill was well worth it. With its sloping green lawns and fishing boats on the shingle beach beyond, it was definitely worth the odd bead of sweat.

He walked through another twitten past St Clement church, first to the bakery; 40 breadsticks and 2 baguettes and then the butchers.

"Morning Barty," said the soft-handed butcher.

"Morning Alan, could I have two ribeyes of beef please?"

Alan disappeared into the back and brought back two joints of ribeye beef on a rectangular aluminium tray, with the shallow up-turned edges that retained the blood. Alan held up each one, showing Barty. First the diameter - four inches was ideal as Barty always cut to the same thickness for those wanting either rare or medium done steaks, and a five or six inch diameter joint would be more weight and therefore more cost per portion. Then Alan shook the joints to demonstrate that they were good and firm; he knew floppy and slimy was not for him.

"Perfect Alan, I will take them both, how much are they?"

Alan put them on the scales. Barty knew they would be between £12 and £14 per pound, and the cost of making a mistake with a steak, was generally around £6.

"That's £195, would you like us to deliver, or would you like the weight for a little resistance training over-the-hill?"

"Thank you, Alan." Barty gave him a look that confirmed delivery was the correct choice. It was 9.30am. Barty would have to get a wiggle on. He had bookings at 1pm, and a new dish to prepare: a gazpacho soup. He used the Hungry Monk recipe of tomatoes, cucumbers, onions, olive oil and garlic. This from the famous home of the banoffee pie in Jevington, which had once nestled in the South Downs outside Eastbourne. Earlier that morning he had picked tomatoes and cucumbers from his greenhouse and the other vegetables were to be delivered to the Imperial after 10am.

He lived in West Hill in an Edwardian, redbrick, end of terrace house. He had bought it for three reasons: it had a good-sized south-west facing garden, the road was to its north and its sitting room was flooded with light. It was arranged over four floors. Leaving the road and pavement, entering a small porch paved with encaustic tiles, up a stone step and through the front door to a similarly encaustic paved hall. In front was a flight of stairs, with turned pitch pine balusters and hand rail. The distinctive yellow and red grained wood was imported from the Russian Baltic states throughout the 19th and early 20th century, and was much employed in the great housing boom of the Edwardian period.

As one passed the stairs on the left, and walked to the sun in the back, there was a small bathroom, with a four-panelled pitch pine door. Inside was a Royal Doulton loo, with wooden seat and large cistern above, both united by a vertical copper pipe. The pipe wasn't green, more rose gold, polished weekly by his effervescent cleaner, Hayley. Beside the loo was a three-stage pavilion bamboo stand housing back issues of Private Eye, Antiques Trade Gazette and random cookery books. The walls were paved with framed photographs and certificates, memories of his childhood and former career as an auctioneer. Opposite was Barty's favourite door, the cellar door. As it swung open, brick steps led down to a vaulted space the size of the ground floor, arranged as a large open space with two smaller rooms enclosed by open, grilled metal doors. In the larger room was a four-foot diameter circular table with three turned legs, formerly a rather grand picnic table. Barty was a great fan of three legs, always even on the roughest of ground. He had once left a restaurant in London after only one drink, as he couldn't face its jiggling fourth leg. Around the table were six chairs. Nowadays Barty had fewer friends; a life of smiling in the auction world had taken its toll. He preferred the company of strangers; just shallow dips into the lives of others. Conversation formed from a mutual interest of wine, food, art and antiques, history and travel. It was a foolish man that would turn down an invitation to Sunday lunch at Barty's. Normally, drinks in the sitting-room and, if sunny, barbecue pulled lamb on the terrace. In the winter, it was rib of beef in the cellar, surrounded by thousands of wine bottles, some in racks but mostly in original wooden boxes. It didn't take many glasses before Barty started opening bottles that were rarely seen in Hastings. The cellar was lit by the best wall lights he could buy, after all, he was replacing daylight. Upstairs at the threshold of the cellar door, looking south towards the garden, was a small but perfectly formed kitchen, arranged with sink under the window, between an undercounter fridge on one side, and dishwasher on the other. Working in professional kitchens had taught Barty that a rinsed plate entering a dishwasher is a lot cleaner on exit. If he stood with his back to the sink and looked through to the sitting-room, in front there was an oblong island housing a four-ring gas hob with the electric oven beneath, surrounded by a mixture of open shelves and drawers, housing pans, plates and cutlery. Barty's best china and glass were in a dresser between the two windows on the north front wall. When he cooked, he could chat with his guests who generally fell into his deep linen-covered sofas. If Barty looked to his left, through two pairs of floor-to-ceiling double doors lay the south west terrace and garden beyond. When he had bought the house, it had only a single door from the kitchen to the terrace, with two sash windows in the sitting room. He remodelled these three openings to house the matching pairs of floor-to-ceiling double doors, which spilled onto the terrace and his garden beyond. On purchase, he had decided that he wasn't going to cut grass, so the garden was divided into rooms: some brick-paved and some cobbled, a mixture of flooring and oversized terracotta pots from Spain or the Greek Isles but also a number of two-handled lead urns, all bought as 19th century from overcautious auction houses. Barty was confident they were 18th century, after all, the big garden boom with it's star, Capability Brown, was the last quarter of the 18th century. The terrace was 'peopled' with old garden chairs and tables, all auction and antique market finds. It is surprising what you can accumulate in 10 years. There were distressed tub-shaped Lloyd Loom chairs, bamboo chairs from Hong Kong, clubby teak armchairs and French café chairs, all scattered with continental zinc-topped wine tables. He had a table and chair for every position of the sun. Not that he had much time to rest, as the glass houses occupied kept him well: big terracotta pots of basil; tomato plants in raised beds amongst strange curly cucumbers that seemed to grow an inch a day. He popped home on his way back from the butcher to collect the cloth bag of garden produce that he had picked before breakfast and made his way downhill to Queens Road.

"Morning Barty, your vegetables have arrived," said Al.

Chapter 7

Hastings

Lionel decided to limit himself to just two small glasses of white Burgundy. The Horse and Groom's bar staff were shocked by his request for water. Lionel and water were rarely coupled, especially in a public space.

"Just a small beaker," Lionel had said whilst lowering his voice, but Lionel's low voice was normal volume for most.

June behind the bar had great delight in approaching him with the offending glass. "Water for Lionel," June announced.

"Only the beaker, June and what's all the fuss. Never seen a man drink water before?"

"Certainly have, but never you, Lionel."

It was too much for Lionel. He left the Horse and Groom and walked the short distance down Norman Road to number 52. This is why he liked to do his jobs in the morning, then from noon he could do what he wished, but the last thing he wanted to do was breathe alcohol over the Chairman and especially his wife Sunny. He had just settled upstairs when the doorbell rang. Justin and Jamie were early, Justin always was.

"Afternoon team," Lionel said, as he turned and pointed to the bronze.

The bronze was now resting on a pair of mahogany folding coffin stands, probably Irish and bought from Norman years ago. At the time Lionel thought "what am I going to do with them" but they were of such quality he couldn't resist. They were too high to rest a tabletop on, but they had become invaluable display stands, being strong enough for a body, they could support most items, even large bronzes. "If you two take the bronze I will bring the stands," said Lionel.

Jamie and Justin made light of the heavy bronze group, strapping it just inside the van's roller shutter door.

"I have some tables and chairs for Barty, is that alright?"

"We have an empty van. Is it for his house?" said Justin, unfolding blankets.

"No it's for the Imperial. I was hoping we could pop down after we've been to The Crest."

"That's fine," Justin said, whilst stacking the chairs.

Once loaded, Lionel locked the shop door and hopped into the cab, sandwiching Jamie in the middle.

"Justin you have been to The Crest before, haven't you?"

"Yes of course! Sunny is always buying something, especially from Battle Auction Rooms."

Lionel relaxed, well as much as you can in the cramped cab of a Ford Transit, and went through his sales patter. He knew the Chairman was a tough customer. More familiar with buying companies than antiques, he was used to dealing with bigger fish, maybe even tricky Russian fish! The figures were: bought for £750, hoping for £2,500. That would sort out food and wine for the next couple of months, as unlike Barty, Lionel didn't cook. Lionel's second wife was a superb cook and only rare comparables to her cooking were to be found in restaurants. That's why Lionel relied upon pork pies. His third wife would be chosen on her ability to raise a pie. He was pushing 60 and it was too late for salads and beans. He was sure his genes would carry him through another decade, or two. After all, he took no pills yet and, with no car, Lionel walked everywhere.

Back to the job in hand. As Justin climbed the steep road to The Crest, Lionel looked back from West Hill's lawns down the hill to Queens Road. Smart, painted Regency terraces made way for later mid-Victorian terraces. Then working its way down hill, like terraced paddy fields, Victorian houses fell into Edwardian four to five storey houses. The steeper the incline was, the greater the opportunity for floors. As it levelled, short terraces joined Queens Road terminating with either corner pubs or shops. Back to the top, and beyond the lawns, there were only a clutch of houses on the headland; The Crest being the furthest and so the nearest to the cliffs, but it remained unseen from the lawns as two large Edwardian villas had its north side and a small terrace of red brick Edwardian houses shielded its west. They entered the Crest by car through an opening in a high boundary wall. There was no need for a gate as few knew the house was there, over a cattle grid that kept Bertie in and the uninvited out. Once in front of the house, a perfectly formed white stucco villa with five semi-circular steps led to its raised front door, to either side of which were two pairs of sash windows with a run of five matching sash windows above on the first floor, all topped by a triangular parapet. Before the merry selling party got out of the van the Chairman, Sunny and Bertie were arranged on the front steps.

The Chairman waved whilst whispering to Sunny:

"Down the steps pronto, the last thing we want is Lionel in the house."

"Don't be mean, darling," Sunny said softly.

"Afternoon Lionel, Justin and Jamie, I can't wait to see the treasure," Sunny called out as they moved to the rear of the van. Justin pushed the roller shutter up with a clatter to reveal the bronze horse and rider. "It looks impressive from this height," Lionel thought.

"I have brought two stands, do you have a place in mind for the bronze?"

"We thought, through a gap in the yew hedging at the end of the walk against that boundary wall. Can Justin and Jamie carry it?"

"Mrs Chairman," as she was known to Justin, "do you have a wheelbarrow?" "Certainly. Darling, would you bring it around. It's by my potting shed."

The Chairman left with Bertie at his heel, reappearing moments later with a big metal barrow. Soon, loaded on a bed of blankets with Jamie on the handles and Justin steadying the bronze, the party moved off with Lionel trailing. The mahogany stands were heavier than he had remembered; after all they were made to bear coffins and, as Lionel knew, some bodies could be bigger than his! As the party came to the end of the walk, Lionel quickly placed the stands just off the wall as Justin and Jamie lifted the bronze from the barrow. Once placed on the stands the whole party walked away back up the yew walk. Lionel waited for Sunny or the Chairman to turn, and remained silent when they did. A pause can be a powerful tool in negotiations.

Sunny spoke first.

"It looks good there. What do you think darling?"

"It does, it really is big enough to fill the space," the Chairman replied, "and the stand is about the right height too."

"Come on Lionel, what's your best price?" said the Chairman, with unmistakeable directness.

"I have yet to show this to anybody else..." started Lionel, but was promptly interrupted.

"Lionel don't give me a load of old flannel, I asked a direct question, what's your price, please?"

Lionel was now feeling pushed and was tempted to say it wasn't for sale, but he caught Sunny's smile and thought better of it.

"Four thousand pounds."

Sunny looked at the Chairman, much like Helen of Troy might have done to have launched a thousand ships.

"I will give you three thousand, and no more," retorted the Chairman.

"Done," said Lionel trying not to smile.

"Thank you, darling," Sunny said to the Chairman.

"This calls for champagne," she said, looking at the Chairman, who quickly walked off to the kitchen. Better keep Lionel in the garden he thought, as he opened his drinks fridge in the kitchen. He looked at a bottle of Perrier Jouet and thought a little too good. Luckily somebody had given him a Sainsburys own-brand champagne, that would do nicely.

With the champagne chosen, he asked Ping, their Sri Lankan housekeeper, to follow with five glasses and some soft drinks. As the Chairman approached, he noticed Lionel was smiling and chatting a little too much.

"Marvellous," Lionel said, as he saw the drinks party approach. Not only now rich, but rather thirsty, Lionel's afternoon had turned out rather nicely.

The Chairman poured and Ping handed the bubbles around.

"To the bronze's new owners," Lionel said, just as the Chairman was about to issue forth.

"Can we return the stands to you in a couple of days, after our gardener has made a suitable plinth?" Sunny asked.

"Of course, but would you kindly cover them with a couple of waterproof sacks, as they are mahogany," Lionel ventured.

"I can do that," volunteered Justin, "as I have a couple of old feed sacks in the van". "All's good then. Chairman, thank you for your business, and please...

cash preferred."

Chapter 8

Hastings

If Lionel was effervescent, it wasn't a stream of bubbles in the champagne glass; it was more hot springs in Iceland. The short journey down from West Hill to Barty's Imperial was accompanied by whoops and excited tales of past deals done and profits made. To say Lionel was on top was to understate the mood in the Transit van's cab. Before Justin could park safely, Lionel was out. He then crashed through the Brewing Brothers' side door and descended the stairs to Barty's cellar restaurant and made his way to the kitchen.

"Champagne, my dear friend Barty, you lovely man, the bronze is sold."

"Well done, a good price?"

"The best price. Isn't Sunny lovely? We placed it on my trusty coffin stands at the end of their yew walk. Barty, the bronze looked perfect there. What do I always say? It's placing, placing, and placing."

Lionel didn't give himself time to draw breath.

"Let's have some champagne."

"Go upstairs and ask the Brothers, I think they've got a couple of bottles of Ruinart," said Barty, who was cleaning the last of the mussels.

"Just the ticket, remember Rebecca, the second Mrs Lionel? I wooed her with Ruinart."

"Go on, get upstairs, I haven't got long before my first booking at 7pm."

"Right ho! Which one of Pru's lovely daughters is on tonight?"

Barty didn't answer, he just waved his chef's knife.

Lionel crashed out and shortly returned with a bottle and three glasses.

"Would you pop upstairs quickly? Justin has brought the outside tables and chairs in the van and he wants to get off home."

"Sure." Barty removed his apron and followed Lionel. Justin was folding his blankets on the back of his van and the tables and chairs were now on the pavement. The tables were circular between two foot six inches and three foot in diameter, on three concave legs held by metal hoops at their waists. There were three tables and eight chairs, all with arms and concave backs. Barty sat in one and jiggled about. The chair flexed and sighed, he knew they would be comfortable.

Lionel could see what Barty was thinking, "They're too good for the pavement Barty, and it will be a pain for the Brothers to bring in and out daily."

"You're right. Polly and I had difficulty looking after 20 covers yesterday, let alone rushing up to outside tables."

"I've had such a good day, you can have all the tables plus the chairs for two hundred pounds, what say you?"

"Would Justin deliver them to my home?"

Justin nodded

"I'll take them at two hundred."

"Thank the lord for that. The champagne will be waiting and warming."

Lionel gave Justin £100 cash for carriage and returned to the kitchen. Barty had pulled out a stool for Lionel and put the champagne in an ice bucket, as Ruinart deserved only the very best. Lionel settled on the stool and smiled. Barty handed him a glass and they both toasted Jack and the bronze.

Barty put some breadsticks in the oven. He had made a mackerel pâté after the lunch service. It would go well with the champagne.

"Barty, are you all ears?"

"Of course I am, what was the price?"

"All in good time, Bartholomew," Lionel took the bottle from the bucket and recharged their glasses.

"The Chairman was brusque and Sunny was, well, sunny. We set the bronze on my pair of trusty coffin stands, which stand higher than you expect. So you're almost at the horse's eye level with the jockey's eyes looking down upon you. Suddenly, instead of being quarter scale the group becomes half size. After setting it up, just off the wall and midway between two yew hedges, we all walked away, and after 10 yards we collectively turned, and it just looked perfect." Lionel continued, almost forgetting his champagne. "Sunny was the first to speak, but it was sold when we'd turned."

"Come on, how much?"

Barty handed him a ramekin of mackerel pâté with a now hot breadstick.

"Delicious Barty, can I stay for supper?"

"Of course you can, but first the price."

"Three thousand pounds."

"No! Well done," Barty raised his glass. "More champagne?"

"£3,000 should keep me on good terms with you and other restaurateurs for a while," said Lionel.

At that point Phoenix swung through the kitchen door.

"Evening boss and hello Lionel."

Lionel leapt to his feet. "Hello gorgeous," Lionel retorted. "My, you are wearing dangerously little."

"Lionel, remember that you can't say things like that anymore," Phoenix said smiling. "Rubbish, I pose no threat to man nor beast. They are just words fashioned as compliments. There aren't many who can carry off such a 'dangerously little' look as you. Of course, your mother could in her youth, couldn't she Barty?"

"Pru was gorgeous, still is. I remember her in her Biba dresses hopping in and out of E-type Jags," Barty said, with more reserve than Lionel; after all, he was the girl's boss.

"Sit down Lionel, there is hardly room for Phoenix and me in this kitchen. Phoenix, here is this evening's menu. I have replaced the lobster bisque with smoked mackerel pâté, and we have only three Wellingtons left. We had a bit of a run on them at lunchtime. Please check the candles. We have three tables booked tonight: a two, and two fours, the first four is for 7pm.

Pheonix left, taking her miniskirt and bursting shirt with her.

"I sometimes envy you. I don't work with sirens like Phoenix and Polly. By the way how is Pru?"

"I don't know. I haven't seen her for a while. The girls say she is busy, lots of commissions, and I know she has just drawn the Chairman's dog, Bertie."

"Funnily enough, saw one of her pastels at Ford market a couple of months ago; a rather good Jack Russell."

"Lionel come for lunch on Sunday? I will invite Pru and the girls too."

"Yes please."

"Now what does a champion antiques dealer want for supper?"

"Ribeye steak, medium rare, please."

"Do you want it in here, or on table one?" Barty said, whilst putting another breadstick in the oven.

"If I'm not in the way, in here please, but chuck me out if it all gets a bit too busy."

"Don't worry I will. Peppercorn sauce or garlic butter?"

"Peppercorn please, and do you have another breadstick? Delicious, where do they come from?" Lionel asked, while raising his glass.

"The bakery in the High Street, they buy me time. You know what it's like as soon as you've ordered, your enzymes get going and 10 minutes seems like a fortnight. But if you can nibble something, all is rosy."

Lionel finished the champagne and had a carafe of Côte du Rhône with his steak, whilst Barty and Phoenix started getting the first checks out.

"That was lovely, I will pay the Brothers upstairs. What time on Sunday?"

"Come for one o'clock."

Lionel went upstairs and settled his bill, then walked back to Norman Road. Still time for just one more drink in the Horse and Groom. He felt like celebrating!

Chapter 9

Hastings

Lionel woke later than usual; 7.30am was practically a lie-in. It had been a good day and one drink at the Horse and Groom had turned into three. He now walked down to the newsagents, picked up his paper, chatted in French to the Belgian owner and returned just in time for the postman. In a plastic wrapper was the Antiques Trade Gazette newspaper, organ of his industry. The national broadsheet would have to wait today. Lionel made himself a cafetière of coffee and settled down in his Lloyd Loom chair. The front cover was normal stuff: some regional auctioneer with a Chinese Kang Hsi vase, estimate £500-£800, surprised at £32,000; no doubt to be later sold in a Hong Kong auction for £300,000. It's all about reach, Lionel thought, as generally financial mandarins don't cross the thresholds of Birmingham auctioneers as they are more likely to be lured into a five-star Hong Kong Hotel with associated fine wines and nibbles. Further, into the paper were the auction reports and then to the letters page. Amongst the normal whining letters about the damage done to the antiques trade by daytime television antique shows, was a photo of some bizarre rural animal/human trap with text urging the reader to identify the sadist who invented it. Lionel was more interested in television antique shows. Not that he watched them. Difficult when you don't own a telly, but it didn't stop him holding the view that without the red and blue team competing at Newark or Ardingly, the trade would be in an even more parlous state than it is now. Did it ever cross the letter writer's mind that IKEA and the roguish practices of West End antique dealers and their restorers, who had spent decades making up pairs and longer sets of chairs, might have eroded the public's confidence in the antiques trade? Furthermore, everybody wanted labels and signatures now. Fewer people were prepared to take the risk on an unsigned picture. 'Victorian school,' or 'after Sir Frank Brangwyn' was no longer good enough. Where was the signature? Amongst the letters was a charming one about buying in Continental markets and extolling the virtues of Tongeren market in Belgium, held every Sunday in the mediaeval walled town. Lots of choice and lots of Belgian beers all within reach by van or Eurostar.

Lionel turned a couple of pages and then saw a bronze horse and rider under the 'Stolen' section. The blood drained from his face first, and then from his arms as he lowered the newspaper to his knees. He read on: "Stolen from Norfolk estate, a quarter-sized bronze group of horse with jockey-up, 1980's casting, with verdigris coloured oblong stand. Reward offered for any information leading to its return. Ring Mercy Penfold at Antiques Trade Gazette."

Lionel put down the paper and picked up his phone.

"Barty, have you looked at the Antiques Trade Gazette yet?" Lionel almost whispered. "No, why?"

"Turn to page 54," Lionel whispered.

Barty padded to his front door and retrieved the plastic bagged newspaper from the encaustic tiled floor, ripped it open and quickly found page 54.

"Oh, is that your bronze?" Barty's voice dropped too.

"I can't say for sure. We know it's not unique, but the timing would fit. Oh dear, what should I do?"

"Ring Jack now and put him on notice, and don't spend the £3,000."

"Will do, but will you help me trace it back? Barty, my name will be mud in Hastings and beyond."

"Lionel, nobody knows anything yet, and you didn't approach any other potential buyers, did you?"

"No, thankfully the Chairman rang first thing, and so I didn't contact any one else."

"That's good, so it's Jack, Justin, Jamie, the Chairman and Sunny then?"

Lionel interrupted.

"Do you think any of them subscribe to the Antiques Trade Gazette?"

"Let's hope not, and even if they did, who reads the Stolen pages?"

"I do."

"Well, let's hope others don't. Ring Jack and find out when he bought it, where he bought it and from whom," said Barty in a sort of 'taking control' tone.

Lionel paused and then asked rather meekly,

"Should I inform the Chairman?"

"No, certainly not. Let's try and get to the bottom of this and then we should know what to do. Now ring Jack, and report back."

"Will do, thanks Barty. For once it seemed so easy!"

"Don't worry, let's get busy and resolve this."

Barty put down his phone. Poor Lionel, just when he thought he was in the money.

"Jack, it's Lionel here, do you take the Antiques Trade Gazette?"

"No, should I?"

"Of course you should. Where are you now?"

"I'm in a salvage yard in Portsmouth."

"I will WhatsApp pictures to you. Ring me when you get them."

Lionel took two photos, one of the whole page, and a detailed one of the stolen announcement. It wasn't long before Lionel's phone rang, but before Jack could speak, Lionel asked:

"Do you think it's our bronze?"

"I have a terrible feeling it might be. What should I do? This is all new to me," Jack said.

"Firstly, don't tell anybody about the bronze. Did you offer it to anybody else before me?"

"No, you were my first and only potential buyer."

"Jack, when did you buy it?"

"Last Sunday, at a car boot just off the M4 near Heathrow airport."

"I know the one, and who did you buy it from?"

"A round fellow with a curious nose."

"Does this nose have a name?"

"He is called Beacon and he operates from a rather tired Renault van. You know, those light blue ones."

"Did you get a receipt?" Lionel asked rather hopefully.

"No, the Beacon doesn't do receipts."

"I didn't expect he would at that price. Now Jack, my friend Barty is going to help me trace this and when we find out who stole it from this Norfolk estate, Barty will then advise us what to do next. Do you know whether this Beacon has a shop?"

"No, I don't know."

"Well, is the car boot on this Sunday?"

"Yes, it's on every Sunday."

"Well, go and grill him. No, on second thoughts, buy a

couple of items from him, give him a cup of tea, and make some enquiries about the bronze. Say it's stuck, you can't sell it and to you, it's dead money that you could be spending with him. Suggest it needs a little story. Like 'where it's come from' may just help shift it."

"Will do."

"I will be with Barty on Sunday so call after 12 noon and, in the meantime, don't discuss this with anybody else, got that?"

"By the way, have you sold it?"

"Of course I have. This is why it's such a mess. Speak to you on Sunday." Lionel rang off, and slumped further into his chair. "What a pickle," he thought. Well at least he had Barty, better give him an update.

"Just had a long chat with Jack, who has the same sinking feeling as I do. He bought it last Sunday at a car boot near Heathrow from a man named Beacon."

"Odd name," said Barty.

"It appears that the man has a spectacular nose, hence Beacon, as in Belisha Beacon."

"It sounds like a relative of that lady who ran the Colony club in Soho. What was her name?"

"Muriel - her nose was quite extraordinary. Back to the point, Jack's going this Sunday to speak to the Beacon. May I come round at noon as I've asked Jack to call then, and it might be good if we were together?"

"Of course. You can prep the runner beans."

"See you at noon. Thanks Barty."

Lionel put down his mobile phone and quietly thanked the lord he hadn't bragged about his sale last night in the Horse and Groom. This was too much. He was used to gentler mornings.

He looked at his watch face, 10am; only two hours before he was in the Horse and Groom again.

Barty took the Antiques Trade Gazette out to his terrace and sat in one of his new chairs. It was made of bamboo, but now painted white by some fool 30 years ago. It was comfy, with good arms and a concave back. Barty turned to page 54 and reread the advert. He wondered where in Norfolk this estate was. He had occasionally gone on buying trips, travelling to auction rooms in Diss and then to antique shops in Holt, Cromer and Kings Lynn; sometimes staying in the Victoria Inn in Holkham. Barty remembered the Victoria Inn for the walk to the beach, especially in the evening when the light was falling and all manner of ducks were circling home, and its truly delicious fish pie. He tended to remember places by food eaten. Professional interest, he supposed Barty was looking forward to a little detective work. He had done none since he retired from his auction business. Then it was all about tracing an object's story, it's provenance, as the antiques trade called it. Provenance added both value and gave comfort to buyers. A good story could transform an object from an ugly duckling to a soaring swan. Barty felt sorry for Lionel. For all his bluster, there was a good guy who just wanted to be liked. He knew Lionel's second wife, Rebecca, she had loved Lionel but found him just too selfish to live with. Barty, with Jack's help, would work back through the bronze's line of ownership. He knew that each buyer would have believed the seller had good title. It was only when a seller became reluctant to give details, that he knew he would be getting closer to the thief. He also knew that goods could change hands quickly. The theft probably happened only weeks ago and he knew he would have to move fast once Jack reported back on Sunday. Luckily, he had Sundays, Mondays and Tuesdays off.

Chapter 10

London

Beacon, real name Derek Laidlow, liked to load his van on Fridays. The jumbo car boot fair off the M4 started at six in the morning and, if Derek was to get his usual pitch, he would need to be on the road before five.

Derek Cyril Laidlow lived in Hammersmith, London, not far from the river Thames, his parents having bought the house in the 1950s. It was in a typical Victorian terrace, red brick with white painted mouldings to its doors and windows frames. Inside the front door was a small hall with parquetry ceramic tiled floor and stairs in front. To the right was a front room with angled bowed window and fireplace. Beyond a set of folding wooden shutters was a small dining room with the kitchen and downstairs loo at the back. Upstairs was divided into three bedrooms and the bathroom off the landing. The unusual thing about the Laidlow's house was a gap in the terrace between theirs and their neighbour's house. The gap was the reason why Derek's father had bought this particular house, as it allowed access down a narrow track to a large garage, with just enough space to turn and park a van. Some years ago, Derek had replaced the big double doors of the timber-clad building with a large cast-iron framed Crittall window, which was divided into 12 panes of glass, adjacent to a wide strapped hinged door. It was from this garage that the Beacon ran his antiques business; mostly house clearances.

"That's where the bargains are," as the Beacon was often heard to say.

The Beacon was helped by his wife, and their young nephew, Colin. Whilst the Beacon and Colin were away on house clearances, Mrs Beacon manned the shop, ably assisted by her kettle. Only repeat visitors came, as there were no hoardings on the street. The Beacon only sold to those he knew and the rest was sold every Sunday at the jumbo car boot fair but, if anything stuck, it was straight to the auction rooms in Putney. The Beacon and Colin were a good team; the Beacon did the talking and Colin did the work. Colin was six foot tall and slim. He wore jeans and a t-shirt and loved his Puma trainers. He both wore and collected them. He had long blonde hair which he was forever sweeping back with his left hand. Colin's obsession with Puma trainers puzzled the Beacon, whose only concession to dress was a brown felt trilby hat which he had found in a house clearance in Chelsea. Made by Lock & Co. of Piccadilly, it fitted him perfectly and Mrs Beacon said it added tone. It needed to, as the Beacon wasn't slim like his nephew; more apple-shaped. He wore an open short-sleeved shirt with the first three buttons undone, enough to reveal some pretty impressive man boobs. Underneath his shirt tails, as he always failed to tuck them in, was a sturdy brown leather belt holding up a pair of brown moleskin trousers. The look was finished by a pair of short brown leather boots, again from another house clearance in Fulham. Rather proudly, the Beacon had not been in a clothes shop in decades, or many other shops, for that matter, as his lightbulbs, screws, mugs, saucepans, plates etc came from house clearances. Mrs Beacon wore Dior and Ralph Lauren just like the fashionable ladies in Chelsea, but her designer clothes happened to be second-hand. Colin, who lived two doors up with Mr Beacon's sister and brother-in-law, would not dream of wearing second-hand clothes. His uncle Derek paid him every Friday in cash, which enabled Colin to spend his Saturday mornings in the high street shops of Kensington and Chelsea searching for new Puma trainers, always kept in their boxes and stored in his bedroom. It was these boxes that had reduced his room by a shoe box length, as they made-up a false wall, not dissimilar to a shoe shop storeroom. Derek's father Cyril had been both a scrap dealer and house clearer, who had bought three houses in the same street before prices became ridiculous, but mid-1980s ridiculous now seems rather cheap. Mr. Beacon let the house next door to three students, who paid him each £700 pounds per month. Life was rather comfortable for the Beacon but it didn't stop him working. He loved rootling through the lives of others. All manner of solicitors and smarter antique dealers had his mobile number.

Derek's van currently housed the contents of a clearance in Richmond that they had done on Thursday: lots of Edwardian inlaid furniture, burr maple 1930's bedroom suites, and countless items of bone china tea and dinnerware. Derek had given £150 pounds for the clearance, as there were three single mattresses and associated boxsprings to get rid of and commercial waste was so expensive. It cost him £30 per item in the Hammersmith and Fulham recycling centre, which was only around the corner, but the round-trip still took him half a day. The light blue Renault van was full to brimming by the time they had loaded the second-hand clothes rail on the back. Saturday was the Beacon's day off, whilst Mrs Beacon, or Dot as she was known, pottered around the Sainsbury's Megastore with her sister-in-law; Derek strolled down to the riverside pubs of Hammersmith, first of which was the Rose and Crown. The Beacon normally started with a pint of beer, and it was normally Fuller's London Pride, as the brewery was only up the river in Chiswick. After a couple of pints, the Beacon moved onto gin. His favourite was Plymouth gin, but he had to move to the Wheelwrights next door as the Rose and Crown didn't stock it. Not that it mattered, as the Beacon had friends in all of the pubs. It's amazing how many others kept to a similar routine or always seemed to be there.

"Morning Reg."

"Morning Derek, how's tricks?" said the landlord of the Rose and Crown.

"Good thanks. It's been busy. Had a clearance in Richmond. Lovely house, just a pain to park. Played cat and mouse, all week, with the gestapo."

This utterance turned a few heads but it was Derek's name for traffic wardens.

"Don't tell me, they only slapped a ticket on the brewery dray on Monday. It's a shame the brewery doesn't use horses any more, as I'm sure a couple of 18-hand shire horses would made short shrift of a traffic warden."

"Anybody been in yet?" said Derek looking around him.

"No, but expecting Doddy any moment now. It's only eleven o'clock Derek."

The Beacon's partner in crime was Doddy, so-called as he looked like the late comedian Ken Dodd, both sharing tousled black curly hair and irregular teeth. On cue, there was a clatter from the pub's swing double doors, and in walked Doddy.

"Morning Beacon, morning Reg, all good?"

"All good," said Reg. "Is it a London Pride?"

"No. Guinness today. I missed breakfast this morning."

With that Doddy produced a book from his man bag, or 'sacosh' as he called it. After all, it was the French who probably started wearing these bags first. He handed the tome to Derek.

"It looks good Doddy, a full grained calf binding with some bright gilt tooling. Derek looked at the spine.

"Golden Cockrell Press, the clue is in the name Doddy, where did you find it?" "Picked it up in Portobello this morning. You know the tables by that sci-fi loo, the one people get trapped in."

"I know," said Reg.

It was where the pavement widened and this was now filled by a cylindrical ribbed silver spaceship, masquerading as a coin-operated loo. Who it served was in the luck of the user, for if the door did not open, the occupant would be subject to the facility's pre-programmed cleaning routine. Many a user had been rescued squinting and smelling of bleach.

"How much did you pay for it Doddy?"

"Fifty pounds," said Dodd.

"Drinks all round Reg, Doddy has bagged himself another bargain."

"What's it worth?"

"Well, see this fellow on the frontispiece, Eric Gill? He is only one of the greatest book illustrators, and here it says number seven of 175 copies."

"So quite special then?" Doddy enquired.

"On Monday, take it to a couple of dealers in Charing Cross Road, especially Lipmans, and don't take anything below £500."

"You're joking Derek."

"No I'm not, it's in the bones Doddy, as my old man would say."

From that moment on, Derek and Doddy made their way along the riverside calling in at all the pubs and having double gins all the way until finally coming to a halt at their favourite Italian restaurant, Dolce Vita. This being a shallow building with large plate glass windows, with a row of neat circular tables outside, each with a pair of chairs facing the river. Once through a heavily weighted brown suede curtain, one emerged into a light-filled and oak-panelled interior. Small rectangular tables were laid with white linen table cloths, sparkling glasses and bright silver-plated cutlery. The menu was unneeded as Derek and Doddy always ate the same: lasagne, it acted like a sponge to their excess of alcohol. They only ate a main course, and were in and out within half an hour. Derek wished Doddy well after lunch. "Be lucky," were Derek's traditional parting words. Then a 25-minute walk home for a snooze in front of the television before Mrs Beacon's steak and kidney pudding. She had a special way with pastry. After supper, Derek and Dot walked to the river and back, allowing stomachs to settle. Then bed for Derek and some game shows on the telly for Dot.

The next morning he rose at 4.30 am, made himself a cup of tea and picked up a tin containing delicacies prepared by Dot. He walked through the garden and unlocked the van. Once safely inside he reversed and noticed Colin in his wing mirror, looking good in bright red high-top trainers. It took only 20 minutes before they were in the short queue to the boot fair.

"Morning Beacon," said the organiser, taking his entry fee. Derek popped in row one, nearest the public parking field, which was almost empty at this early hour, bar a couple of vans, one of which was Jack's Mercedes sprinter. Jack had been counting the hours down to meeting the Beacon again.

Colin was loading when Jack turned up with two cups of tea. Luckily Colin was of a generation that drank only Red Bull or water.

"Morning Beacon, got a spare tea here, any interest?"

"Thank you young sir," said the Beacon in a rather courtly manner. He always used this sort of language for selling.

"Flatter the buyer," his old dad had always said.

"It's Jack and the small fellow is Clive."

The Beacon didn't stroke dogs. He had been bitten once as a child; five stitches and two days in bed, he hadn't risked it again.

"Remember the heavy bronze group of horse and rider I bought from you last week? It's been a little slow to sell, and I wondered if it had come out of one of your more glamourous house clearances? Say an old actor or society figure, somebody with a story, that I could add to the bronze?"

The Beacon looked up from his polystyrene cup of tea, and the morning light caught his nose, a big warty affair, made up of different shades of red and purple, magnificently highlighted with dark thread lines. It was truly splendid and once caught sight of, it was difficult to avert the eyes.

"The bronze came from an old friend of my father's, Ray in Wandsworth, just over the bridge, and he ain't no actor or society figure."

"Does he have a shop?" This was going better than Jack had expected.

"Not exactly, more a yard. Ray's a scrap dealer like my old Dad."

Chapter 11

London

Jack couldn't wait until noon to inform Lionel of his success but, being early, he decided to text.

"Bronze bought from Ray @ Wandsworth Bridge scrapyard. Rgds Jack"

Now Jack had passed the problem on he found temporary relief and concentrated on the job in hand: the pursuit of bargains.

Colin was rearranging coat hooks on a clothes rail, the journey must have spilled some of the vintage clothing on the van's floor. There were a few buyers around so Jack made off for other vans which were slightly more ahead on the unpacking front. There was a good backgammon box amongst a trestle table top of junk; he had seen a similar one in Lionel's shop. He picked it up and there was a rattle of counters or, as Lionel referred to them, 'stones'; a term he said reflected the game's Middle Eastern origins. The board being furrows in the sand and the stones, quite literally, different coloured stones. As Jack picked up the large oblong box he admired the geometric patterns, like mosaic flooring just a lot smaller. He carefully inspected the surface for losses. Jack, like the keen sponge he was, remembered that Lionel said most of these decorative boards were made in Damascus, the Syrian capital, and sold to tourists when Europeans still travelled in the now troubled Arab countries. He opened it; the hinges were good and so too, the mosaic inlay inside. The 'stones' were made of turned bone, not ivory. The former is lighter in weight and is more open pored. Fifteen were stained red and fifteen were left in their natural state. The red-stained counters were the same vivid colour as chess pieces, the ones with elongated figures made in the Chinese port of Canton. Maybe the stones had been added, after all, the box must have been early 20th century, a souvenir, possibly bought by a wealthy Edwardian tourist travelling the Mediterranean aboard a private steam or sail boat. Jack had once taken a date to Waddesdon Manor in Buckinghamshire, where he had seen exotic octagonal tables in the billiard room, whose mosaic inlay reminded him of the box now in his hands. Those exotic Ottoman tables, like this box, might have been bought during carefree summer cruises, with no worries about maximum baggage weight associated with today's aircraft travel. Those floating palaces had ample and unrestricted storage below decks. It was these sort of stories that Jack had hoped the bronze might have had, and not Ray the scrap dealer. He couldn't think of anything less glamorous.

"What's your best price?" Jack asked an already seated dealer.

"Fifty-five will buy it now as you are the first to pick it up today."

"And maybe the last?" Jack countered.

The small man shifted in his folding chair. His cheese cutter flat cap hid thin mousy hair and partially covered his little beady eyes, all above a small moustache.

"How do you see it then?" said the owner of the rather mean moustache.

"Firstly, where is it from?" Jack wasn't taking any risks today.

"India? I think," said the owner of the thin cap.

"No, not country of manufacture. Where did YOU buy it?"

"Clearance near Shepherd's Bush. All nationalities around there," said the thin cap. "Thirty pounds," it owes him nothing being part of a house clearance, surmised Jack.

"Thirty eight and it's yours," replied the moustache.

"That's kind, but this time I'll give you forty," said Jack, letting the Indian attribution go, as it doesn't pay to be cocky. "But only on the condition the next time you get anything similar, especially octagonal tables, you'll keep them on the van for me. I'm here first thing every Sunday."

"Will do," said the still seated beady eyed man.

Jack bagged his purchase in a blue IKEA shoulder bag and made his way back to the Beacon. A third of his van was now unpacked and the clothes rail was crammed. On the rail he saw the unmistakable sandy colour of a Burberry raincoat. Removing it from its hanger, he slipped it on. It was too big, but perfect for somebody older, say in their 40s. He took it off, but kept it over his arm, and scanned around the van. Not much, just spindly chairs and delicate tables, but then he noticed a heavy leather upholstered chair towards the front of the van.

"Can I look at the leather armchair?" he said to the Beacon.

"Of course young Sir, be my guest."

With this, the Beacon pointed to a set of metal kitchen steps - only three treads, which perfectly bridged the gap from ground to van floor. Jack pulled the chair to the open face below the van's rolled shutter and sat in the seat. It was comfortable in a clubby way: its serpentine back supported his lower lumbar region, and its scrolled top rail held his head without forcing it forward. The arms were wide and upholstered in a brown open-grained leather; the whole back with shallow buttoning. Once Jack had established it was comfortable, he got up and turned the chair over on the van's floor being careful to lay a blanket down first. If he was to buy it the last thing he would want to do would be to explain scuffed leather to a buyer such as Lionel. It was certainly heavy, surely heavy enough to have a maker's stamp. He checked the underside of the rails for such a maker's mark, but there was none.

"Beacon, how much for the chair?"

"Three hundred pounds young Sir, but there is a little discount for the pair."

"What, there is another?" Jack tried not to sound too surprised.

"Yes, further down the van, just below the Luton. Colin should unearth it shortly."

"Did they come from a good home?" Jack asked, still nervous about 'good title'. "Richmond, to be precise. We had a house clearance there this week. One chair was in the downstairs sitting-room and another upstairs in the study; hence why they're in different parts of the van."

"Beacon, I will take the pair at £550, and how much for this?" Jack held up the Burberry raincoat which was still on his arm.

"You can have that for free, young Sir, you being a repeat customer."

Jack peeled off the bank notes, the same notes Lionel had given him for the large bronze, and waited for Colin to free the second chair from the grip of too many fussy Edwardian chairs and delicate tables. Jack loaded his purchases into his Mercedes Sprinter van and headed off for a bacon roll, Clive's favourite stand. As they walked, Clive barked a "little bacon never hurt anybody". After a mug of tea and a bacon roll, he and Clive did another tour of the car boot field. It was full now, but the serious house clearers in the large battered vans were all thoroughly combed. What bargains that may have been borne to the field were now elsewhere; only old stereos, ladders and buckets remained. Jack walked back to his van and thought he would give Lionel first option on the chairs and backgammon box, plus Clive would love a walk on Hastings beach.

In Hastings, Lionel woke at seven and it wasn't until he collected his newspaper that he looked at his mobile. On the screen was an alert for a new message from Jack: "Bronze bought from Ray @ Wandsworth Bridge scrapyard. Rgds Jack"

Not ideal thought Lionel, those scrap yard boys are generally on the rough and ready side, but hopefully Barty would know what to do. After consuming most of the Sunday Times, especially the arts, food and drink pages, plus a more careful read of the world news, as it was sensible to be up to speed with Barty and Pru in the room. Lionel put down the newspapers and walked upstairs to shower and shave. He then selected a Turnbull & Asser shirt, a light blue gingham check, no collar stiffeners today as an open collar sat better without them, and his trusted navy blue linen suit. The look was finished with an orange silk square which was teased into his top left breast pocket. He wanted to look his best for Pru and the girls. Before Lionel left his house he needed a present for Barty. No point in taking wine as Barty would be offering something much, much better. The folding fez bought from the vintage clothes shop, Xanadu at the end of the road would be perfect. Run by a delightful mother and daughter team, on his way to the shops in London Road, making it just too easy for Lionel to pop in every other day to check new arrivals. He had bought the fez along with three others a couple of weeks ago. One had a beautiful woven straw structure, to which was sewn the distinctive red felt outer layer, with a long black silk tassle on top. He thought that it would buy Barty another 20 minutes in his garden as the air cooled after sunset. The other two could be rolled much like a panama hat and put in a coat pocket. Lionel chose one of the scrunchable fezzes. It seemed to fit all head sizes and he thought Barty would wear it on his terrace. Lionel put it in his coat pocket. He checked his phone, wallet and keys and pulled his front door to. He walked down Norman Road and then turned right to the sea. It was a 20-minute walk to the end of Queens Road, then a further 20 minutes to Barty's front door. A forty-minute walk would leave Lionel absolutely ravenous.

Barty, like Lionel, had been up since 7 o'clock. His first job was to assault the leg of lamb. With a small paring knife he made numerous slits, into which he pressed garlic and rosemary, before rubbing it with olive oil and seasoning with salt-and-pepper. He would let it stand until he put it into his kettle barbecue which stood purposefully outside on his terrace. He would light the barbecue later, say at 10 o'clock. Last night the restaurant was packed; Phoenix managed to turn three tables. It had been a good week for Barty. He had little costs, Polly and Phoenix's wages and the food, he didn't get involved in the drinks, as they were sold by the Brewing Brothers in the bar upstairs. The Brothers paid for the electricity, gas, water and rates to which Barty made a small contribution. The arrangement worked well; he concentrated on the food and they made money on the drinks. He hoped to clear £1,500 a week, which afforded him a good lifestyle from a four-day week.

The door bell rang and Barty opened his front door to find a rather flushed Lionel wearing a fez.

"A present dear friend," Lionel said, as he removed the fez and handed it to Barty, who immediately put it on. It fitted perfectly.

"Thank you, I'll have difficulty taking this off."

"Don't then, it takes years off you. What's cooking?" Lionel said as he walked through the small hall corridor into the large airy sitting room.

"A leg of lamb from Romney Marshes, runner beans from West Hill and Parmentier potatoes, as I love a little chopping on Sundays. White wine?"

"Oh, yes please," said Lionel, falling into an armchair.

Last night, after a drink with the Brothers, Barty had clambered home and put three bottles of white burgundy in the fridge. Barty now cut the foil, pulled the cork, and poured the wine into two long-stemmed glasses. He handed Lionel a glass and they toasted "Friends, family and food".

"This is heaven! What alchemist made this?" said a smiling Lionel, whose breathing after his 40-minute walk had almost reached a more regular, resting rhythm.

"It's Domaine Roulot 2010. Nice and peachy isn't it? Now what news from young Jack?" said Barty, whilst removing par-boiled potatoes from a pan.

Lionel produced his mobile and read the short message:

"Bronze bought from Ray @ Wandsworth Bridge scrapyard. Rgds Jack."

"This will need some thought. Maybe after lunch we should plot our next steps. Here's a bowl; would you kindly go into the garden and pick lots of runner beans, fill the bowl to brimming please."

Once Lionel had walked outside, Barty took a stool and made some notes at his kitchen island. Asking a scrapyard owner about a stolen bronze was never going to yield results. This would need some careful thought. He paused and took a sip of wine. Life was good and he didn't want Lionel's mishap to rock their charmed world. Lionel re-emerged through the sitting room's double doors, holding a brimming bowl of beans.

"You've enough for the restaurant out there," said Lionel smiling.

"I occasionally take some down, but I really need twice as many canes. Saying that, I would rather have the room for asparagus. Only two more years to wait now."

"Why, how long does it take?" Lionel enquired, whilst draining his glass.

"First year sowing; second year cutting; third year harvesting and then an annual crop for 10 to 15 years. Just think, in two years' time we will be enjoying the asparagus season."

"Let's drink to that," Lionel said, proffering an empty glass. Barty realised he wouldn't be able to keep up with Lionel; that's why some houses had both butlers and cooks as it was difficult being both.

"Lionel, you're my butler today, the white wine is in the fridge, so too, the tonics. It's your job to look after everybody's drinks, including yourself, is that understood?" said Barty firmly.

"Loud and Clear," said Lionel whilst topping up both glasses.

The doorbell rang, Barty put down his knife, rinsed his hands and opened the door to Pru and her girls.

"Welcome Pru, how lovely to see you," Barty kissed her on both cheeks and waved at the girls behind.

"Come with me, I have a surprise in the sitting-room," Barty said, whilst leading the girls through the hall.

"Pru," Lionel said softly, and rushed to kiss her. He had always rather fancied her.

The girls all had a gin and tonic with ice and lots of lemon slices, masterfully prepared by Lionel.

"l like the fez Barty," Phoenix said, "very Marrakesh."

"It fits so well I forgot I had it on. It's a present from Lionel."

"How's Pru?" said Lionel.

"Really busy. Everybody seems to have fallen in love with their dogs. Rather excitingly I've been asked to stay in Norfolk to draw some pugs for an old friend."

"Oh really, where in Norfolk?" enquired Lionel.

"It's near the coast, a rather grand estate called Kooling Towers."

Chapter 12
Norfolk

Clem made his farewells to his Ma and Pa and took the two steps down from the caravan to its surrounding concrete pad, closely followed by Tom and Scan, who were quickly re-joined by their small retinue of terriers. Something was troubling Clem. Although his Pa was no longer physically strong, he still managed to be in charge. As one sense recedes, another takes up the slack, and in Terry's case he could no longer fight the young lions but he was still able to control them. From the beginning of time, 'Divide and Rule' has been a useful tool for many an elderly statesman. There was something in his Pa's manner that didn't sit well with Clem. As he knew, honesty and his father didn't go hand in hand. Clem led the way to their black Toyota pickup truck. It was a twin cab with large diameter alloy wheels. Clem took the driver's seat, Tom the front passenger seat and the fox-like Scan the backseat, leaning forward to be between his two elder brothers.

When all the terriers were in, and the doors safely closed, Tom turned to Clem and said, "Was Pa telling the truth?"

"I'm sure he was," Clem said, couching the truth from his younger brothers.

"It seems odd that a casual thief would go for something so near to the house," replied Tom.

"I can see why people think it was us, we're local, strong and with a certain reputation, but the only thing I have ever taken from Sir Roger are pheasants and rabbits. I haven't even been up his drive, and wouldn't even know where that bronze stood. Do any of you know who might have lifted it?"

Scan handed two rolled cigarettes to Tom whose job, as second-in-command, was to light both and hand one to his elder brother. As the three brothers smoked they fell into thought. Clem wanted to find out who had tarnished his name, Tom was concerned his Pa wasn't telling the truth, and Scan was worried about a conversation he'd had at a wedding only a month ago. The three brothers' cousin, Kezia, had married someone from Essex. Brandon, Kezia's new husband, had two younger brothers similar in age to Scan, and after a few drinks Scan had talked about their childhood antics in the woods of Kooling Towers.

"I'm not sure, but I may have said the wrong things to the wrong people,"ventured Scan.

Both Clem and Tom turned their heads around,

"What are you talking about?" said Clem.

"You know at Kezia and Brandon's wedding, I got on with Brandon's younger brothers."

"Yea," said Clem, "what were their names?"

"Cliff and Albert. Cliff was the short and stocky one in the Adidas, and Albert was tall and ginger in the red Puma quilted jacket."

"I remember Albert," said Clem. "His hair managed to clash with his jacket!"

Scan continued.

"I spent a good deal of time telling them about our adventures in the woods of Kooling Towers and how the house was vast with splendid gardens. Well I remember the tall one, Albert, asked me did the Towers have any garden ornaments. I thought at the time, it was an odd thing to ask, when all our talk was of catapults and air rifles."

"That's weird," said Clem. "Anyways, let's get going, those hedges in Holt aren't going to cut themselves."

With that, the Toyota moved through the metal gates of their site and took a left on the road for Holt. As Clem drove he thought of Kezia, and her wedding day. His favourite cousin Kezia had always been a sort of orange colour from about the age of 12. She was tall, five foot 10 inches with long limbs and a flat stomach. Her face was a sort of oval, with a button nose, good cheekbones, and ridiculous false eyelashes. She wore a uniform of large hooped gold earrings, gold or pink sequinned boob tube and miniskirt, with trainers rather than heels, the only concession to her young age. Clem and Kezia had always got on. There was a spark about his younger cousin. She, like him, was leader of her little pack, which was made up of sisters and cousins all of various ages and shapes, but united both in orange skin colour makeup and clothes.

Kezia and Brandon met at an earlier wedding; he strutting around amongst his younger brothers, and Kezia flirting. Whether there was a 'grab' or not, their courtship was quick, and a wedding day set, allowing just enough time for a spectacular wedding dress. The chosen dressmaker didn't normally do wedding dresses but Kezia and her little posse often went to Norwich's grid system of market stalls opposite the Town Hall, the owner of one of these stalls had recently graduated with a first-class honours degree in fashion design. She made figure hugging dresses with short bottoms, in fine wools and silks. Kezia was the perfect clothes horse; something on the hanger came alive on her gangly giraffe-like frame. Whilst still studying in her final year at Norwich University, the 'graduate' had opened her stall in the market and Kezia had quickly become her willing muse. This relationship was only possible if the posse of sisters and cousins were dispatched elsewhere. After all, the graduate had a brand to grow and a gaggle of boisterous travellers chewing gum wasn't going to add much glamour, whereas Kezia did.

When Kezia removed her hooped earrings and wriggled into one of the graduate's dresses, she quickly became the talk of the market and it wasn't long before teenagers and twenty somethings found her stall and 'trying on' quickly turned to buying. It was on one of these days when Kezia had influenced a merry band of buyers, that the graduate had offered to make her wedding dress.

"You have been a star, a proper glamour girl, and on your wedding day I would like to make you a dress fit for a princess."

The graduate lived with her boyfriend in a 'shed' on his parents' smallholding just outside Holt. To say shed was to underplay the structure. The boyfriend, a builder called Dave, put up the structure in only a month. A fibrecrete base, that shining beacon of recycling where concrete becomes stronger by combining a problematic landfill material, fibreglass; which when shredded and added to the concrete mix, allows the concrete to expand and contract without cracking. This magical base was only interrupted by a single soil pipe and mains water feed, and from it rose four courses of bricks then timber studs for the walls. The walls were clad on the outside with black painted corrugated tin along with timber tongue and groove planking on the inside. Both linings sandwiching wool insulation, and all under a pitched slate roof. Russell, the roofer, beat a personal best of three days from the tile battening to cementing the semi-circular ridge tiles.

It was to the 'shed' that Kezia's wedding dress party descended. Taking the lead was her mother, June, various aunts including the boy's mother Pearl, plus various sisters and cousins. Instead of it having two bedrooms, Dave had fitted the second bedroom as a workroom, a light filled space with a centrally placed rectangular pine table to which the graduate had pinned a padded linen cover, so as not to stain or damage any precious silks or wools. Below a metal framed Crittall window was a large brown leather Chesterfield sofa, which was now filled with June, Pearl and perched on top was the remaining pack of sisterhood.

The graduate knew travellers paid big money for wedding dresses. She also knew this might be her chance to get at least two years' rent on a shop come workspace in Holt. The market in Norwich, was great in the summer months, but spring and autumn showers often damaged her stock.

Once settled with glasses of Prosecco, Kezia and the graduate disappeared to the next door bedroom, leaving the sisterhood to party in the workroom. As the Aunts turned their attentions to the three bottles in the ice bucket, there was a certain stillness in the bedroom next door. Kezia stood naked, save for a red coloured thong, whilst the graduate slipped the brilliant white dress over her outstretched arms. Then Kezia turned around as the graduate pulled up the concealed zip at the back of the dress. As the zip rode up it seemed to magically pull every fibre taut, giving Kezia a body not seen since the naughty 1890s. Kezia turned and looked in the mahogany framed cheval mirror, the bodice gave her boobs and an even better waist. The skirt was short, as there was no point in hiding

Kezia's race horse legs, and at the back, was the all-important train. The dress turned Kezia into the Princess that she had long dreamed of being. She turned and hugged the graduate with an unmistakable grip of thankfulness, walked next door, while the graduate hung back in her bedroom. Firstly, she heard gasps, then tears and finally clapping and wolf whistling. After more glasses of fizz and numerous cigarettes, the cash was counted and the graduate was left in the still of her workroom with empty glasses, full ashtrays and THREE years' rent on a workspace in Holt.

A small ceremony in the Roman Catholic Church in Holt was followed by a large reception held at a rather surprised golf club. The club boasted only nine holes but had a cavernous function room with a 20-foot bar. Greed had got in the way of judgement, and Kezia's father and brother had reversed a categorical 'No' with a £5,000 deposit. Most of the girls brought their own drinks but the boys wanted Guinness and lager on draught and the sales of these would more than compensate for the smuggled-in pre-mixed vodka and cokes.

After all, as Kezia's father said,

"There'd be fierce competition at the bar and how would a manager and two teenage boys cope with orders of 16 different drinks!"

Clem remembered Kezia had never looked prettier and Brandon had an easy way with him. Clem had heard that money stuck to Brandon and he hoped he would be kind to his younger cousin. The night ended with only the one scrap, younger boys fighting for position, and Terry and Pearl being dragged semiconscious from the golf club. It was a good night, now slightly tarnished by Scan's recollection of chats about garden ornaments.

Tomorrow, Clem would drive to see Brandon, it would be good to see Kezia in her new home.

Once in Holt, Clem sent a text to Brandon and shortly received a call back.

"All alright?" said Brandon.

"Champion," said Clem. " We are passing your way tomorrow. Will you be about?"

"Sure, business in the morning, but back at noon. Kezia would be keen to see you, and the boys."

I'll text the postcode, see you tomorrow."

Brandon hung up and as he did so he dropped a semiconscious creditor to the floor. A bloody nose would remind him to pay the outstanding debt and fast-accumulating interest. The man was a fool to gamble and an even greater fool to use Brandon's money to do so.

Clem returned his mobile safely to his inside pocket and said to his brothers,

"We are off to Brandon and Kezia's tomorrow. Let's find out what Brandon and his brothers actually do."

Chapter 13

Norfolk

Sir Roger was quietly seething. There had been no response to his advertisement and subsequent reward in the Antiques Trade Gazette; nothing back from Anita at The Swotter Arms and Lou hadn't heard anything from Terry or his boys. It was a dead-end thus far. He knew he would lose the odd five-bar metal farm gate, but he hadn't expected a theft so close to the house. Even his interview with the police had yielded nothing so far.

Detective Inspector Kevin Smythe had come from the main police station in Norwich. When Sir Roger rang through to his local police station in Sheringham, the Inspector decided to pass it up the line to Norwich. Kooling Towers was a well-known estate and Sir Roger was well connected within the county. Sir Patrick, Sir Roger's father, had been a good friend of a much-respected former chief constable, Sir Michael Steele; both had played rugby at Blackheath Football Club before the war. As a young constable in training, Kevin had heard Sir Patrick speak at his passing out ceremony. The man and his words had left a lasting impression upon him, so when the call came through from Sheringham station, Kevin leapt at the opportunity to interview Sir Roger at Kooling Towers.

Detective Inspector Kevin Smythe lived with his wife Helen, a former WPC, who had left the police force when their second child was born, but hoped to return to Norwich police station when her children started secondary school. Like Kevin, her father Frank had been in the Norfolk Constabulary and had been one of Norwich's most feared desk sergeants. Frank had dealt with matters in a more immediate way: a word there, a cuff here and even a 'gentle' touch with a truncheon. As her father would say, "alot of paperwork saved."

Frank's Chief Constable had been Sir Michael Steele and Frank did all he could to best serve Sir Michael. As children, Kevin and Helen had grown up with both their fathers continually quoting Sir Michael:

"What would Sir Michael think?"

"What would Sir Michael do?"

To say he had an influence, was to severely underplay his role.

Kevin and Helen lived in a 1970s house on the outskirts of Norwich. It sat in a quiet residential road, with well-tended front gardens and considerately parked cars. From the first-floor bedrooms they had sight of Norwich's Cathedral tower, and when the wind was in the east they could hear the City's many chiming bells. The house was sun-filled and immaculate. Breakfast, lunch and supper were taken around a 1970s teak G plan table; the Smythes believed in conversation. As far as Kevin and Helen were concerned, children and electronic tablets didn't mix. Sir Michael would have surely agreed.

Kevin was excited about his interview with Sir Roger. He had had his hair cut in honour: a smart anvil-shaped affair, as his hair had been 'at attention' from boyhood. A grey flannel suit, regulation white shirt and a Norfolk constabulary Rugby club tie completed the look. That morning he kissed Helen and the children, who all chimed "Good luck," as Kevin left the drive in one of the station's unmarked grey Hyundais. He arrived at Kooling Towers just before his 9.30am appointment. The front door was opened by the housekeeper, May.

"Good morning Detective Inspector," May said, before Kevin could even introduce himself.

"Sir Roger is in the library, please follow me."

"Thank you," replied Kevin, who was slightly taken aback by the formality of his greeting.

This housekeeper seemed to be better briefed than his colleagues in the Constabulary. As May led Kevin through the hall, she enquired whether he would like tea or coffee. Kevin hesitated but May reassured him that Sir Roger was having coffee.

"Well, coffee for me then too please."

May knocked and, without waiting for a reply, she opened the library door. The impressive oak-panelled room was fitted with library bookcases, each shelf neatly arranged with calf-bound books: library editions of Shakespeare, Dickens, Trollope etc. Opposite the door, and amongst the bookcases, sat Sir Roger in a tub-shaped leather chair next to a laid, but as yet unlit, fire. Sir Roger rose to his feet, which he always did for Lady Daphne and other women.

"Good morning Detective Inspector."

"Good morning Sir Roger."

"Please have a seat," he said, indicating to a matching armchair opposite his own.

"Thank you."

Kevin settled and brought out his black, folding notebook in which was a card that he handed to Roger. Sir Roger inspected the card and said:

"My father's great friend was a former chief constable, Sir Michael Steele."

"I had the honour once of hearing your father address new recruits saying that, "the discipline of the army was easily transferred to the constabulary."

"Two great men, your father and Sir Michael."

Sir Roger noted the sincerity in which the young Detective Inspector spoke, and remembered Michael's words:

"Good men make good police officers and poor men become bent coppers."

May returned with a pot of coffee and laid the tray on a table covered in newspapers and magazines. The table dominated the library, Sir Roger's father had bought it from his old regimental headquarters when his former regiment had been amalgamated with the Grenadier Guards. Rectangular, with an inset gilt-tooled leather top, over an arrangement of six frieze drawers, on triangular-shaped tablet ends with powerful, carved claw feet. The whole table shone with a reddish mahogany glow. It was very special to Sir Roger and always reminded him of his heroic father.

"Black or white Inspector?" asked Sir Roger.

"Black, thank you."

Sir Roger dispensed both tea and coffee in his household, as Lady Daphne was always just too busy.

"If I may take all the details, Sir Roger."

Sir Roger opened an A4 day book in which he had made some notes with Cecil the gardener.

"We believe the bronze was taken on Saturday night or early Sunday morning. May, who you have just met, noticed its removal when she walked to work on Sunday morning."

"What date was that Sir?"

"It was the first Sunday in June."

"That would be the third of June. Do you think the incident occurred during the day or night?" enquired the Detective Inspector, whilst earnestly writing in his notebook.

"I believe it was in the early hours of Sunday morning. Cecil, the gardener, was awoken by May's dog Punch barking at just after 1am."

"Did this Cecil look out of the window Sir?"

"No, regrettably he didn't. He dismissed the commotion as Punch barking at a fox or a badger. Punch is a Jack Russell with honed terrier instincts."

"Did your gardener notice anything else?"

"Cecil did say, after the theft was discovered, that it may have been a van Punch was barking at. Certainly, the damage to the grass verge at the mouth of the drive would suggest a van or a small lorry with twin tyres on its rear axle, Cecil has photographs of the damage."

"Thank you. I would like to interview Cecil afterwards?"

"Of course, Cecil is looking forward to helping and can walk you around the garden."

"I have been sent good photographs of the bronze. Was it valuable?" ventured Kevin.

"No not really. I acquired it years ago from a local auction room."

"Which one Sir?"

"The one in Diss. Lady Daphne and I try to go to the view days. Some marvellous things turn up there."

"Thomas Gaze, Sir?"

"That's the fellow. Lovely lady who runs it, works like a Trojan."

"Do you know roughly when you bought it, and possibly for how much?"

"Thankfully I found the saleroom receipt, dated Friday 6th June 1997. Hammer price was £550 plus buyer's premium and associated VAT. It comes to just under £650," said Sir Roger. He liked accuracy.

"It's not old you know, probably cast in China or the Philippines in the 1980s when metals were considerably cheaper."

"Thank you Sir Roger."

Kevin was pleased with the original sales receipt. He liked a paper trail.

"Before I interview your gardener, do you have any suspicions as to who might have stolen the bronze?"

"My first thought was that it was the work of Terry Kindly and his boys at that site in Lucky Slap."

"They are well known to us Sir Roger. May I see your gardener now?" said Kevin, rising from his seat.

"Of course, I will introduce you to him. He is waiting outside."

Sir Roger then led Kevin through the hall, past a drawing room into a circular glass conservatory, the likes of which Kevin had never seen before. He and Helen had added a conservatory to their kitchen last year, but it was nothing like this one. Above Kevin's head were thousands of rectangular panes of glass, held by metal ribs which ran from the ground to a central point at least 12 feet above his head. The interior was shaded by a grape vine that wound its way around a painted metal internal ladder system, lying only six inches off the metal ribs and glass panes. The 'ladder and vine' model hadn't been offered to Kevin by Bob, the owner of Norwich's foremost conservatory company. He would tackle Bob later on that.

A set of double doors opened on to steps and then a large, beautifully lit terrace, beyond which was a small garden. This, he believed, was called a parterre, full of interlaced low cut box hedging. One of Helen and Kevin's favourite programs was the BBC's Gardeners' World and he was sure the presenter's garden, Long Meadow, had something similar. In the centre of the hedging stood a rather strange statue, inappropriate, he thought.

"Cecil, this is Detective Inspector Smythe of Norwich police station. I will leave you now Inspector. Thank you for your attention and I hope you are successful in recovering our bronze."

"Thank you Sir Roger; I will report back shortly."

Sir Roger walked back through the conservatory, thinking a man like Kevin would do his best to recover their bronze.

Kevin turned his attention to Cecil now.

"Good morning Cecil, may I have your surname for the record?"

"Trowel, Cecil Trowel, Sir," replied Cecil, who decided to wear a suit and tie today. He hadn't met many detectives before and, if Kevin had been Morse, he would have hired a dinner jacket and black tie!

"Do you have photographs of the damaged verge?"

asked Kevin gently, as he could see Cecil was ill at ease.

"Yes, on my phone."

"Would you send them to either this email or my mobile number," said Kevin, handing Cecil his card.

"Can I get May to do that. She's more technical than me."

"Now, would you show me the plinth from which the bronze was taken?"

Cecil led the Detective to the hornbeam walk. Kevin inspected the pylon-shaped plinth and noted its repair. Sir Roger obviously ran a tidy ship. Then he paced out the distance from the plinth to the drive. Cecil volunteered that they must have used a wheelbarrow and then pointed out damage to the grass verge of the drive, still showing signs of a van's rear twin tyres.

"Sir Roger suggested that it might be the work of Terry Kindly and his boys," said the Detective.

"Do you have any suspicions Mr Trowel?"

"Terry has been a nuisance in the past but not recently. I believe he's not a well man now."

"What about the boys?"

"I very much doubt it. They may be young and clumsy but they are no fools. They have played in these woods since they were little boys and I don't think they would wish to jeopardise that.

Furthermore, knowing the boys, especially the eldest Clem, I wouldn't be surprised if he wasn't making his own enquiries as to whom had been thieving on Kindly's Manor!"

Chapter 14

Essex

Clem, Tom and Scan waited for the roads to settle. The drive to Kezia and Brandon's place was a good two hours away and there was no need to add rush hour traffic to that. They left shortly after 9am and drove south towards Ipswich. Clem was keen to see Kezia in her new role as wife. Had she changed, where did they live and what was Brandon's family like? Clem knew that they lived near Rayleigh in Essex, but was it in a house, a caravan or some half-way measure like a prefab chalet on bricks? Clem's thoughts were broken by Scan.

"What do you call a fly without any wings?"

Both Clem and Tom knew the answer but they would never spoil Scan's punchline.

"A walk," said a chuckling Scan.

"For Pete's sake, Scan, that's not the first time we have heard that one!"

"I've a new one."

"Ok, fire away," said Tom.

"How does Moses make coffee?"

This was new to both Clem and Tom.

"How does Moses make coffee?" Clem repeated.

"Hebrews it!" said a chuckling Scan.

This time, all three boys laughed. If they were going to travel for two hours, they might as well be laughing than staring blankly at the road. The boys carried on talking and laughing until they stopped outside Ipswich, crossing the Orwell Bridge their stop was The Suffolk Food Hall. A cavernous farm shop with a fearsome reputation for homemade sausage rolls. Clem parked his Toyota furthest from the farm shop's entrance under the shade of a tree. The terriers needed shade and Clem knew that three travellers emerging from a pickup truck drew unnecessary attention. Anyway, it was good to stretch the legs. Clem bought the sausage rolls whilst Tom got the teas from another counter. Scan secured a table with a clear sight line to the Toyota. He loved their terrier dogs and he didn't feel comfortable if he couldn't see them. The feeling was mutual; they all stared back from the passenger window with their back legs on the seat and front paws on the window sill, continually trying to nose their way out of the two inch gap at the top.

"These are good," said Scan, taking a bite from his sausage roll.

"What does Brandon do?" said Tom.

"Much like us, I would think, odd jobs here and there, but I know he's not a builder," replied Clem.

"Why not?" said Tom.

"Builders normally drive vans and Brandon's got a four-door Mercedes and it doesn't look like it lugs power tools and accro props."

"Nor dogs," interjected Scan. A man without a dog raised suspicion in Scan.

"Let's get on, and find out," said Clem, putting down his empty cup.

The dogs went wild as soon as the remote unlocked the pickup. Once inside with dogs settled they resumed their journey to Rayleigh.

Clem was expecting a quiet lane and an unmarked entrance, give or take the odd fly-tipped washing machine or rubble sack. None of these marked Brandon's site, just two substantial brick-built gate posts capped with concrete model dogs. Once through the posts, there were two rows of floating homes, surrounded by larger floating ones. By floating, I mean held aloft on several courses of bricks. Little was mobile at Brandon's, but it did seem settled except for the usual unruly clutch of kids. Much like terriers, they were immediately on to the unknown pickup, putting both hands on the vehicle's windows whilst keeping their feet on BMX pedals.

"Who you for?" came the cheekiest boy.

"Brandon and Kezia," Clem replied feeling strangely uncomfortable.

"They're on the right," said the cheeky boy to his crew.

"Which one?" Clem replied

"That would be telling."

"Brandon's our brother-in-law, which one is his?"

"Steady sister," said the boy, "I don't know who youse lot are?"

"Nor do I, and one more 'Sister' and I will be opening this truck door!"

Luckily, for the BMX kids, a door opened on the nearest floating home and Kezia appeared, waved and smiled.

As Clem, Tom and Scan jumped from their truck doors, so did their dogs who promptly scattered the unruly kids. Much like 18th century coaching dogs would have dispersed robbers and highwaymen, the kids' ankles on BMX bikes were just the right height for their fiercely loyal terriers.

Kezia stayed in the doorway, seeming almost fearful to alight on the ground. She still looked like a giraffe, all long limbed, in short skirt and a crop top. Clem was the first to climb the two treads into the doorway. They hugged, his nose briefly becoming entangled in her huge hoop earrings. After hugging and kissing all three, Kezia turned and led them into a light-filled salon. Below large windows was a stainless steel sink and draining board, sunk into white work tops with white undercounter cabinets and matching hanging cabinets all with gold coloured handles. The sun was streaming through the window and seemed to bounce off every surface. Beyond a small right-angled return of cabinets stood a large cream leather sofa with deep seats and low backs. To Clem it looked brand new, in fact, all looked untouched.

Kezia broke his silent inspection.

"Tea, boys?" As she said this, she opened a cupboard and removed a sparkling kettle, filled it from the sink and plugged it in. Then she took cups from another overhead cupboard and tea etc. assembling them all in front of the kettle. Clem thought this was odd. His Ma kept everything on the side and he knew his aunt, Kezia's Ma, did the same.

"It is so lovely to see you all," said Kezia as she made the tea, while the boys stood rather awkwardly filling the spare space in the kitchen.

"How's all at home?" Kezia said, without turning around.

"All's good with Ma and Pa, although Pa is rarely allowed out. His poor heart has taken the spark from him and Ma is more keeper than wife now. No real change. Come on, less of us, more of your news. What's married life like?"

Kezia didn't turn around, but continued to fuss over the tea when she spoke.

"Things are fine, but since the wedding I haven't done a lot. I mostly stay here bar the odd trip out."

"Brandon, what does he do?" asked Scan.

Clem and Tom both looked at Scan and then turned back to Kezia. They were keen to know the answer to the question, but hadn't had the courage to ask.

"He's fine. I don't see a lot of him, he's always working with his brothers," said Kezia, turning with two outstretched mugs: Clem and Tom first and then one for Scan.

"What's his work?" Scan probed.

"I don't know, he really doesn't talk much about work."

"Are we going to see him?" Clem asked.

"He knows you're coming today. He normally gets back around six," said Kezia.

"He said to me that he would be back around noon, and it's now after 1pm,"'said Clem.

"Shall we go into Rayleigh and grab something to eat?"

"I'm not sure I should leave now," said Kezia as she put the kettle and other tea things back into their allotted cupboards.

"Come on, Kezia, you always jumped at the chance of going to Norwich, surely Rayleigh has somewhere for food?"

"I'm not sure when Brandon is getting back," she said, almost anxiously.

"Message him," said Clem.

"I would but I have no mobile, Brandon's taken it for repair."

"I'll call him then." Before Clem dialled, Kezia reached out and lowered Clems' phone.

"Let's go," she said.

She ushered her cousins to the door. Outside, all was calm, no BMX gang; the terriers had kept them safely in their homes.

She reviewed the interior of her floating home and then closed the door.

"Aren't you going to lock it?" said Clem as he held open the front passenger door for his cousin.

"No need, nobody would dare enter, and Brandon's mother opposite, keeps a close eye."

The terriers scrambled over the central armrest to nuzzle Kezia. They loved her, as she loved them.

"I have so missed them," said Kezia, scratching their excited upturned bodies. "Why don't you get a dog?" asked Scan.

"Brandon doesn't like dogs."

"Why?" replied Scan.

"He thinks they are messy, all paw prints on the floors and jumping up on his clean trousers. That would be too much!"

Clem steered the pickup truck through the brick gateposts. Kezia's shoulders fell and she reached and touched Clem's arm.

"I've missed you."

"We have all missed you too, you're alright, aren't you?"

"Of course, it's just different and sort of lonely. Before, I had my gang of girls and lots of family. Now, I just have Brandon."

"What about his family?"

"They're all around, but it's just not the same. There's little laughter, not like the constant ribbing of Terry and Pearl and the warmth of my family. I loved my wedding and know that it will be different when we have our own kids, but it's just this in between time."

"I'm sure it will get better. You will have beautiful girls and strong boys," said Clem. Rayleigh was not far from Kezia's. They found a bakery off the high street with tables outside and a parking space. Once the dogs were shut in the truck, the party settled, ordered filled bread rolls and soft drinks. Kezia sat re-arranging her limbs several times and drank with a straw in her bottle. Clem thought she could have been 15 again; she seemed far too young to be married.

Clems' thoughts were broken with the beep beep of an incoming message, which read: "I'm at home, you got Kez?"

"Brandon's at home, let's finish and go. I want to properly meet this husband of yours," said Clem, as he finished his cheese and ham roll. The rest followed, carrying half-finished rolls and Cokes to the truck. Scan never finished anything as he always left a little for each of the dogs. As they drove through the brick gateposts, Scan thought it was odd that they should be topped with concrete dogs, seeing that there was little love for them here, or maybe he thought the last two dogs were cast alive in concrete!

Outside the floating home was Brandon's big black Mercedes. If a car could look menacing, this one did. Standing beside it were Cliff and Albert, Brandon's two brothers. Albert's hair seemed to be even redder. Kezia smiled but didn't speak. She walked past Brandon's brothers, opened the caravan's door and ushered her cousins in. He was sitting in the middle of the cream sofa, perched on the front edge wearing black trousers, cut short to show a pair of brown Gucci suede loafers. He was on the phone. He didn't stand up, but just raised a single finger in acknowledgement. He didn't talk much, just listened and then said,

"See you tomorrow, noon".

He then got up, beckoned Clem and his brothers over, shook hands and bade them to sit on the sofa. He kissed Kezia and took four beers from the fridge.

"Isn't Kezia looking good," Brandon said, as he distributed the beers.

"Not as good as she looked at the wedding, what girl does?" Brandon added.

"It's a nice home," Clem said.

"Kezia keeps it nice."

As he spoke, he brushed his right trouser leg, for no apparent reason, maybe more habit than need.

"I like it just so. Too much mess outside. I like it nice inside."

"Are Cliff and Albert coming in?" Clem asked.

"No, best left with the car," Brandon said changing the subject. "How was your trip this morning?"

"Fine, stopped once near Ipswich and then easy all the way here. How's things with you, we were chatting in the car trying to work out what you do for a job?"

Brandon paused, then stroked more invisible dog hairs from his right trouser leg.

"I'm a people person, I help them out," he said, whilst individually staring at Clem, Tom and Scan.

"A sort of caring," he added, "anyway, it's been lovely seeing you boys but Kezia and I have a date, don't we Kez?" Brandon looked over at Kezia who was quick to register a change in plans.

Kezia looked at Clem.

"I'm sorry but we have to go!"

The boys got up, kissed and hugged goodbye to Kezia whilst Brandon was once again on his mobile. But he did raise a single finger in acknowledgment of their departure!

The boys walked past Cliff and Albert who cheekily said in unison,

"Be careful!"

As they drove through the gateposts Scan said,

"Do you think Brandon cast the last two living dogs here in concrete?"

The brothers silently smiled.

Once they got on the open road Clem said,

"I hope he's being kind to Kezia."

Clem turned to Tom and Scan.

"Let's wait out of sight, just to see if they do go out. Something tells me they're not going anywhere."

Clem found a side road, then turned around to have sight of the passing traffic. Nothing passed.

"We will give it another 10 minutes and then we will go."

"Scan remind us, what did Cliff and Albert say about those garden ornaments, when you were telling them about Sir Roger's place?"

"They didn't ask too much. It was just weird that they asked at all, as we were talking about pheasants, rabbits and catapults. It was just so out of the blue."

"Do you think Brandon and his boys are capable of taking a heavy bronze?" said Clem. "No, I don't think it's their line of business," countered Tom, "but I do think they may have tipped somebody off and, most likely, somebody from their camp."

Clem didn't wait the full 10 minutes, as he knew Kez and Brandon weren't going anywhere.

"But how do we find out? I didn't see any garden ornaments there," said Scan.

"I know who will," said Clem.

"Who?" replied Scan

"Pa."

Chapter 15

Hastings

Pru and the girls left at 4pm, after much praise for both Barty's delicious lamb and runner beans. Barty closed the front door and rejoined Lionel in the sitting room. "That was truly delicious," said Lionel. "I still see Pru as twenty you know, and her girls are lovely. You're a lucky fellow Barty; I wouldn't mind working with those two gorgeous girls. It would keep me young."

"I tell you what it's great for and that's tech! They helped me download both WhatsApp and Instagram. I'm not sure anybody would find my restaurant now without Instagram. You should get it Lionel. It would help you migrate from collector to seller!"

"Are you saying that I don't sell anything! What about the 30 years at Norman Road and the same at Ardingly Antiques Fair."

"Come on, Lionel, you're rarely in the shop after noon and Ardingly is only six times a year!"

"You know I'm at my peak in the morning, selling in the morning and marketing in the afternoon!"

"What, chatting in the pub in the afternoons, is now marketing!" said Barty laughing.

"Of course it's marketing, as loose talk often sells antiques! Take the Chairman and his lovely wife, you wouldn't have known about that bronze had it not been for you being in the Horse and Groom!"

"Ok, you have me there, and that's what we need to discuss now, the bronze, but whilst we do, I have a rather special bottle of wine."

Barty left the room and descended the cellar steps, re-emerging minutes later cradling a horizontal bottle.

"This will need decanting," Barty said with pride.

"So will I after this afternoon, so what's the bottle?"

"It's a 1980 Chateau Lynch-Bages, Paulliac."

"Sounds delicious, decant away, dear friend," as he got two new glasses in readiness. Barty took his time with the bottle: good things rushed tended to spoil.

"How do we, as gentle middle-aged men, approach South London scrap dealers? I'm not sure that either one of us has the menace for the job."

"We don't have menace but we do have brains. Young Jack did well to find out where Derek had bought it and it's now our job to find out who sold it to this Ray of Wandsworth. We do know that it came from a Norfolk estate. The advert in the Antiques Trade Gazette said so, but how many hands did it pass through between theft and scrapyard?"

"If we take the scrapyard as the centre of this timeline, we know that it's passed through Derek's, Jack's, your hands and now, currently, resting with the Chairman. That's four!"

"Would the Antiques Trade Gazette tell us from where or whom it was stolen?" enquired Lionel.

"I don't know, but when I was an auctioneer I tried to avoid stolen goods!" "Don't you have anybody you could ask?"

"I used to deal with a very efficient lady who handled auction advertising, but it's some ten years ago now and she was too good to stay there long. I will try, but today is Sunday and this lovely wine isn't going to drink itself."

With that, Barty poured. Lionel toasted his host. As soon as the wine touched their lips, the nastiness of theft was forgotten.

"This really is delicious," said Lionel, whilst raising his glass to the window. "What a light colour for a red, especially as it's spent most of its life in a dark cellar. I do wish we got lighter with age!"

"It's so unfair," Barty replied.

"Don't I know. I even walked here today, a full 40 minutes."

"But did you throw in the odd 50 metre sprint, to raise the heartbeat?"

"If somebody saw a 60-year-old man in a suit and fez running along the promenade, they would either call an ambulance or a policeman. The first for the inevitable ensuing heart attack and the second to alert of a potential street mugging. It's a bit like a balance sheet having two sides. It's the food and wine going in, let's call them 'calories', a rather vulgar word, to be balanced with exercise going out. In my case, the balance is firmly tipped to goods in, rather than goods out. It's cruel that the older you get, the more able you are to buy better food and wine, but the less able you are to burn it off. As we get larger our tailors get richer. It takes at least three square metres to cover me!"

"Lionel, don't be so morose, we can't do anything about it now, let's enjoy this bottle. Do you know Pru is off to Norfolk to paint those pugs. Maybe she could do a little digging for us. Norfolk's a big county but I'm sure the landed gentry are pretty close knit."

Barty too, forgot about telling the Chairman and Sunny that their lovely new bronze wasn't strictly theirs!

Chapter 16

Hastings

The next day Barty woke at 6.30am, donned his dressing gown and pottered down to his kitchen. A cup of tea first with whole milk, he needed the calcium, strong bones prevented broken ones. As he stirred in a brown sugar lump, he noticed two gold finches pecking on his bread. He was a veteran bread maker, sourdough and focaccia, and any hard ends were hooked in a wire hoop hung from a branch of one of the umbrella plane trees outside his kitchen window. It was lovely to see the finches, but unless he stood stock still the birds took fright. It was a beautiful sunny morning and the bright light caught the finches' red, white and gold plumage. Barty couldn't stand by his sink all day. He moved and they flew into the branches above. He had two plane trees side by side, each carefully tied to large horizontal grids of bamboo, which provided a frame to tie the shoots. He had planted them only four years ago and the trunks had doubled in diameter. They already provided green shade for a French metal table and pair of chairs below. If the weather was fine, he normally had his first cup of tea there in the morning sunshine but he didn't want to disturb the feeding birds so he took his tea, mobile phone and offending Antiques Trade Gazette to the veranda on the south side of his sitting room. Settling on one of the chairs that he had recently purchased from Lionel, he leafed through the Gazette to find the stolen page. He re-read the advert ... 'Taken from Norfolk Estate'. That narrows the field he thought. At the top of the page was a contact name, Mercy Penfold. Barty thought, what a great name, as he punched the given contact number into his mobile telephone. On the third ring the call was answered.

"ATG, Mercy speaking, how can I help?"

The voice was business-like and clipped, in a sort of English girls' boarding school way.

"Hello, my name is Barty and I was enquiring about the large bronze of racehorse and jockey stolen from a Norfolk Estate."

"I know the one; it's in our current issue."

"Do you have any measurements for it?"

"I do," said Mercy.

"But first, might I take your full name and contact number?"

This threw Barty but before he could decide to opt or not, Mercy pressed on.

"I have a number displayed on my handset ending in treble eight. Is that the best number for you?" Mercy then paused, allowing the caller to fill the gap.

Barty thought, "she's good". There was no getting away without giving his surname.

"Hix, Barty Hix."

"Thank you Mr Hix, and your mobile ending in treble eight, is that the best number?"

"That's my best and only number. Do you have the measurements?"

"I do," said Mercy.

"But would you kindly tell me, why do you want to know these measurements?"

Barty had reckoned on a little 'cat and mouse' in this enquiry, and he was pleased that he was on his own, without the anxious ears of Lionel trying to 'help'.

"I have seen a similar casting and I want to be sure this one is not somebody else's!"

"That's fine, I hope you don't mind my asking, but there is now a reward for its successful recovery." Mercy then paused, to bring the caller metaphorically closer; she then expanded.

"The owner contacted me on Friday and offered a reward of £1,000 for information leading to the bronze's return."

"Thank you, that's very helpful."

"The bronze had been bought from auction, so we were able to recover the measurements from the catalogue listing. May I ask, from what part of the country are you speaking?"

"I would rather not say," said Barty, feeling he wanted to stop the call now.

"Mr. Hix, no place, no measurements," Mercy paused again.

"Hastings."

"Hastings, on the Charing Cross line?"

"Measurements please?" said a despondent Barty.

"Its measurements are roughly a quarter size of a living, breathing racehorse and jockey," Mercy continued, "it stands four foot high including plinth, four foot six inches long, and the plinth measures 4 foot by 14 inches." Mercy paused and then said,

"Are you able to help the Gazette with any further information Mr Hix?"

"No, not at present, but out of curiosity, would you tell me the name of the Norfolk Estate?"

"I'm unable to disclose the name of the Estate, but should you have any information, would you please be sure to contact me, Mr Hix?"

"Of course I will. Goodbye."

Barty ended the call and went inside to make another cup of tea. He wanted to think before he called Lionel. Whilst he was considering his next step, Mercy at the Gazette was calling Kooling Towers in Norfolk.

"May I speak to Sir Roger?"

"Who may I say is calling?" answered May the housekeeper.

"It's Mercy Penfold from the Antiques Trade Gazette, regarding the bronze." "Please hold the line and I will try to connect you."

May then put the call through to the library where Sir Roger promptly lifted the phone.

"Sir Roger, I have Mercy Penfold from The Antiques Trade Gazette."

"Thank you May, please put her through."

"Good morning Miss Penfold."

"Good morning Sir Roger. I have just ended a call from a man wanting to know the measurements of your stolen bronze."

"Marvellous. Are you able to tell me from where he was calling?"

"Yes, Hastings on the south coast. I made the caller aware of the reward and I will follow it up tomorrow morning."

"Thank you Miss Penfold, I will call Inspector Smythe and inform him of this development. I will look forward to your news tomorrow. Goodbye."

Sir Roger ended the call and rang the number on the Detective Inspectors' business card. It was a direct mobile number and not a general switch board for the Norwich Police Station. The call was answered promptly.

"Good morning Sir Roger."

After his visit at Kooling Towers, Detective Inspector Kevin Smythe had added Sir Roger to his contacts list.

"Good morning Detective Inspector. I have just received a call from the Antiques Trade Gazette, saying that they have today spoken to somebody asking after the measurements of the bronze. The lady at the Gazette said the enquiry was from a man in Hastings on the south coast."

"Thank you. Would I be able to have the woman's name and I will call her directly," said Kevin, with a whiff of excitement. Funny how a simple classified advert in the right paper can flush out a potential lead. Sir Roger gave the Detective Inspector Mercy's contact details and replaced the handset with the merest hint of a smile.

Meanwhile, in Hastings, Barty rang Lionel.

"Morning Lionel, I have just spoken to the Stolen Page lady at the ATG, she has given me the measurements of the bronze. Did you measure the bronze before you sold it to the chairman?"

"No, I didn't. A little too much detail for me, but I did leave the bronze on my coffin stands, which I said I would collect later."

"Well, give the Chairman a call and arrange for you and I to collect them either today or tomorrow and I will bring a tape measure," said Barty.

Lionel called the Chairman and arranged for he and Barty to collect the stands. The Chairman couldn't resist teasing Lionel.

"Surely you can manage two stands on your own or is the gout playing up?"

Lionel ignored this, saying he was the muscle and Barty had the car. Lionel rang Barty.

"We can go anytime this morning. The gates are going to be open and their gardener will be there. Could you pick me up and then I will buy you a drink at the Horse and Groom afterwards."

"Let me dress and have some toast, I'm still in my dressing gown. I will pick you up within the hour."

Barty went inside and checked on the goldfinches, who were still eating his bread. He made himself a coffee with frothy milk and just a touch of chocolate sprinkles on the top, toast with his own marmalade and just a bit too much butter! Then dressed and out, locking his front door and unlocking the BMW. Barty had bought his navy blue BMW twenty years ago from a lady who only used it for her weekly shopping trips. It was manual and immaculate and he couldn't bear to part with it. Ten minutes later he was outside Lionel's shop in Norman Road. He knew that Lionel would be waiting, so he beeped the horn once. Lionel turned his swing sign from 'Open' to 'Closed' and then locked his heavy glazed shop door.

"Tape measure," he said holding the instrument aloft, "have you the measurements from the ATG?"

"Of course I have. Buckle up and let's go and see the Chairman," said Barty.

"I'd rather see Sunny," said Lionel smiling.

They were soon through the Chairman's cream-painted heavy wooden gates and parked on the circular gravel drive behind the gardener's van. They found him working on a new plinth for the sculpture. He was getting on well. The pylon shaped structure was formed from cement blocks, which he was now cladding in knapped flints. Lionel opened the exchange.

"Hi, we have come to collect two mahogany folding stands."

The gardener put down his bull-nose trowel and flint and said that they were in their tool shed for safe keeping.

"Mr Gunner said you would be calling."

"Good work with the flints and I like the tapered sides," said Barty.

"Yesterday, Mrs Gunner gave me a drawing of the design she wanted and, once issued, results are expected!" the gardener said with a cheerful smile, "I will just fetch your stands."

Once the gardener had disappeared behind a hedge, Lionel took out his measuring tape and read off the height first:

"Four feet," and then the length, "four feet six inches."

Barty reminded him,

"and the plinth measurements?"

"Four foot long by fourteen inches wide," Lionel said.

"Oh bollocks!" said Barty, "it's a match."

Chapter 17
Norfolk

Detective Inspector Kevin Smythe took Sir Roger's call on his mobile whilst at his desk in Norwich main Police Station. The Station stood next door to the Town Hall. Both were made of Portland stone in the Art Deco period of the 1920s. Kevin's desk stood below a south-facing window which looked onto the market square and the grid of stalls beyond, one of which was rented by the graduate who made beautiful clothes of wool and silk. Kevin sat with his back to the window and was bathed in sunlight during the summer months from 11am to 3pm. The light wasn't great for his desk computer, but it was a small inconvenience for the benefit of both; vitamin D and the pleasure of a warm back. Whilst speaking to Sir Roger, Kevin made notes in a standard issue notepad. As a police recruit, the importance of note taking was constantly impressed upon him and, for Kevin, it was an integral part of his job. He punched in the number for Mercy Penfold at the Antiques Trade Gazette.

"Good morning Gazette, Mercy Penfold speaking."

"Hello, my name is Detective Inspector Kevin Smythe and I'm speaking from Norwich CID. I have just been given your name by Sir Roger Swotter, and he tells me you have received an interesting call this morning?"

"That's correct. I took a call from a man in Hastings, wanting to know the measurements of the bronze horse and jockey featured in the stolen section of our paper this week."

"To confirm, we are talking about the same one stolen from Kooling Towers, Norfolk?"

"The very same Detective Inspector. I gave him the measurements plus informed him of the reward."

"Reward, what reward is that?" said Kevin.

"Sir Roger called me on Friday to offer a reward. He was irritated that the advert published on Tuesday hadn't got a single enquiry," said Mercy, "and he was keen not to lose a moment, as he put it."

"Mercy, what is the reward?"

"£1,000," retorted Mercy, noting a little irritation on the other end of the line.

"£1,000," said Kevin, unable to hide his annoyance. Afterall, it was his job to recover the bronze and not Sir Roger's.

"May I have the caller's name and did you take his contact number?"

"I have both his name, Barty Hix and his number..." said Mercy.

"And did he say why he was ringing?"

"Let me check in my day book."

Like Kevin, Mercy was also a fastidious note taker.

"Mr Hix said 'he had seen a similar casting and he wanted to be sure that this one is not somebody else's'."

How considerate thought Kevin.

"Thank you Mercy, you have been most helpful. If Mr Hix should contact you again, will you call me immediately?"

"Of course, Inspector. I said to Sir Roger that I would call Mr Hix tomorrow."

"Mercy, I would prefer it if you left this to me now. I will inform Sir Roger of your help and please call me if you have any further enquiries," said Kevin firmly.

"I will Inspector."

"Mercy, one further thing before you go. Do you have a point of contact at Brighton's Antiques and Stolen Goods team?"

"I do," Mercy said, pausing long enough for Kevin to come back.

"And may I have the person's name and number?"

"You may, but I thought I was being stood down?" Mercy knew she was pushing it but she was bright, and knew when to push and when to ease off.

"Mercy, may I remind you that I'm a policeman who wants to do his best for Sir Roger," said Kevin firmly.

Mercy pushed again.

"And so do I, Detective Inspector. My contact at Brighton's Stolen Antiques Squad is Sergeant Arnold on Brighton 01273....358."

"Thank you Mercy, I will give both Mr Hix and Sgt Arnold a call today and I may give you a call later, as I may need your help. I imagine this isn't the first antique you have tried to recover."

"I have a 32% success rate of recovery, the highest figure of any of my predecessors on the stolen classified desk, and this desk has been here since the paper's first publication 60 years ago."

"Impressive. Thank you, Mercy. I will call later."

Kevin hung-up and immediately looked up Barty Hix on Facebook. Nothing. Then he tried Instagram, typing in #Bartyhix, and up came a picture of a well-covered man. Possibly late 50s or early 60s, and wearing a panama hat. Below was a good grid of images, mostly of food and a couple of video clips. Kevin liked these short videos as they opened a more intimate window on a person: the voice, the mannerisms and their surroundings. Kevin clicked on the first clip. It showed Mr Hix standing behind a kitchen island which was formerly a large butcher's block, raised on a solid looking stand; the square section legs united by a simple slatted shelf, which was stacked with a variety of large pans and mixing bowls. There were a couple of orange pans and lids. Kevin knew they were French, Le Creuset, as he had given his wife, Helen a similar one for Mother's Day. He also knew they were expensive and Barty had three of them! On the butcher's block near his hand was an opened bottle of white wine. Kevin could make out 'France' on the label; next to it was a large glass with a splash of gold coloured wine. He and Helen had watched Keith Floyd's cookery programmes many times and his constant prop was a similar looking glass of wine, just fuller. Mr Hix had a chef's white jacket on, covered with a blue and white striped apron. Behind him was a stainless steel sink with central chrome mixer tap, below a large Victorian sash window. Over Mr Hix's left shoulder was a stainless steel extraction unit and hanging from the sides were a number of kitchen utensils: ladles, whisks, tongs, slotted spoons etc. Kevin clicked the play arrow in the middle of the frame and the video sprang into life. Barty picked up his glass with his free right hand and said:

"Welcome back viewers, bottoms up! Today I will show you how to make Sri Lankan flatbreads."

As he spoke he picked up a small glass mixing bowl.

"First add 250 grams of best gluten-free flour, roughly a large wine glass in measurement. I use Dove's flour. Then add half a quantity of coconut water." He poured it from a carton into the same, now empty wine glass.

Kevin thought this sounded nice and simple, and might impress Helen and the children with it. He could even save the cost of a naan bread from their weekly takeout curry.

Mr Hix continued:

"Take a pinch of table salt, stronger and cheaper than sea salt, a teaspoon of onion seeds and some chopped coriander. If you don't have coriander, use parsley or chives or any other soft green herbs, as these will add colour to your flatbreads. Now kneed your dough in the bowl first then, when it comes together, stretch the dough out, keeping it in the bowl; cover with cling film and allow it to rest."

Then Mr Hix shook a little flour from the packet onto the butcher's block. He spread the flour with one hand, rubbed his hands together and then covered a wooden rolling pin with more flour. He cut the dough in half and made two round balls, took one ball and started to flatten it with the rolling pin. He reminded the viewer not to press hard and to turn the dough by 90 degrees on every roll. After six rolls he had turned half a tennis ball to a perfect eight-inch disc approximately 1/8th inch thick. He then made an apology to the viewer for forgetting to put a large saucepan on the medium/hot ring. Kevin noticed it was a gas hob, nice and fast. Whilst the dry pan heated up, he rolled the other ball of dough. Once completed, he put the first flatbread in the hot pan; urged the viewer to leave it for a minute until "you could smell toast" and then he turned it over. "Remember," he said, "the less fussy you are, the better it will be." Once he finished one side he took an old wooden-handled steel slice and turned the flat bread over, showing how it was now coloured with brown patches but you could still see the green of the coriander. The whole clip lasted no more than two minutes. Mr

Hix spoke clearly and worked quickly. He had obviously done this many times before. He signed off with: "Happy cooking and bottoms up," and with that, he raised his glass and smiled. Very impressive thought Kevin, he liked his cooking and he was sure he would like the man. he picked up his phone.

"Good morning Mr Hix, my name is Detective Inspector Smythe. I'm with Norwich Constabulary."

Kevin pressed on, he wanted to startle Mr Hix.

"I understand that you rang the Antiques Trade Gazette in response to a bronze featured in their stolen pages?" Kevin paused.

Poor Barty needed more than a pause, he needed a seat and bottled oxygen!

He always thought the police were rather slow. He obviously hadn't reckoned on Detective Smythe. Regaining some composure, Barty responded

"Good morning Detective, I rang the ATG because I had seen a similar bronze group and I was keen to know its dimensions."

Kevin responded immediately,

"Mercy Penfold said, and I quote, 'I have seen a similar casting and I want to be sure this one is not somebody else's'." Kevin paused again, as he felt a certain anxiousness at the other end of the line.

"Where is this similar casting Mr Hix?" Barty knew he had made a mistake when he chose to explain his motive for ringing the Gazette, Mercy must have been taking notes.

Terrifyingly, it was word for word.

"The casting Mr Hix?" Kevin prompted.

"I saw a similar one in the back of a van at a car boot."

"Which car boot, and when?"

"It was on the M4 near Heathrow Airport."

"And when was this Mr Hix?"

"Over a week ago, it's held every Sunday," said Barty.

"Can you recall the make and colour of the van?'

"No."

"Thank you for your help Mr Hix, that will be all for now, but I may need to take a statement. Is this the best number?"

"Yes, it is."

Barty hung up, collapsed into his sofa and concentrated on breathing.

Sugar! This detective is not going to be shaken. Lionel, Jack and I need to find both the thief and owner before this Detective Inspector knocks on my door!

Chapter 18

Hastings

After a couple of minutes of raising and lowering the diaphragm, Barty managed to regularise his heartbeat. He was just too old to tell lies, hence his couched untruth to Detective Inspector Smythe. The bronze had been at a car boot, but not when Barty first saw it. The measurements and timing confirmed that the bronze, now sitting in the Chairman's garden in West Hill, was the same one taken from a Norfolk Estate two weeks ago.

Barty rang Lionel. The phone hardly rang before Lionel picked up.

"Morning Barty, what news?" Lionel tentatively whispered.

"Too much to be honest. I have just got off the phone to Detective Inspector Kevin Smythe of Norfolk Constabulary."

"Oh my goodness," Lionel replied, nervously twisting in his Lloyd Loom armchair.

"The clock is ticking now and we need to get moving. I have three days before I open the restaurant again on Thursday. I think it's best if I come over for a coffee now and we write a game plan together."

"I have a terrible feeling this is no game Barty, more a crisis," Lionel whispered.

"Why are you whispering, are you on your own?"

"Of course I am. I have always whispered bad news and shouted the good," said Lionel, whispering again.

"Lucky I am coming over. I can hardly hear you on the phone. See you in ten!"

Barty immediately left the house and walked to his parked car. He removed a flyer from his windscreen wiper: about a new fresh pasta bar, 20% off until Saturday at The Courtyard next to the Promenade. Delicious, he thought, and a stone's throw from Lionel in Norman Road. He popped the flyer in his trouser pocket and opened the car door. It was already warm and the BMW's tobacco coloured leather seats smelled lovely. Barty had had the seats reupholstered soon after he bought it by great upholsterers in Hastings, Hayward & Son. The lady from whom he had bought the car, only used it for a weekly shop, but she had three dachshunds who had scratched the back seat. Although he liked dogs, he had never owned one and, after the bill from Hayward & Son, he was unlikely to. Barty drove to the sea front and turned right along the coast road to St Leonards. The sea was calm and the sun sparkled off the small rippling waves. There were lots of happy people walking along the promenade with few cares, unlike him. He found a space outside Lionel's shop, it was one of Barty's super powers; where he hoped to find a parking space, he usually did. He walked into Lionel's shop. A bell rang and Lionel popped his head around a painted leather four-fold screen. He looked pale and anxious.

"Coffee is upstairs," he whispered, "I'll just close the shop."

He swung the 'Open' sign to 'Closed' and led Barty up to the top of the house. His kitchen-cum-sitting room was on the top floor, which allowed him to see over the houses with clear sight of the sea and pier beyond. Barty had brought a black A4 day book with him, which he now opened; turned to a fresh page and wrote 'Monday' in the top right hand corner.

"How do you want your coffee?" enquired Lionel.

"White please, do you have one of those frothers?"

"No, but I could blow through a straw?"

"No thanks, I don't want your breath in my coffee!"

"What's wrong with my breath!" Lionel said indignantly.

"I don't know, but I don't want to risk it," said Barty.

Barty turned his day book by 90 degrees and drew a line from side to side. On the right side he wrote 'Chairman and Sunny, Hastings', and on the other he marked it and wrote a question mark and 'Norfolk'. Barty then marked the line in the middle and wrote 'Beacon M4 car boot' and then he filled in the names and places between the Beacon and the Chairman, Jack and Lionel. The spaces were from Norfolk to the M4 car boot. Lionel, looking intently at the timeline, pointed out:

"We know, or think we know, that the Beacon bought it from his friend Ray at Wandsworth Bridge Road scrapyard, London. Can we mark that?"

"Of course we can."

Barty marked the line to the left of the Beacon.

"There are three owners to the right of the Beacon and only two to the left. I bet you that the person who stole it from Norfolk, sold it to the scrapyard on Wandsworth Bridge Road," said Barty who was now getting excited. Even Lionel had stopped whispering.

"Do you fancy going up to London and asking Ray, the scrap dealer, who he bought it from?"

"Not on your nelly," said Lionel. "I seem to get hot and my throat goes dry when I go up to town these days."

"Come on Lionel, you're not that old."

"Is there another way? How about Jack, calling in on this Ray of Wandsworth?" volunteered Lionel.

"What a good idea. But how could Jack lure the information out of Ray?" Barty paused, he had an idea.

"Ray, the scrap dealer has never met Jack before. What if Jack takes a load of mixed metal with a bronze amongst it?"

"Then if Jack sees this Ray, does a deal, it might just get Ray talking." Lionel said, warming to the role of Detective!

"In summary, it's a call to Jack. What about the unknown of the Norfolk Estate. When did Pru say she was going to Norfolk?"

"I think it was today," Lionel said, "so why don't you text one of your waitresses to make sure?"

"I will do it now." Barty messaged and quickly received a reply from Polly.

"Mum left today. Invited for lunch at Kooling Towers and she's staying for three days."

Good, thought Barty, I will call her tomorrow and do a little fishing.

"Hello Jack, it's Lionel here. Barty has had an unwelcome call from DI Kevin Smythe in Norwich. We need to get our skates on before the police start calling on us."

Lionel then outlined his plan.

"I'm on it," Jack said over the speaker.

"We are leaving it to you, you're street smart, and you can certainly think on your feet." Then Barty added

"You've got to get Ray into your confidence in order to get nearer to the seller who, we believe, is the thief."

"Good luck," Barty and Lionel both said in unison as Lionel ended the call.

"Progress?" said Barty.

"Definitely." Lionel then looked at the time on his phone.

"I know it's only 11.30 but I'm thirsty, shall we repair to the Horse and Groom?"

"No," said Barty, bringing out the flyer from his pocket.

"Let's go and try this new fresh pasta place by the pier."

"I hope they sell Chablis," said Lionel, "you know, I can't do Sauvignon Blanc". "Come on Lionel, don't be so fussy. You can't do London. You can't do Sauvignon Blanc. You have obviously been on your own for far too long!"

Chapter 19

Norfolk

It took Pru just under four hours to drive from Hastings to Kooling in Norfolk. She and her girls shared a black Volkswagen Golf car. Pru had had Golfs since their first introduction in the 1970s. The hatchback boot had worked well, consuming all manner of painting easels, picnic baskets, folding chairs and luggage. Her father, a long-gone, retired army officer always reminded Pru:

"Any fool can be uncomfortable!"

She remembered him fondly, raising a glass in an old campaign chair, whilst Pru and her siblings sat cross-legged on a tartan picnic blanket. Too many years on exercise had made her father uncomfortable with lunch indoors.

"Lunch is always best taken outside; improves anything from a salad to a pie," he would say to visitors, as he led them past a perfectly good dining room into the garden. Bizarrely, her father had spent many years abroad and had difficulty with the cold, so latterly lunch outside was rarely done, but much talked about!

As Pru drove through the village of Kooling she noticed a rather splendid 16th century inn. She had been to Lavenham in Suffolk before and this looked like it had come from there: a jettied timber frame with pastille coloured plaster. It looked at

odds with the neighbouring houses which were all brick and
flint. The bricks did the structural stuff, window openings and
corners and the round flint cobs did the infill. These rounded
stones were all set in horizontal rows, the stones or cobs were
slightly different in size but the repeated strings gave them
uniformity. In one of these flint and brick houses was a village
shop. Pru parked and walked inside. She had half an hour
to kill before she was expected at Kooling Towers and she
needed some dog treats. These were the secret weapon of her
profession and she was going to need a lot of bribery to keep
the attention of pugs, let alone four! Plus, she wasn't sure if she
was drawing Sir Roger's dog too. Lady Daphne, or Daphne
as Pru knew her in her London days in the 60s and 70s, was
dismissive of Sir Roger's labrador. Suddenly Pru noticed that
she was being watched by a small apple-shaped lady who
smiled with a perfect set of white teeth, too perfect for a
woman in her mid-fifties.

"Morning," was ended by a high-pitched whistle.

Pru was slightly wrong-footed but proceeded,"Morning, I'm
after dog treats." "Small or l...swee?" the apple-shaped shop
keeper whistled.

"I'm sorry," said Pru, "small or what?'

"L...swee, are they small or large?"

"Four pugs and a labrador," said Pru, now getting the
intonation of the whistles. "Ah, that will be Lady Daphne up at
the Towers," said the whistler.

"That's right."

"Lady Daphne has a monthly order of treats. I will get you some."

She disappeared and returned with one box of each treat.

"Will that doooo?" she whistled.

"Perfect," said Pru, "you have some lovely peonies and lilies outside."

"That's my Jim's. I keep shop and he grows the fruit, veg and flowers," she beamed.

"They are superb, may I take a bunch of each please?"

"Of course, that will be £10 for the treats and £22 for Jim's flowers. Take your pick on your way out.

"I will," Pru said, as she laid £32 in cash on the counter.

"Goodby...swee," the apple-shaped whistler called out.

Pru closed the door and chose two bunches of flowers, they smelt terrific. As she closed her car door, she chuckled and said to herself, "This is going to be fun."

Kooling Towers was just minutes away from the village shop. A good looking lodge house with similar brick and flint cob work marked the entry to the drive. Instead of square openings for windows and front door, the lodge had arched openings in a gothic revival manner. Pru noticed some repairs to the verge: iron stakes and rope keeping the newly sown grass seed undisturbed. She drove through some elaborate iron gates, all freshly painted in Atlantic blue. Pru thought that would be Daphne's hand as, when Pru knew Daphne in London, she worked in Pimlico Green assisting the legendary Martin Spooner, antique dealer and interior designer, who always answered the phone as "Big Carol!". He had the flamboyance of a drag queen but the wardrobe of a man. The Americans, who were big buyers in the 1960s and 1970s, loved Big Carol for his stories, his indiscretions and generous hospitality. As Daphne used to say, "Work with a free drinks bar!" But she was sensible, somebody had to be. As Big Carol bought and sold antiques, Daphne safeguarded the look of the showrooms and dealt with shipping and sales contracts.

They were a great combination. Big Carol would ply the champagne and sell the antiques for huge prices, and it was Daphne who made sure that the bills were paid. All went very well until a young Sir Roger walked through the door. He had spotted a pair of leather chairs in the window. Before Big Carol told him the price, he urged him to try them out. Whilst seated, a Moorish octagonal table was placed by his side, followed by a glass of champagne, then another. You could have almost bought a mini car for the price asked, but delivery was included! Daphne was used to Big Carol's routine, but as she took the rather handsome young Roger's address at his father's house in Norfolk, Daphne saw security, dogs and possibly a title in this now tipsy young man. After a couple of phone calls regarding delivery, Daphne got a date and six months later Roger and Daphne were married in St. George's, Hanover Square. Pru hadn't been invited to the wedding, as she moved in very different circles. She had gone to Chelsea School of Arts and lived in World's End, the other end of the King's Road to Daphne, who lived in some splendour off Sloane Square in a red brick first floor apartment. She had always liked and admired Daphne, almost a girl crush, and she was looking forward to seeing her again. Pru passed the front porch. Parked beside a green Range Rover was an old Golf cabriolet. Daphne had kept her car, the one Big Carol had bought her. Pru took the flowers and walked beneath a vaulted entrance hall, which was open on three sides and big enough for a car to pass through. The blind side had a pair of massive metal bound doors. One door opened and May stood waiting.

"Good afternoon. Please come with me, Lady Daphne is in her sitting room."

Pru walked up three wide stone steps into a square shaped stone paved hall. They turned left and walked along a corridor, dotted with furniture and pictures between tall windows and cushion covered window seats. Pru followed May, walking on brightly coloured Caucasian runners which covered wide oak floorboards.

"What lovely flowers," said May.

"I bought them in your village shop."

"I thought they looked like Jim's. You're lucky to get them, as most go to a florist in London. Is your car open and may I have your keys? I will get Cecil, to take your luggage to your room."

"Oh, thank you," said Pru handing her keys to May. May then stopped, knocked on a door and walked in. Amongst a burst of barking, she heard, "Is that you Pru? How lovely," and a tall figure rose from a sofa in the middle distance. As Pru approached Daphne, she was reminded how elegant she was. Daphne kissed Pru on each cheek and bid her to sit beside her.

"These are my darlings that I would like you to draw."

With that, two pugs leapt up beside Daphne on the sofa whilst two struggled to get airborne. They were quickly scooped up and all four pugs licked their owner and stared at their visitor.

"May, would you kindly tell Sir Roger that Pru has arrived. We will have the champagne here, please?"

"Big Carol would approve, wouldn't he Pru?"

The two fell into talking of the good old days in swinging London, peopled by characters and coloured by fun. Five minutes later, May brought in a tall glass vase, followed by Cecil bearing an ice bucket and bottle. May took the flowers and arranged them in the tall glass vase.

"What lovely flowers Pru, they look like Jim's. You remember the florist diagonally opposite us on the Green? Jim has supplied them since I moved to Norfolk twenty years ago."

"I had such a funny time in your village shop, the lady kept whistling," said Pru.

"That would be Mary's loose dentures," said a voice from the door. Pru turned to see Sir Roger being handed the champagne bottle by Cecil.

"How lovely to see you again Pru. Good drive here?" As Sir Roger spoke, he opened the champagne and poured three glasses. He handed Pru her glass, and kissed her. Once Pru's arrival was toasted, Sir Roger took a match and lit the laid fire. Although it was warm outside, Lady Daphne always needed a fire. Their chatter was interrupted by May saying that there was a call for Sir Roger.

"I will take it in the library, thank you."

May went back to the kitchen and put the call through to the library.

"Sir Roger, it's Detective Inspector Smythe."

"Thank you, May. Good afternoon Detective Inspector, any news?"

"Sir Roger, after speaking to a very helpful Miss Mercy Penfold at the Antiques Trade Gazette, I have now spoken to the caller who was enquiring after the measurements of the stolen bronze. He comes from Hastings and it is my feeling that he knows more than he is saying."

"Excellent Inspector, will you interview him?"

"No, I will get the Brighton antique squad to do that."

"Good work Inspector, and I look forward to hearing how they get on. Goodbye."

Sir Roger rejoined Daphne and Pru and refilled their glasses.

"What's the occasion?" said Daphne, who was rarely given a second glass so quickly.

"You know that rather earnest detective that I told you about? He's only spoken to a man in Hastings in connection to the bronze!"

Pru's ears pricked up at the mention of Hastings.

"Poor Roger has just had a large bronze of a racehorse with jockey up stolen," Daphne continued, "it sounds like your Detective Inspector is getting closer, Roger."

Chapter 20

Norfolk

Pru was feeling a little light-headed. She wasn't used to having champagne before food and such a lovely bottle too. May called lunch, and Daphne led them into a beautiful bubble-shaped conservatory.

'What an unusual room,' said Pru.

"It's known as an onion shaped conservatory built in the 1820s, when the Towers were given a romantic Gothic makeover. Which Swotter did the changes, Roger?"

"It was Sir Cloudesley. He made a fortune in herrings, feeding the naval fleet."

"I never knew you were fishermen, Roger."

Daphne said this as she winked at Pru. It was obvious during their courtship that Daphne was in charge, and Pru remembered Daphne telling her of the young man sitting in one of Big Carol's red leather library chair. It was love at first sight. Pru saw a tall young man staying longer in an antiques shop to buy a pair of chairs he could ill afford, just to get a date. To Daphne, Sir Roger was still that young man. He was an exemplary husband, who had remained kind and thoughtful. Plus, he had kept his figure, just like his impressive father, Sir Patrick. Even when it was diagnosed that Daphne would be unable to conceive children, her husband never showed any regrets and redoubled his thoughtfulness. He had provided a charmed life for her, keeping her always warm, in a house that had historically been cold, surrounded by dogs that loved her and supported by a loyal staff who greatly admired her. When Sir Patrick had had Koolings, there was a butler called Sykes who lurched from pantry to front door; more gatekeeper than loyal servant. Later, when Sir Roger inherited, Daphne slimmed the staff down to May and Cecil. Lou, as gamekeeper, came under Sir Roger's sole direction.

May had not been a cook, but Daphne had seen a quiet efficiency in the young village girl who occasionally helped out at the Towers and had had the foresight to enrol her in a famed cookery school in Cornwall. The course was six weeks long and May had loved every second. She had excelled to such an extent that she still received an annual Christmas card from the owner which was proudly pinned above the Aga. As Daphne had rightly thought, the produce of the Norfolk coast was very similar to that of Cornwall, it just came into season a couple of weeks later, and it was the fruits of this investment that the household enjoyed today. May entered the room followed by Cecil: she, with a tray of small plates and he, with another ice bucket and a bottle of white wine. May laid the small plates in front of Daphne first, then she took the wine from Cecil and poured each glass two fingers full. She had already filled the water glasses, it was something that Bertram's in Cornwall instilled in their students, 'It's all in the prep, everything must be just so.'

"May, this looks delicious, what is it?" said Daphne.

"It's cured brill with ginger and spring onion curd," said May.

"Do start Pru," said Daphne, as May left the room.

"This is scrummy; what a fabulous yogurt," said Pru, as Daphne tasted hers.

"May has found this rather strange producer of buffalo milk who makes a yogurt from the curds. That was one of the many great things of Bertram's, they taught their students to be inquisitive. They took them, not just to markets, but to farms as well.

"Cecil often drives May to hidden farms in Norfolk to find uncommon produce." Twenty minutes later, the next course arrived, again borne by May, who placed a new plate in front of all three: a smoked mackerel fillet on a bed of spinach, with bertolli beans in tomato purée. The colours were vivid. Next May refilled the wine glasses to the preferred two fingers level. Then she topped up the water glasses. Before leaving, she cast her eye over the party to make sure all was well and, once satisfied, she quietly left.

"Now Pru, I haven't seen you for ages, how's life?" said Daphne.

"It's good, we are all very happy on the South Coast. After Richard left us, I moved to Hastings, where the girls quickly found friends at school. It was difficult at first financially, but I was introduced by a lovely new friend, to a lady who drew pet portraits in Sussex and Kent. I started drawing with her in her studio and we quickly became friends. She taught me how to use pastels properly. At Chelsea, we had charcoal sticks in life drawing classes, but I had never used pastels before. I thought they were rather old fashioned, but now I know why those 1920s society portraits in pastel are so good. It's so quick, you catch the moment and, in turn, the person. I then started using oil paints as a wash, which gives an added depth. To cut a long story short, Marjorie liked my work and said I was her rightful successor. She then started referring me to her old clients and I'm now doing two or three animal portraits a week and at £950 each, it has given me financial stability."

"Well done you, Pru, but you haven't given up your abstracts?"

"I have rather, you know. I remember as students in the 1970s we weren't allowed to paint anything that was representational."

"Roger has a solid black labrador, Sampson, and I'd rather hoped you might do an abstract painting of him?" said Daphne.

Sir Roger looked at his wife in surprise but didn't say anything.

"I will happily give it a go again. I'll have to do some studies of Sampson before I return to my studio to properly concentrate on it."

"And the girls, how are they?" enquired Daphne.

"Both happy and very different. The eldest, Polly, works hard at her studies; she is taking her Oxbridge exam soon, and Phoenix is pretty and arty and hopes to follow me to a London Art School."

The party was interrupted by the presence of May.

"I have laid out coffee in your sitting room. Would you like Cecil to walk the dogs?"

"No thank you May. Let Cecil get on in the garden, as Pru and I will walk the dogs after coffee."

A walk in the garden would be good for Pru to observe her darling pugs and her husband's labrador. Sir Roger took a coffee to his library and sat in one of the chairs that he had bought all those years ago in that Chelsea antiques shop.

Whilst in Hastings, Barty sent a text to Pru.

'Hope you have arrived safely? What's Kooling Towers like? You left your pashmina here! Love Barty x.'

After coffee Daphne, surrounded by a pool of dogs, led Pru to the hall.

"Do you want some wellies?" Daphne asked.

"No thanks, I have some in the car."

Daphne opened the front door and they both walked to Pru's car.

"I see you've still got your Golf. You know I was slightly envious of that."

"I wanted an ordinary Golf, but you know what Martin was like. He had never bought a company car before, and I'm not sure that he had ever driven one, as he much preferred to be driven. Anyway, he took me to the Volkswagen showroom and I pointed out a standard Golf. We sat in it and then Martin directed the most extraordinary questions to the salesman.

"Did it come with a drinks fridge?" and "would it know the way to The French Horn in Sonning!" After ten minutes, he became bored, as he always did, and then pointed to a very glamorous cabriolet in the front window saying,

'We'll have that one!'

"I said don't be ridiculous, but he wouldn't listen. He knew that I'd love it and he, as you know, was always so generous.

It must be on its last legs now," said Pru, opening the boot of her own car to retrieve her blue calf-high wellies.

"I just can't bear to part with it, and it seems to squeeze through it's annual checks. Such happy memories. I do miss Martin," said Daphne.

After walking around an immaculate garden, they went between two large yew trees and left into a wide walk bordered by hornbeam hedges. At the end stood a pylon-shaped flint plinth.

"That's where the large bronze horse used to stand. Roger has been preoccupied with its recovery since it went over a week ago. You know, he placed an advert in the Antiques Trade Gazette. I remember Martin used to be invited to the annual editor's lunch.

Roger has only had one response to the advert. Funny that it should come from a caller in Hastings."

Pru decided to ignore this observation. Hastings had a reputation but it had really improved recently.

"Which room would you like to paint in?"

"I don't know," said Pru.

"I believe that they will be more settled in my sitting room. I can read on the sofa and they should be quiet for at least twenty minutes."

"That's perfect. I will make some quick studies this afternoon, which will help me decide on a composition for tomorrow," she said, as she was keen to get going.

Once inside, she was shown up to her room by May, to retrieve her sketch book and materials.

She also looked at her phone: a new message from Barty. She read it and wrote back 'excellent news re. pashmina, was wondering where I'd left it! Just been shown empty plinth of stolen bronze horse, Hastings connection, rather embarrassing! Love Pru xxx'.

Barty's phone went bleep, bleep, he picked it up and rang Lionel. Lionel answered with a whispered,

"Hello?"

"Pru has messaged, the bronze was stolen from guess where?... Kooling Towers, and she mentions a Hastings connection......the clock is definitely ticking!"

At that, Lionel dropped his phone.

Chapter 21

Norfolk

Pru woke up well before breakfast at nine. She opened the curtains and returned to her rather large bed. She had a double bed in her home in Hastings but not as large as this; nor was it as high. She felt like a child again, jumping up on to the mattress. She criss-crossed three pillows so she could sit up and survey her room. Her immediate environment was comfortable and she recognised the white-work counterpane bought from Casa Pupo. Daphne had worked opposite this 1970s treasure trove in Pimlico Road and her sheets and pillow cases were all from there too. Either side of her vast bed were a pair of lamps fashioned from old Chinese porcelain vases. They, in turn, stood on two similar 18th century night commodes with raised galleries that retained books, glasses and bottled water. This would have once hidden chamberpots behind sliding tambour shutters, but now mercifully superseded by an ensuite bathroom. At the foot of her bed was an old and comfortable two-seater sofa with smokey blue heavy linen upholstery. Beyond this was an elegant dressing table with a 3/4 gallery, over two frieze drawers, each fitted with a pair of sharply turned wooden handles. The circular legs were both ring-turned and tapered, which disappeared into gilt brass capping and castor feet. On the table was an over-the-top heart shaped mirror, the porcelain frame modelled with multi-coloured flowerheads topped with a rather rude pair of chubby pink cherubs. It looked like the artist had surprised two naked Beryl Cook figures in an overcrowded rose garden. Serving the dressing table was a blue coronation stool. Pru had seen a lot of these in Lionel's shop. He loved them, collecting different kings and, of course, queens, of the twentieth century. Often they had embroidered royal cyphers, stamps on the stretchers and limed oak legs. Either side of this trio of furniture were two tall windows with inset window seats. To the right, on a blind wall, was a large three-door wardrobe into which May had unpacked her clothes. This was very spoiling and, after a life time of putting away her two daughters' laundry, it was most welcome. Finally, to the left of her bed was a door leading to her bathroom with a large bath, the sort Pru could properly wallow in. She heard barking dogs outside and decided to dress and take a walk in the garden. As she closed her bedroom door she had doubts on which way to turn for the stairs. Luckily the hall was dotted with standard lamps and tables and the nearest one had a small black framed notice with 'HALL' and an arrow beneath. Reassured, Pru walked the thirty yards to the galleried stairwell, which was hung with larger family portraits, Victorian big game trophies and decorative fans of old swords and rifles. Once through the front door, she turned right and followed the line of the house. Walking around to the west side she passed through one garden room with giant topiary figures, another garden room dotted with small box balls, then a border room, all connected with either brick or flint cobbled paths and, if there was no hard path, she found neatly mown grass, cut so short that it was like treading on carpet. On a raised gravel terrace near the house on the south side, she came across Cecil who was in the middle of watering the agapanthus, planted in giant terracotta pots.

"Morning," Pru called out.

"Morning Madam," Cecil replied.

"Watering in June, is that normal?"

"I just want to give these young ones a head start, Madam."

"It's Cecil, isn't it?" said Pru.

"It is Madam," said Cecil Trowel, who always liked a touch of formality.

"Please call me Pru."

"Thank you Madam," Cecil replied. He had learned early on, that addressing all as Sir and Madam saved a lot of remembering.

"Congratulations, the garden looks fabulous."

"Thank you Madam. We have just over a week before we open the gardens here for the cricket."

"By the look of things, you are already ready."

"We would be if I could get the grass to stop growing and the flowers from wilting," said Cecil.

"As it's a nice day, May has laid breakfast in the conservatory. Just carry along this terrace and you will find the steps on your right, Madam."

"Thank you, Cecil."

As Pru walked to the conservatory, she thought how lucky Daphne was to have Cecil and May. Both seemed to have two jobs: May, housekeeper and superb cook and Cecil, gardener and also willing footman.

Pru stepped through the open doors of the conservatory and found Roger and Daphne with attendant dogs: Sampson, sitting on the ground looking up at his master, and the pool of pugs sitting on a chair next to Daphne.

Roger stood up and offered her a seat next to him.

"Morning Pru, did you sleep well?" said Daphne.

"Like a child. What a lovely high bed," replied Pru.

May magically appeared and placed a plate of yogurt topped with blueberries.

"Not that lovely yogurt again?" said Pru.

"It is," said Daphne, "May never forgets a compliment."

"I have just walked around your garden and bumped into Cecil. He tells me that you are having an open garden soon."

"We are, we normally host six a year, all for different charities. The next one is for the village cricket club. We try and take two professional cricketers each season. My grandfather, Sir Noel, had a sister who married a tea planter from Nuwara Eliya in Sri Lanka. Every year, we take two promising cricketers, obviously not test cricketers, but ones who might be in the future. We usually hold a special fundraising home game on Sunday with an Open Garden on the Saturday, but this year, we have decided to use the tent for my birthday party on Saturday and roll both Open Garden and cricket match into the one day on Sunday. It's not just teas and cakes. May also serves quiches and salads in the tent, whilst Cecil and Lou, the keeper, run the bar. We hope to raise enough to cover the players flights and some spending money, as we put them up for free in the coach house."

"Now Roger, may Pru have Sampson this morning, to sit for some studies?"said Daphne, touching his arm.

"Please do, I'm off to see Lou. It appears that we are missing some items from both the big lunch tent and my special ticket tent," he answered whilst standing up and pushing in his chair.

"Not the sweet one with the scalloped pelmets, that we used for your fortieth?" said Daphne looking up at her husband.

"Yes, Lou said something about missing poles and tent pegs. It won't be a problem as if we need replacements, we have plenty of time to cut and paint some more."

With that, he left the ladies to their coffee.

"He is still lovely," said Pru.

"I know, I'm a lucky bean. There was a time when I thought I would be looking after Martin and the shop forever. Then one day that lovely young man walked into the shop and bought those chairs that he could ill afford. Martin used to tease me. He knew that he was the one. Martin really was odd, full of contradictions, but beneath all that bravado was a man who loved both his clients and friends. Come on Pru, let's get going before I get too sentimental!" Daphne led Pru to her sitting room, followed by the pugs. Wheezy little things, thought Pru.

Sampson had no time for the pugs. His breeding and training was for the sole purpose of retrieving fallen game.

"Whilst we have Sampson, would you like to do the studies of him first?" said Daphne.

"Definitely. Yes please."

On grey paper, Pru got Sampson's profile and shape and then, with brown pastel crayons, his irises and with a thin oxide, painted his highlights. After three A2 size studies she felt happy. She would convert the browns and whites to more vivid colours, say greens and blues in her abstract work.

"I think I have got him," said Pru, showing a seated Daphne her preliminary sketches.

"Very good, how do you do it!" said Daphne, "You know this fund-raising weekend? Well, it also just happens to be Roger's birthday. Do you think that you might be able to finish the painting and then I could give it to him for his present?"

"Of course I will try, what size would you like it? Four foot by two foot six inches?" asked Pru.

"No, much bigger. You've seen the height of the walls here. Small things tend to get lost."

Pru continued, now recording the unruly pugs; Josie, Connie, Bunny and Bunty, and after numerous studies she alighted on a composition that she thought might work. The hours slipped quickly away, only to be interrupted by the welcome routine of lunch. More champagne in the sitting room, followed by two delicious courses in the conservatory, then coffee and more drawing in Daphne's sitting room. All was completed by 4 o'clock and it was agreed that Pru would leave a day early to give her more time in her home studio. Abstracts may look haphazard, but a lot of time goes into their conception.

Pru left Koolings on a cloud; it had been a spoiling stay and she didn't really want it to end. Arriving in Hastings and before going home, she decided to call in on Barty. She could collect her pashmina. She knew it was his day off and, if she was lucky, he might be home. It made no odds if he wasn't, as she only lived around the corner. She had an easy run and found herself on his doorstep in no time. She rang Barty's door bell holding a pot of May's delicious buffalo yoghurt. As Barty opened the door, she thrust the pot his way.

"This is for you. It's the most delicious yogurt from buffalos in Norfolk."

"Wow, how was your stay?"

"Dreamy. What a place. They really looked after me and I did some good drawings. I finished the pugs but have been commissioned to do an abstract as well," said Pru.

"Not of a dog?" asked Barty.

"Yes, a rather noble black labrador called Sampson. He really is his owner, Sir Roger, in dog form!"

"What would Marjorie say?"

"She would love it," Pru continued.

"The abstract is to be Roger's birthday present. Daphne wants a big canvas and I have just over 10 days to do it and I may need you or Lionel's muscle to deliver it. You have access to a van, don't you?" asked Pru.

"Lionel has a new young friend with a large Mercedes van. I'm sure we can borrow it."

"I must get home and start. I haven't painted an abstract for such a long time, I'm so excited, toodaloo."

Barty stepped outside and waved her off from the pavement. Once back in his hall, he saw Pru's pashmina neatly folded on the second step of his staircase.

Chapter 22

Hastings

Jack was already in his van when he took the call from Barty and Lionel. He had pulled over and turned off the engine. Even Clive knew his master wanted to think. He moved away from the gearstick, being his normal bench seat position. Jack ran antiques, not scrap metal, and where was he going to get a van full from? He needed the metal before he could call the Beacon. He took his phone and rang Lionel back, it rang once.

"Hello?" Lionel whispered.

"It's Jack, Lionel. Before I call the Beacon, I need a van full of metal but I don't know any scrap dealers and the only house clearer I do know to ask, is the Beacon! Can you help me?"

"It's Jack," whispered Lionel to Barty.

"He wants a contact for scrap metal."

"Tell him we'll ring him back," said Barty.

Lionel ended the call and started a roll call of names.

"Metal Mickey, Brassey Mick..."

Barty interrupted him. "Was everybody christened 'Michael' in the metals game?"

"Only in Sussex," said Lionel with a smile.

"What about those second-hand catering equipment firms?

There is one up on the Ridge, isn't there?"

"Yes, there is. I bought an old steel Hobart dough mixer from them. It's just before you get on the Rye Road."

"Well, let's finish this pasta and go," said Lionel calling Jack back.

"Jack, leave it to me and Lionel. Can you come to Hastings tomorrow?"

"I can get to the shop by 10 o'clock and I have a little parcel of goods you might like. See you tomorrow, but please confirm that you have a load ASAP and then I can ring the Beacon."

"Righty ho. Call you later."

"Lionel, you pay. Here, take this flyer from the Brewing Brothers, it's worth 20% off as The Courtyard is their new adventure and I'll look up the address of 'Pettits'." Lionel paid a young man with an impressive moustache at the bar, saying:

"That was delicious. The pasta melted, leaving the best bit, the rabbit ragu. Thank you, we will come again."

Lionel returned to the table and found Barty juggling glasses and a phone.

"That was great Barty, so quick, it makes your service look slow at the Imperial," Lionel teased.

"Steady, I never keep anyone waiting more than twelve minutes, unless of course, they don't have a starter. The starter is the magic weapon of the restaurant trade. It's small, simple and quick but, best of all, it buys the chef time to assemble the more complicated main course. You've been with me in the kitchen, I'm like a whirling dervish."

"More spinning top, and a large one at that!" said Lionel.

One of Lionel's legions of faults is that he never knew when to stop. He just assumed everybody was as thick-skinned as he was.

"Thank you. I see myself more as a James Martin, all prepped and ready to go."

"You're more Keith Floyd; all blazer and cravat gently sweating like your onions."

"Shut up; let's get on."

Barty pushed the door open and left it to swing in Lionel's face.

"Don't be such a tart, Barty. You know I think you are the embodiment of James Martin, you just happen to dress like Keith Floyd!"

They crossed the coast road, and walked up London Road then into Norman Road to Barty's car, ribbing each other all the way.

"What's the name of this catering place?" Lionel asked, settling into the passenger seat.

"It's called 'Pettits' and, unusually for commercial kitchen suppliers, it's owned by a cheery fellow called Robin."

"I have never met a wrong Robin," said Lionel.

"What a lovely smell this car has. It doesn't smell like a beamer, more one of those great boat-shaped Jaguar Sovereigns of the 1980s." Lionel continued: "I have a friend who once bought a Sovereign. He sold it after six months as nobody would let him out of junctions. He concluded that it was the most hated car on the road, putting it down to either jealousy, or the fact that government ministers were photographed getting in and out of them." By the time Lionel had stopped blathering, Barty had turned into the industrial estate. They drove past the normal offerings: tyre centre, paper supplier, car stereo fitters, and double-glazing fabricators until they got to Pettits, recognisable by a large pile of stainless steel double sinks, twisted steel cladding and everything else that might be torn from a pub or hotel kitchen. Barty parked his precious car a good distance from every pile but, before he was completely satisfied that his car was out of harm's way, a small forklift truck shot out of the gloom of the unit. It was driven by a wild-eyed young man in brown dungarees, who quickly nosed his machine into a pallet and lifted a strapped steel undercounter cabinet, which he then swung around, and disappeared with into the gloom of the unit. Before Barty and Lionel entered the dark unit, a small door to the side of the rolled metal shutter opened and Robin Pettit emerged. He wore a checked shirt and blue overalls, a red spotted cotton handkerchief tied around his neck and a great big plate of a flat cap. It was a cap that looked like it had never left his head, as Barty had trouble in identifying either the pattern or the material. Mr Pettit removed his hand-rolled cigarette from his mouth and spoke.

"Good afternoon gents, what are you after; sinks, cookers, cabinets or pans?"

"None of those," said Barty, "we are after scrap metal."

"Scrap metal lads normally drive small tipper trucks," said Robin Pettit, nodding at the polished BMW.

"I recognise you," the cap wearer continued looking straight at Barty.

"Didn't I sell you that old Hobart dough mixer, the one with the wonky bowl?"

"You did," he replied.

"Did you take it to the welders that I recommended?"

"I did."

"I bet it's as sweet as a nut now."

"It is and I use it daily," said Barty.

"I remember young Robin saying it was a devil to get down the stairs, to a basement kitchen?"

"You remember correctly, the kitchen is downstairs under the Imperial on Queens Road."

"The size of a large child, that mixer. Used to think there was somebody staring at me when we had it in the unit."

Lionel was beginning to worry whether these fond recollections of mixers sold would ever end.

"Do you have any metal we could have? We are happy to pay the best price." interrupted Lionel.

"I don't," said Mr Pettit, "but my son Robin might."

Just then, the wild-eyed youth re-emerged at speed, on his fork lift. Before he could nose into another pallet, Robin senior whistled. No ordinary whistle, this one could topple vases. Robin junior shot over to his father's side, still seated, and said: "What's up Dad?"

"These two gents want some scrap," his father replied.

"What now and in that?" Robin junior looked at the BMW.

"No, we have a large Mercedes Sprinter van."

"I remember you," Robin junior retorted. "That heavy mixer to a basement kitchen on Queens Road."

"Yes, that's me," Barty replied.

"Weren't you once an auctioneer?"

At that young Robin jumped off the forklift seat and shook Bartys' hand, the speed of which surprised him. In fact, this young man seemed to do everything at top speed.

"What was I saying yesterday, Dad, about the Spread Eagle in St Leonards?"

His father nodded.

"We were saying that we needed an antiques expert to cast an eye over the place before I clear it."

"The Lord works in mysterious ways," said Pettit senior.

"At your service," said Barty, "and my friend here is an antiques dealer on Norman Road."

"Praise the Lord," said Pettit senior.

"There's no chance you'd look at the stuff now?" said Robin junior.

"Be delighted, if there was some scrap metal in it?" said Barty.

"Of course there is. Follow me and I will sort you out."

Knowing Robin junior had only one speed, Barty enquired of the address, just in case they lost him at a set of traffic lights.

"It's on the approach to Warrior Square train station, north side," said Pettit junior, as he climbed into a long white van.

"See you there." He then lurched off before Barty and Lionel had even got in the car. Five minutes later, they found Robin's van outside the closed pub. Barty hated the look of the perforated metal panels that companies fixed over windows and doors. The life seemed to seep through those little holes. Robin junior had opened the front door to let some light in. It was lucky it was a sunny day as the electricity had been turned off. It certainly was closed.

Barty called out, "Hello."

"Just coming," came the reply, as young Robin walked from behind the bar.

"Let me show you the items that might be antiques."

As Barty and Lionel's eyes adjusted to the low light, the objects started popping out. Behind the long mahogany bar and mirrored shelves, were the usual advertising whisky water jugs, large china sherry brandy barrels with burgundy-coloured hoops, various optics caging large upside-down spirit bottles and numerous tankards. The furniture around them was pure 1970s reproduction: dark stained beechwood tables and tub-shaped chairs.

"What about those?" Robin pointed to advertising mirrors printed with frothing tankards.

"I'm afraid they're the same era as the furniture, 1970s," said Barty. "Regrettably, this pub must have suffered a refurbishment," said Lionel, wistfully thinking of his local Horse and Groom which, thankfully, had been saved the indignity of modernisation.

Robin junior could see the disappointment of both Barty and Lionel.

"No matter, this old Victorian place has many rooms and we are only in the saloon bar. The public one is through here, but you will need your phone torches. I've tried the outside door but I just can't get it to open." Robin led the way to a small room off the saloon bar. It measured no more than 14 foot square, and was served by an extension to the bar counter, with a small fireplace opposite. Dotted around the room were four circular copper-topped tavern tables with oak square tapered legs and knopped turned feet.

"Do you like those, Lionel?" Barty said.

"Yes I do. Looks like this room survived the refurbishment."

"There is more like this upstairs," called young Robin.

"Lead on," said Lionel, his senses heightened by the copper-topped tables.

"Those tables are as rare as hen's teeth," Lionel whispered to Barty, as they trailed Robin up the stairs.

They walked along the first-floor landing and then into a big sitting room. When the pub was built in the 1880s this room was probably intended as a 'function room' and the second floor would have been the tenant's accommodation. But in recent decades, to get the right tenants, the living quarters were extended to include the first floor rooms. Luckily, the windows on the first floor were not shuttered. Barty noted a large leather sofa and two matching armchairs, a reproduction d-end dining table with six regency style dining chairs, and then he saw an oak standing corner cabinet and almost matching cupboard. Both had copper straps as door hinges and green glazed panelled doors, on the top frieze of the cupboard was written in copper lettering, 'Praise the Lord'.

"Do you like those two?" asked Robin.

"Yes, I do," said both Barty and Lionel in unison.

"Anything upstairs?" said Lionel.

"Not sure, take a look," said Robin.

As Lionel walked around upstairs, Barty said to Robin: "There are some nice bits of furniture here, for which I am sure Lionel will give you a price, but we really wanted to fill a van with some scrap metal."

"Don't worry, the kitchen hasn't been updated since the 1970s. The fittings have no commercial value and I have been paid to strip it all out. Come with me." As they walked onto the landing, Lionel was coming down the stairs.

"Anything?"

"Nothing, do you mind if I have a look at those cupboards again?"

"Sure. I'm taking the chef down to the kitchen. Join us when you are finished."

Robin was right, the kitchen was full of big pots with missing handles, a big dirty range with missing knobs, now replaced with jubilee-clipped wooden pegs. Perfect, thought Barty.

"Is it for you?" enquired young Robin.

"It's perfect. Let's recover Lionel and hopefully agree a price."

Lionel was still upstairs, now inspecting the back of the display cabinet.

"Checking for worm, none found."

"Now young Mr Pettit, I will give you £1,000 for the four circular tables in the public bar and the two oak cupboards on the first floor."

Robin paused, as he normally dealt with the kitchen trade, bartering over stainless steel sinks, which he knew the price of, was one thing, but he knew little about antiques, let alone their values.

"What say you?" pushed Lionel.

"Give me £1,200 and another £200 for the metal in the kitchen and it's all yours. Remember, the more you take the less I have to clear."

"Done. So fourteen hundred. Here's £400 for now and I will bring the remaining cash tomorrow."

Lionel always carried cash, a little seed money, he called it. After all, if there was no consideration, there was no deal.

"When can you collect?" asked Robin, trousering the cash.

"Tomorrow at 9.30 in the morning. Would you help us load it?" asked Lionel.

"Happy to. See you here tomorrow." Lionel and Barty thanked young Robin and drove off to The Horse and Groom.

"What a day," said Lionel. "Maybe our luck is turning."

"Real progress, we now have the bait for Ray. Just the thief to catch now. Give Jack a call and get him down earlier, say 9am. I wonder how that Detective Inspector is doing?"

Chapter 23

Brighton

Detective Inspector Kevin Smythe, or 'Anvil' to his colleagues, had gained his nickname, not only because of his haircut, but also on account of his immovability. It was said of him once that, when set on a particular path, he just didn't deviate. This trait had served him well. A combination of doggedness and tenacity had seen many of his investigations concluded when, mid-term, they seemed hopeless. As he sat at his desk in Norwich, doubts were beginning to creep in. He had come under some ribbing from his colleagues for pursuing the theft of 'garden ornaments'! Especially as it was from the home of a titled landowner. The bulk of CID's work was the investigation of domestic abuse, sexual violence with the very rare murder and lots of fraud. Theft, unless large scale, was the role of the beat bobby, neighbourhood watch and insurance companies. Kevin knew he couldn't spend too much time on Sir Roger's bronze, but was aware that if he recovered it, it would greatly enhance his standing within the county. He wrote in his notebook the leads he had to date. Mr Barty Hix in Hastings was just too much of a coincidence. The reward of a £1,000 offered by Sir Roger. The potential help of Mercy Penfold at the Antiques Trade Gazette. He wished he could involve

Mercy more, as she was eminently capable. But this was a police matter, and there were certain protocols he had to follow. He needed to speed the investigation up as it was drawing attention from both his colleagues and his superiors. Plus, he had his annual review later this week and he really couldn't afford the time to go to Hastings. It was 9am, he was unsure whether Mercy would be at her desk, but over-thinking had never troubled 'Anvil' before. Kevin rang the number in his notepad and within three rings, it was answered.

"Gazette, Mercy Penfold speaking."

"Detective Inspector Kevin Smythe here."

"Morning Inspector, how can I help?"

"Mercy, I fear that I was too quick to dismiss your offer of help yesterday," Kevin continued. "I have a lot on currently and I wondered whether you would unofficially assist me in the recovery of Sir Roger's bronze?"

"Have you rung Mr Hix?"

"I have, and between you and me, I believe he knows more than he is letting on."

"Have you rung Sergeant Arnold at Brighton?"

"No," said Kevin.

"Would you like me to call him, Inspector?"

"Yes please, and Mercy if we are going to work together, please call me Kevin."

"Thank you, I will call you later, Kevin. I just hope Sergeant Arnold is on duty."

"Good luck." Kevin hung up.

Whilst DI Smythe returned to his normal duties, Sergeant Arnold's telephone extension in Brighton rang. There was a time when most antiques stolen in Great Britain ended up in Brighton, but those days had gone. Was it the disappearance of the Brighton knocker boys or the redevelopment of its railway station car park that heralded the end of Brighton's Sunday Antiques Market, or was it the crash in antique furniture prices? His colleagues on the auction reporting desk used to say that 70% of regional auctioneer's sale total would be furniture, and the remaining 30% was silver and jewellery, china, glass and pictures. This was now reversed, with furniture contributing only 20% of regional sale's total. Sergeant Arnold organised open days of recovered antiques, where the public would hope to find their grandmother's brooch or grandfather's pocket watch and, if found, ownership was often claimed with an incidental family photograph or a post code marked with invisible ink. Sergeant 'Arthur' Arnold, so named after the first great television antiques expert, Arthur Negus, whose programmes like 'Going for a Song' paved the way for so many of the BBC's current programmes: Antiques Roadshow, Bargain Hunt, Flog It, Antiques Road Trip and its now more crafty cousin, The Repair Shop. 'Arthur' had trained under the great Inspector Wallace, who had started the Brighton Antiques and Stolen Goods Squad in the 1970s. This was when streams of white Ford Transits travelled up Brighton's London Road, heading to Wales, Gloucestershire, Yorkshire, Lancashire and Cornwall; in fact to every town and village in the land. They knocked on doors with cheery hellos and told the householder how very desirable the first thing that they saw was.

"You know, that bench, I'd give you a grand for that," when 'a grand' was worth more than a good holiday. Cheered by this good news, the knocker might be invited over the threshold to see more, as greed is a powerful driver. Once inside, the knocker would give prices on numerous items, invariably low prices on the most desirable items, say a large four glass table clock, its gilt brass frame looking slightly tired. This would be dismissed as yet another French carriage clock, but did the householder have the clock's leather covered travelling case? If a total price was agreed for the 'parcel', the 'knocker' would hand over the cash for the table clock and two other items, saying that he would be back later for the 'bench at a grand,' as he didn't have room in his van, just now. He would leave with the pieces that he wanted at a cheap price and never return for the bench that even on a good day, might fetch no more than £50. Once the vans were filled or the cash ran out, the 'knocker' boys would return to Brighton on Thursday or Friday to see the bigger dealers in Brighton's South or North Lanes, often queues forming to see the more ballsy dealers. Generally, prices were paid on the whole contents. The four glass table clock would be offered separately making ten times what was paid for it. Then the cash would be spent with wives and partners in pubs and restaurants. Some might sell at the station market on Sunday morning but most would be sleeping off two days of partying, before doing the whole thing all over again on Monday.

Arthur, like Wallace, knew all the players: the big antique dealers who bought parcels from the backs of vans and the knockers who filled those vans. If a policeman called from Suffolk saying that a daughter of a mother living on her own had been bullied into selling her family's antiques, there was every chance that Arthur or Wallace might know the 'knocker' concerned. If they had a good description, it was then their turn to do the knocking! They had to be quick though as, if they were not, the goods would soon be in a steel container crossing the Big Pond to America. By keeping the sellers and buyers apart, super profits were made and to ensure this, shops often displayed 'Trade Only' signs. It was a perfect market for two decades until a troubled fellow, Richard Reid, sat on a plane with explosives in the heels of his boots. They didn't explode, but as far as the American tourists were concerned, they might have done. Plus, America had developed a more relaxed furnishing style. It was either terrorism or fashion that ultimately pulled the rug on American demand for English antiques.

Mercy rang Brighton police station and asked for Sergeant Arnold's extension. After five rings, the phone was answered by a woman, "Sergeant Arnold's phone. WPC Tredwell speaking."

"Morning. Is Sergeant Arnold about?"

"May I have your name, caller?"

"Mercy Penfold." Mercy imagined Miss Tredwell to be short and sure-footed, most likely wearing highly polished Doc Martin boots.

"Sergeant Arnold is currently not at his desk, but is expected to return soon," Miss Tredwell continued, "may I have your number too?"

The gathering of information started at first contact, as instructed to new recruits of the police force.

"It's Mercy Penfold from The Antiques Trade Gazette in London and my number is......778"

"Thank you Ms Penfold, I will get Sergeant Arnold to call you back. Goodbye."

"Ms Penfold," confirmed Mercy's suspicions that WPC Tredwell's larger sized uniform was struggling at the seams.

How wrong she was! Miss Tredwell was tall, blond and arresting in appearance. She was one of three daughters of a well-known Brighton knocker boy, who had initially wrestled with his eldest daughter's desire to become a police woman. He blamed Morse, Rosemary & Thyme and Jack Frost detective dramas on television that his wife and daughters incessantly watched. Mercy had Barty Hix's name and number, but little else about this mystery caller, other than Kevin Smythe said he lived in Hastings. Mercy knew from older colleagues that Hastings and St Leonards had been thick with antique dealers. It was one of the stops that the Continental dealers made on the south coast's Folkestone to Honiton route. They called into shops and warehouses as they travelled west: Sandgate, Rye, Hastings, Eastbourne, Brighton, Worthing, Arundel and beyond, filling their vans with Globe Wernicke bookcases and carved oak refectory tables, all to put in their showrooms in Belgium and Paris. Often older dining tables were paired with contemporary designer multi coloured ply and chrome legged chairs. She wondered how Barty Hix fitted into this current antiques world, but her musings were broken by the ring of her telephone.

"Gazette, Mercy Penfold speaking."

"Morning Mercy, it's Sergeant Arnold. Good to hear from you. What's missing now then?" said Arthur in a cheery voice.

In fact, Arthur was always cheerful. He loved his work, his town and his wife.

"It's a large bronze group, a quarter sized study of a racehorse with jockey up," said Mercy.

"Is it valuable?" questioned Sergeant Arnold.

"It was bought at an auction room in Diss for under £700 in 1970.

"That sounds cheap, for a quarter size bronze study?"

"It's not old, made circa 1980s, cast when metals were considerably cheaper."

"I know the type," said Sergeant Arnold, "Containers of bronzes used to come into Newhaven from the Far East. Now I come to think of it, I have seen quite a few in the Brighton shops over the years. Why the interest, Mercy?"

"A number of reasons really. The gentleman who has reported it stolen is an aristocrat, Sir Roger Swotter of Kooling Towers in Norfolk. Secondly, he has offered a reward, £1,000, and thirdly, I'm keen to come through for him."

"Ok, Mercy, do you have any leads?"

"Yes, I took a call from a Mr Barty Hix in Hastings, asking after the measurements as he said 'he'd seen a similar casting'."

"His timing is a little suspicious," said Sergeant Arnold, "would you like me to pay this Barty Hix a call?"

"That would be splendid," replied Mercy, "when could you do it?"

"Hold on, I just want to ask Helen what's scheduled for tomorrow."

Mercy heard him call out.

"Helen, have we got time for a visit to Hastings tomorrow? It's about an hour away."

"We are snowed under this week getting ready for our Open Weekend. Monday, first thing?"

"Did you hear all that, Mercy?"

He deliberately hadn't covered the mouth piece with his hand.

"Sorry, we can't do it any sooner, but we will have hundreds of people hoping to be reunited with their stolen antiques this weekend."

"Thank you, Arthur, Monday will be fine. I will email you the details of both the bronze and Mr Hix." Arthur replaced the handset and said to Helen Tredwell:

"She's a nice girl, that Mercy; keen as mustard. Why don't you send her details of the Open Weekend? You two should meet. You know, she has turned that stolen desk at the Gazette from a curiosity to a valuable recovery tool." "Sir Roger, Kooling Towers, Barty Hix and a bronze racehorse. It all sounds very PG Wodehouse to me!"

"It does too. I have put Mr Hix in for a 7am on Monday, Sarge."

"Excellent Helen; always best to catch them out with an early morning knock. Would you inform Mercy Penfold for me?"

Chapter 24

Hastings

Jack arrived outside Lionel's shop in Norman Road just after 8am. He rang the bell and tried the door. It was open. Lionel had already picked up his paper and wine gums from the Sikh brothers on London Road and had left the shop door unlocked for Jack. Exercise is exercise but too much, especially up and down stairs, might be fatal for a man of Lionel's age. Jack walked in and called up the stairs.

"Lionel, it's Jack. I have some bits on the van."

"I'll be right down," called out Lionel, whilst easing a tray of sausages into the oven. Lionel found Jack outside with his van's rear double doors open. He had placed a step on the tarmac below the opening for Lionel. He had made the step out of heavy ply shuttering. It had four sides and a top held together by four two-inch square corner posts. These posts, which were glued and screwed from the inside, projected beyond the bottom edge of the box's corners and now, having become worn, had in turn become more stable. In the middle of the top step Jack had jig-sawed an open figure of eight which allowed him a handhold. Carpentry was one of the things he liked about the antiques trade. He always left a bid on a table with a wobbly leg or the open armchair with stained upholstery. He had put a shed behind his parents' garage in Cobham, Surrey. Theirs was a three bedroomed 1930s house on a quiet road on the M3 side of the town. Beside the brick and pebble dash house, was a garage and it was behind this that he had put up a small green painted corrugated iron structure made from reclaimed materials, as he wanted the neighbours to forget it had not always been there. He had panelled half of the interior with some old Scotch board, and this enabled Jack to form a workshop area. His tools were hung on nails with stencilled shapes to remind him where they went. His father, an ex-engineer, had told him, "if you weren't organised, half your time was wasted in looking for your next tool, screw or particular sized nail". It had wired lighting and power sockets from the adjacent garage's fuse box. This workshop allowed Jack to repair the cheap and broken, in the hope of selling at improved profit.

Lionel placed his left foot on the box and stepped onto the van's plywood floor.

"I like the step, a nice courtesy, not lost on an old antiques dealer such as myself," said Lionel.

"Now, what have you got to show me?"

Jack worked quickly removing the ties and blankets that secured his load.

"I'm trying to think 'Downton Abbey' meets 'Grand Designs', something old and something new!"

"Steady Jack, I'm not your bride! I like the baltic pine pot cupboard and you have a second, a pair! Well done, this feels a bit like Christmas," Lionel said whilst thinking Norman's days might be numbered.

"And the luggage rack." Lionel lifted it up and turned it over, it had a makers' oval brass label reading, 'Thomas Squirrel and Sons, Worcester Lane, Cheapside'.

"Not bad, Jack! We have a pair of pot cupboards, Mr Squirrel's luggage rack and that backgammon board. Any stones?"

"All 30 are present, plus a pair of wooden shakers and die."

Lionel opened the book-like hinged board, and took out the shakers; heavy he thought, and beautifully turned. The interiors were ribbed, "a nice touch", thought Lionel.

"Jack, a word from the wise, these here shakers are made of the heaviest wood in the world, lignum vitae. They use this wood for the bearing of a ship's propeller. It's incredibly hard and its natural resin in the wood lubricates the shaft. A win-win! Man working with nature; the virtuous circle that we all seek. Now, talking of virtuous circles, how much are these goodies to Uncle Lionel?"

"£225 for the pot cupboards. The luggage stand with the makers label £75 and the board, shaker and stones £125. That's £425 in total."

"Jack, this is Uncle Lionel. You're the runner. I'm the retailer. Now try again.

"£325 and I'll throw in a large sausage sandwich for free!"

Before he could answer, Clive barked... for the sausages and not the £325!

"Is that a 'yes' for Uncle Lionel?"

"It is, but only if there's a sausage for Clive."

"Of course there is. Now let's get them in. I'm starving."

Over sausage sandwiches and coffees in Lionel's upstairs kitchen, Jack outlined how he was going to approach Ray at the scrapyard.

"Nervously?" said Lionel. "That's how Barty and I would approach Ray in the yard. Is the Beacon willing?"

"He talked about being too busy at first, but when I mentioned that I would have an empty van afterwards and was keen to buy stock for Ardingly, suddenly his diary was magically clear!"

"Good stuff, here's some seed money." Lionel gave him £325 in cash for the antiques. "Now, may I come with you in your van? The pub is just up the road and we are meeting Barty and Robin there at 9am."

Lionel and Jack followed Clive, downstairs. Lionel locked the door then struggled into the van's passenger seat. Once in, he gave Clive another sausage. "Stop that Lionel, otherwise I will lose Clive to you."

"Alright, but I know Clive will burn it off. Now we need to go up the London Road, and then you will see the metal shuttered pub on your right."

As Jack started the engine, Lionel suddenly called out,

"I've forgotton the bronze."

Lionel left the van and popped back into the shop and returned with a 4 foot object covered in a grey blanket.

"What's that?" asked Jack as Barty placed the wrapped object in the passenger foot well beside him.

'It's a bronze figure of Venus, it's a reproduction. I gave £350 for it, only on account of it's size. That Jack, is your bait for Ray."

"Come on, we can't be late for young Robin. You know, I never went in this pub," Lionel continued. "It's funny how you get used to one spot and fail to venture forth, even on one's own doorstep."

"There's young Robin's van. I will pop in and ask Barty to move his car so we can load nearer the door."

Inside, Lionel walked past the bar, following the sound of pots and blackened pans being thrown into large wheelie bins. Young Robin was feverishly throwing what wasn't new into the bins with practiced accuracy.

"This is all yours. Take it out now and we'll have another full load on your return," said Robin. Lionel snatched the bin back on its wheels and left before he was hit by a flying pan. It didn't take long before Jack's empty van was full of old catering equipment, including a large six-ring gas range.

"That's a good load," said Robin, "and don't take anything less than £200 for it". As they wished Jack good luck and waved him off, Lionel asked Robin if he could have another look around.

"Of course, and anything upstairs is yours, as I've more than enough to deal with downstairs."

"That's most kind," said Lionel.

"Here's the £1,000 balance owed."

"Thank you, and remember, the more you take upstairs the less I have to clear, and when will you be picking up the cabinets and tables?"

"Hopefully, later today on Jack's return to Hastings," said Lionel. "I will call you." "Come on Barty, let's have a look at those cabinets again."

"Sorry Lionel, I need to go and do my ordering for the Imperial, I haven't given a thought to what I am going to cook yet. This saga has rather consumed me."

"I'll give you a call when I have news from Jack. Maybe we could meet up for supper?"

"Excellent. I should be organised by then, see you later."

Barty popped his head into the kitchen to say goodbye to Robin and narrowly missed being struck by a large stainless steel shelf.

"Sorry," said young Robin. "This is about the only thing of value in here, as chefs are always adding shelves to kitchens and this one is large enough to be cut down."

"I'm off. Thanks for your help with the metal."

"My pleasure, and remember Pettits for any kitchen equipment. Did you know that Dad collects old kitchen utensils? You should see some of the slicers he has!"

"Tell him I would love to call and see them one day, but I have a restaurant to get to. Bye."

As Barty left, he shouted upstairs.

"Bye Lionel, maybe see you later?"

Lionel was too busy to hear; he was now in discovery mode. Often, when he knew something should be there, it took another turn of the room to find it, whether it was in the smalls' section in an auction room with all that china and glass or with the metalware, or the glorious miscellaneous section, including everything cased: microscopes to stuffed fish and birds. He knew there was nothing in the small kitchen upstairs, as he had checked the cupboards twice. He went around the sitting room once more, but there wasn't anything of note. "Odd," thought Lionel, as the cupboards were by 'Shapland and Petter' a maker of great repute. He remembered that the second-floor bedrooms were furnished with rather poor post-war utility bedroom suites. Maybe he should push himself to have another look. This time he checked inside the wardrobes and chests. Again nothing in the small bedroom, but in the large wardrobe in the big bedroom were two old cardboard boxes. He lifted one of the large boxes onto the bed, he had an inclination that it contained a vase, it certainly felt like one item. He opened the box and started removing the old newspaper which was yellow and dated 1st August 1963. He pulled away more newspaper to reveal a large Chinese enamelled porcelain vase. He put it down and checked the other box. It too had a matching pink ground vase. Lionel put it back and sat on the bed. It was just too much excitement at this hour of the day. He had one more brief look at both, re-wrapped them and put them in their boxes again before taking them downstairs and placing them in the larger cupboard. To say Lionel floated back to his shop was to underplay it. He smiled, he waved, and he even sang.

Chapter 25

London

Once underway, Jack called the Beacon and arranged to meet him at Ray's yard on the south side of Wandsworth Bridge.

"I'll get there for noon, young Sir," the Beacon confirmed in his preferred Dickensian way. Whilst Jack drove, he tried to formulate a strategy. Although he was new to the antiques trade, he was learning quickly. He hadn't wasted hours keeping shop but had honed his skills on the road. An antique runner's shop is his van; smalls in the cab and furniture in the back. He knew what to tie, and he knew what to blanket first as any dealer will be intrigued by what they can't see. His parents had been keen fans of the television series 'Lovejoy,' and he remembered one episode, in which the star, Lovejoy, had covered up a 16th century oak bible box with a grey blanket. The covering had hidden the box's recent restoration but also had acted as a magnet to an inquisitive buyer. The episode had stayed with him so he always had something covered in the back. This time, he had added the wrapped bronze of Venus to the middle of his load. The trap was set, but how was he going to persuade Ray to slip up, and reveal the identity of the seller of the horse and jockey bronze. After all, it would be incriminating. Surely scrap metal merchants shouldn't be buying stolen metal, be they garden bronzes or lead from church roofs. He knew that Ray would be more guarded with a stranger and less so with the Beacon who he had obviously known forever. He would let the Beacon play the central role in the sale of his load. He found the yard without too much difficulty, as you could see the hills of crushed cars from the roundabout. Once inside, he parked next to the Beacon who was with a similarly gnarled-looking man.

"Morning, Derek," Jack called out and before he could reply, his gnarled friend said to Derek:

"Who's your *china*, Del?" (*China Plate* = mate.)

"This Ray, is Jack. He has become one of my young customers at the Heathrow car boot. He is new to the game and showing promise."

"What, in rag and bones?" said the gnarled man, who Jack sensed to be Ray.

"Well, it's not the metal, otherwise you wouldn't be here, Del. Come on young man, show us what you've got in the back of your beer." (*Beer can* = van.)

As Jack opened the double doors of his van he wondered whether Wandsworth had its own dialect. He knew that the Beacon formed his sentences as Dickens might have done for Victorian readers. His father had told him when he had been an electrical engineer on rigs off Aberdeen, that some people spoke or used smatterings of Doric. The Welsh had their language too, but for Jack, born and raised in Cobham, Surrey, '*china*' and '*beer*' were a little off centre. Jack opened the doors and stood aside. Ray just had a quick look and quietly calculated the load.

"Let's get you on the weigh bridge and work back from there shall we. He directed Jack to a large metal plate in the yard. Once on briefly, he was instructed to go over to a pile of aluminium, and before Jack could stop the van, a man mountain of a youth, stripped his load. Then Ray motioned him to the plate again. The whole procedure took no more than five minutes, during which Ray and Del stood side by side. Ray opened the back doors before Jack could get out of his cab.

"Got any steps?" asked Ray.

Jack placed his ply box on the ground and Ray hopped up followed by the Beacon, who had clocked the wrapped object tied to the side of the van. Ignoring the old range and twisted metal, they both went for the tie and blanket. Lovejoy was right, the grey blanket is a magnet. Jack watched from outside the van as the two *chinas* unwrapped the bronze.

"This is more you Del," said Ray.

"You had m' last one, didn't you?"

"I did,'"said the Beacon, "and I sold it to young Jack here."

At this, Ray edged away from the bronze and looked at Jack.

"How much did Del ask for the...?" Ray paused and then remembered, "the 'orse and jockey?"

"Oh Ray, don't break the dealers code; once sold, nobody knows!"

"I was asking your *china*, not you," Ray snarled.

Jack was caught between the Beacon and his snarling mate.

"I paid the going rate," replied Jack ambiguously. I bought that horse for scrap weight and I sold it to Del as art. I would be pissed off if I've been taken for a plum!"

At this the Beacon brought out a hip flask from the inside pocket of a rather loud tweed jacket; no doubt, from one of his many Mayfair house clearances. The Beacon then slipped off a silver sleeve cup from the bottom of the flask, poured a good measure of golden liquor in, and passed it to Ray. Once drained,

188 | Barty — A Tale of a Stolen Bronze

Ray passed the cup back, which the Beacon refilled and passed to Jack. Jack didn't normally drink spirits, but something told him that he should, much like an earlier explorer would have done with an indigenous tribe, hoping not to cause offense just to stay alive!

After the Beacon had, in turn, finished his cup, all seemed much more relaxed, so relaxed that Ray now urged the Beacon and his *china* to his office to settle up for the load.

"What about the bronze and metal?" said Jack, unaccustomed to the new bonhomie mood.

"Give me your keys and young Ray will sort out the van," said Ray.

Jack looked at the Beacon, who motioned him to go with it. There was trust and there was trust, and this tenuous trust didn't extend to the well-being of Clive. Jack opened the van door for Clive and then threw the van keys to the man mountain, who must be young Ray. 'I wonder what he was fed on as a child?' thought Jack. 'Obviously iron!'

Past a gleaming, burgundy-coloured Bentley, they climbed a set of outside steel steps, passing a secure ground floor office peopled by working women. Once on the top step, Ray opened a metal door to a large airy office, with unrivalled views over his kingdom. Then, from behind a large table, he opened the middle drawer of a filing cabinet, from which he brought a bottle of brandy and a pack of ginger ale cans. As he mixed the 'horse's necks' he phoned.

"Jackie, any ice in yours?" asked Ray.

Moments later, the clang of heavy steps on steel treads announced a rather large lady.

"Here's your ice," Jackie said, as she plonked a bag onto Ray's table.

"Don't push it. We have a pile of VAT returns to do today, and here's the young man's read out." With that, she left.

"Your Jackie, still cheery!" said the Beacon.

"Just like her old Mum," said Ray, "frightening, but efficient. You know, I never touched a ledger with her Mum, and I haven't touched a computer with our Jackie." Ray added the ice to his and the Beacon's drinks, and asked Jack what his poison was.

"Mine's the ginger ale thanks. I've got to get back to Hastings after I have seen what Derek's got."

"Perfect, young Sir. A couple here, and then you can take me back to Fulham in yours." said the Beacon.

"As long as it's only a couple," Jack replied meekly, as he knew Ray was a man of fragile moods.

"That's quite a read out!" interrupted Ray. "Aluminium's up again. Your *china* is a lucky lad."

"What do you think your load has come in at?"

"With the bronze or without?"

"Without of course. Del can buy the bronze, as he's here!"

"Two hundred and twenty?" said Jack.

"Two fifty," said the Beacon.

"No, I wish it was. Four hundred and twenty, bank transfer or cheque?"

Jack was having difficulty keeping up.

£420? I'm sure young Robin Petit said, 'Don't take anything less than two hundred,' and his father had always said, 'buy country, sell city.' A rather less anxious Jack sat back and listened to the two old traders.

"What did you give me for that large bronze group Del?"

"Don't tease me. I know that you could reel off every deal that you've made this quarter, and to the pound!"

Ray smiled.

"I gave those ladies £150 for that bronze. They shouldn't have taken my offer, it was too low. But I know one of them lives around the corner, and London traffic ain't that friendly to horse boxes. Come on young man what did you give Del here, for the group?"

Jack looked at the Beacon who mouthed 'dealers code' and then said,

"Come on Ray, stop pushing, let's have another drink?"

Ray poured them both another horse's neck and pushed Del a little further

"What are you going to give this young lad for his bronze beauty?"

"Nothing Ray, I always does swaps for some items in my store."

"Did you take anything else from the ladies in the horse box?" probed Jack.

"No," said Ray, who seemed to grow friendlier with every swig.

"I said to Mandy, the one with the short hair and leather jerkin, that there wasn't much call for working lawnmowers around here, as I pointed to the hundreds of glass and steel apartment blocks opposite. It's a scrap metal price here and there ain't no premium for self-propelling metal. Her pretty mate Maxine gave me the eye and heaved her chest, but that doesn't work with me. I don't like *tea leafs*. Not a nice pair. They seemed chippy, resentful of the gardens they work in. I bet they have never even met the owners. You know some of those 'ouses over the water in Chelsea have acres of garden, full of sculpture, garden seats and pots. They even tried to sell me old china flower pots!"

"I'm always buying flower pots for Ardingly Antiques Fair. You don't have their number?" Jack ventured.

"Oi, have you heard of the metal merchants' oath?" said Ray
"No," said Jack.

"Well it's no names, no numbers, and I have slipped up on the
names bit! Now pick up your £420 from Jackie. Bye Del, and bye
young man. Remember, if it's metal and heavy, bring it to Ray."

Jack called into the office below and Jackie gave him a cheque,
a printed receipt and his van keys. Before he put Clive in the cab,
Jack checked to see if the bronze was still in the back.

It was. All was in order and now with both the Beacon
and Clive in the cab they set off for Fulham. He had got close:
names but no phone numbers. Just two light-fingered gardeners
who appear to have the only horse box in South London. After
Jack had run the Beacon back to his store in Fulham, he then
sifted through his latest house clearance, a small house in
Hammersmith. The Beacon had definitely gone into a slower
gear ever since draining the silver sleeve from his hip flask.
In fact, he seemed to have dropped his Dickens dialect and
become much more chummy. The Hammersmith house must
have belonged to a 1970s hipster. The furniture could easily be
arranged into an early Conran photo shoot. There were a pair
of circular bamboo chairs that floated in black painted iron
stands, two matching circular bamboo coffee tables with lovely
bent legs, held together by small circular stretchers, a couple
of interesting bamboo standard lamps, and two tile-topped
oblong teak coffee tables. Jack said:

"All this group needs is an orange carpet!"

"Funny you should say that," said the Beacon gently swaying.
"There was one, but too much moth, so we tipped that. People
need to spring clean regularly, if you don't move the furniture,
you will leave the moth undisturbed."

The Beacon then made for a similar filing cabinet to Ray's, opened the middle drawer and out emerged a very well-stocked bar.

"Now, nothing goes to waste on a clearance," the Beacon said, as he poured himself another brandy and ginger ale. He then opened a bright orange coloured SMEG fridge and took out an ice tray. Once the desired cubes were emptied into what looked like a regimental snare drum, the Beacon relaxed into a Regency cane library chair. He had certainly done alright from the humble house clearance game.

"Now young Jack, you want the bamboo?"

"Yes," said Jack. "So that's six items. The oblong coffee tables?"

"Yes please, and what about the chair you are sitting in?"

"This chair will cost you the bronze and the other eight items, say £200."

"That's very kind of you."

"I like you, Jack, and so does Ray. It normally takes years to get up his stairs." "That's why I asked you. Often an introduction from a friend generally speeds up trust."

"Now I must load up and go. My friends in Hastings are expecting me and I will see you on Sunday at the car boot."

"Look forward to it," said the Beacon, as he raised his ice-filled glass.

"Be early. Colin and I have a good flat clearance in Barons Court tomorrow and Friday."

"I will bring you a cup of tea at six o'clock, and thanks for your help today."

"Do not speak of it, kind Sir."

Chapter 26
Norfolk

After Brandon and Kezia didn't show, Clem drove straight to his Ma and Pa's in Lucky Slap. Whilst Tom and Scan joshed and smoked, Clem thought that he had got no further by visiting Kezia. Brandon remained a mystery. He was definitely self-assured. Clem was pretty certain now that he and his brothers were not involved in the theft from Kooling Towers. He had a lot of questions for his Pa as he knew the Rayleigh lot much better. They arrived at five and his mother, Pearl, was preparing tea.

"Come in boys," said Pearl, "we are having toad in the hole; any takers?"

"Yes please Ma," Scan replied giving her a kiss. Their father Terry was on the phone. Since his heart attacks, Terry couldn't ply the roads as before. As he used to say, "A little tarmac here and a dusting of gravel there". He and his brothers used to knock on the better-looking houses; Terry in his trusty hi-viz tabard and sign-written truck 'Drives to Last'. He was good at giving lots of spiel. They would "be in the area re-surfacing for the highways and would have surplus tarmac going cheap". He knew how to play that funny thing called greed. Just like a big fish on the line, by the time that he had walked down the drive, the fish had landed. He would then take his surveyor's wheel from the truck and measure.

Later, when done, came the catch. The drive was not a single strip one yard wide, and 200 long, it was 3 yards wide, so not the 200 square yards at £6.50 per square yards but 600 square yards. Terry then took the homeowner through the inevitable distress and anger, with little touches of menace and compassion. In the end a deal was struck at twice the length. It always worked and it always followed the same pattern. The homeowner begrudgingly admiring his chutzpah and charm, but there was never repeat business. Terry put down the phone.

"Hello boys, what's up? Pearl, have we got enough toad for the boys?"

"I've just asked them and they're staying."

"Sorry, I was on the phone to your uncle Pat. Give the boys a beer Pearl."

"Alright. Scan, there are some cold ones on the bottom shelf."

"Your Ma allows me a beer when we have visitors. Thank the Lord you came"

"Just the one, Terry," Pearl added, as she whipped up the mixture for the batter: four eggs, self-raising flour, milk and salt. She would add some more of the cooked sausages to go around.

Scan passed the cans around and Clem said, "we went to see Kezia today".

"How is she?" Terry had always been fond of his pretty niece.

"I'm not sure," said Clem. "She seemed somewhat lost. You know, she was the leader of the pack here, but at Brandon's she's sort of lonely".

"She will find her feet, look at your Ma. She was tough as a teenager and just got tougher as a Ma! I'm sure once Brandon and her have kids, things will settle."

"But what if she can't have kids?" retorted Clem.

"Of course she will, remember Kezia is one of ten! Do you want me to have a word with Uncle Pat? He would be well cross if his little princess wasn't being looked after."

"No, don't do that Pa, but its a mystery, what Brandon does?"

Terry took a swig from the can and continued.

"Your Uncle Patrick knows the Rayleigh lot better than me. Something to do with his mother's uncle. They were a commercial lot. No tarmac or roofing, more, a sort of security, I think." Terry then called to Pearl:

"Patrick's mother, wasn't her father a good fighter?" Pearl joined the boys and Terry on the sofa.

"Alfred, Patrick's grandfather, was a celebrity in his day. I can still picture his caravan. It was beautifully painted, a traditional wooden affair. How his wife brought up your Auntie Rose and her 5 siblings, with all that travelling too, I'll never understand. Alfred was a boxer, you know, the bare-knuckle stuff. There was quite a circuit in the 1930s, and fights were arranged and travelled to. None of Alfred's sons inherited his boxing gene, but they did inherit their mother's talent for figures. Alfred's wife opened a book when her husband fought. There were, of course, other bookies too, but she made the money. Sometimes, even against Alfred. He never knew, but he was very surprised when they moved to a lovely house in Leigh-on-Sea. She was smart, Rose's mum, and she looked after Alfred who became like a child towards the end; too many knocks to the head. It was so sad to see that lion of a man speaking like a child."

"Maybe Brandon got the money gene from his great grandmother."

"But again, do you know what Brandon does?" pressed Clem.

"I don't, do you Pearl?" said Terry.

"No, I don't know. Give Pat a call. I've got to get going with the onion gravy."

Terry redialled Patrick's number. He and Terry were like brothers, having married Terry's older sister Pearl, and like Kezia, she had been a real beauty in her day.

"Patrick, the boys have just been to see Kezia today, and briefly saw Brandon. They can't work out what he does."

The reply came back, "I know he has never lifted a shovel. We had a fun night before the wedding, which ended in some arm wrestling. He has soft hands but hard arms and hard eyes too, sort of inky. Your big sis thinks there is something of the night about him. He's in finance and, with those eyes, I would say a loan shark. Did the boys say how Kez was?"

"Yes, all well Pat. Come over and see me. Pearl's got me under house arrest."

"Bye Terry. You should be behind bars. Love to Pearl."

"Come and see me soon Pat?" Terry put the mobile down, "Kezia's married to a loan shark".

"He's a chip off his great grandma," Pearl added.

It slightly confirmed what Clem had thought, but Cliff and Albert looked too stupid. Theirs must be a driver's role. But it still left the question: why their interest in garden ornaments?

"Pa, you know about Sir Roger's missing bronze. You don't have any idea who may have taken it? As local gossip has it, it's us, the Kindlys from Lucky Slap." "Who's saying that, son?"

"Stringer in The Squirrel said something about Jess loosening her mouth off at The Swotter Arms," replied Clem.

"That Stringer's a little rat. He's too settled with Mike at The Squirrel. Why don't you pay that Jess a visit at The Swotter Arms. See what she knows, but watch that Anita, she's tough as your Ma." Terry continued, "The problem at The Towers is they keep opening the place allowing any old diddy in."

Clem smiled, it was nice to be reminded that there was other riff-raff about.

"Pearl, how's that toad getting on? The boys are famished," called out Terry.

Pearl ignored him, she had chopped the onions then sweated them down. Now she added water, a splash of her sherry and beef gravy granules.

"Clem, why are you interested in the bronze?" asked Terry.

"I don't know Pa, but we have always been on good terms with Lou, the keeper."

"What about the pheasant heads?" said Terry. "We made good money that night."

"You're in no shape to go hunting around woods at night now, and nor would we want to. We feel sort of settled here, and I don't like people taking liberties, which they then lay at our door."

Terry interrupted, he had heard enough.

"I told you Pearl, we would all go soft if we stayed. It's happened. I can't move now and my boys are turning into policemen!"

"Calm down, you can't afford another turn."

"I will have one if I hear any more of this. Promise me boys, you will travel a bit before you settle down. It will sharpen your wits, having the old Bill moving you on."

"We will Pa, but we just want to right this wrong. There is no harm in asking Jess what the village gossip is. We need a lead. All we have now, is suspicion towards us, and it ain't us."

"It will be somebody clocking it on one of the Tower's Open Days. Pearl tells me there are posters everywhere for one next Sunday. Some cricket do?"

"You may be right Pa, but we will ask Jess first."

After Pearl's toad in the hole the boys left for The Swotter Arms saying, "This would be a first for the Kindly family, walking over the threshold of The Swotter Arms." Clem hoped it was one of Jess's shifts. As was his normal practice, he chose a parking spot farthest from the Arms. He then asked Tom and Scan whether they would mind staying put, just while he checked the lay of the land. Clem was careful to choose the public bar on the left. He knew Anita would be in the saloon bar to the right. He walked into the open arch, where once coaches would have rolled in, and took the left-hand door. The top half of the door was glazed, allowing a visitor to check if the bar was crowded or quiet. He paused to see whether Jess was behind the bar. He couldn't see anybody, and the room looked quiet. He pushed the swing door open and heads turned to see who had entered. Clem was tall and well-built with thick black hair and dark brown eyes. He never knew why people stared at him. Did they see the gypsy in him, or a good-looking man in his prime? He acknowledged their stares with nods and moved to the empty bar. He sat on one of the eight empty bar stools and waited for service. Within minutes, Jess came through the same swing door and bobbed under the closed bar counter. Somewhere between the "Hello," and, "what can I get you?" Jess recognised Clem.

"You can't stay."

"Why ever not?"

"Anita wouldn't like it."

"I only want the one lager."

"Go on then. Carling or this nice German one 'Dortmunder?'" She asked. "I would go for the German. That's what my old Grandad used to say."

"Jess, the jester, I thought you were just teeth and tits."

"Oi Clem, you won't get this pint if you carry on like that! Now, what can I do for you, master Kindly?"

Jess and Clem had been in the same class at school. She had always fancied Clem; it was his broad shoulders and unguarded smiles. Both Jess and Clem had left school early: he for the call of cash and she because she had found the whole 'learning thing' a complete mystery. She was a chatterbox, so bar work was perfect, and Anita was like another Mum, just stricter. She passed the pint to Clem.

"I thought you and your brothers were more at home in The Squirrel?"

"I came to see you, Jess," said Clem.

"On account of me looks? Why so long, handsome?" Jess teased.

"None of that. It's about a missing garden statue taken from The Towers," Clem continued as Jess tried to concentrate. "Stringer at The Squirrel was mouthing off that you had said we might have taken Sir Roger's bronze."

This put Jess on the back foot. She knew Clem was direct, as he had been the one who had asked the cheeky questions in class. Clem stared at Jess and waited for her response.

"I never said that you had taken the garden thing, just that you and your brothers were the prime suspects."

"Jess, this ain't a TV drama. What's all this 'prime suspect' business? It's me, Tom and Scan. We wouldn't want to piss off Lou or Sir Roger. We are so busy with gardening. It seems like nobody wants to climb a ladder anymore. We have almost cornered the market in hedges over seven feet, and there are a lot of them around here. Anyways, who told you we are the 'prime suspects'?"

"Cecil and Lou came in here on Monday wanting to know whether Anita or me had heard anything."

"Had you Jess?"

"No. I knew that your names were a lazy call."

"It was, and it sometimes hurts, but as time goes on my skin gets thicker. Not yet the rhino level of my old man, but still thicker than most. Jess, it wasn't us. Is there anything that has aroused your suspicion? Think hard, it's important."

Jess thought for a moment then Clem prompted her.

"Pa thinks Sir Roger's a fool to keep opening his garden. It could be anyone who visited The Towers lately."

"Cecil and Lou said the thieves used a truck with twin tyres on their rear axle; that's why you're the 'prime suspects'. You still have that tipper truck don't you?"

"Yes, we do, it's for towing the wood chipper. We need the twin tyres as we are often on soft ground. You know, trailers and horseboxes have twin tyres too?" Suddenly something registered with Jess.

"You know what? We had a horsebox here overnight about a couple of weeks ago. Two women they were loud and with a different accent."

"What sort of accent?" said Clem.

"It wasn't from here, more London."

"What were they driving?"

"Don't ask me! I have never owned a car, though I think it might have been one of those old Volvos and the horsebox wasn't very big. I had a look at it as you know I like horses."

"Jess, when was this?"

"They came in a couple of Saturdays ago. They had dinner, took a double room and didn't stay for breakfast. I remember, I was on that Sunday breakfast and they didn't show."

"Do you stay overnight when you have rooms?"

"No, no need, as Anita lives here."

"Do you keep a record of guests?"

"Only in the diary with all the table reservations."

"Would you have a look for me?" Clem pulled out his broadest smile and touched her arm over the bar.

"Anita keeps it with her by the landline in the saloon bar. I will pop over and look."

A couple of minutes later, Jess returned waving a waitress pad.

"This is exciting. I have the owner of the horsebox: a Ms Maxine MacKenzie. I didn't have you down as Morse, Clem." Jess said smiling, she was enjoying this. "Any address?"

"None, she paid cash. We don't normally take addresses down, only if they want a copy invoice for expenses. But Anita remembers one of them saying they had driven from London."

"So two of over nine million odd people! That shouldn't be too hard then! Here's my number, if you think of anything else, call me."

As he slipped his 'No Hedge Too High,' card over the bar, he cheekily stole a kiss. As Clem opened the door to leave, he turned and waved and then he noticed that Jess was blushing. Clem walked to the truck waving the slip from Jess's waitress pad and said to Tom and Scan.

"Pa was right, I think we have our thief".

Chapter 27

London

Mandy and Maxine tried to escape London and their normal lives every couple of weeks. Life had not turned out the way they would have liked. Both inseparable friends from school, a regular state school in Wandsworth, South London. They had had fun together in their teens and early twenties.

Mandy got married in her mid-twenties and was divorced by her forties. Divorce sounds messy and protracted, but it was not so in her case. She had been married to a gambler. Her divorce wasn't a division of assets, just a walk from her repossessed home back to her mother's third-floor flat. She was stuck with a mother who would have preferred to have lived with either of her two other children.

Whereas, Maxine had never married, and as an only child, she had inherited her childhood home. A three-bedroom mid-terrace house in Tooting, within sight of the Common and enough room in the front to park both her Volvo estate car and a small horsebox. Maxine's earnings were spent on a horse called Peter, who was in livery stables just outside Epsom. It was with her car and horsebox that she and Peter explored old Surrey villages and ancient bridle paths. But it was never for long, as there was always her son Kelvin. Kelvin was on the spectrum, or super needy, like he was as a child. Maxine's mother had said, "That child is too clever by half, watch it girl, as he will have you!"

How right she was. Kelvin was like a drogue anchor trailing behind a boat. As hard as Maxine worked, Kelvin would drag his heels. He had started on the wrong foot; a mistaken legacy of one of the endless summer music festivals. Maxine could hardly remember Kelvin's father, except he was short and drunk but super attentive at the time. Such was her and Mandy's lifestyle she didn't even know that she was pregnant until it was too late. Mandy and Maxine often shared beds, boys and sometimes both at the same time. But that was then and now, the only beds they shared were those they weeded. If only Kelvin wasn't around, Mandy would live in Tooting with Maxine. She had always fancied Maxine but both knew their friendship would break if Mandy and Kelvin had to share the same space.

Over the years, Mandy and Maxine had refined a list of wealthy clients. They liked those they didn't see. Whose contracts came through property agents or personal assistants. As long as the gardens were weeded, cut and tidied, everyone had done their job. It didn't matter that extra billable hours were added, when they were younger, it was the wallets and drugs of drunks they stole, but now it was garden benches or bronzes, as so much could be blamed on a wider, lawless society. The property agents and the personal assistants soon found replacements happily billing their clients for their time. The service system worked. A pyramid of subcontracting only made possible by the very wealthy at the top and the 'perfunctories' performing at the bottom.

Mandy could mow a lawn with enviable stripes, having learnt her craft with Wimbledon tennis ground staff, whilst Maxine went through the beds and borders with her magic hoe. "Little and often," her father had taught her. After so many years they worked as one. There was no duplication, just application. But when work was over, that's when reality hit. Mandy with her sour mother and Maxine with the relentless Kelvin. It was weekends when the two friends would escape. Mandy had no problem leaving her mother. Her cheery wave and goodbye was met with a sarcastic, "Don't worry about me!"

Whereas, Maxine left Kelvin in bed, as with no school, he would sleep until hungry and then shuffle to the sofa to play whatever computer game was in fashion. He didn't need physical friends as he had so many online. The friends who would 'forget you,' as Maxine called them.

If only Maxine could capture that feeling between closing her driver's door and turning her ignition key; a glorious pause where responsibilities ebbed and a new adventure began. It only took 15 minutes to Mandy's. She would be on the pavement, smiling with home-made cappuccinos. She did the planning and Maxine did the driving. She wasn't the best driver and the small horsebox behind her exaggerated her errors, leaving clipped kerbs and tyre-marked verges.

It was on one such Saturday morning that they left for the further reaches of Norfolk. Mandy kept an eye on open gardens, be they for local charities or the National Garden Scheme. You didn't need local knowledge anymore as everything was now on smart phones. The gardens normally opened around 10am and closed at 5pm. They might make this one for lunch if there was little traffic. Her smartphone said just under four hours, but experience told them to add another half an hour for the horsebox.

"We might arrive for lunch," said Mandy

"Remind me, where is this garden?"

"It's called Kooling Towers, conveniently in the village of Kooling. It's just North of Holt. Do you remember where we took that cast iron garden seat from?"

"What! That incredibly heavy green painted one?"

"Yes, the one modelled as ferns that we rolled over the hedge."

"How that hedge survived!"

"Well, that fern seat came from a garden just outside Holt, and Kooling Towers is no more than five miles away from there."

"I remember now," said Maxine, "the hedge was the boundary to the highway. We retrieved the horsebox, loaded it up and off we went in broad daylight."

"That bench covered the whole weekend: bed, breakfast, dinner and fuel. I sold it to that tall rude bloke in the Lillie Road, £500 in cash."

"Let's hope we have the same luck this weekend. Where are we staying?"

"I've booked a room in the village. At The Swotter Arms. It looks great but just a little near if we pinch anything. You did remember the wheelbarrow?"

"Yes, of course, it's in the horsebox."

"That's my girl," replied Mandy.

Traffic was light and the Volvo and attendant horsebox made good time. They drove through the village, past The Swotter Arms, the lodge house and straight down the drive. Excitement grew with just a touch of nerves. It was the rush of blood that made them feel alive. Just before the big house, they were directed off the tarmac drive into a mown 'stick and string' temporary car park. Volunteers in high-viz tabards shepherded them towards the entry desk.

"Two pounds each," Mandy said as they both walked towards the lunch tent.

"They can't have inflation in Norfolk."

The lunch tent was packed with a small queue in front of a starched linen-covered table. On it stood various dishes: a bean salad, shiny with a dressing, another with coleslaw speckled with black onion seeds and two stemmed circular dishes elevating sliced quiches. One with sundried tomatoes and the other with wilted spinach and goats cheese. Every dish was colourful and bright; there was no beige fare here. Mandy chose two different quiches, as they always shared, and heaped another plate with mayonnaise potatoes and salad. Meanwhile, Maxine picked a bottle of white wine, which came with an ice filled bucket and two glasses.

"This is delicious," said Mandy refilling their wine glasses.

"I could happily stay too, but we've come a long way to see this garden and we will share a bottle at the pub later. Hopefully our room has a bath."

"Come on, let's have a look around as we've got to pay for all of this somehow."

It took them an hour to identify a large bronze of a horse and jockey.

"It's perfect," said Mandy patting the horse's bottom. "It's screened by hedges and a short distance from the drive."

"But how on earth will we carry it?" replied a slightly less sure Maxine.

"Remember how we rolled the fern bench?"

"Yes."

"We will do the same thing here, but more knock than roll."

"I don't get it."

"We will topple the bronze off this plinth into a blanket-filled wheelbarrow, and that way, we will never have to carry it. Then it's a quick push along the walk, up the ramp of the horse box and home."

"You make it sound so easy."

"It will be. There's a full moon tonight. Let's walk the route back to the car and see where we can turn the horsebox around."

From the bronze to the drive was no more than 50 metres. Once on the drive, it was right for the house and left for their car park.

"Let's walk to the house first," directed Mandy.

On the way, they passed a parking area with bins outside, what looked like a kitchen door.

"Could you back in there?" asked Mandy.

"Yes, comfortably," replied a more confident Maxine.

"Brill. It's down the drive, turn here, load the bronze, then off. Simple."

"Let's get to the pub. Early dinner, early bed, then back for the bronze."

Maxine and Mandy recovered the Volvo and trailing horsebox. Slipping quietly back down the drive, past the lodge house, and then left on the main road to the village. Maxine parked carefully off the road behind the pub, backing the trailer against the hedge with the nose of her Volvo pointing towards the road. If they were to make an early morning dash for the bronze, she would need a straight run at it. They recovered their overnight cases from the backseat and made their way through a tidy garden over a wide cobbled path. A path that would have once taken horses and carriages, through the inn, to the stables at the rear. The edges of the path were now peopled by tall standing plants:

hollyhocks and giant yellow flowered fennel, all with alchemilla mollis strewn around their feet. There was something truly beautiful about this invasion of pointing. It was a lucky place that suffered such elegant marauders; most paths were colonised by docks, nettles and couch grass. As gardeners, Mandy and Maxine appreciated this random beauty. Once in the former carriage arch, they turned left through a heavy swing door into a sort of airlock, devoid of furniture bar oak panelling to breast height. Pushing through a matching door with glazed side panels, they came into a large brick-floored and oak-panelled saloon bar. It was the idealised pub interior, something an American tourist would wish for. Seated at the bar was a handsome woman soundly built in Guernsey jumper, corduroy trousers and sensible shoes. She was chatting to a young girl, wearing a crop top barely covering impressive breasts and flaunting a perfectly taught tummy.

"Good afternoon, you must be our room," said the sensibly dressed woman. She continued as she stood from her bar stool:

"You have a choice. The biggest bedroom we have, comes with a large bath and a kingsize double bed, or we have a twin-bedded room with shower only."

Before Mandy could speak Maxine chipped in:

"We will take the large bath, please. I can't think of anything nicer than a good soak after the drive we've had. It's a long way here, from London."

At this, Mandy darted a 'shutup' look at Maxine.

Anita had a landlady's sixth sense for trouble. "Would you two like a drink before we show you your room?"

"I would love a gin and tonic," replied Mandy.

"Coming right up, and your friend?"

"Sorry, I'm Mandy and she's Maxine."

"We would like a bath," said Maxine ignoring the 'what drink' question.

"Jess, why don't you show Maxine room 4 and I'll make a G&T for Mandy."

Jess took the key from the hook behind the bar and led Maxine out through the airlock, back into the open archway, and through another door marked 'Bedrooms'. Once through the door, there was a small lobby and the flight of stairs beyond. Maxine watched the girl carry hers and Mandy's bags up the stairs. She did it so effortlessly. This girl had it all: long legs, flat stomach and tumbling hair. Maxine had dressed the same when she was younger. She still had the figure; riding Peter had kept her legs slender and her tummy tight, but she no longer had the devil-may-care attitude, that often comes with youth.

After passing two other doors on the bedroom landing, Jess dropped both bags and unlocked a tall door. A pair of large sash windows lit the room and to her right was a large-sized bed with a well-stuffed headboard.

"You're lucky. Anita doesn't give this room to anybody. Try the bed, it's really high." Maxine hopped on to the bed and gave it a bounce, bending and straightening her arms to lift her bottom up and down on a well sprung mattress.

"It's lovely, makes you feel like a child again. Where is the bathroom then?" "Through this door."

Jess opened a painted door to reveal a large pedestal sink and associated mirror, typical of the 1920s. To the left, Maxine could see a substantial arrangement of chrome bath taps at the head of a pale green bath.

"That's perfect, thank you."

"No trouble, here's the key, see you downstairs."

As the door closed behind Jess, Maxine slipped off the bed, walked into the bathroom, put the bath plug in and turned the hot tap on. Better to warm up the enamelled bath and then add cold water at the end.

Whilst Maxine bathed, Mandy stayed and chatted in the saloon bar below. This was not in the 'Good Thieves' manual, as preferred behaviour was to be quiet and unnoticed at all times, but Mandy was now free of her mother, and enjoying her new-found company.

Bathed, brushed, and restored Maxine retrieved Mandy from the bar. They took a small table under one of many diamond-patterned leadlight windows. The table was oblong with rounded ends and unusual brass strapped edges. It had the look of a ready missile or shield once used in bar fights, but now saved with all its bruises by a pinned brass edge. In spite of, or maybe because of, their long friendship, they never ran out of conversation. Mandy and Maxine didn't just sit and eat, they talked and laughed too. First course was a soup, a hot courgette and mint, made delicious with a proper chicken stock, followed by a smoked haddock, mashed potato, egg and cheese dish. Delicious, much like a Sussex smokie, just in Norfolk! Polished off with a blackberry and apple crumble, with a stomach settling spoonful of yoghurt. All three dishes shone. If food had a heart, it was from this kitchen.

They paid and quietly slipped away, making vague mutterings about breakfast at 9.30am. Quickly to bed, their last task was setting the alarm for 4.00am. We all have internal clocks, maybe even many. Too much fun at the bar and your liver will wake you at 3.00am, sometimes 3.01am or even 2.58am. How on earth does it know? Maybe it does an early morning shift, and if its task ahead is too great, it inevitably starts grumbling. It's that grumbling which wakes the once happy reveller. Best let the landlady wake at 3.00am, visit the loo, return to bed and drift off to sleep again before they stir at 4.00am.

The alarm sounded, wrenching them both from a deep sleep. Just like in their gardens, they moved quickly and efficiently with wheels rolling at 4.15am. Back past the lodge house, up the drive and past the bin bay. Maxine backed her horsebox into the kitchen area, reversing the turns on the wheel to allow a smooth return to the drive. Once level with the hornbeam walk, Maxine stopped squarely on the drive. It wasn't worth risking a soft grass verge. She and Peter had once been stuck on a normal looking verge in Surrey. It was the dew that had made her wheels slip initially, all too soon they were up to their axles. After two hours, a tractor and £100 cash for repair of the householder's grass, Maxine had vowed never to venture onto a verge again. They stopped, she lowered the tailgate and Mandy righted the wheel barrow and heaped it high with folded grey blankets. As Mandy took the handles and pushed off, Maxine kept a steadying hand on the top of the tower of blankets. Once by the plinth it was Mandy who produced a crowbar from the wheelbarrow. As Maxine created a nest of blankets in the barrow, Mandy eased the crowbar under the bronze stand.

"Ready," Mandy whispered.

Maxine took the barrow's handles and replied quietly, "yes".

A moment later with a soft thud, the bronze fell on its side into the nest of blankets.

It was then that they heard the barking.

"Quick, let's go."

Surprisingly, the bronze felt light in the barrow. Luckily it had fallen with much of its weight over the pneumatic tyre. As they neared the tailgate, the barking seemed to get louder.

Mandy quickly tied both the barrow and bronze to the side of the horsebox with a thick webbing strap. Then they lifted the tailgate and scurried into the Volvo. As they passed the semi-detached cottages on the drive, Mandy checked that there were no lights on. Not far afterwards, they left the drive by the lodge house onto the highway, but in her panic to get away, she forgot the horsebox and cut the corner, driving over the grass at the mouth of the drive. Mandy said nothing, what's done is done. Their pressing aim was to get far away as soon as possible.

Chapter 28

London

Mercy Penfold was frustrated by events thus far. She had been effectively told to stand down by DI Kevin Smythe, and her friend Sergeant Arnold couldn't do anything until Monday. Whether a knock on Mr Hix's door would rattle a new lead, she didn't know. There was no point ringing DI Smythe with her findings. He could ring Sergeant Arnold for himself, but she could ring Sir Roger, after all, he was her client. She decided to call him.

"Good morning, Sir Roger's residence, May speaking."

May liked to mix it up, sometimes it was, 'Kooling Towers', sometimes it was 'Sir Roger's Residence.' There was no rhyme or reason for the difference, just her mood.

"Good morning May. It's Mercy Penfold at the Antiques Trade Gazette here. May I speak to Sir Roger, please?"

"I regret to say that Sir Roger is out. Would you like to leave a message?"

"Would you please tell Sir Roger that I have spoken to Sergeant Arnold in Brighton?"

"Will do. Thanks for calling Miss Penfold."

Another frustration thought Mercy. It was just one of those days. Mercy's mother had always told her and her sister, Grace, that there was no such thing as dead ends, just roads with smaller openings, and it was their job to discover those openings if they were to pursue life as her mother had done. Her mother, Rose, and her parents, had all travelled from Tobago in the West Indies, when she was only three. Her father Leonard had, like all saintly first-generation immigrants, taken a menial job on the London Underground. First, he swept station platforms, moving quickly on to the ticket office and then, when the opportunity arose, he trained and qualified as a train driver. This gave him both the money and the time to help his daughter Rose. Rose was bright and did well at secondary school in Streatham. Much to the joy of her parents, she achieved a first-class degree in English Literature at Bristol University. Whilst at Bristol, she met a very bright mathematician. He was tall and dark. Albert was also the son of immigrants wanting to find a better life for their children. They were a popular couple at the university: Rose had all the words and Albert had all the numbers. When Albert wasn't studying, he was playing cards in the University Bridge Club. In his second year, he was promoted to the first team and in his third year he had little room to live in, as the silver trophies that he had won were edging him out. Shortly after university, Albert and Rose were married with her father's blessing, in her church in Streatham and then on to a private dining room in Claridges. It turned out that Albert's father was a trusted investment banker for many wealthy African families, who were keen to get their money into a hard foreign currency. Albert's father spoke their language and was beyond discreet, something that he installed in his son. Discretion and trust were much like holding a bridge hand close. As a wedding present, Albert's family gave them a small house in Kensington. He wanted his grandchildren to have the same start that his fellow white colleagues had been given, and it was in this rarefied environment that Mercy and her sister Grace grew up. They had the fight and purpose of their parents and grandparents, but also the polish of their fellow private school classmates. Both girls had followed their parents to Bristol. Mercy inherited her mother's genes and read History of Art, whereas her sister got her father's and read International Statistics. Mercy was the only employee of the Gazette to arrive by taxi every day. Her father wanted her chauffeured but Mercy didn't want to stand out from her peers as she said to her parents, 'my colour is enough difference. Throwing wealth in too, would just be too much!' As her colleagues at the Gazette arrived in the morning complaining of late trains, slow buses and flat tyres, Mercy kept a careful silence. This was her first job in the art world. She had decided against the museum route as it took too long. She was in a hurry to be an editor of an art magazine; words and art, were for her, the magic combo, and that's why results mattered, as all were stepping stones to that editor's desk.

"Gazette, Mercy speaking."

"Good morning. May said you rang earlier," with vowels like Sir Roger's, there was no need for names; his speech was his unique DNA.

"Thank you for returning my call Sir Roger," There was a pause, so Mercy pressed on, "I wanted to update you with actions thus far."

"Go on," said Sir Roger.

"I have spoken to my contact at Brighton, a Sergeant Arnold, and he is going to see our caller in Hastings."

"Did he say when Mercy?"

"Yes, an early Monday morning knock as Sergeant Arnold called it."

"I wouldn't like to be our man in Hastings," said Sir Roger, "but can't he go any earlier?"

"No, regrettably he is tied up with an open weekend for recovered antiques. They are put on display in the hope that owners will reclaim them."

"That sounds good. Have you ever been?"

"No I have not, but I think I will. I'll call you on Monday regarding Sergeant Arnold's visit to Hastings. Goodbye."

Mercy went into her emails to write to Sergeant Arnold regarding his open weekend, but there, in her inbox, was a new, unread email entitled 'Recovered Antiques - Open Weekend, Brighton' and the sender was a WPC Helen Tredwell. She opened it and wrote down the details in her daybook. She would catch the train to Brighton, and maybe take her mother too. There was no point in asking her sister, Grace, or her father as they both worked on their fund in Mayfair, day and night with her father saying:

"There is a market open somewhere in the world."

The fund had been her father's 'baby' since leaving the employ of his investment bank. He moved his investors west to a lovely terraced Portland stone townhouse off Grosvenor Square, and was thrilled that his younger daughter had joined him. He managed the investors and she spearheaded a small team working on algorithms and computer coding, a brave new world of pure maths or 'Silicon Valley magic,' as Albert referred to it. Mercy rang her mother Rose and booked the train tickets for Saturday, saying that the traffic would be a nightmare, and further, the venue was only a short walk from Brighton's main line station. She was looking forward to putting faces to the names of Sergeant Arnold and Helen Tredwell.

Chapter 29

Hastings

After leaving the Beacon in Fulham, Jack called Lionel's mobile. It was answered immediately.

"Hello Jack, how did you get on?" he whispered.

"Metal's gone."

"I don't give a damn about the metal, old love. Did Ray spill the beans?"

"Some and some," replied Jack. "It's 5 o'clock now. Do you want to see me this evening?"

"Yes please. I rather wanted to pick up my items from the closed pub."

"That's fine, I will come now. I should be with you in about two and a half hours, but it may be later."

"Don't worry about that. Barty has invited us for supper at the Imperial and I have a spare room here. You can stay the night and Clive can have a walk on the beach in the morning. Does that work?" said Lionel.

"That would be great. I would only be in the workshop at home and I wouldn't mind a good blow out. I haven't had a thing since your sausage sandwich this morning."

"I will make the calls and tell you what's going on," ended Lionel.

Lionel called Robin junior first.

"Robin, it's Lionel here. Young Jack is running late. Any chance I could pick up tonight?"

"Sorry Lionel. I'm in Rye delivering a six-hob oven range to a restaurant on the steepest street you've ever seen. It nearly took me for a swim in the harbour. What about first thing tomorrow? I'll give you a hand."

"That's fine, see you at nine tomorrow?"

Lionel had wanted to ask if anybody had been there today, but he didn't dare. His two boxes in the cabinet had to remain a secret for now. He redialled.

"Barty, Jack is coming down tonight, any chance of some supper? Happy to take you out?"

"Don't be silly, I have more than enough here. Has Jack got any news?"

"Some and some, he said."

"My life hasn't been this stressed since the third Mrs Lionel left me."

Lionel's mind wandered to the two boxes in the cabinet again, all alone in a closed pub. What happens if someone breaks in or young Robin left a ring on in the kitchen, and the pub burnt down, shattering both porcelain vases in the subsequent blaze? He told himself to stop worrying as he remembered the electricity had been turned off.

"Lionel are you still there?"

"Yes, but I could do with a drink."

"Come over here, lots of white Burgundy and you could help me juice a box of lemons."

"I'll walk over, I want to clear my head. See you in about 40 minutes."

Lionel got back on the phone and arranged with Jack to go straight to Barty's Imperial, as they could catch a taxi back to Norman Road which would give Jack and Clive a good walk to retrieve the van in the morning. Lionel locked up the shop and walked to the seafront. He crunched through the big pebbles until his legs hurt then he returned to the asphalt promenade. He picked up the pace as his thirst drove him to Barty's door. The Brewing Brothers was open. Lionel paid his respects and climbed down the steps to Barty's cellar restaurant. He swung open the kitchen door to find Barty flattening chicken breasts with a wooden rolling pin.

"Evening, Lionel. Open the fridge to your right and pour us both a glass of wine. I have a white or a rather nice rosé."

"Rosé first, I need a thirst quencher," said Lionel smiling at the task. He took two wineglasses from the long stainless steel shelves above the prep table, and poured two healthy glasses of rosé. He held on to both until Barty had washed his hands, as raw chicken and salmonella come high on the kitchen hygiene list. Barty took the extended glass and said, "Bottoms up."

"What's this weekend's menu?" Lionel asked.

"Well, I'm doing chicken schnitzel or, as they call it now, breaded chicken, and you're juicing those lemons for the sticky lemon and thyme sauce."

"Well, set me up with those lemons, then I can get on!"

Barty reached under the prep shelf and brought out a large box filled to the gunnels.

"I've never seen so many lemons," said Lionel, as Barty handed him a knife and stainless steel squeezer.

"First take some blue roll and put it under your chopping board, then it won't move. Then chop the lemons in half, twist on

222 | *Barty – A Tale of a Stolen Bronze*

the squeezer and pour the juice into this jug. That's the first, only another 49 to go!"

"I need a top up," said Lionel making for the fridge.

"Stay where you are. Rosé refills only on every 15 lemons done. Got it?" instructed Barty.

Whilst Lionel got into the rhythm of juicing lemons, Barty was mixing plain flour, water and table salt in a mixing bowl. Once brought together, he wrapped it in cling film and placed it in the fridge. He then took four large beetroots and four equally large celeriac, and peeled them. He removed the cooled dough from the fridge and rolled it into a long sausage and divided it into 8. He then rolled each section into eight-inch diameter discs, and wrapped each vegetable with the dough. Once all eight hard root vegetables were covered, Barty placed them on a rectangular metal tray with parchment paper lining, and slid the tray on the bottom shelf of the oven. Lionel was beginning to get bored with squeezing lemons so Barty topped up both glasses.

"What are you doing wrapping veg in dough?" enquired Lionel.

"I'm 'salt baking' them in a slow oven. Once cooked through, after 2 hours, I will let them rest, then I will break off the dough cases and cut them into three-quarter-inch thick steaks, and store in the fridge. When I need them, I cook them like a steak. The slow cooking in the salt dough does the work and I just caramelise them in the pan. Blessed is the veggie. I think this is the first menu where I have equal vegetable dishes to meat and fish!"

"I hope you have a steak for young Jack and me?" said Lionel, hopefully.

"Celeriac or beetroot?" teased Barty.

"Very funny," said Lionel returning to the tyranny of squeezing lemons.

"Your heaven, my hell, and if hell's as hot as this kitchen, I will be in purgatory and you will be in heaven, Barty."

After 40 minutes, Lionel put the last lemon skin in the box, grabbed a stool and sat down.

"Are they all for a sauce?" said Lionel.

"Not just a sauce for the schnitzel but also for my special salad dressing."

"I like your French dressing, the white one."

"Yes, my secret dressing with the French Viandox. Are you hungry?"

"Of course I am! What's on offer?"

"Well, I made some taramasalata today because they had some cod's roe at the fishing huts. I will make some flatbreads or we could have some sourdough."

"What's quicker?" asked Lionel.

"There speaks the Epicurean. I will toast some sourdough, then."

"Give me another job. If hell's a kitchen, I might as well get used to it."

"It's runner beans for you."

Barty placed a trug of runner beans picked this morning from his garden. "Top and tail them, pull the strings off the edges and cut on the diagonal into one and a quarter-inch pieces and then when done, put in this pan please."

Barty took Lionel's empty glass and rinsed it under the cold tap.

"Now, how about that white Burgundy?" offered Barty.

"Pour away, dear friend."

Lionel raised the glass and tasted.

"Delicious. Hell with wine, I could live with that."

Barty laughed as he returned to prepping the steaks and, as Lionel concentrated on the runner beans, he boiled some new potatoes. He had deliberately never installed a deep fat fryer in his kitchen which, anyway, was far too small to accommodate such a smelly appliance. Barty was a gentleman chef and not a fryer. His solution was to boil new potatoes, cool them and store them in the fridge. When needed, he cut them crossways and pan fried them adding salt, pepper and thyme. They tasted like chips, but just had a different shape. As they both found their groove, peeling, cutting and boiling, stopping only for more wine, they in turn, were interrupted by the sound of paws on the restaurant floor announcing the arrival of Clive and Jack. Once Clive was settled with a bowl of water and the steak trimmings, Jack was sent upstairs for a pint. The three convened at a circular table, nearest the kitchen door, Barty bringing a bowl of taramasalata and toasted sourdough.

"Dive in," invited Barty.

"Now Jack, how did it go with Ray?" asked Lionel.

"He was much like the Beacon, but without the warty nose. He has quite an operation there, and you should see his Bentley, big and gleaming, rather at odds with the crushed cars around it."

"We've got the picture," Lionel said, urging Jack on, "but what about our thief?"

"Ray was cagey, but he weakened as he was anxious to know how much the Beacon had got for the bronze. He had given £150 for the bronze .....and here is the clue. Ray bought the bronze from a horse box full of the contents of a couple of garden sheds: flower pots, old mowers and garden tools."

"But who sold it to him?" pressed Lionel.

"Well that, Ray wouldn't say, talking of the 'metal merchants oath,' being 'no names and no numbers,' but he did mention that two ladies owned the horse box. One with short hair and a leather jerkin, and the other rather glamorous. Ray added, that there weren't many horse boxes in South London!"

"Good work," Barty said. "It's more than I expected you to find out. Did the Beacon help?"

"Yes, he was great. I wouldn't have got far without 'me old *china*.' Ray operated on a short fuse and the Beacon's silver sleeved hip flask turned the mood back in both our favours."

"The loose talk of lady gardeners and the horse box, were only given in Ray's office after a couple of drinks."

"Ah, loose talk costs lives," said Lionel.

"So," said Barty, "we have two women, who may or may not be gardeners, but they own a horse box. Why would you bring a horse box into South London, when there is a scrap metal merchants in every big town in Great Britain? I would suggest our lady gardeners, and likely thieves, live in South London not far from Ray in Wandsworth."

"Well done Jack," said Lionel, "one step closer. Now let's feed the lad, Barty."

"I bought a fillet of beef today. Lionel and I will have the ends and you, Jack, can have a proper one, plus, I make a Béarnaise sauce. I will leave you two to work out our next step. Lionel, sort Jack out for a beer, and ask the brothers for a couple of bottles of Côte du Rhône, please."

Barty disappeared into the kitchen, brought out the loin of beef from the fridge and cut both ends off leaving the best bit for Jack. That left him a potential seven steaks for the specials board tomorrow. He returned the loin to the fridge and waited for their steaks to come up to room temperature. He had learned long ago to do the last part of a dish first, as it was the one that got forgotten. He put a pan of water on a low heat, and in another saucepan, a whole pack of salted butter, cubed for greater surface area. Then in a shallow pan, he put a small glass of white wine, the juice of 2 lemons, thank you Lionel! A teaspoon of black peppercorns and a sprig of fresh tarragon. He then added a finely cut shallot and reduced this liquid by half. He passed the shallots and liquor through a sieve into a shallow, stainless steel mixing bowl, which he put over the gently simmering pan of water. To this bain-marie, he added 3 egg yolks and whisked until the mixture became as thick as double cream. Then, still whisking, he added the now melted butter, steadily, as the trick was not to let it curdle. Once the sauce was done, he set this aside and started to boil the runner beans. On the remaining hobs, he heated a large pan for the steaks. He oiled and seasoned both sides of the meat and cut up some new potatoes. He added the steaks to one pan and the new potatoes to the other. He turned the gas down under the steaks and after a short while turned them over. He added a couple more knobs of butter which, when melted, he spooned over the three steaks. Once cooked to medium rare, he removed them from the pan and placed them on a metal tray to rest on the pass. Now he checked the runner beans: two more minutes. He tossed the slices of new potatoes, strained the beans and mixed them in butter and garlic. Barty added these to a bowl that they could all share. He warmed up the Béarnaise sauce in the bain-marie, plated up the steaks and 'chips,' and added a pool of sauce to each plate. He carried Lionel and Jack's plates through first, and returned to retrieve his; wine glass, plate and bowl of beans. He didn't normally get applause when he served food, but he did on this occasion. The table fell silent for the first couple of mouthfuls.

"Congratulations to my dear friend, the Gentleman Chef," said Lionel.

"Hear, hear," added Jack.

The three happily continued to eat, drink and chat until midnight. Lionel, Jack and Clive decided to walk back to Norman Road, and Barty climbed up West Hill to his home. A good day, but how was he going to find two lady gardeners with a Volvo and horse box?

"Easier in South London, than Gloucestershire," he thought!

Chapter 30

Hastings

Pru lived in a small terraced house at the bottom of West Hill, whereas Barty lived in one of the bigger red brick houses near the top. Pru's house was painted mandarin yellow and her neighbours were pink and pale blue. In fact, the whole street looked like a Pantone colour chart, which had been arranged by a small child. When Pru bought it ten years ago, it was a small two-up, two-down. She had the front bedroom and the girls, Polly and Phoenix, shared one at the back. When the girls started secondary school, Richard, her ex-husband, gave Pru enough cash to secure a small mortgage to add a two-storey extension at the back. This enabled Polly and Phoenix to have a bedroom each and for Pru to have the kitchen that she had always wanted. It was a Bohemian affair, old painted pine furniture had been re-arranged to form a bespoke kitchen. Anytime Lionel had something shabby in pine, he always sent it around to Pru. Lionel was no fool. He had always liked Pru and, more importantly, loved her cooking. As he said to Norman,

"Deliver this to Pru in West Hill, and take no money, as it's for food not cash."

Pru did her prep and cooking on an island in the middle of her north-facing kitchen. On her east wall, she had a sink below a Yorkshire sash window. Instead of the windows going up and down, they went sideways. Not as freely moving so she often waxed the bottom runners, but in their favour there were no complicated ropes and weights. Either side of the sink were pine-topped planked boards and the open space below had a deep shelf, enclosed by printed curtains. The print had an Omega workshop feel: pastel pinks, yellows and blues. These hid a vast collection of kitchen equipment; mixing bowls, jugs, plates, salt cellars with mottos such as 'Many Friends, Few Helpers'. After her divorce she had heeded this motto and when she came to live in Hastings, she decided to choose her new friends from helpers! It had worked; both Barty and Lionel would drop anything to come to her aid. Both had been kind in their own ways; Barty employing her girls which had given them enormous independence, and Lionel with surprise deliveries when she was furnishing the extension. It was still a rare fortnight that she didn't find a box in her front porch; a Dartmouth pottery fish jug, a strange kitchen tool or a measuring jug. Lionel spent his life pottering around antique, junk and charity shops and couldn't resist buying; the merry-go-round of some strange addiction.

On the west wall of Pru's kitchen was a pair of French doors which filled it with afternoon sun. Either side of the doors, she had two similar 1920s oak bookcases with glazed top sections sitting on bases enclosed by blind cupboard doors. Lionel had bought them from the offices of a now defunct regional newspaper. They were made to house old press cutting books but were now replaced with Pru's enormous collection of cookery books. To these, she couldn't resist adding a drawing, the odd vignette in the margin, or a note of what had worked for her. Under her ownership, the cook books were work in progress. Some had drawings of her daughters measuring ingredients, standing on stools to get nearer to the worktops or of dogs tucking into the finished dishes. Barty had often said, 'You should send one of your more animated books back to the publishers. They might produce a new edition with your added drawings."

Pru was tempted but she had more than enough work with her dog portraits. Her books recorded the events and flows of her family life. They started with her marriage to Richard, cooking from Constance Spry and Elizabeth David, in a little flat in Hammersmith. She and Richard had met at Art school. She had thrived in the freedom of the 1960s but he turned out to be too graphic, a realist with little emotion. He had quit Chelsea Art School after the first year and converted to Architecture at University College London. It was Pru who worked in shops and restaurants to support them both whilst he qualified. He was good in this new world, and it wasn't long before he started earning enough money to allow them to have the children that Pru had always wanted. When the two girls were eight and seven, Richard was working long hours and often on far away projects. It was too much, his work became his life, and his junior assistant Megan, his pleasure. The end came with a foolish phone call from Megan to their, now bigger home in Richmond. Pru and Richard had inevitably been drifting apart and the girls were her world. They divorced on reasonable terms and Richard had always tried to help financially, hence the two-storey extension. The mortgage element of the finance was small enough for Pru to maintain her independence. As he said, "Let's keep the loan small, banks don't normally lend to artists."

The island in Pru's kitchen was seven foot long by three foot wide. Sunk into the top at one end was a 4-ring gas hob, given by Lionel from one of his many house clearances. Her old oven had been replaced with a commercial turbo fan oven from Barty, which stood on the plank worktop opposite her island hob. This oven, unlike the last, when set at 180 degrees actually delivered the correct temperature. Pru didn't have to squat down to look through the glass door to check on culinary progress. The rest of the island's surface was kept clear except for a constantly used mahogany book rest. Below this work surface was a random arrangement of cupboards and drawers, all formerly old chest cupboards that Lionel had sent her way. Around the island sat four odd stools at which Pru and the girls had their coffees, teas, food and chats. The leisurely lunches and suppers were eaten on a circular table opposite the hob end of the island. It was at this table that the girls had done their homework, whilst Pru cooked. The best brains were often made on well-fed bodies. She made herself a coffee and walked through the kitchen door into her studio, converted from a former dining room. It had a north-facing Victorian sash window providing the even light that she required. Not that she was able to do much painting at home, as most was completed quickly in her clients'. It was only possibly highlights, dates and signatures that she added later. This time she had been commissioned to do an abstract painting of a very formal dog, Sampson, who of course was a thoroughbred and carried his breeding in his upright manner. It was a challenge beyond her normal medium of pastel and required acrylic or oil paints. She thought the latter suited Kooling Towers with all its old oil portraits. Pru had placed a five foot by three foot canvas on her largest easel and propped up numerous studies of Sampson against jugs and vases on an old chest of drawers. Sampson was a black labrador, whose only other colours, were a pair of brown eyes and pink lips. She was going to have to work some magic with vivid colours to bring him alive. She sketched out an outline of the pose. He was to be sitting on his hind quarters looking straight out from the picture. Pru wanted to capture Sir Roger's dog in one of those serene moments that are often the measure of a man or beast. Once she had a rough body, which was one and a half scale, she worked on his broad head adding ears, eyes and mouth, strong shoulders, stiff front legs and bent back legs. As she worked down his body, she started seeing shapes, a circle here, a triangle there. Then, just as colours began to join shapes, she heard a key in the front door.

"Anybody at home?" called out Phoenix.

"In here darling," replied Pru.

Phoenix floated in and said: "Wow, that's a big canvas. Who's the dog?"

"This is mighty Sampson, Sir Roger and Daphne's labrador."

"The outline looks impressive. I'm starving and I have to get to Barty's by four. His text read; 'Late night with Lionel, could use a hand before first booking shows up.'"

"Do men ever grow up?" said Phoenix.

"Lots do, but there is truth in 'stay young and remain fun'. You wouldn't want your mother hanging out with puritans, would you?"

"Fat chance of that happening with Barty and Lionel as your chums. Shall I toast something or is there something in the fridge that could be revived?"

"I have hummus, salad or some veggie lasagne?" offered Pru.

"Would it be greedy if I had a little of all three? I need reviving after a rather long lecture on Roman Architecture. Talk about throwing people at a problem. Tens of thousands were used to build Rome and it still stands today. I bet our new study block at college won't last that long!"

"Come through and chat to me in the kitchen," said Pru.

"I will be down in a moment, I just want a quick shower and change first."

Five minutes later, Phoenix was sitting on a stool chatting to her mother.

"Have you got a deadline for the dog?"

"Daphne wants to give it to Roger for his birthday next Sunday, and I have been invited to stay for the weekend. I feel very honoured and I was hoping Lionel might organise delivery, as it's just too big for our car."

"If there's a sniff of antiques, Lionel will be more than willing. Isn't Daphne's place rather splendid?"

"It certainly is. There are enough antiques in Norfolk to keep Lionel busy for the rest of his natural life."

"What are your plans for the dog portrait?" asked Phoenix as she tucked in to her heated-up lasagne.

"It's going to be an abstract, all shapes and colours."

"Good luck with that. I saw your studies next door. He looks quite a formidable black dog."

Phoenix finished her plate, kissed her mother and left for Barty's restaurant. Pru walked back to her canvas, sat down and, for the first time, had doubts about an abstract black labrador.

Chapter 31

Norfolk/Brighton

Clem, Tom, Scan and attendant school of terriers returned to their caravan. It had been a good day for Clem. It was a day of girls: firstly his favourite cousin, Kezia, and secondly Jess. She, like Clem, had always been the cheeky one in class and they often found themselves sitting next to each other in the front of the classroom. Clem had taken the lessons in, but he wasn't sure how much Jess had understood. She had always been fun and sparky, and tonight showed Clem that her sparkiness was still there. Before the boys slept, they had a beer and reviewed their options.

"So we have Maxine MacKenzie and friend in a Volvo towing a horse box. If we were coppers, we would have started with the name."

"That's what Pa called us today. Coppers."

"I prefer detectives," retorted Scan.

"What's our next move?" Tom asked Clem.

"Pa has been right all along. He has a gut feeling for these things. He's been around the block and he just knows how people tick," Clem continued. "He said the Towers were fools to keep opening their garden. He also spoke of any old riff-raff being let in, and said, we would be the first ones the coppers would point a finger at."

The boys smiled at this.

"But he's right. I bet you that Maxine MacKenzie and her friend cased the joint at the last open garden, stayed that Saturday night, and took it in the early hours. The damage at the end of the drive was the horse box cutting the corner of the verge on to the road.

"Surely they close the gates by the little lodge house?" volunteered Tom.

"I thought they did," said Clem.

"Maybe they forgot. We know Sir Roger has another Open Day next Sunday for the Cricket Club. Ma spoke about the flyers around the village. We have a busy week next week. That bungalow in Sherringham with the overgrown garden, the owner rang me. They are putting it on the market and they want it cleared and tidy for the weekend, as they have a House Open Day on Saturday."

"I remember the one," said Tom, "it's a big job, and it would be a lot easier if we could spread the wood chippings on site."

"Thankfully the couple have a swing and rocker for the grandchildren. I said we should put chipping under it."

"By the time we chip all those lower branches, you won't be able to see the swing," interjected Scan.

"We can put those chipping circles around the tree bases too. You know how good that looks. Job done."

"Yes, until the rabbits and badgers start scratching around them."

"Well, if we can lose all the waste in the garden, Tom won't have to keep lugging it back here."

"So what about catching this Maxine then?" said Tom.

"I say we forget it for the moment. Let's concentrate on the Sherringham bungalow, and then stake out the Open Day next

Sunday. I will give Jess a call tomorrow. She will keep eyes out for a horse box or a booking at the Swotters. We have a name and we have a vehicle; now all we need is the bronze."

In London, Mercy and her mother, Rose, were waiting on the Brighton line at Victoria station for a very different sort of Open Day. Theirs was Sergeant Arnold's Stolen Antiques weekend. He held these three times a year in a large church hall in Station Road.

These events had been the initiative of his predecessor, Detective Inspector Wallace, some 20 years back. They offered hope for the people who had lost valuables and all too often sentimental items. A burglar sees only gold, silver and gem stones, which means money. But to the householder the small silver brooch was given to a grandmother by a son who never came back from the Western Front, a small tangible link to a lost relative. Scrap value to a thief £5, value to the family, immeasurable.

Sergeant Arnold had witnessed many times, the joy of owners being reunited with their precious possessions. It was far and few between, but over the many years, it had equated into a goodly number. He and WPC Helen Tredwell, had worked hard to catalogue and number all the items that had once been evidence in trials, or just seized goods that had been tagged and stored in secure warehouses. Barcoded tags would mean little to the public, so each item was given a number and brief catalogue description. Sergeant Arnold was lucky to have Helen Tredwell, being the daughter of an old knocker boy. She was brought up with the technical terms of the antiques trade. She knew the difference between a court cupboard and a chest, a fruit spoon and a tablespoon or a gold watch chain and a guard chain. Talk about recruiting from the enemy, Helen had been a godsend for Sergeant Arnold. Until her arrival, he had done all the cataloguing himself. Now she did it, plus the posting on the internet. It was the silver maker's name or assay dates that alert a homeowner to the possibility of recovery. Sergeant Arnold and Helen stood back and surveyed the hall. The doors opened at 10 o'clock and Helen had had a good number of enquiries.

"Well done, Helen. All looks good. Let's hope we have some success today."

"I'm sure we will Sarge. The more we move today, the less we have to move at the end!"

"Agreed Helen. Remember, Herod's decision remains with me and I will need proof, be they old inventories or photographs. Nothing is ever clear cut, but you get a feeling whether it is right or wrong," he continued. "Who's on the door today?"

"Sergeant Gravett and Constable Turner," Helen replied.

"Good, that means it will be a steady ship. Will you ask them to open up. Let the day begin!"

Mercy and Rose arrived at Brighton station shortly after 11am. They decided to stop for a coffee and croissant in a little French café, a short walk from the station. There had been no buffet car nor trolley on the train, and Rose was hungry.

"When your grandfather worked for the underground, before it became the acronym TFL (Transport For London), he had a card that allowed us discounted travel on all underground and railways. Your grandmother and I used to take train trips at the weekends or in the holidays, when my father was working. It was such fun and your grandmother made fabulous picnics; cold creole chicken or ribs, pineapples and coconut water. My mother chose the towns where we could stay for an hour, have tea or coffee then return home before your grandfather returned from work."

"Was Grandma always home for Grandpa?"

"She was and she always liked to be, as your Grandpa had worked hard to give us a better life here. It was your grandmother's small way of showing her gratitude. Plus, he loved hearing about our adventures. When he retired, they did similar journeys and always with exotic Caribbean picnics. They loved Britain as Britain had been kind to them. They wouldn't believe how we live now. Your Grandma and Grandpa only met Albert's parents once, at our wedding."

"Do you remember them as you were only small when they died?"

"I do," replied Mercy, "I remember Grandpa lifting me onto his knee and taking my arms to replicate the motion of an old-fashioned train. His smile was so lovely and his movements, so gentle. I really enjoyed staying with them."

"It's wonderful that you remember them. In the early days of our marriage if your father was going somewhere interesting for his old bank, I would join him. I loved Amsterdam, New York and Tel Aviv, and I knew how much my parents loved having you and Grace to stay. I knew my father had a weak heart, but I thought that my mother would live forever. After your Grandpa died, she missed him too much, she knew we were all well and settled, I think she just died of a broken heart. It is good to be able to tell you all this, so you and your sister know where you come from. I know you will be successful and I have a feeling that you will have a happy and rewarding life, just like me and your father. My life has been much like my mother's; the same love, just in a different part of town. Come on now, I'm getting too sentimental, don't you have a policeman to see?"

"I do, but it's great to know more about Grandpa and Grandma."

Whilst her mother went to the loo, Mercy paid at the till and simultaneously checked her phone for the hall's location. It was a short walk away, just off the main road to the Clock Tower. On entering, Mercy and her mother were asked for their names and contact details. In return, she asked to be introduced to Sergeant Arnold.

"Please follow me, Miss Penfold," said Constable Turner as he led her to a happy-looking man, at the far end of the hall.

"Sergeant, this is Miss Penfold."

"Thank you Constable," said Sergeant Arnold. "How good to finally meet you Mercy, we must have spoken fortnightly since you took over the Gazette's stolen desk."

"It's great to see you too, and I wasn't expecting to see so many people or antiques. Any reunions yet?"

"Only one so far: a pair of large pink ground Staffordshire pottery vases. A couple from Weybridge had them stolen from their parents' home. Nothing nasty, just a knocker boy taking advantage of an elderly couple. Now, I must introduce you to Helen, who has become my right arm on the squad."

Sergeant Arnold turned and called out in the direction of two WPCs: one tall with blond hair held in a ponytail and her colleague who was as wide as she was high. To Mercy's surprise, it was the tall blonde who turned around and called out, "Yes, Sergeant."

Helen approached Sergeant Arnold and Mercy with the grace of a rather large cat. It took Mercy a couple of seconds to register that the beauty approaching wasn't the seam-splitting WPC she had first envisaged. Sergeant Arnold did the introductions and afterwards said,

"Helen, why don't you show Mercy around? You two should get to know each other."

"Mercy, do you like jewellery? Come with me and let me show you this amazing emerald and diamond necklace."

"May my mother join us?"

"Of course," replied the gorgeous Helen, "remember, this is a public open day and we are a lot less formal".

Mercy made the introductions and Helen led them to a glass counter display cabinet. On it's top shelf sat an open red Morocco leather and velvet lined case, housing a beautiful emerald and diamond necklace.

"Oh, how beautiful," said Mercy's mother.

"It's stunning," said Mercy.

"Have you ever featured this in your pages in the Gazette?" replied Helen.

"No, and I would remember this beauty," said Mercy.

"She remembers everything," chipped in Rose, "since she was little, she remembered it all: peoples' names, books read and pictures seen."

"Sergeant Arnold always says that the Gazette is lucky to have you," said Helen, turning back to the emerald necklace.

"This won't have been in the Gazette. It was taken from a security box in Central London. It either belonged to a Russian, or a thief and I doubt either will come here to reclaim it. That's why we have the two uniformed policemen on the door. As Sergeant Arnold says, "It wards off the chancers and thieves, plus we have the whole site covered by CCTV."

Mercy then mentioned the ongoing investigation into the recovery of the horse and jockey bronze group.

"I'm looking forward to paying your Mr Hix a call on Monday with Sergeant Arnold. He has a disarming way with people.

After the initial shock of the knock, Sarge will settle them down and find out all that they know. Afterwards, I'm sure he will let you know how we got on."

"That would be good," replied Mercy, "I see the trains to Hastings leave Brighton every half an hour. We might go and have a look around."

"Why not, it will give you a feel for the town. Get off at Hastings mainline station, walk down the hill straight to the sea, once on the coast, turn left for the Old Town passing a large amusement hall, you will then see a pedestrian road called George Street. It has lots of antique shops and at the end, turn left on to the High Street where there are lots more independent shops."

"Thank you, Helen, I think we will do that. Any recommendations for a late lunch?"

"I would take your mother to The Crown in the Old Town. Somebody will show you where it is, it's really good."

"Thank you for being so kind to us and will you say goodbye to Sergeant Arnold? I see he is rather busy with an excited family; it looks like another recovery!"

On their walk back to the station Mercy asked her mother,

"Would you like to continue this adventure in Hastings?"

"Yes, lets. I remember the last time I was in Hastings I would have been either ten or eleven."

"I'll give your father a call. He said, if he could, he would like to join us. You know what he's like. He hates missing out and we might even get a lift back to London!"

Chapter 32

Hastings

Little changed Lionel's morning routine, but the vases in the wrong place did. Last night, Lionel, Jack and Clive had walked back to Norman Road along the seafront. He had done all the right things for a good night's sleep walking there and back to Barty's Imperial; a total of about one and a half hours, plus he had drunk enough to snore like a wildebeest. The only fly in the ointment was worry. After his third failed marriage, he had pledged not to complicate his life. He bought and sold with payment at time of transaction. He gave no credit and asked for no credit. He lived alone, with the good fortune to have enough space to zone rooms for particular uses. The shop on the ground floor was for antiques in and antiques out. Mistakes and dead stock were sent every quarter to a saleroom. They generally sold for what they had cost. Using the basket of eggs principle; some you win and some you lose. On the first floor, Lionel had a good-sized sitting room with big, light windows overlooking Norman Road. It was comfortable with both sofas and armchairs. The walls were paved with pictures, oils, watercolours and engravings, and all had their original frames. He was a stickler for contemporary frames, as he said that artists were fussy fellows and had strong views over which frame would show their work to its best. On the same floor, looking towards the sea, he had his bedroom with kingsize bed between a pair of bamboo sidetables. On circular plate glass tops stood large lamps, converted from japanned tin tea canisters. They were the sort that would once have lined a Victorian shop, painted green, red or black with gold numbers to help identify the different varieties of loose tea. Lionel liked simple linen shades, and on/off switches that he could reach with his last waking movement. The bedroom housed his extensive collection of clothes: some bought secondhand as happy finds, but mostly from London in more affluent times. Bizarrely, he had stayed roughly the same size. His height at 6 foot 2 inches had helped him. He never drank beer and didn't own a car so he tended to burn what he ate and drank: 2,500 calories in; 2,500 calories out. By the time he went to bed he hoped for a zero balance. Therefore, he was able to wear shirts, trousers and suits that he had bought 20 years ago. Like everybody, he had his favourite suits. He liked cool navy blue linen in the summer and loud tweeds in the winter, the sort that PG Wodehouse would say, "Were not oft seen away from a West End stage." As he put on his blue linen suit that morning he thought of the late fashion designer, Jean Muir, who said, "There is only one colour, and that is navy blue." Such a great colour steeped in history. A bit like the discovery of European porcelain, the re-discovery of dark blue happened in Germany. The man responsible was one of Europe's most colourful figures. Johann Conrad Dippel was actually born in Castle Frankenstein in Germany in 1673. Once home to a mysterious theologian and a passionate dissector, who believed souls could be transferred from one corpse to another and thus becoming the inspiration for Mary Shelley's masterpiece, Frankenstein.

In his 30s Dippel had become fascinated by the proto-science of alchemy but, like so many, including his fellow alchemist Johann Friedrich Bottger accredited with discovering the secret of porcelain, he had failed to turn base metals into gold. Instead he focused his attention to find an elixir of immortality in the form of Dipples oil, a compound so toxic that two centuries later it was used as a chemical weapon in World War II; certainly not the elixir of immortality! To cut costs on his Berlin laboratory, Dippel lab-shared with a Swiss pigment maker, Johann Jacob Diesbach, a fellow scientist involved in the lucrative business of producing colours. One fateful evening around 1705, when Diesbach was preparing a batch of crushed insects, iron sulphate and potash in a reliable recipe for a deep red pigment, he accidentally used one of Dippel's contaminated implements. The following morning the pair found not the expected red, but a deep blue. The immense value of the substance was immediately clear. The recipe for Egyptian blue used by the Romans had been lost to history some time in the middle ages. Its substitute, lapis lazuli, consisted of crushed Afghan gemstones, sold at astronomical rates. This discovery of a stable blue colour was literally more valuable than gold! Within a few short years, the recipe had gone into factory production. It was used extensively in painting, wallpaper, flags, postage stamps and became the official uniform colour of the Prussian army. People seemed drunk on the stuff. Indeed, they were actually drinking it. By the mid 18th century, the British East India Company was even dying Chinese tea 'Prussian Blue' to increase its exotic appeal back in Europe.

Jack had slept in one of two guest bedrooms on the second floor, with Clive on a blanket on the floor between his master's bed and the door. It was Lionel's pacing on the floor above that woke Clive up. Clive crept up the stairs to see Lionel making a percolator of coffee. His approach was rewarded with a torn piece of bacon as he laid out rashers in a dish for bacon sandwiches. Clive went downstairs and licked his master on the nose. Jack didn't need an alarm. Clive seemed to know when to wake him: 5am on Sundays for the Heathrow carboot, but most days at 7am, unless it was Ford Market on Thursdays, or Ardingly or Kempton fairs. Jack got up and threw on his normal uniform of blue jeans and white t-shirt with calf length brown 'dealer' boots. Although he spent many hours driving his van, he just seemed to burn his calories; his calorie balance sheet was always in the minus. As Jack called up to Lionel he could smell bacon being grilled.

"Lionel, morning. I'm just going to take Clive out for a walk."

"Fine. Tea or coffee? The bacon sarnies will be ready in 15."

"Coffee please, I won't be long!"

After a short walk Jack rejoined Lionel in his kitchen. They ate the bacon sandwiches with ketchup and drank black coffee.

"What's on the van?" asked Lionel, "anything for me?"

"I hope so, I have a lovely Regency library chair."

"Goodie," said Lionel, "let's get on. It normally takes me 40 minutes to walk to The Imperial."

"Do you want the bed stripped?" asked Jack.

"No need, you are the first person to sleep in that room since I furnished it. You never know, you might need it again and, if so, I will have to name it 'Jack's room'."

Lionel quickly washed up whilst Jack cleaned his teeth and made the bed. The walk along the beach back to the Imperial took longer as Clive slowed progress, too many seagulls to chase and too many interesting smells to sniff. Further, when he was put on the lead to walk up the Queens Road, it was Lionel and Jack's turn to slow progress with their compulsive window gazing. Reunited with Jack's van, they drove the short distance to the closed Spread Eagle pub. It was 8.30 am and Robin junior wasn't due until 9 am.

"Let's find a coffee, I can't just sit around here for half an hour," said Lionel.

Three shops down, there was a bakery doing takeout coffee. They took them outside whilst Jack rolled a cigarette.

"Do you smoke, Lionel?"

"Years ago, when I was your age, but fortunately I lost the taste for it in my thirties. I have tried the odd cigar since then after a good lunch with friends, but it is the one thing that guarantees me a headache, and I just don't want to complicate my life with that in the morning," he continued, "Now, when young Robin opens up, I want you to go upstairs and find the larger of the two cupboards, the one with the copper lettering saying 'Praise The Lord.'

"Why that one?" said Jack interrupting.

"Well inside this cupboard are two boxes. Would you pack these out with blankets so when we man-handle the cupboards down the stairs, the boxes remain secure. Best strap up the doors. Have you got any webbing in the van?"

"Of course, that was an early lesson for me. A Victorian bookcase toppled over coming out of Kemp Town fair, and the replacement glass was so expensive."

"That's good," Lionel was getting a little tetchy as he didn't normally experience interruptions.

"When the boxes are secured and the doors strapped, call down for a hand with the lifting."

"What's in the boxes?" enquired Jack.

"If you do as I say, I might show you, but it's very important that those boxes are really secure."

"I have it. All clear and understood. If I see anything for Ardingly, can I make Robin an offer?"

"No need, anything you want, by my understanding, is ours to take."

With this, the two watched young Robin draw up in his van and reverse it into a space at a speed most people wouldn't drive at! He left his van at a run, and unlocked the ungainly metal shuttered pub door. Lionel found watching young Robin exhausting, but he did admire his energy. Jack went to the back of his van and grabbed a couple of webbing straps and a large bundle of grey blankets. As he passed behind and through the saloon bar, he heard Lionel and Robin in the public bar. He moved quickly up the stairs, along the landing and into the sitting room. He opened the twin doors of the 'Praise The Lord' cupboard and rearranged the two old cardboard boxes so they now sat side by side on the bottom shelf. Then he packed the empty space with blankets and, once satisfied that they wouldn't move, he closed the doors, locked them and tied the webbing straps around the cupboard's middle. He secured the single door of the corner cabinet with a similar strap. Once done, Jack walked down to find Lionel and Robin behind the bar looking at the advertising tankards and ashtrays.

"Jack," Lionel said, "Robin says if you want any china or glass here, it's all yours. Why don't you make up some boxes for Ardingly. It's good to have some smalls to decorate the furniture."

"You will find some empty fruit boxes in the dry store next to the kitchen," said Robin.

Jack filled six boxes with a mixture of jug-handled bobbly glass tankards, lots from Manns, Courage and Whitbread breweries, ashtrays from the seventies, old spirit bottle tops and a vast array of bottle openers plus some undamaged 'Sherry' and 'Brandy' barrels. Then they removed the two cupboards from upstairs, Jack on the bottom end and Robin at the top, with Lionel supervising from the foot of the stairs. Once everything was loaded, Lionel took Jack for one last tour of the pub.

"It would be silly to ignore the opportunity of free stock for Ardingly," he told Jack. As he said this he spotted a couple of stools in a dark corner.

"Take those, Jack, they have got more stretchers than rungs on a ladder, and they have elm seats. Plus, if you partially hide them with a blanket, someone might even think they are a pair."

Jack loaded them on the van. They said their goodbyes to young Robin and drove the short distance down the hill to Norman Road. When parked outside the shop, Lionel got out and unlocked it.

"Let's get the goods in!" he said. Jack placed his box step onto the tarmac and started to untie the tables and cupboards from the sides of his van.

"Don't bother moving the cupboards," said Lionel, "Would you like them for Ardingly?"

"Yes please," said Jack.

"Give me those two cardboard boxes from the larger cupboard and the 4 copper topped tables. By the way, what did you get from the Beacon?"

"Let's get your boxes and tables off the van and then I will show you."

Lionel carried in the four matching circular topped pub tables, and thought the Horse and Groom will love these. Otherwise, he would offer them to Barty or Welsh Huw in Courthouse Lane. He then gingerly took out the two cardboard boxes. By the time he had carefully placed these on a table at the back of his shop, Jack had released the library chair and all of the bamboo. Lionel inspected the group, and said

"How much for the library chair?"

"Nothing," Jack replied.

"What do you mean, nothing?" Lionel queried.

"Well, the Beacon swapped it for your bronze of Venus, so I suppose it's yours."

"Well done, that's a great swap, and what about the bamboo standard lamps, would £150 buy them?" ventured Lionel.

"No, make it £200 and then I will have covered my diesel too."

"That's fine. Give me a hand in and then I can give you the cash."

Jack bid Lionel farewell and drove to the seafront to give Clive one last walk along the beach. After an easy run back to Cobham, he suddenly remembered that he had forgotten to ask Lionel what were in those two old cardboard boxes.

Chapter 33

Hastings

Mercy and Rose caught the next train to Hastings. It was a small 2 carriage affair taking them past Sussex University at Falmer, through Lewes, Eastbourne, Bexhill and finally to Hastings. The journey took just over an hour but there was so much to see: the South Downs, Pevensey's Roman Castle and flashes of the sea as they neared Hastings. All the while, Rose told Mercy of her journeys with her mother. Mercy loved it; the train seemed to trigger tales of her grandparents that she had never heard before. Her mother, as an only child, had been her parents' total focus. The subsequent pride they must have felt when she graduated with a first class degree in English Literature, was almost beyond words. Her mother also told Mercy about the surprise her parents had on first meeting her father.

"Your father and I were consumed with university life, but he also found time to play bridge at ever higher levels. He told me that he loved counting as a boy and, as he grew, his love of numbers was followed by more and more complicated arithmetic. This stretched to a fascination with both the order and randomness of playing cards. Funnily enough, although he pursued numbers, we both loved the same thing: patterns. He saw patterns in numbers and I saw them in words."

"We were just too wrapped up in our own worlds to properly include your grandparents whilst in Bristol. I do regret it now, but they were so remarkably selfless and loving that they never commented. I always rang home and they were content that I was happy. It was a relief for them to be introduced to your father after our graduation ceremony. I could tell that, by the way my mother looked at your beaming father, as we posed for photographs, with our gowns and mortar boards. Your father and I had decided not to introduce our respective parents to each other that day. One surprise was enough. After the ceremony and photographs I took my parents to a little restaurant in the docks where Albert and I had celebrated all the landmarks of our relationship: anniversaries, exam successes, birthdays and even times when things hadn't gone so well. The restaurant was small, just 30 covers, and was run by an all-embracing lady who, like my parents, had come from the West Indies but, unlike my parents, she was a showman, loud, jolly and cuddly. Over my three years at Uni, Jenny Lynn became my 'Bristol Mother' and it was to her that I ran, when life got too much. She was married to a lovely man called George, who was white, tall and quiet. He left the talking to her whilst he cooked in the kitchen. Jenny Lynn always said she was the better cook, "but somebody had to be front of house". The thing was, knowing the meals she cooked me, I would say the restaurant was better served by George in the kitchen. I knew their routine, and on days when everything seemed too much, I would turn up at 10 o'clock whilst they would be getting ready for lunchtime service. I would walk in trying not to cry, and Jenny Lynn would give me a big hug and that's when I would start crying. Then George would magically appear with hot chocolate and the most delicious thin homemade coconut biscuits. Within 20 minutes, I would be restored and sent on my way, with a Caribbean food parcel for my lunch. If my problems stemmed from your father, Jenny Lynn would say, "wait until I see him and I will spank that tall boy!" Of course, she never did, as she really liked him and knew he was the man for me!"

"Wow, I never knew about Jenny Lynn and George," said Mercy to her mother. "Do you still keep up with them?"

"No, sadly they both died when you were in your teens though they did come to our wedding. I remember Jenny Lynn swathed in bright Caribbean colours and George wearing a grey flannel suit. They looked so different but they really loved each other. They needed to, as they both lived and worked together. They loved our reception at Claridges, as they had never been. In fact, except for Albert and his parents, nobody within our small wedding party had. It could have been such a stiff do, but everybody could see your father and I were so happy, that it dissolved any awkwardness. Albert's father had instructed the waiting staff to give each of the guests a special cocktail made of white rum, melon and mint. It was long and refreshing plus had the magic effect of broadening smiles. By the time we walked from that lovely panelled ante room into the dining room, the group of 20 people had gelled into one."

"Who gave the speeches at your wedding?" Mercy asked with interest.

"My father spoke, then Albert's father followed by Albert. He didn't want a best man so, being your father, to surprise us all, he had asked Jenny Lynn to stand up. She was excellent filling in all with details of our 3 years at University, and what a genius your father was at cards and my love of writing plays."

"Were any of your plays performed or published?"

"None were published but two were performed by one of the uni theatre groups. I have the scripts somewhere at home."

"Did you continue to write when you left university?"

"No, life got in the way, your father worked so hard. We had you two and like my parents, I put all my energies into you both."

"I would have loved to have met Jenny Lynn. Did you see or hear from her and George?"

"We did, as your father's bank had a back office in Bristol. It was perfect so whilst he had meetings with his staff working on new trading systems, I drank hot chocolate with Jenny Lynn. She put our wedding cocktail on the menu and called it 'Claridges' and George named a pudding, 'Coconut with Rose'. There was never any rose: it was rice pudding made with coconut milk and then a teaspoon of passion fruit seeds on top. You know how they look like frogspawn? George used to call it tropical caviar. They kept both on their menu right up until it closed."

"Why did they close the restaurant?"

"The whole dock area was being redeveloped, and they were offered a sum of money that they just couldn't refuse. It was perfect timing as they were both running out of steam, and Jenny Lynn had always wanted to show George where she had come from, St. Lucia the island that she had left as a small child."

"It sounds like a happy ending."

"It was as it happened. She had a cousin who owned a restaurant on the coast out there. She sent me photographs. It stood on stilts, half in the water. As Jenny Lynn worked, George started painting. He soon found his groove and his hot colour abstracts became popular."

"Oh, did George do the paintings in our kitchen and Pa's offices?"

"Yes, they are all George's work. They had a wonderful

retirement there and it was a shame that your father and I never visited them. To compensate, he would always buy two of his paintings every year. He never asked the price, but just transferred a sum that would make George and Jenny Lynn's retirement worry free. That's your father, generous, but sadly little time!"

They were both so engrossed in conversation that they nearly missed their stop in Hastings. Once through the station, they walked down hill to the seafront. They turned left past a crescent of Regency houses, with a church at its centre, and then past some amusement halls before they came to a pedestrianised opening of George Street. This was a street with enormous charm, small shops and restaurants on either side. WPC Helen Tredwell was right; there were lots of antique shops; Mercy and her mother were soon dipping into them, with her mother holding up items and saying,

"Your grandparents had this!" or, "I remember these when they were being sold new!"

It took them about an hour to cover George Street, and then they turned left up the High Street. Her mother couldn't resist a rather strange but beautiful corkscrew for her father, in the most wonderfully crowded shop. When they left, they suddenly felt exhausted and hungry. Mercy asked for directions to The Crown from a rather elegant man attended by two border terriers. He offered to take them there but Mercy declined the offer, as she knew that her mother would say something embarrassing. After walking past a pottery and more antique shops, they crossed a busy road and up a small lane that framed The Crown beyond. Opposite the pub was a rather large navy blue Mercedes. Rose waved at the driver and said,

"Your father has beaten us!"

Mercy held the door for her mother and once inside, there was her sister Grace and her father. He stood to kiss them both, took a bottle of champagne from an ice bucket, opened it and poured four glasses. After handing out the glasses, he made a toast.

"To my daughter, Mercy, who got us out of the office."

As he sat down, her father said, "and why are we in Hastings?"

"It's a long story Pa."

"We have all day, go on."

"Well, you know I run the stolen desk at The Gazette?"

"Of course I do. We take The Gazette at the office. It's amazing how many of our clients read it whilst waiting in reception."

"Two issues ago we featured a stolen bronze from a Norfolk Estate and last Monday I received a call from a man wishing to know the measurements of this bronze. Well, the caller lives in Hastings!"

"Wow, is my eldest daughter turning into a Detective?"

"Not exactly, but I do want to recover this bronze as it's about time I left the stolen desk. I want to move to Auction Reporting and it would be good to leave on a high."

"Do you want me to find this guy's address? You know us bankers, we can find out most things."

"No, he is getting a call from Sergeant Arnold of the Brighton Antiques squad on Monday morning, and his assistant said she would call me up after."

"Well, if you need me, just ask. Have you had a fun day?"

"It's been lovely. Ma told me all about Jennny Lynn and George. Grace do you know about their 'Bristol' parents?'

Grace looked shocked.

"It's not as it sounds," said her mother, "Albert you tell the girls about them, but let's order first."

As a waitress took their order a tallish gentleman in a blue linen suit finished his glass of Chablis, folded his copy of The Telegraph, stood up and quietly left the table next door.

Chapter 34

Hastings

As the tall gentleman in the blue linen suit closed the pub door behind him, he quickly crossed the road and walked towards the High Street. After some 100 yards, he turned and made sure that nobody had followed him. He then dialled a number; it rang 5 times then the answer machine message started. He ended the call and tried again and again. Barty must be busy. It was on Saturdays that he did both a lunch and dinner service. Maybe, just maybe, he had some stragglers chatting over another bottle of wine or coffees. If Barty wasn't going to pick up, he needed to get there. He walked to the High Street, climbed up a steep street past the church, then up never-ending steps past some lovely jettied and tile hung town houses. Once on the grass, he reached the summit of West Hill. Arriving on the top, he stopped and caught his breath, first looking behind him at the fishing boats resting on the beach. He often reminded visitors that Hastings has the largest beach-based fishing fleet in Europe. You would have thought with those numbers they might have built a harbour by now. He then glanced towards the Crest where the Chairman and Sunny had erected 'that bronze', and a small shiver ran down Lionel's back. He made his way across the common and then down two flights of stairs, named Whistlers and Noonan Steps, passing the house where the author of The Ragged Trousered Philanthropist, Robert Tressell once lived. He always stopped to read the description, but on this occasion he didn't. He quickly acknowledged the staff in The Brewing Brothers as he made for the cellar restaurant steps.

Barty was sitting with a group of regulars, they were drinking wine with the exception of Barty who was nursing a coffee. He motioned to him to come to the kitchen as he opened the swing door.

"What is it Lionel, you look like you've seen a ghost!"

"I think I have, but not a ghost of the past, one of the future!"

Barty pulled out a stool for Lionel and said

"Sit down and catch your breath, I will get you a glass of rosé."

"Thank you," said Lionel as he took the glass from Barty.

"Now tell all," said Barty.

"I was sitting in The Crown having a quiet read of the Telegraph, when in walked this elegant and well dressed man with, I presume, his daughter, they ordered their most expensive bottle of champagne. I notice these things. They were then joined by, I assume, his wife and another daughter."

"How do you know this?" Barty interrupted, "Were you introduced?"

"No I wasn't, but I was sitting on the table next door and I could tell that they were a family by the way they greeted each other. Now will you let me get on?'"

"Sorry, go on."

"They had come to Hastings to get a feel of where a 'caller from Hastings' lives."

"Why?" asked a rather shocked Barty.

"Because he was the caller to the Gazette who enquired after measurements of a stolen bronze statue from a Norfolk estate!"

"Was one of them Mercy Penfold from the Gazette?" Said a rather shocked Barty.

"I don't know, but I guess yes, and I hate to say this, but the police are knocking on your door on Monday morning!"

Barty didn't say a word just poured himself a glass of rosé too! Typical, Barty thought. He was only trying to help Lionel, and now he was the one who was getting the police visit. Lionel broke the silence,

"I'm sorry Barty, the police should be knocking on my door and not yours."

"No, it's my fault," said Barty. "I shouldn't have called the Gazette but I just wanted to make sure that your bronze was the missing bronze."

"I think we can all be pretty certain of that now," said Lionel.

"Did you overhear anything else?"

"Yes, Sergeant Arnold is the policeman paying you the early morning call. I have heard of a Sergeant Arnold. I believe he runs the Antique and Stolen Goods squad in Brighton."

"Well, I have until Sunday to be in or out on Monday," said Barty thoughtfully.

"Lionel, you will have to leave me now as I have 22 people booked in tonight. Thankfully, I have both Polly and Phoenix helping. Let's both sleep on it and chat tomorrow."

Lionel bumped into the effervescent Polly and Phoenix as he left The Brewing Brothers, and walked down Queens Road towards the seafront. As he passed a set of traffic lights he noticed a large and very polished navy blue Mercedes queuing on the London bound side of the road. He made his way to Norman

Road, he thought of his friend Barty. It did seem unfair that he was to be questioned by the police and not Lionel himself, the only good thing of it being that he would be absolutely useless in interview and Barty would be so much better. By the time he had weighed up Barty's strengths and his weaknesses, he had passed his door straight to The Horse and Groom at the top of the road. Talking about weaknesses ...

"Afternoon all," Lionel called out as he entered the crowded bar.

June, all too soon, was at his side with a glass of Chablis.

"Thank you, and which pie do you have on today?"

"Your favourite Lionel."

"Not the chicken and tarragon?"

"Yes and I have some fresh spinach!"

"Yes please, June," said Lionel, re-engaging with his friends.

At The Imperial, Barty thankfully didn't have the luxury of thinking time. He was going through the menu with Polly and Phoenix,

"For starters, we have bruschetta .." before he could continue, the girls groaned, "Not again!"

"Only joking, yesterday's bread is today's croutons!" he said in triumph.

"It's too hot outside so we have a cold gazpacho soup with said croutons. The toppings of the much maligned bruschetta are now on a side plate: mozzarella, basil and small pickled cherry plum tomatoes from my garden."

"And croutons?" interrupted the cheeky Phoenix.

"Very funny," sighed Barty as he continued.

"Plus homemade taramasalata with the grissini breadsticks. Try some, I have a small bowl here."

"They are lovely," said Polly, "what are the seeds?"

"They're sesame seeds, I have baked two batches of them; so we have enough to give a pot of sticks per table, as nibbles. Forget that, let's go wild and give every table a small bowl of taramasalata with breadsticks, free from us to them. You never know it may improve the tips and, talking of tips, I have mananged to get a case of Miraval Rosé wine, made at the vineyard in the south of France where Brad Pitt and Angelina Jolie were married. £5 commission for every bottle sold. Polly, would you add it to the wine chalk board at £49 a bottle."

"And the mains?" pressed Polly.

"I have seven fillet steaks with a Béarnaise sauce and pan fried rosemary new potatoes, a breaded chicken schnitzel with a lemon sauce and green beans, and a fish curry with red rice. It's a fun looking dish as I have used turmeric in the sauce: it's yellow, red and green with the coriander."

"So the same colours as the bruschetta then; it's the Italian flag again," added Phoenix.

Not quite right, but Barty ignored this and carried on, "and for the veggies we have either a beetroot or celeriac steak. I salt baked them yesterday and will pan fry them and serve with a miso sauce. Finally there is pudding; lemon tart with raspberry sorbet, and of course, Bakewell tart ice cream. We have 22 booked for tonight, starting with a table of four and two at 6.30. So Polly, if you could chalk up the boards and Phoenix, would you fill the water glasses and carafes and make sure that those wine glasses are gleaming, please. Thank you and let's have a good service."

Barty returned to his kitchen and retrieved two lemon tarts from the oven. He allowed them to cool and then cut each one into ten slices. He portioned up bowls of taramasalata. Two people could share a bowl and he would add parsley and lemon just before they went out. Polly came through the swing door and said,

"I have an invitation from Mum for lunch tomorrow. I told her how busy we have been here."

"That's so kind, I would love to come."

"Mum has texted Lionel too. We all really enjoyed Sunday lunch at yours and she is keen to return the invite."

"How's your mother's abstract painting getting on?"

"Well, I think. You can see it tomorrow."

"Let's get through tonight first, and if we get any walk-ins, we can squeeze them in at the end and remember to use the boys, they can hold them upstairs at the bar while you turn the tables down here."

The service went well. Phoenix sold 3 bottles of Miraval Rosé and Polly squeezed two walk-ins, one table of six and another of four.

"The taramasalata worked," said Barty dividing the tips. The kitchen got half and front of house got the other half, so Barty kept £80 and Phoenix and Polly each got £40, plus Phoenix got another £15 for the Miraval sales.

"Here are your tips and I will bring your wages tomorrow. I'm just too tired tonight," said Barty.

"That's fine. Is everything away in the fridges?" Polly asked.
  Barty nodded.

"Well then, give me your apron and go home. Phoenix and I will tidy up. See you tomorrow for lunch at 1pm."

Polly held out her hand until Barty relinquished his chef's apron.

"Thank you. See you both tomorrow," He dragged himself up the hill to his home. He didn't dare sit down but quickly showered and went to bed. He was soon asleep and slept soundly until 3am when he woke with a start and pottered to the loo. On his return he was about to have a glass of water as was his custom but he had forgotten to bring one up. He padded downstairs to the kitchen. As he filled his glass from the kitchen tap, it struck him, there was no need to recover the bronze, just REPLACE IT!

As Lionel said, it wasn't unique. There were lots of matching groups of jockeys and horses which had been imported into Britain during the 1980s, and made in far cheaper foundries in China or the Philippines, when the price of metals were considerably lower. Their mission next week was to find an exact replacement. Much like parents did with a child's dead goldfish, only their search would be harder. He would be 'in' for Sergeant Arnold on Monday and would try and buy some time.

Barty went back to bed and slept like a child, who hadn't lost his goldfish!

Chapter 35

Hastings

Barty woke at 9.30am the next day. He hadn't done that since he was in his twenties. He went downstairs and made himself a pot of Earl Grey tea. It was already sunny outside, so he took his pot, mug and phone to a table beneath his umbrella plane trees. After a few reviving sips, he turned on his mobile phone and texted Lionel.

"Let's concentrate on a replacement bronze. BW's Barty."

He had enough time for another mug and a slice of toast with marmalade before the phone rang.

"Good morning, Lionel."

"You sound jolly."

"I have just had the best night's sleep in decades," said Barty.

"Well you would make a very relaxed condemned man. Have the police messaged you to say they are no longer coming?"

"No, sadly not, but I can brave out that visit. I think I have found a solution to our dilemma. We must find a replacement bronze! Hundreds of our bronze were cast in the '80s. I have seen quite a few in my time. You bought it for £750 saying it wasn't that old and you sold it for £3,000, also saying it wasn't that old. Let's find another one."

"You're a genius."

"Thanks."

"Once we have another, what do we do then?" questioned Lionel.

"Well, here's the thing. We put it back where it came from, and then the Chairman and Sunny will never know where theirs came from."

"The Chairman would love to know it once came from Kooling Towers, the seat of the Swotter baronets: you know how he loves a name!"

"Leave it, Lionel. Let's concentrate on finding a replacement but, once found, how are we going to replace it without anybody finding out?"

"When you and I deliver Pru and her abstract painting to Kooling Towers."

"So we have a week?"

"No, we have 4 days if we are to return it with Pru on Friday."

"Anyway, get your thinking cap on and I will see you at Pru's. Remember, it's crucial that Pru never finds out otherwise, she would be compromised and we might lose a dear friend."

"I'm totally with you. I would absolutely hate to hurt Pru."

"I will leave you now and call Jack. See you at 1pm." Lionel hung up and called Jack.

"Morning."

"Morning Jack, can you talk?"

"I can in a moment. I'm just doing my final rounds of the Heathrow carboot. Let me get in the van and I will call you back in five."

After grabbing a cup of coffee and settling Clive, Jack rang Lionel.

"All good?"

"Yes fine. There's been a change of plan here. Barty's had a brainwave. We are going to replace the bronze and not pursue the thieves, and by doing so, the Chairman's bronze can stay where it is."

"Wow, that sounds much simpler."

"Regrettably not. It all hangs on finding another bronze exactly the same. Are you still at the carboot?"

"Yes, why?"

"Go and see the Beacon and tell him that the person you sold the bronze to wishes to buy another one for a friend's 50th. Say it's all very last minute but your buyer is willing to pay top money."

"Are you, Lionel?" said Jack.

"I don't want to but, I have this terrible feeling that I'm going to have to! Go and speak to the Beacon and I'm sure he will spread the word in West London. In fact, tell him we will pay him £1,000 finders fee, if he can secure a matching bronze."

"Will do."

"Don't worry about calling back today. Call me on Monday after the police have been."

"What police?"

"It's a long story which I will tell you about tomorrow. In the meantime, get looking for another quarter size horse and jockey, and leave the rest to Barty and me."

"OK, and give my best to Barty."

Jack and Clive headed back to the Beacon and his nephew Colin.

"All right young Jack, are you missing something?" enquired the Beacon.

"You could say that! Remember that large bronze you sold me?" The Beacon looked blankly.

'Of the horse and jockey?' Jack prompted.

"Yes, of course I remember; sorry bit slow today. Doddy and I rather overdid it yesterday." In contemporary parlance, as he seemed to have dropped the Dickens dialect, now that he knew Jack better.

"Well, the person I sold it to, wants another one for a friend's 50th."

"Bronzes don't grow on trees, young Jack. They are cast in foundaries in far and distant lands."

"I know that Derek, but the one I bought from you was a 1980's reproduction cast in their hundreds or thousands, and sent by the container load to Britain. There must be another one out there. Will you help me find one? There's a finders fee for you, if you do."

"I will do my best, when is the 50th?"

"This coming Friday!"

"Well I best be damn lucky. We only have one clearance and that's on Wednesday. Do you want me to keep that Chesterfield on the van?"

"I forgot that, I will bring the van over now."

Lionel's call had thrown Jack. He had already paid the Beacon £250 for the brown leather chesterfield sofa, and he was going to pick it up when the crowds had cleared a little. Jack loaded up and drove home to Cobham for Sunday lunch with his parents. It hadn't been the easiest of weeks.

In Hastings Pru was giving Barty and Lionel Coronation chicken, the great Constance Spry recipe from the Queen's 1953 Coronation. It was hot outside and Barty needed to restore the minerals. The chicken would do that. The girls had texted that Barty was on his knees last night, so Pru decided on a restorative chicken with coronation sauce; it always tasted better on the second day. She finely diced the onions and put them in a pan with some oil, then she gently caramelised them and added some tomato paste, a bay leaf, wine and curry powder. She cooked it all off and then added the tinned apricot, which she had liquidized. She added 2 more slugs of the wine for good measure. Pru remembered watching a lovely episode of Floyd on France in which Floyd had watched a busy French chef add the wine both at the beginning and the end of the sauce 'for the flavour.' Pru would add this mother sauce to her mayonnaise. She then made a salad, cutting anything hard into straws, including carrots and red staining beetroot. Then she tore the salad leaves and cut the tomatoes crossways to expose their seeds and added toasted pine nuts for crunch. She cooked the rice, added some oil, garlic salt, pepper and finely chopped spring onions. She managed to prep everything before the girls came down for breakfast.

"Morning Mother," said Polly looking a little sleepy.

"Good night, was it?" asked Pru.

"Good fun. After tidying up the restaurant we went out with the team from Brewing Brothers. There was a DJ playing at The Courtyard, then we came back to the Brewing Brothers for a lock-in."

"That sounds excellent. Is your sister up?"

"No, but I will take her a tea as I want to borrow some clothes."

"Here's two mugs of tea. Go and wake up your sister."

After she returned home she went into her small garden and picked some mint and sweet peas. Pru had trained her sweet peas on a bamboo lattice and made a real effort to pick the flowers every other day. To make the process easy she kept a small flower trug and a pair of snips outside, under a box seat next to her Green Joanna. It was into the mighty Joanna that she put all her vegetable peelings, coffee grouts and cardboard. She watered the contents occasionally to help its digestion! It went in the top as waste and came out at the bottom as top plant feed. A virtuous circle for a little garden which she accessed by a split stable door in the west wall of her kitchen. Pru filled her trug with sweet peas which she now arranged into four jugs. One for the sitting room coffee table, one in her studio, and the remaining two for her kitchen, island and table. She opened a bottle of rosé and returned it to the fridge. Now she was ready she went upstairs to change. When she had added the 2-storey extension, she had divided a section of her bedroom to form a small ensuite bathroom. She had a shower and a loo behind a wall, and to maintain the complete length of the south wall, she had a free standing marble topped sink set into an old chest of drawers. By installing a broken wall she was still able to have sight of the pair of sash windows from her king-sized bed. She showered and chose a floaty cotton dress. It was approaching 1pm and she knew Lionel would be on time. Pru called upstairs for the girls to get ready and took the wine from the fridge, filled a water jug and polished all the glasses with a cloth, whilst she waited for the bell to ring. Barty was first, carrying a cardboard box of wine.

"Morning Pru, I promised the girls they could try this special Rosé."

"Thank you Barty, let's get it in the fridge," said Pru as she led Barty into the kitchen.

"Will you pour us this chilled rosé, and we will wait for the girls before trying yours."

They were soon interrupted by Lionel who gave Pru a bunch of freesias in a moulded celery vase.

"Both yours my dear. Found the vase yesterday in a charity shop by the station!"

"Thank you Lionel. What a shame that I haven't got any celery!"

Said Pru.

"One step ahead," responded Lionel, as he magically produced a brown paper bag containing a head of celery from his outside pocket.

"Lionel you must stop bringing me presents," said Pru.

"Only when you agree to marry me," said Lionel trying to bend down on one knee.

"Well I'd better get used to the presents then, as you and I are beyond marriage. We are just far too independent now."

Pru turned to Barty

"Can you see Lionel giving up the Horse And Groom to stay in with me every night Barty?"

"No I can't, and I might get jealous if you were always together and forgot to include me."

"That's agreed," said Lionel. "No more talk of marriage. The last thing I want is to call time on our selfish lives." He then added, "Bit dry around here?"

"Lionel!" said Barty reproachfully.

"Come on Barty. We are amongst friends here. We can speak our minds, circle of trust?"

"Stop complaining Lionel and open the bottles in the fridge."

Pru called out to the girls who appeared minutes later.

"Here is Brad and Angelina's Rosé," said Barty, "it's made in the South of France where not only Brad Pitt married Angelina Jolie, but where the former owner of 'Miraval' had a recording studio in which the blessed Pink Floyd recorded some of their, The Wall album."

"It's delicious," said Phoenix.

"Well that is a relief as I have brought three bottles of it! Now, how is your abstract coming along Pru?" asked Barty.

"Well, I think it's ok, but it's not finished yet. Girls, why don't you show these two the picture next door whilst I deal with the food?"

Polly and Phoenix led the way to the next door studio. They stood each side of the picture and said in unison, "What do you think?"

"Well, it's definitely a dog," said Barty.

"How can you tell?" enquired Lionel cocking his head to one side.

"It has the upright manner of a male black labrador. I see the blue is the black and I like the green ground."

"It's big," said Lionel.

Polly cut in, "Be nice to Mum, as she's unsure of it so far, and keeps saying she hasn't done an abstract for years."

"Lunch," called Pru from the kitchen.

Lionel was first in.

"This looks yummy," as he took in a multitude of dishes arranged on the island.

"Help yourselves. Now what do you think of the picture?"

"It's bright and large," said Lionel.

"Magnificent," chimed-in Barty.

"And that is why, my dear friends, I want to ask a huge favour. Would you both like to help me deliver it to Daphne's house in Norfolk?"

Lionel looked at Barty and both simultaneously said, "Of course we would!"

Chapter 36

Hastings

Barty couldn't sleep, it was 3 in the morning. He had had a lovely lunch at Pru's. Her Coronation chicken was delicious. He had got home at 5pm, done a bit of gardening, and had tried to read the Sunday newspapers, but he couldn't concentrate on anything bar that police visit tomorrow, which was now today! He didn't know at what time they would call but imagined it would be early. After lying still for half an hour and concentrating on inflating and deflating his diaphragm, he gave up, put on a dressing gown and climbed downstairs. He made a cup of tea and sat down in his sitting room. What was this Sergeant Arnold going to ask him? Probably the same questions that the Detective Inspector from Norfolk Constabulary had asked previously on the telephone. Barty got up, made himself another cup of tea and retrieved his daybook. If he was going to be plausible, he better be organised.

-Why had he rung The Gazette? Answer: He had seen a similar bronze at a car boot just off the M4 at Heathrow and wanted to check whether the measurements were the same.

-Why are you so interested in the measurements?

-Do you go to this car boot often? It seems a long way from Hastings.

-Do you have the name of the dealer on whose van you saw the bronze?

-Are you an antiques dealer, Mr Hix?

-Are you the thief, Mr Hix?

Barty thought there were so many questions that could be asked, and there was little point in second guessing them. Better to get his story right and as close to the truth as possible. He had seen the bronze on the back of a van, but it had been on Jack's van outside a pub in Hastings and not in a car boot off the M4. All he needed to do was convince the police that his enquiry was a dead end. After all, he didn't have the bronze and, in fact, had never owned it. Barty continued to proof his story until he felt tired and returned to bed.

The knock, when it came, was more a series of sharp wraps. He jumped out of bed, cursing that he had forgotten to put his alarm on as he had meant to.

The second set of sharp wraps were accompanied by,

"Mr Hix, it's the Police."

Barty was half way down the stairs still wearing his night attire of a white T-shirt and sarong. He turned the key and opened the door. In the porch, a little too close to the door was a cheery looking policeman with a very beautiful WPC behind him. It was the cheery policeman who spoke,

"My name is Sergeant Arnold of Brighton Police Station and this is WPC Tredwell. Would you confirm your name is Mr Barty Hix."

"Yes, it is." Barty then noticed he was barefoot.

"I'm sorry you had to wait, I was fast asleep."

"The easy sleep of the innocent, Sir. May we come in?"

Barty was slightly thrown by the 'easy sleep' comment but

this was no ordinary police officer. Here was an experienced policeman confident enough to joke at 7am in the morning, plus have a supermodel as his back up.

"Of course, please do come in, the sitting room is on your right."

"After you, please, Mr Hix."

Barty led the way in and motioned towards the sofa.

"Please sit down. Would you like a tea or coffee, as I'm going to have a sweet tea. The shock of your knock has made me a little unsteady."

"You sit down Mr Hix, Helen here will make the tea."

Helen Tredwell moved like a cheetah towards the kettle in the kitchen, and within minutes she had found mugs, tea, milk and sugar. The learned skills of a detective thought Barty.

"Now we are all settled Mr Hix, I would like to inform you that this interview is not under caution, but we may take notes. Are you happy with that Mr Hix?"

"Yes." said Barty.

"I head up Brighton's Antiques and Stolen Goods Squad, and we have been asked by Norfolk Constabulary to investigate the theft of a quarter scale bronze group modelled as a racehorse and jockey. We are here in response to your telephone call to a Miss Mercy Penfold at the Stolen Desk of the Gazette. Am I correct so far, Mr Hix?"

"You are."

"Why did you call Miss Penfold at the Gazette Mr Hix?"

Barty was expecting the cheery policeman, whom he had let into his home, to morph into a sort of human cobra, as he couldn't seem to shake the intensity of Sergeant Arnold's eyes.

"I wanted to know the dimensions of the bronze group."

"Didn't the advert in the Gazette give the measurements Mr Hix?"

"Mr Hix, didn't the advert give those measurements?" Sergeant Arnold pressed.

Barty wished that he had looked at the advert again earlier this morning when he was preparing for this interview. Which wasn't going as well as he had hoped for.

"The advert said it was quarter life sized and gave an overall height."

When Barty finished he saw WPC supermodel pass her phone to Sergeant Arnold who then spoke.

"Helen has just shown me a scanned cutting of the advertisement in the Gazette which gives both a height of 4 foot and a length of 4 foot 6 inches. So why, Mr Hix, did you need to ring the Gazette for the measurements?"

This was not going at all well thought Barty. He had prepared for a roster of questions and hadn't expected to be pursued on this one. His foolish, foolish call to the Gazette.

"Why ring, Mr Hix?"

"I had seen a similar bronze group..."

"At the M4 Heathrow car boot which is held every Sunday?" interrupted Sergeant Arnold.

"Yes, that's right it was ...."

Again Sergeant Arnold interrupted with greater intensity.

"Did you buy the bronze Mr Hix at this car boot you speak of?"

"No Sergeant, I did not."

"Did you measure the bronze Mr Hix?"

"Yes Sergeant, I did."

"So why did you ring Miss Mercy Penfold at the Gazette, Mr Hix?"

Barty was beginning to panic, then it struck him, the plinth!

"I had measured the depth of the plinth as I had wanted to set it on top of my garden wall." Sergeant Arnold looked at WPC supermodel who quickly referred to her phone and showed Sergeant Arnold.

"Did Miss Penfold give you the measurements of the plinth?" asked Sergeant Arnold.

"Yes, she did." Barty decided to keep things brief.

"What were those measurements Mr Hix?"

"The plinth measured 4 foot by 14 inches, and my garden wall is a standard 9 inches so it would overhang it, and look stupid."

"May we see this garden wall, Mr Hix?"

"Yes, of course."

"Lead on, Mr Hix," both Sergeant Arnold and WPC supermodel stood up. She towered over her senior by a good foot. Barty led them through the central pair of doors on to his terrace, and then along a cobbled path to a short wall with a soldier line of 9 inch capping bricks.

"Is this the wall?"

"Yes," replied Barty.

Then without speaking, the WPC loaded what must have been a measuring app onto her phone, she laid it on the bricks width ways and showed the reading to Sergeant Arnold.

"Thank you for your time, Mr Hix here is my card. If you can think of anything more, please don't hesitate to call me. Would you show us out please."

Barty walked ahead and led them back to the terrace and through the sitting room to his hall. He opened his front door, and they left without a further word. He didn't normally drink in the morning and never before 8am, but he needed one now. He went to the fridge, found a half open bottle of white Burgandy, poured himself a large glass, and sat down on the first seat he could find. He sat there, just staring at the front door. Barty allowed himself time to think. He knew Lionel and Jack would both be up and anxious to hear his news, but they could wait.

Had that just happened?

Why hadn't he set the alarm, and had he got away with it?

Chapter 37

Hastings/London

As Sergeant Arnold climbed into the driver's seat, fastened his seat belt and closed his door, he turned to Helen and asked,

"First impressions?"

"Not the whole truth," replied Helen.

"Spot on, but do you think he stole it?"

"No."

"Right again, Helen. Will you inform Detective Inspector Smythe of Norfolk Constabulary of our findings. Until someone finds this missing bronze there is little more we can do."

After 15 minutes Barty had replaced his empty wine glass for a black coffee and then settled into his armchair to make a call.

"Morning Barty," Lionel whispered, "have they been?"

"They've been alright, and guess what? They caught me asleep."

"But I thought you were going to be ready for them."

"I planned to be, but I woke at 3am, worked out what I might say to them, then returned to bed without turning on the alarm! I did the whole interview in a T-shirt and sarong!"

"How did it go? When did they come?"

"They came, on the dot of 7am; stayed no more than 15 minutes. It was harrowing."

"I'm so sorry Barty. It should have been me. Shall we meet up?"

"Good idea, come for breakfast. I have eggs, bacon but no bread. Would you mind walking past the bakery by Warrior Square Station?"

"Of course I will. Anything in particular, sourdough, croissant?" ventured Lionel.

"A cottage loaf please, see you in an hour," Barty then hung up and climbed upstairs for a bath. His best thinking was either done on a walk or in the bath.

Once the call was terminated, Lionel rang Jack.

"Morning young man," Lionel could hear the background noise of the van.

"Where are you heading?"

"I am going to Hammersmith to team up with the Beacon and his friend Doddy."

"Who's Doddy?"

"He's another old friend of the Beacon's, Doddy seems to cover the West End, but mainly books."

"Don't worry Jack, just remember it's all about serendipity. I have walked into many an old bookshop and bought the table beneath the books or the ornaments on a catalogue-strewn book shelf." Lionel didn't wait for a reply but signed out with,

"Go forth young Jack, and lead your motley search party. You do have the measurements, don't you?"

"I remember its length 4 foot 6 inches but I don't have the other measurements."

"I'm seeing Barty shortly, so I will get him to text you them all. Plus, I have some good photos of the bronze that I took to sell the fellow, and then you have something to show to this Doddy. You have some cash?"

"I have £1,500 in cash and I have 2 cards so that I can get another £500."

"Hopefully you won't need more, but just ask if you do. Remember when you find one, it's cash and load immediately, even if you have to put it in a black cab. Good luck and stay in touch."

Lionel took his jacket from a hook behind his kitchen door, grabbed his wallet and keys. The bakery in the street leading up to Warrior Square train station was next door to one of Lionel's lucky shops. It had a normal plate glass front but had the advantage of a loading bay immediately outside, on which the owner kept his large yellow Mercedes van with its back doors permamently open. It was in the van that the freshest stock was to be found. Over the years he had bought some real finds: a Tibetan bronze Buddha, a box of 5 Delft blue and white 'dry drug' jars, and any number of Chinese vases. As he used to quietly say to Barty:

"Norman provides my living and the ex DHL van provides my cream!"

Regrettably, it was too early for the van, but not the bakery, which smelt wonderful. Lionel chose a white cottage loaf which he popped into a black string bag. Much like the half head of celery yesterday, Lionel kept all manner of items in his outside jacket pockets. He never left his home without 2 string bags, vital for antique purchases, also his keys, mobile phone plus a tailor's tape measure. There was a world of difference in the value of a chest of drawers under 3 foot, plus when did a plate become a charger? 12 inches, of course! Lionel kept his reading glasses in his top left pocket where they fought with his orange silk hankerchief. Normally when he went for his glasses, he got his silk handkerchief too. Lionel did his loop of station approach and back to the seafront. It was far too early to ascend the three hills to Barty's so he took the straight line East. Longer and flatter was his preferred option. When he knocked on Barty's front door, Barty nearly dropped the glass bowl in which he was mixing his eggs and cream.

"Morning dear fellow, how are you?"

Barty gave his largest smile. It was the relief of a friendly face and the smell of freshly baked bread.

"Come in, what a morning!"

"Tell all, dear friend," bringing out the cottage loaf from a brown paper bag and pocketing the string bag automatically.

"First, do you want tea or coffee?" enquired Barty.

"You know me Barty, tea first thing, and then coffee 'til noon."

"Come on, how did you avoid arrest?"

"Don't joke about it. I was genuinely scared! I don't think I have been that frightened since I was caught going to the pub at school," he said whilst he added salt and pepper to the egg mix.

"That Sergeant Arnold had the eyes of a cobra: once locked on, it was impossible to leave his gaze, and his assistant, Helen, was aptly named obviously after Helen of Troy. Her face could definitely have launched a thousand ships. When they rose to inspect the garden wall, she was a good foot taller than him. It was really quite comical, if it hadn't been so terrifying."

"Why on earth did they need to inspect the garden wall? Did they search for the bronze?"

"No, I told them that I didn't buy the bronze at the car boot because I had wanted it to sit on my garden wall, and the plinth was too deep for my 9 inch wall."

"Did they buy that?" questioned Lionel.

"I think so, without the bronze they've little to go on."

Barty cut two slices of bread, put them in the toaster and melted a knob of butter in a small frying pan. Once melted he swirled it around and then added the egg and cream mix off the heat. After lowering the flame, he returned the pan to the hob and slowly turned his mix over. He got two warm plates from the oven, buttered the toast whilst his scramble, still slightly runny, was spooned onto the toast. He placed two rashers of streaky bacon on each plate, finally adding some cherry tomatoes, which he had already roasted. Both were sprinkled with chives. It was a work of art, thought Lionel.

"That looks delicious."

"Grab some cutlery Lionel, and we can have it outside on the terrace."

Once seated at Barty's new French café table, the two ate in silence. On finishing, Barty asked,

"Where are we going to find this replacement bronze?"

"Obviously, I have been thinking about this. Brighton and Lewes are good places to start. Both have a reputation for Antiques and racing, with Brighton and Plumpton racecourses nearby."

"Good call. I remember when I was an auctioneer in the 1980s a lot of the shippers used to get containers from the Far East, full of Chinese water buckets, Korean elm furniture, reproduction bronzes, big porcelain gold fish bowls and barrel shaped garden seats. What about racing headquarters in Newmarket? I used to sell a lot of items for two brothers who rented converted mushroom sheds near Stanstead. I went there once and they were unloading two large containers full of imported repro, all packed in brown cardboard tied with string. I'm sure that I saw one of those horse and jockey groups there."

"Well, shall we do Brighton and Lewes today and tomorrow, then Newmarket on Wednesday?" asked Lionel.

"It's a good start and Jack is looking too?"

"Yes, he is. I called him this morning, and he was already on his way to see the Beacon and a friend called Doddy. Oh I nearly forgot! May I have the measurements of the bronze, as I promised to text them to him."

"Funnily enough, they are engraved on my mind!"

Whilst Lionel texted this information to Jack, Barty cleared breakfast away, and ten minutes later they were in Barty's BMW heading towards Brighton. As one search party was started, another was truly underway.

Jack picked up Derek, aka Beacon, and Doddy from the Beacon's house in Hammersmith. As the senior man, Derek took the passenger seat and Doddy shared the middle seat with Clive. Jack was to be their driver. First call was a couple of large junk shops in Hammersmith. Derek would say,

"That will do nicely there," pointing to a place with double yellow lines.

The first time Jack exclaimed "I can't park on double yellows."

"Course you can," came the reply from both Derek and Doddy.

"It's only reds you have to watch". Jack went with it, as he was instructed to stay in the van so he could easily move if a warden approached. After twenty minutes they returned. Doddy clutching something wrapped in tin foil. Once in the cab, he distributed sausage sandwiches with brown sauce. Then Derek imperiously announced, "Fulham, Lillie Road."

When they arrived Derek pointed out another empty double yellow line and the two once again, disembarked. Jack watched them move down the street taking one shop each and bizarrely, exiting these alternate shops both at the same time. This process continued along the street and when they returned Doddy was carrying a plastic carrier bag. In the cab he bought out a can of coke for Jack, and cans of Guinness for himself and Derek. Once the ring cans were pulled and first sips taken, Derek announced the next destination.

"Chelsea, Lots Road."

Soon another double yellow was pointed out and then Derek and Doddy disappeared into the furniture cave and various other shops. Again they returned with Doddy carrying a second carrier bag. Jack was handed another coke and Derek and Doddy cracked open more cans of Guinness.

"Victoria, Pimlico Green," Derek uttered, again they searched and returned with more drink.

"Mayfair, Dover Street," Derek said this time. Whilst they were out of the cab, Jack's mobile phone rang.

"Hello Lionel."

"How are you getting on?"

"I really don't know. I'm unsure whether I'm a driver to a search party or part of a drinking game!"

Chapter 38

Brighton/Norfolk

As soon as WPC Helen Tredwell returned to Brighton Police Station she placed a call to Detective Inspector Kevin Smythe. It rang twice before it was briskly answered.

"Detective Inspector Smythe speaking."

Helen liked using 'Sirs' and 'Mams' as there were so many titles in the police force.

"It's Constable Helen Tredwell from Brighton, Sir," she pressed on, "Sergeant Arnold and I called on Mr Barty Hix this morning at 7am."

"How did you find him, Constable?" Detective Inspector Smythe interrupted.

"Sergeant Arnold believes that he knows more than he is letting on, but he also believes he is not our man."

"How so, Constable?"

"He had a very straight forward manner and a plausible reason for not stealing the bronze."

"And that was, Constable?"

"The base of the statue wouldn't fit his wall."

"Sorry Constable, I didn't catch that."

"Mr. Hix has a 9 inch garden wall and the bronze's base is 14 inches deep, as he explained to us, 'it just wouldn't fit'."

"Well, I have heard some alibis in my time, but not 'fitting on his wall' must surely be up there. Would you ask Sergeant Arnold to call me when he is free, preferably soon."

Detective Inspector Kevin Smythe ended the call and then mouthed "fit on his wall!"

Kevin was getting that sinking feeling again. He had put his name forward to something that he couldn't accord proper time to, and this was the result.

"It wouldn't fit on his wall!" He muttered.

Helen left her desk and went in search for Sergeant Arnold. He knew everyone in the station and pretty well everyone beyond it. His nerve centre was a circular table nearest the till on the south side of the canteen. Anybody new or on their own would be beckoned over. Colleagues were never reluctant to join 'Arthur'. He was warm and kind and knew how to listen. In return he had built up an enviable reporting system; traffic wardens would inform of more vans than normal outside 'Junk and Disorderly' in the North Lanes or Michael's in Ship Street, so he knew exactly who was doing the business. He followed his canteen stint with a daily stroll around both Brighton's North and South Lanes, calling in and having a chat with the dealers and runners. As Arthur told Helen,

"You can tell when something's up, when a van is being unloaded. If the van doors are carefully closed between trips, you know they are up to no good, and if they are using blankets when there is no rain, then you definitely know that something needs investigating." As expected, Arthur was at his usual round table talking to three traffic wardens.

"Cup of coffee, Helen?" Arthur asked as his assistant approached.

"Yes please Sarge."

To which he called out to Pat on the till.

"Coffee for Helen, Pat."

Pat turned to her colleague in the bowels of the kitchen,

"Skinny coffee, for the skinny one."

"Coming up, Arthur." she relayed back. He was her favourite policeman and she was happiest when 'King Arthur' was at his round table!

"Sarge, DI Smythe at Norfolk would like you to call him."

"Very well, Helen, all good?"

"I don't think he liked the news," informed Helen.

"Let's have these coffees first, and then I will call this DI in Norfolk before doing our rounds as it might pay us to give everybody the heads up about this statue. You never know, it could turn up in Brighton!"

Barty was going to follow the coast road to Brighton, and then he remembered how long it had taken him before. So he decided to take the A27 with every intention of covering Brighton first, and then Lewes. However, after slow traffic, he was keen to get searching, so they pulled off at Lewes. After carefully parking, Lionel and Barty walked through a twitten on to Cliffe High Street, and into their first Antiques Centre. After the normal "hellos" with the ladies at the counter, they pressed onto the stands.

"Lionel, you take the right and I will cover the cabinets and stands on the left." Most stands or pitches follow a similar layout; free standing furniture in the middle, bookcases, shelving, mirrors and pictures covering the back wall and side partitions. If the large bronze group was on a stand, it would be in the free standing area.

They both agreed in the car coming to Lewes that this shouldn't be a silent search. Spreading the word was hopefully the best course of action. After looking everywhere, and finding nothing, they stopped for a late lunch at Bills. It was kind enough weather to sit outside. Barty ordered a half bottle of french rosé, that came in a small glass carafe with moulded tumbler glasses. He thought a heavier glass was just right for pavement tables; far less likely to be blown over.

"This is good," said Lionel holding up his glass to the light.

"That's the problem with rosé, it just slips down. It's 4pm now and there is little point in going to Brighton, especially on a Monday as the shops that aren't closed today, will soon be closing anyway."

"Give Jack a call? He may be having more luck than us."

Lionel dialled,

"How are you getting on?"

"Well the bizarre drinking game continues. My current position is outside a large junk shop in North London which, thankfully, has a forecourt, so for the first time today I'm off double yellows!"

"Where are you two?" replied Jack.

"We are in Lewes. We have done all the antique shops and centres in the Cliffe but have run out of time for Brighton. We had a couple of people that remember seeing similar groups but nothing concrete. Have Derek and Doddy had any sniffs?"

"I wouldn't honestly know," said Jack, "Derek gives directions, Doddy nods approval, and then they drink Guinness until the next shop. They have done that six times now. I have noticed that both seem to be weaving a little, as they return to the van. Now I'm 'legally' parked I will go and check up on them."

"I would love to meet this pair," said Lionel.

"The Beacon seems to have a network of friends in low places.

His friend Doddy, hasn't uttered a word in the van yet! Speak to you later."

"Have they had any luck?" Barty asked Lionel.

"None at present. It appears he hasn't been able to leave the van all day, but he is now parked legally so, for the first time, he is going to join them."

Their food arrived. Barty was having the cod fillet on a bed of spinach, white beans and tomatoes, whilst Lionel had chosen the sausage and mash with onion gravy; one of his favourites. So the healthy colour of the Italian flag for Barty and the all brown for Lionel.

Lionel's phone rang.

"It's Jack," whispered Lionel to Barty, "Hello."

"Hi, nothing to report here and we are calling it a day, whilst they can both still stand. I will give you an update when I have dropped them off. Bye."

"No good news from Jack," confirmed Lionel.

"We know that Sir Roger lives in Norfolk and we know the bronze was made and exported into the UK over 30 years ago. What we don't know is where Sir Roger bought it. There are a lot of antique dealers in the wilds of East Anglia. Let's give Brighton a miss tomorrow and head to Newmarket instead."

"Agreed. I think we would have more of the same in Brighton as we had in Lewes today."

"Let's go straight to the home of racing, Newmarket, and work our way east. "That will be fun. I haven't been on a buying trip for years," said Lionel.

"When we get home, let's go through the Gazette and internet to find the bigger trade warehouses up there. I think that they are the most likely places where we will find our bronze. We want salvage yards and converted farm buildings where stuff is moved on pallets by forklift trucks."

"I agree," said Lionel.

Back in Norfolk, Detective Inspector Kevin Smythe's call with Sergeant Arnold had shed no further light on their visit to Mr Hix in Hastings, but Sergeant Arnold did ask if he had any other lines of enquiry, to which Kevin Smythe suddenly thought of the Kindly family in Lucky Slap. Sir Roger had suspected them but his gardener, Cecil Trowel, was dismissive. Maybe Kevin should back the owner and not the gardener. He could make a detour on his way home it wouldn't take long; this was just a chat, not an interview. In the car on the way to Lucky Slap, he made a call to report in his visit. Not to the Police Station, but to his wife Helen. When he pulled into the travellers' site, he was met by the normal melée of dogs and kids. He knew Terry and Pearl's home was the largest and he also knew their boys lived next door. Luckily, there were no big trucks to be seen, so he might be able to catch Terry on his own. Kevin checked his tie and knocked on the caravan door. Pearl opened the door, recognised Kevin and shouted inside, "It's for you, Terry love."

With that, she walked past Kevin and disappeared into another caravan.

"Come in, come in," said Terry from inside.

When Kevin walked in, Terry said, "I'll come quietly officer. Don't be rough with me. I'm not a well man.'"

"Very funny, still got the old humour then Terry."

"To what do I owe this pleasure?"

Although Terry was older, they had both been around the block together. Kevin had never arrested Terry nor, to his knowledge, had any other policeman. Even though the Kindlys had always seemed close to the trouble, they had never actually been caught. Maybe they were just lucky.

"Did you hear about the bronze stolen from Kooling Towers?"

"I hears alot of things, now I'm around Pearl all day!" Terry said with a smile.

"There's talk that it's got something to do with your boys."

"My boys are different Inspector. Every generation is different, and since we moved to the Slap here, it's been kind to us. The boys were always in Sir Rogers woods; this place is home to them and I knows they wouldn't take the piss."

Kevin knew that too. Clem, Tom and Scan were hardworking and generally polite. He had never seen them swagger about or heard of them pushing people around; they were more into gardening, than tarmacking. Kevin looked at Terry who could sense that Kevin also knew his boys were decent lads.

"Inspector, my Pearl said that the whole area is plastered with advertising for a Cricket Club fundraiser at the Towers on Sunday. Well, before that bronze was taken Sir Roger had another open garden. We both said he was asking for it! You knows, all the years I did tarmacking, I never advertised as you gets the wrong sorts."

"Garden visitors drive Honda Jazzes, not twin-tyred tipper trucks," responded Kevin.

"But not all twin tyres are on tippers Inspector. A great many are on horseboxes and trailers, and generally towed by Land Rovers."

The old sage of Lucky Slap needed to speak no more. With a "take care of yourself, Terry" Kevin left the caravan and got in his car and started thinking, really thinking.

Chapter 39
Norfolk

Barty and Lionel left Hastings early the next morning. They had identified a number of larger dealers, from Newmarket in Suffolk to Holt in Norfolk. As a sign of commitment to the task ahead, Barty had booked two rooms at The Victoria Inn in Holkham. A shared twin room would have been cheaper, but he felt they were too old to share, just imagine the snoring! Barty had texted two brothers who rented a sprawling collection of converted mushroom sheds. As they steered the BMW into the yard, they were reasssured by a large number of steel containers. To save lots of looking in artificially lit sheds, they showed the brothers a photo of the bronze group. They both recognised the Horse and Jockey, as they had sold them in the past, but they had none in stock at present. Before they left, Barty showed them their list of dealers that they intended to visit, asking if they had left off anyone who might be able to help. The brothers added one in Woodbridge and one in Felixstowe. Next stop was Newmarket, the home of British Horse racing. It had an ordered otherness about it. All the grass verges were cut like prized lawns and fencing was newly painted. They passed the National Horse Racing Museum, a former palace and racing headquarters to Baron de Rothschild. They parked Barty's car under the shade of a curbside tree, thankfully not a dripping lime, and dipped into a couple of antique shops, always showing a photograph first. No joy in Newmarket after a good hour, but the list of ten large warehouses still remained.

"Give Jack a call," said Barty, once they were moving again. Lionel got through within a couple of rings.

"He is in the van," Lionel said as he got through.

"Morning Jack, how's tricks?"

"Good thank you. I'm at Kempton antiques fair. Nothing as yet, but a dealer I know from Albert Road in Southsea, recommended that I should call in Arundel and then I think I will poke around Chichester and Portsmouth."

"What about Derek and Doddy?" Lionel enquired.

"They are old enough to get their own driver, but rather kindly, Derek said they would try a couple of places they know in Hertfordshire," Jack continued, "they were funny: Derek with his brief orders; Doddy with his nodded agreements and swinging carrier bag of Guinness. In the end I managed to get Doddy to speak. I asked him why he only bought 2 cans at a time as surely it was so much cheaper to buy a multi pack. He said, "They're colder of course!" to which Derek nodded. Five words in eight hours! Even Clive has more to say than Doddy. In fact we are quite enjoying having the cab back to ourselves again."

Lionel had put his mobile on loudspeaker so that Barty could hear the news.

"Jack," Barty joined in, "we have done our call in Stanstead and admired lovely Newmarket too, but if we are successful in locating a bronze, would you come up and collect it?"

"Of course I will, I have a dealer friend in Beccles who I'm keen to visit. I have bought and swapped numerous things with him at Ardingly, and I have always said that I'd come, but of course, never have."

"Good luck today," said Lionel, "and give us a call if, heaven forbid, you find one."

"Where to Barty?"

"Let's go North to the coast. I have never been to Kings Lynn; everyone tells me that the architecture is fabulous. Let's lunch there and then tick off that dealer near Fakenham Racecourse."

"Perfect," agreed Lionel settling into the tanned leather passenger seat.

"Remind me Barty, how much did Hayward's charge you for redoing the upholstery?"

"Leave it, Lionel, otherwise you're out walking!"

After a tour of the finer buildings of Kings Lynn, including the stone and flint chequered Guild Hall, Barty parked near the Customs House and walked to the Bank House Hotel. They ate their lunch in a Brasserie style restaurant, both plumping for the breast of roast guinea fowl with chorizo lentil casserole. It was a good job that they weren't sharing a room thought Barty! After lunch their search started in earnest by ticking off the list of dealers who might or might not own a forklift truck, which included Norfolk Reclamation that boasted not one, but multiple forklifts, sadly no replacement bronze.

As they left the yard, Lionel said,

"It would have been a lot easier if they had stolen a bronze figure of a lion. I reckon we could have replaced a quarter sized lion at least three times!"

They went from converted farm buildings to town centre spaces. In some, they were offered tea and coffee; in others, it was just a cheery greeting, but in none were they ignored. The same pattern was quickly adopted. Barty showed the dealer a photo of the bronze group on his phone and then he would show their 'dealer list' asking, 'have we missed anybody?' Whilst Lionel walked around the stock. Bizarrely, the same warehouse in Felixstowe, kept being mentioned, with caveats like: "he's an odd one; be sure to ring first," and "he either likes you or he doesn't."

After visiting a lovely couple outside Fakenham, who had converted an old dairy into both holiday lets and antiques showrooms, they called it a day and headed north to the coast, and their rooms for the night.

The Victoria Inn stands at the gateway to Holkham Park, and opposite a long drive to Holkham beach. It was just after 5pm when they checked in, dropped their bags in their rooms, and walked to the beach. After 15 minutes they were on the golden sands amongst fragrant pine trees: the smell of the South of France in Norfolk! Barty and Lionel had every intention of walking to the water's edge but it was low tide and it would take them too long to walk back to the Inn, especially as Lionel was getting itchy for the bar. As they returned, a flight of ducks landed right in front of them, what a sight. Once, over the threshold, Lionel took the lead to the bar rubbing his hands together on his final approach. A little too keen thought Barty as Lionel asked the barman for the wine list.

"Tonight is on me, Barty. I do appreciate how you have helped me and I still have the Chairman's £3,000."

"Lionel, you may well need that and possibly more, especially if word gets out that we are searching for an exact replacement. Supply and demand, and we know from the last couple of days, that the supply is non existant!"

"Barty, how often are we away from Hastings? I haven't been on a buying trip for years, and Norfolk is charming. You know, in the Old Town we have walls of flint cobs set in rows, like courses of bricks? Here we have whole villages of them. It's like a picturesque idyll. We're only 4 hours away from Sussex, with its houses clad in painted timber or mathematical tiles, and we land in Norfolk where it looks like the Dutch have only just left: Flemish gable ends, wavy walls and Roman roofing tiles. Beer or wine?"

"Beer for me. I will try the Adnams, that is their local one."

Lionel ordered a pint for Barty and a bottle of Macon-Villages white Burgundy, which arrived in a wine cooler along with glasses and food menus.

"How lovely," Barty said whilst perusing his menu.

"They have a 'Plat du Jour.' I have often thought about offering that at the Imperial."

"You're only open 4 days a week. How would that work? Plats du Mercredi, Jeudi, Vendredi and Samedi?"

"Talking of opening, I better post an Instagram that I will be closed this weekend. I did it 2 years ago when I was struck down with flu and, luckily, I haven't had to close down since."

"That's kind of you to close." Lionel said while raising his glass.

"Shall we share some starters?"

"That would be useful as it's half pleasure and half work for me. I would like to try both; the tempura avocado with harissa oil, plus the prawn and smoked salmon thermidor."

"Perfect, and I'm going for the Venison carpaccio with the celeriac remoulade. What is a remoulade?"

"It is a cold sauce similar to a mayonaise, made the same but with the addition of grated celeriac, mustard and lemon juice."

"Sounds delicious, almost forgotten about the venison carpaccio. Can you see a day when you swap the order of food on a menu, putting the veg first, say, like 'Yorkshire puddings, roast potatoes, honey glazed carrots with roast beef?' "

"I'm sure it's around the corner. My weekly veg bill is now the same as my meat and fish. Vegetables are still cheaper, but we are eating so much more of them."

"What are you having for your main?" Lionel asked.

"I will have the Plat du Jour of course, sole meunière and boiled potatoes."

"Any sides? I see they have the work of the Devil here, sautéed cabbage and chestnuts."

"I wouldn't mind the Greek salad. What are you going to plump for?"

"I will have the oily fish, the whole mackerel, nature's butter, and as we both are having the fish, shall we stick to the white or there is a very good Rosé from the Western Cape of South Africa: Vondeling, my friend Nick in Bristol recommends it."

"Perfect, let's go for that."

"You do the ordering whilst I quickly post the Imperial's closure for this weekend, and I'd better message the Brewing Brothers as well. It's a blessing that I did so well last weekend. It was a full house every day!"

Barty and Lionel carried on the easy chatter of a long friendship and shared interests. The food was delicious and they both retired to bed absolutely exhausted, in the hope that tomorrow would finally be 'their day.'

Chapter 40

Norfolk

Being early risers, Barty had walked to the beach and this time, he was rewarded with a high tide, the water had that silky surface of a calm sea and Lionel, in the meantime, had decided that he was going to walk around the village surrounding the Park gates. He admired a thatched roofed pavilion housing a metal water pump. The design might have been taken from a Regency landowner's guide to estate architecture, in that every building, both humble or grand, had flintwork, stepped brick gables and detailed joinery. The two men met, had breakfast together, and then left for Holt, which had two entries on Barty's list.

Regrettably, yet again, both drew a blank, so they pressed on. As more of the list was ticked off, the mood in the car began to fall.

"Surely there is another one somewhere," said Lionel.

"What if we can't find one, should we pinch the Chairman's back?"

"No, that Sergeant Arnold would be straight on to me. A matching bronze stolen from a house no more than half a mile from mine, plus you Lionel, as the seller? He's no fool. He would soon make his own conclusion and we would be in for the high jump!"

"We've just got to keep on looking."

"Let's check in with Jack. I wonder how he got on yesterday?"

"Nothing in Arundel. Some great shops though. Saw a bronze horse without the jockey in Chichester and then went around a scrapyard in Portsmouth. The only bit of bronze they had was a propeller, so it's a nothing from me!"

"Can you help today?" asked Lionel.

"Yes, of course," said Jack. "I decided to sleep in the van last night. Clive and I found a quiet spot in the New Forest and we are heading into Bournemouth now. I was told that there are masses of antiques shops on the Christchurch Road, and from there, I'm heading to Dorset. It's a bit like stepping stones. I visit one place and the dealer tells me about another. Hopefully, I will find this bronze before I get to Land's End!"

"Good luck, dear boy," Lionel said before ending the call.

"He's certainly got the bit between his teeth," said Barty.

"I'm not sure that I have the stomach for horsey analogies now," replied Lionel.

"Where next on our list?"

"Two in Norwich, the 'City of church bells'."

"Let's hope that we are on the hour there then!"

"The first stop is in the City Centre by the Town Hall."

Barty and Lionel fell into their routine, showing photos and quickly walking around the stock.

As Barty parked the BMW, he was unaware that only yards away was Detective Inspector Kevin Smythe in Norwich Police Station. 'Anvil' had fallen back on his gritty resolve and was determined to rescue this investigation. Both Sergeant Arnold in Brighton and Terry Kindly, had urged him to look at what was nearest. If Terry was right, and the bronze had been stolen after an Open Garden, then why shouldn't the thief come back for seconds, especially as he hadn't been caught so far? Kevin had the weekend off and he liked cricket, and Helen and the children would enjoy visiting Kooling Towers. He would ask her tonight and, if agreed, he would then ring Sir Roger.

Barty and Lionel exhausted more antique emporia and then they travelled to Woodbridge.

"Another wonderful town," exclaimed Barty, "with so many antique shops but none with a replica bronze." Before the one way system in Woodbridge released them, they called the warehouse in Felixstowe. Lionel's phone rang several times and as he was about to hang up a rather rude,

"What?" bellowed over the loud speaker. The volume of the word startled both of them.

"We would like to have a look at your stock."

"What sort?" came the voice again, but Lionel was catching on, "Bronze sort."

"I've lots of bronzes, mostly expensive."

"Any of horses?"

"Some, and lions too!" Lionel raised his eyebrows at the mention of lions.

"May we come and see you?"

"What, now?"

"Yes, we will be with you in 20 minutes."

"Well, get a move on. I close in 40 minutes promptly at 5pm." With that he put his phone down.

"Well, he wins the customer care award for the East of England!" Lionel said to Barty.

"We were warned that he was rather rude but if he has our bronze, he is charm personified!"

Thankfully the old factory units outside the dock area were very easy to find, in what would have been once a railway good's yard. Barty saw an old white Mercedes Sprinter van next to a couple of old 700 series Volvos, the mules of the antiques trade. They parked and walked from the light into the gloom of a warehouse and as their eyes adjusted they saw row upon row of furniture. The rows stretched as far as the eye could see in the dull artificial light, which was so bad that Barty started feeling depressed and he hadn't even found the grumpy owner yet. Nothing was stopping Lionel though, as he marched up the corridors calling out,

"Hello!"

After what seemed the tenth "Hello" a rather loud "Yeah" came back from the end of the building. Lionel approached him with a jovial greeting,

"I rang about a bronze."

"I know," said an impressively large man; big hair, big bones; almost a different species.

"May I see them?"

"You could if you were in the right place, they are over in the other building but hurry. I close at 5 sharp."

Lionel picked up a bewildered and blinking Barty on his way out. They both crossed the yard and dived into another similar warehouse, this time it was filled with 'smalls,' but nothing in here was small. The vases were floor vases, standing 5 feet high. There were large 4 foot diameter porcelain gold fish bowls enamelled with gold fishes and green lilies, and dotted amongst all this colour was the familiar dull gold of bronzes. Not one bronze figure, but many, as though a whole container had just been emptied and its contents arranged around the warehouse.

There were horses, dogs and lions of course: some quarter scale, some half and some even life sized. Lionel and Barty flashed a look and a smile to one another. Were they finally close? The warehouse was full of large items, pinball machines, one armed bandits, even painted circus flashings, all gaudy with colour, and amongst this jumble of items Barty and Lionel found themselves searching with greater purpose. Then, suddenly, there was a cry,

"Eureka!"

Barty negotiated the dividing corridors to find Lionel stroking the horse much like a winning owner.

"You clever fellow."

"We have it," Lionel said hugging Barty.

"Firstly, let's measure it," prompted Barty, "just to make sure."

Lionel produced his tailor's cloth measuring tape from his outside coat pocket and then said the measurements out loud.

"4 foot high, 4 foot 6 inches long, IT IS A MATCH."

"And the plinth, just to make certain?" urged Barty.

"4 foot by 14 inches, we have only gone and got ourselves a replacement!"

With that, Lionel performed an impromptu jig. Out of nowhere a large outline emerged in the shape of the owner of the bronze horse and jockey.

"Found something?"

"We have," Lionel was about to add 'my friend' but thought better of it.

"How much is this?"

Now, the large man spoke in more animated sentences.

"Two days ago that racehorse & jockey group in front of you was priced at £3,250, but since Tuesday, I have been receiving calls from fellow dealers saying that there are a 'couple of old fruits' enquiring after a bronze of a horse and jockey."

Barty smarted at the phrase 'old fruits,' but Lionel held out his right hand to signal 'let it go.'

"Well, I reckon," continued the large man, "you two need to buy this, more than I need to sell it?' He paused briefly and then said, "Am I right, gentlemen?" to which Lionel nodded meekly.

"You will have noticed that there are very few price labels, as I keep it all up here." With this he motioned to his large mop of curly hair.

"I reckon that the next auction I go to, I will be giving a lot of 'drinks' to people who called me. The price for cash, as I don't do cards, is a round £6,000."

Both Barty's and Lionel's jaws dropped in unison, whereas the large oaf summoned up a small grin.

"It's past 5 gentlemen. Your answer, please?"

Before Barty could say anything Lionel blurted out,

"We'll take it!"

"Do you have the £6,000?"

"I have £3,000 on me and can pay the final three and collect tomorrow morning?"

"I open at 10am but I must go now as my husband Kenneth has my dinner ready bang on six."

They walked back to the BMW in silence. Lionel handed over the cash and waited for Kenneth's husband to count it. As a receipt, he scribbled on a large brown label marked 'Bronze horse and jockey, £3,250'. Barty and Lionel drove away and stopped at the first garage.

"I need water, a coffee and a little silence," said Barty.

"Rightie ho, you stay here and I will get the necessary."

Lionel too, was a little shell-shocked by the whole experience. They drank their water and coffee in silence then Barty spoke.

"Let's find somewhere to stay and work out how we are going to get the remaining £3,000."

Whilst Barty sorted rooms, Lionel got out of the car and rang Jack,

"We have found it!" Lionel cried.

"Great, cool. What a relief."

"Thanks. Can you come to an address in Felixstowe for 10 o'clock tomorrow?"

"Sure."

"Where are you?"

"Dorchester."

"Well, turn around now, and I will see if Barty can get you a room. I'll text you the address shortly."

Lionel knocked on the passenger window and Barty lowered it.

"Jack's in Dorchester and is now heading our way."

"That's lucky as I have booked us into the Bell Inn, not far from the Dartford Tunnel. I will check if they have another room."

Barty redialled and booked Jack into a room whilst Lionel texted the details: Bell Inn, Horndon-On-The Hill, Stanford-Le-Hope, Essex. A rather grand address for Essex, not the normal Barking, Romford or Rainham, thought Lionel.

Chapter 41

Essex

Barty and Lionel travelled down the A13 to the Thames Estuary, putting some distance between them and the hairy giant of Felixstowe.

"I feel pulverised," said Lionel, "and I didn't even shake the man's hand."

"I think it's a magic combination of relief at finding the bronze, plus that ghastly empty feeling of knowing you have paid far too much for it," added Barty.

"You paid Jack £700 and you sold it to the chairman for £3,000, a profit of £2,300," he continued, "so just the £3,700 to bridge!"

"Thanks! I know you're right though. Reputations must be maintained and losses have to be covered if you want to stay in the swim, but sometimes you look back and wish you had never bought something. The bronze is one of those. Who would have thought a £700 purchase from the back of a van, would have sucked in so much cash, time and energy: Yours, Jack's, mine and even the Beacon's and Doddy's. Tonight, we must plan its reinstatement to Kooling Tower, but first we should celebrate our Felixstowe find!"

At the mention of planning, Barty's mind wandered to how they were going to return the bronze, and Lionel's mind erred to how they should celebrate. What exactly was the Bell Inn's food like and what was the depth of their wine cellar?

After a one and a half hour drive, they finally arrived outside the 600 year old former Coaching Inn. Lionel led the charge. Through the front door he went, and was not at all disappointed by the oak panelling and smell of log fires. Rubbing his hands he approached the bar and asked for a pint of best bitter and the wine list. Whilst he perused the list he took a small sip of Barty's pint, delicious, but definitely not him. If he needed liquid in any quantity, it was water with cucumber, lime or lemon. There was a small choice of wines on the list: the whites included a St Veran and a Viognier. Before Lionel chose a whole bottle, he plumped for a glass of House Champagne. Bubbles befit good times like these. Lionel took Barty's pint and his Champagne to a circular copper topped table with 2 tub shaped wooden-seated chairs. They looked comfortable, and they were. As Lionel took a small sip from the flute glass, he surveyed the room. There were 3 men standing at the bar in suit trousers and ironed shirts. They had the look of business colleagues who had just dropped their bags in their bedrooms. Maybe salesmen or auditors enjoying a pint before supper. They weren't the only people in the bar. There was a couple having an early supper at a favourite table next to the fire: he, dapper in sports jacket and navy blue buttoned cardigan, and she, with ironed hair and a sleeveless quilted jacket. At her feet lay a perky looking terrier. Lionel didn't know the breed but he would ask Barty when he joined him. What was he doing? thought Lionel. He took another sip of Barty's pint. He wouldn't notice. In fact the more Lionel sipped the beer, the more he liked it. A dreadful thought entered his head. For decades he had been needlessly throwing his money over the bar for wine, when he could have been supping beer for half the price. His thoughts were interrupted by Barty entering. He smiled as he handed Barty his beer, the active agent for the rounder figure! Barty raised his glass,

"Congratulations, one large bronze found!"

"Thank you, you have been an absolute brick."

"No need for speeches, the interesting part is yet to come. Reinstating it to its rightful home, at you know where and without anyone noticing. That will be the real challenge."

"I know, and Pru will be in the van with us."

"Let's not worry about that now. We had a plan and half is now completed.

Finding that bronze was the difficult part, and as they say Lionel, all is downhill from here!" Barty raised his glass,

"Let's hope by Monday this saga will all be over!"

"One step at a time, I don't think that I could cope with much more stress!"

At the mention of stress both Lionel and Barty paused and sat in silence. So much had happened in the last three weeks. It all needed a little bit of time to digest. The silence was broken by a single bark and the fast approach of a small brown dog.

"How are you Clive?" Barty said whilst rubbing Clive's shoulders with both hands. Clive liked Barty. Dogs are good at smells and, for Clive, Barty would always smell of a ribeye steak. Jack wasn't far behind.

"Congratulations. Where did you find it?" said Jack pulling up a stool.

"It's a long and harrowing story but first, what would you like to drink?" said Lionel rising from the chair.

"A Guinness please and I'll toast 'the Beacon and Doddy' with every drop!"

"Have you called them, do they know our good news?" said Barty.

"No, I haven't but I will call the Beacon tomorrow. He's more of a morning person!"

"Aren't we all," said Lionel returning with Jack's Guinness.

Chapter 42

Essex/Hastings

Pru had got up early, as Thursday was her last day to tweek the abstract before taking it to Kooling Towers. The canvas measured 6 foot by 4 foot allowing the subject, Sir Roger's noble labrador, to be larger than life. She had conveyed the bulk and presence of Sampson with blocks of blue, fixed on a green background. There was a definite shape of a seated labrador but something was nagging her. It could be any large black labrador and not the quiet, but slightly haughty, companion of Sir Roger. She wanted to convey that telepathic communication between dog and owner. Plus, she wanted Sir Roger to recognise the spirit of Sampson. Daphne was more avant garde in her artistic taste but, Sir Roger leaned towards the more traditional representative school of art. What Pru had been agonizing on, was the addition of detail, some yellow and black, to give an approximation of Sampson's mouth and eyes. She stepped away from the canvas and charted where she might add the highlights to suggest Sampson's broad chest and raised head, both the desired result of continuous and careful breeding. She approached the canvas and added some black horizontal lines to define his jawline, and some verticle lines to shadow his front legs and shoulders, then she stood back. The picture had changed.

Sampson was finally emerging from the blue block that she had been so careful to retain. Too much detail and she threatened the very essence of the abstract picture. She squeezed the Indian yellow oil paint on her palette and wondered whether a fourth colour was too much. No, three was enough for now. She put down her brush and padded into her kitchen. A coffee was needed plus the 'sounding board' of her daughters. She added three heaped dessert spoons of ground coffee to a stainless steel cafetière, and placed this and three mugs on her island, before calling up to her girls and texting Barty.

'What's your ETA to collect my picture? BTW It's 6 ft x 4 ft. Love Pru xx'

Barty was at The Bell Inn in Essex enjoying a lovely breakfast. Whenever he saw kippers on the menu, along with smoked haddock, he knew he was in the right place. He thought fish only got the green light for breakfast, with the addition of a poached egg. Barty looked at his phone and then looked up at Lionel and Jack.

"It's Pru. She wants to know what time we are picking up her picture."

"Can you reply 'will confirm timings tonight' as first we have got to negotiate the Giant of Felixstowe," said Lionel.

"Of course," replied Barty whilst tapping a short text message to Pru.

"I can't wait to meet this man," said Jack.

"More fool you," replied Lionel, "he's not exactly cheery."

"Don't be so hard on him. You and I fell into a big trap of our own making," added Barty, as he cut into his poached egg. The reddish yolk ran over his fillet of smoked haddock.

"That's a great coloured yolk," Lionel said, before lifting a good fork-full of sausage to his mouth.

"It's a marvellous farming secret, the reddish yolk," replied Barty.

"Go on, tell. What's the secret? It must be something to do with the breed of hen?" ventured Lionel.

"No," said Barty. "Any theories Jack?"

"A dye in their drinking water?"

"That sounds a little George Orwellian," added Lionel.

"No, it's more benign than that. They feed the chickens with flowers."

"What, red ones?"

"No yellow ones! The flowers are Marigolds."

'Put to an extremely good use, in my opinion!' said Lionel.

'Well, who would have thought that, two yellows makes a red. We had better ask Pru for the answer to that one!" said Lionel.

"Now less of egg yolks," said Barty, "we'd better settle the bill and get off to Felixstowe, as he opens at 10 o'clock."

"I will pay for the rooms and supper Barty, but would you mind finding a Nat West bank on our route to the giant?"

Ten minutes later they left armed with an address of a bank in Colchester that opened at 9.30. Barty drove with Lionel in the beloved BMW, Jack and Clive following in the van. After stopping off to withdraw the grand sum of £3,000 in cash, they found themselves back at the antique warehouse just after 10. As they pulled up, a large man with curly hair was guiding their bronze horse and jockey on a set of piano wheels, the trusty 4-wheeled 'donkey' of the antiques trade.

"Doesn't it look good," said Lionel to Barty as they parked their car next to the oaf's Volvo estate.

"Morning gentlemen," said the rather too cheery giant,"have you got the money?"

"We have." said Lionel waving a bulging white envelope.

"Good, and a van too, I see."

"Morning," said Jack, "I have heard a lot about you."

"All bad, I hope," came the reply.

"Can a man who holds the stock you want, ever be bad?" replied Jack, who noticed that Clive was keeping a wary distance from the Giant.

Once the cash was counted twice, inspite of a paper band saying £3,000 with the bank clerks initials on it, the bronze was loaded, and the small convoy of BMW and van left.

Back in Hastings, Pru and her two daughters were considering the large canvas in her studio. They stood with cups of coffee, squinting their eyes, trying to find the shape of the sitter.

"What do you think?" asked Pru.

"It's large," said Phoenix, "but I'm not sure that I'm getting a dog."

The three squinted again, then Pru picked up a square headed brush and added two small black vertical lines which showed the weight of Sampson's heavy velvet ears.

"It is beginning to emerge now Mum," said Polly. "Keep going."

"I'm not sure whether I should add some yellow. The black pushes the shapes back and the yellow brings the features to the fore."

"Why don't you try some yellow?" said Phoenix. "You can always take it off."

"I'm not sure if I am brave enough for the yellow yet. I was toying with giving him a block of yellow on his chest, like a bib."

"Steady." said Polly. "Sir Roger might think it's some heraldic device, and I'm pretty sure heraldry and abstract art are diametrically opposed."

"I get your point, but I rather feel he would like that. Sampson is definitely all black or, for the purposes of this painting, all blue!"

"Stop it girls. I want some constructive criticism. It's my last day for any changes as Barty and Lionel pick it up tomorrow and the paint needs to dry overnight."

"Do something with the eyes," Polly said, as she walked in front of the canvas and faced her mother and sister. Looking at them both she closed her eyes. "Dead?" and then opened them, "Alive?"

"That's where your yellow should go, the eyes."

"Let's try," said Pru. She picked up a new square headed brush and dabbed into the yellow paint on her palette, then she strode to the painting and, without pausing, placed two yellow squares where the eyes would be. She turned and asked her daughters, "Dead or alive?"

"Stand to the side Mother, and we'll tell you," said Polly.

"Alive," they said in unison.

"That is remarkable, who would have thought two tiny blobs of colour would transform the dog into a real character. Looking at it now, you feel as if you know him!"

"Why, thank you Polly, that's really kind of you."

"Come on, I'm starving. Anybody for scrambled eggs?" said Phoenix.

"I thought you were vegan," teased Pru.

"Only with her friends!" her sister chipped in.

"Ha ha, you know I'm not a vegan, and for goodness sake don't tell Barty. I will never hear the end of it! 'Are you allowed to carry steaks?'.... 'Watch out, that once had feathers.' You know what Barty and Lionel are like."

"Yes, prehistoric," added Polly.

Pru handed a heavy frying pan to Phoenix.

"Remember, eggs slow." As Phoenix turned on the gas hob.

"I know Mother, and by the way, Barty says exactly the same when I make him a scramble at the restaurant. Just pass me the eggs and cream and sit down. Polly you do the toast. Now tell us about your forthcoming exciting weekend at Kooling Towers."

"I'm hoping to leave tomorrow morning. Barty has yet to confirm what time he's picking me up. They are borrowing the van from a friend to take my picture. Knowing them, it will be late morning, as they will not want to get caught in rush hour, especially on a Friday."

"Don't tell me Lionel's invited too?" said Phoenix beating the eggs, cream, salt and pepper in a glass bowl.

"No, I'm the only one invited to stay for Sir Roger's birthday weekend. Barty and Lionel have booked themselves into the local pub, as they want to explore Norfolk. It's really very sweet of them. They are going to pick me up on Sunday. I will introduce them to Daphne and Roger then, as Friday will involve some subterfuge, because the picture is a surprise present for Sir Roger."

"I should say," said Polly buttering the toast. "How do you hide a 6 x 4 foot canvas, being carried by two old rogues of roughly the same dimensions!"

"Polly, that's unkind, you know how sensitive Barty is about his weight. Thankfully Kooling Towers is very large, with many points of entry."

"Forget about those two," said Phoenix, "what's happening over the weekend?" "Quiet supper on Friday night, picture reveal then party on Saturday and Charity Cricket Match on Sunday."

"Don't tell me that constitutes as an exciting weekend!" said Phoenix groaning.

"The only good news about this weekend, is that Barty has closed the restaurant for your mini-break. Shall we have a house party Polly?"

"Don't you dare!" said Pru smiling.

Chapter 43

Hastings

Barty, Lionel, Jack and Clive had made good time from Felixstowe back to Hastings, going straight to Barty's home in West Hill. Jack wanted to walk Clive so Barty had given him a short shopping list of cockles, samphire and sea bass straight from the fishing huts, asking him to buy first before having a swim, and then collect on his way back. With the exit of Jack and Clive, Barty disappeared into the cellar and re-emerged with a number of interesting looking bottles. Lionel followed the bottles and glasses to the veranda, where they settled and plotted the return of the bronze to Kooling Towers. After a delicious supper, Lionel, Jack and Clive walked back along the seafront to Norman Road. This should be qualified by, Lionel tottering, Jack walking and Clive achieving a fast paced combination of running and swimming. Lionel mused that if that dog could ride a bicycle, he would have triathalons licked!

Lionel woke at 8am after a deep sleep, the first since seeing the bronze. He went to his kitchen, made a cup of tea, sat in his Lloyd loom chair and allowed himself a silent review of yesterday. His musings were broken by the sound of feet on his wooden stairs. Like some medieval knight being preceded by a page, Clive rushed into the kitchen, ahead of his master.

"Morning Jack, kettle's just boiled," said Lionel from his chair.

"Morning, did you sleep well?" this was a rhetorical question as Jack had heard a low rumble of contented snoring from the floor below.

"Slept like a log, and you?"

"Very well. What can I do to help today?"

"Firstly, would you retrieve the van from Barty's, as I want to hide the bronze with a couple of blanketed items of furniture, it's vital that Pru does not see that bronze."

"OK, works well for me. I will walk Clive along the seafront again and I might have another swim."

"Take a sarong. There's a selection to choose from in the bottom drawer of the serpentine fronted chest of drawers in your room."

"Many thanks."

On Jack's departure Lionel picked up his phone.

"Morning Barty, I can't tell you how well I slept. I even forgot about the bronze."

"Did you get back alright?"

"We had a lovely walk home, and thank you for the supper. That sea bass was delicious."

"My pleasure, I have just heard back from Pru, who is using a hairdryer to dry the final touches of paint. Can you pick her and the picture up before noon?"

"Jack's just left to retrieve the van. Do you want to come back with him or shall I pick you up after Pru?"

"After Pru please. What's the time now?"

"It's 8.30am. It will take Jack, say an hour, to return back here. We are going to hide the bronze with a couple of blanketed items. Pru and I should be with you at about 11 to 12."

"Perfect. I have booked us into The Swotter Arms for Friday

and Saturday. I have looked at the menu too. It's a proper pub, lots of puddings and pies."

"Marvellous, I'm looking forward to retracing our steps around Norfolk without the angst of finding a bronze! See you shortly, bye."

Ending the call Lionel walked down the stairs and chose a couple of items that might hide the bronze; a 3-fold draught screen, large and light, also his trusty pair of mahogany coffin stands. Then he trudged up the stairs to his kitchen to make a coffee and went to his bedroom to pack for the weekend. All too soon Jack found Lionel in the kitchen with a cup of coffee.

"Van's outside."

"Splendid, just a couple of items to load, then I'm off. I have left coffee in the pot. Not much in the fridge, but do help yourself. There is also some wine in the cellar. Remember The Horse and Groom at the top of the road, but I'm sure Polly and Phoenix will show you around. You have their numbers?"

"Yes, thanks, but let me help you load first. I've filled the van up with diesel." When Lionel was certain that nobody could see the bronze, especially not even an inquisitive Pru, he lurched off the kerb of Norman Road, and made his way up to her. Pru was excited, she had managed to dry the final touches including her signature and date, and had wrapped the canvas with thick brown paper. After loading, they swung around to Barty who was waiting outside with a leather overnight bag and tea towel covered wicker basket.

"Hello Pru, you are looking very glam," said Barty.

"Dapper as ever," she retorted.

Lionel's only offering was,

"What's in the basket?"

"It's a picnic; every road trip should have one. When the conversation dips, I dip into the basket!"

"Fat chance of that," said Pru.

"What?" retorted Lionel.

"Conversation dipping."

"Smells like sausage rolls?" Lionel said hopefully.

"No clues. Come on, let's get going. I can't wait to see this stately Kooling Towers." Lionel lurched off another kerb, heading for Norfolk.

The chatter in the cab was of the weekend ahead, the abstract picture of Sampson, and how Barty and Lionel should address Sir Roger.

Barty teased Lionel with, 'Your Grace,' but Pru steadied the ship with, 'how about Roger?'

After the relief of getting through the Dartford Tunnel, Barty started distributing the contents of his picnic basket: egg and cress sandwiches first, so small and moreish, they were impossible to refuse. Triangles of brown bread, egg mayonnaise, cress with a touch of salad cream for the vinegar edge and only two bites each. Perfect, Lionel thought. He was a lucky bunny to have Pru and Barty as friends, almost a family. Three single people who put Polly and Phoenix above all else.

"Jack is really looking forward to meeting your girls," said Lionel.

"Who wouldn't be?" added Barty.

By the time they had reached the Elveden War Memorial, the picnic basket was empty. They had managed to demolish everything, including three sausage rolls and a palette cleansing apple each. With only one more hour to go before they got to their destination, Barty steered the conversation around to the gardens at Kooling Towers. He did so, in the hope that Pru might suggest a guided tour, around the gardens, so that he could check out where the final resting place for the bronze might be.

On arrival to the village, she pointed out the village shop and The Swotter Arms, before they turned off at a pretty lodge house. As they drove up the drive, the scale of the place became apparent, and a feeling of excitement gripped the occupants of the van.

Lionel parked and all three disembarked, with Pru taking the lead to the front door. She pulled the bell rod, May opened the door, shortly followed by Lady Daphne.

"How lovely, Pru," giving her a kiss on both cheeks.

"May I introduce my two friends," she said.

"This is Barty on my right, and Lionel on my left," gripping each one on the arm to verify their identification.

"I have heard a lot about you two, and how you have looked after my dear friend. Come in and have some tea."

Daphne turned and lead them to the conservatory. As if pre-planned, May appeared with tea and cake, a lemon drizzle. During tea, it was established that Sir Roger was busy at a County Council meeting, and so a plan was hatched to hide the painting in Pru's bedroom until Sir Roger's birthday on Saturday. On Daphne's excited prompt, they got up and followed her through the house to the van. Lionel opened the Mercedes Sprinter's split rear doors and clambered in. As he discarded the ties and blankets, Barty, Daphne and Pru looked in.

"This brings back memories," said Lady Daphne, "What have you got on the van?"

Both Barty and Lionel tensed. Thankfully Lady Daphne continued,

"Pru, I remember when Big Carol and I used to watch runners peeling off grey blankets in the hope of selling some antiques.

The excitement was tangible. Christmas every day! Big Carol did more deals on that road in Chelsea, than any high street store, and none ever troubled a card machine! As he used to say, 'Amex is for selling, cash is for buying'."

"What's in the back?" this time it was Pru who was asking.

Lionel quickly released the picture, "A hand please Barty."

He hoped that this was enough to change the subject, luckily it was, as Barty grabbed the other edge of the picture.

"It does look large," Daphne said to Pru, "how exciting. I can't wait to see it. Follow me boys!"

As the party approached the front door, it was magically opened by the ever-attentive May.

"Are you alright?" enquired Daphne as she wafted ahead, leading them through the hall and down a corridor. This was new to both Lionel and Barty, not that Barty saw much as he was walking backwards. Lionel had mastered carrying objects always walking forwards. Just before the party turned another corner, Daphne raised her right arm and the party stopped.

"Pru, this is the spot I had in mind. Abstracts need distance, don't they?"

"It should be perfect on this corner especially with this North window," replied Pru smiling.

"Well, shall we unwrap it then and see?"

"No," replied Pru firmly, "it will be more exciting for you both, if you and Roger first see it together."

"You are right. Boys, you can leave it leaning here and May will organise its removal before the birthday boy gets home. Come on, who wants to see the garden? It's all rather exciting outside, lots of tents, bars and bunting."

After walking through the sitting room, the party emerged

on to the South Terrace. The space and light reminded Barty of an even more beautiful Côte d'Azur. Certainly, the Indian Bean Trees filtered the light into a much hotter yellowy green. Daphne led her party through numerous garden rooms til they came across a pretty cream coloured canvas tent with red painted wooden poles.

"That is Roger's prized tent. I commissioned it for his 40th birthday. It's an exact copy of his grandfather's 1920s one," said Daphne continuing, "It will house the raffle prizes. Let's duck under the ropes, we can get back to the house along the hornbeam walk."

As the party manoeuvred around the tent's guy ropes, they passed a pylon-shaped flint plinth. Barty tapped Lionel on his arm and pointed to it.

On returning to the house, Barty mentioned to Daphne that he had a magnum of Vondeling Rosé wine from South Africa in the van, which he would be more than happy to donate to the raffle.

"That's very generous of you. Would you like me to take it?" said Daphne.

'No need, I'd be very happy to drop it off on our way out, as I would love to look at that gorgeous tent again?'

"How kind. Just park on the drive and then you can walk down the hornbeam walk."

"Is that the walk we just took to return to the house?"

"That's right, and have a lovely weekend, you two."

"We will and thank you for the tea. That lemon drizzle cake was delicious."

"Bye boys, have fun in Norfolk," said Pru as she stood next to Daphne.

Chapter 44
Norfolk

"Can we really do it now? Shouldn't we wait for darkness?" said a rather flustered Lionel.

"Can you imagine us carrying a heavy bronze in the dark? Plus, you heard Lady Daphne, Sir Roger is away. Let's take the magnum down to the tent and carefully recce the route first."

They drove the short distance down the drive.

"I can see the top of the hornbeam now," said Barty looking left. "Let's stop here." Lionel stopped the van on the drive, as the verges looked too pristine to park on. Barty retrieved a magnum of Rosé from his overnight bag and made their way to the hornbeam walk. It had a blind end where the branches had been vertically trained just 2 feet off the ground. They both walked to one side and ducked underneath the lower branches. As they stood up they saw the vacant plinth at the far end of the walk. They looked at each other and walked slowly further down, past an opening to their left, both pausing and looking towards an elevation of the Towers only some 50 yards away. Nobody was about, complete silence. They continued towards the empty plinth. Both hearts were thumping. Barty's grip on the bottle tightened as they approached it. It stood in the middle of the walk about 5 foot wide by 6 brick's deep. The top was made up of shallow paver bricks laid with thin white lime mortar lines. The top surface was hip height and either side of the plinth were the tent's guy ropes anchored with large metal spikes. Beyond it and before the blind hornbeam end, was an arched opening to the left which was partially covered by the canvas tent.

"Let's squeeze through here and look in the tent," Barty suggested.

In Sir Roger's tent was a cloth-covered trestle table. On it stood various raffle prizes: boxes of chocolates, tins of biscuits and a few bottles of wine.

"Looking at this lot, your magnum could make first prize," whispered Lionel looking at the table, "Once we have replaced the bronze, won't it stand out?"

"You're right, these guy ropes aren't going to hide anything. We have blankets on the van but it might be too obvious. Let's look for ancillary stuff, crates for china and glass and any other items that the hire companies have left."

They looked behind the raffle tent, nothing, about 10 yards away was a larger tent, presumably for lunches and teas. They scuttled across with Barty hanging on to the bottle, just in case they were challenged! Behind the tent were a number of large blue boxes, a stack of surplus trestle tables, bingo!

"Let's take the tables first. Thank goodness they are the modern aluminium ones, and not those old finger pinching wooden fellows." said Barty.

Quickly, they stacked lots of empty crates on the trestle tables and then bore them like a large stretcher, passing behind the raffle tent through the tight opening to the plinth.

"Have we got enough, do you think?"

"I don't know but it's a start, let's get the bronze and see." replied Lionel, "and I'm sure you can leave the bottle here."

Barty nodded, they strode up the walk, pausing at the opening to check for anybody outside the house. Charged with a combination of excitement and adrenaline, they quickly scrambled into the van and slid the bronze to the back, then looked at each other and said,

"Here goes!"

Once off the van, they placed the bronze on the grass, and Lionel bent down and grabbed the horses two back legs rolling the head towards Barty.

"It will be easier to carry on the diagonal," he whispered.

Somehow, they covered the ground quickly without stopping, once by the plinth, Lionel gave the bronze a final heave, managing to get one corner on the top of a brick edge.

"Hold the balance, and I will come around." As Lionel moved to the head end, they both lifted it up, and roughly slid it into place.

"Looks perfect. I'm sure the jockey would have looked down the walk.'

"Spot on," said Lionel, hurrying to balance the blue crates on the brick plinth. After covering all sides he lent the trestle tables on their ends to hold the crates in place.

"I saw a folded canvas amongst the crates. Grab the bottle, let's retrieve that cover too." Barty was now getting anxious, and carried the magnum much like a priest might carry a crucifix in the presence of evil. They retrieved the heavy tarpaulin and threw it over the crates and trestle tables. Only once all was covered did Barty place the magnum of Rosé on the raffle table.

"Why don't you leave one of your cards with the bottle. Organisers like to know who has donated the prizes, especially good ones."

Then they quickly made their way back to the van, before leaving the walk and turned to check their handiwork.

"Absolutely spot on," said Barty, "it looks like the hire company have stacked their empty crates on the plinth."

"It does too, but let's get going before somebody spots us!"

Once safely back in the van, they drove down the drive past the lodge house.

"I cannot believe that we have just done that. Hooray."

They drew out on to the highway back to the village.

On arrival at The Swotter Arms, they took the right hand entrance off the central coaching arch. Pushing the door open they took in an Inn that hadn't changed much since the exotic Sir Noel Swotter had refurbished it in the early 1900's. Wide elm boards on the floor from which oak panelling rose, covering every wall to a height of 4ft. From then on, the painted walls were paved in pictures. Lionel and Barty turned to each other and smiled a silent 'we've done it' smile. This gentle moment was broken by,

"Evening gentlemen, are you checking in?" said a handsome woman dressed in a navy blue guernsey jumper and jumbo corduroy trousers.

"We are," said Barty, who tended to speak on behalf of Lionel regarding admin matters.

"What a lovely old Inn. Does it have much history?"

"Never mind history, that's all in the past, and won't mind waiting a little longer. Would you like to see your rooms first or a drink?"

"The latter, please," said Lionel springing into speech.

"Two pints of bitter please."

Barty gave Lionel an old fashioned look

"Beer?"

"A recent convert." Lionel shrugged.

"I really liked that beer at The Bell Inn and I pushed myself lifting the br...."

Lionel wasn't allowed to finish. A reflex finger to the lips from Barty brought the word 'bronze' up short.

As the landlady pulled the pints, Barty whispered

"Loose talk costs ....."

"It's done and forgotten."

"Two pints of Camel, brewed in Kooling. I have put you in rooms 103 and 105 at the back, as there is not much traffic noise. Where are you from?" asked the landlady Anita, placing 2 foaming pints on the bar.

"We are up from the South Coast." said Barty.

"Here for the cricket at Kooling Towers?"

"No," he replied, my friend Lionel here is an antiques dealer and he has always wanted to go to the Beccles Antiques Market."

"You'll love it, lots of bargains, but get there early!"

"No need to worry on that score. Antique dealers, like bakers, are morning people."

Chapter 45

Norfolk

Sir Roger returned home ten minutes after Lionel and Barty had safely passed the entrance lodge house. He made his way through the hall towards his study, but he altered his course towards the sound of laughter coming from the sitting room. The appearance of a bounding Sampson confirmed the location of his wife. As he entered the room he found Pru and Daphne seated on the sofa separated by the pugs. Pru stood and kissed Sir Roger, whilst Daphne remained seated and graciously proferred an upturned cheek to her husband.

"I was just giving Pru the low-down of who we have invited to your birthday party," said Daphne.

"Good, but tell me, who was prompting the laughter?"

"Your cousin Willy and Judith."

"You haven't invited Willy, have you? We both love Judith, but Willy, please?"

"He is your first cousin and it's a special birthday, Roger."

"I know, but he might frighten our friends. He hasn't been to the barber's since his father died, and that must be a good 10 years ago! Daphne, have you seen him recently? He's a real fright."

"Don't be so stuffy Roger. Admittedly he is alarming in

appearence but he is also great fun. I was telling the story of Willy taking his mother on her last holiday to Brighton."

"Don't, Pru will get a jaundiced view of us Swotters."

"He sounds a scream and Daphne has kindly seated me next to him," said Pru.

"You will have fun and its jolly lucky it wasn't his father, Uncle Norman. He really had no filter."

At that moment, the dream team of May and Cecil entered the room. May placed 2 plates of canapés on the sofa table and then took the wine cooler from Cecil whilst he held 3 champagne flutes ready for Sir Roger, who did the honours and opened the bottle. As Cecil handed out the glasses, May offered the canapés: smoked salmon on tiny circular cut flat breads and pretty little baked potatoes cut with a cross and topped with sour cream and chives.

"They look so good, May," said Daphne taking one, "it isn't going to burn me?"

"No, Cecil and I have tested one each in the kitchen. They took 45 minutes to bake and 15 minutes to cool," replied May.

"They are absolutely scrummy," said Daphne turning to Pru, "Roger and I watched a killing interview on the television recently, with this most delightful old American lady whose husband had owned an Hollywood studio. They had hosted the Queen for a dinner during a Royal Tour. She recounted that they had staged it in a large studio, filled with Hollywood's finest producers, directors, actors and actresses. This lovely widow then went on to say, how at dinner, she had produced a baked potato from her black patent leather handbag and slipped it onto her plate. The Queen, who noticed the smuggling of the potato, asked, "Do you always carry a baked potato?" and the mogul's wife replied, "Only when my husband takes me out to functions. You never know what you are going to be served, so my cook always ensures that I have a baked potato, wrapped in a napkin. Sometimes, I eat it and other times I just keep it in its napkin and use it like a mini hot water bottle. I'm getting older, and do feel the cold so." To which the Queen retorted, "What a sensible idea."

"What a wonderful story" Pru interjected, Daphne continued,

"This lovely old grandee looked like a powdered teenage girl in a Chanel suit, with her legs dangling above ground from a beautiful giltwood chair. She must have been at least 90 but she had the vigour and figure of a teenager! May, are we having these lovely potatoes tomorrow?"

"Yes, you are, along with Sir Rogers' favourite lamb mince samosas," replied May.

"Marvellous, plus what's the funny bread under the salmon?" enquired Sir Roger.

"It's a yogurt flatbread with dill, Sir Roger."

"Not that buffalo yogurt again!"

May and Cecil retired to work on dinner, both courses of which were to be repeated at Sir Roger's birthday lunch.

"I'm getting rather excited about my birthday. Tell Pru what's happening tomorrow."

"Breakfast at 9am. Afterwards, Pru and I will check the tables, then at 12.30, your guests will start arriving. If it's fine, I think we should have drinks on the South Terrace but if it's too cold or wet, I think we should be in the hall. Lunch will be in the tent whatever the weather."

"Anything in the evening?" Roger asked.

"Hopefully, we will have prized your cousin Willy away from Pru, and the three of us can enjoy a bowl of soup with a debrief in the library."

"What time does the match start on Sunday?" Daphne enquired.

"Normal start for cricket, eleven in the morning."

"How many people do you think will turn up?" asked Daphne.

"Well, last year, we had 200 spectators, plus teams, umpires etc. so, probably about 250."

"May and her team served 180 lunches last year, didn't she Roger?"

"Well, talk of a good cook travels. What with the entry fee, food and drink sales, we raised more than enough to keep our 2 talented Sri Lankan players for the season."

"What time are your friends picking you up on Sunday Pru?" asked Daphne.

"I should imagine around teatime, as I know they are getting up early to go to the Beccles Antiques Fair then, knowing them, lunch!"

"I look forward to meeting them. Daphne said they are very kind to you and the girls," said Sir Roger.

Daphne rose. "Come on Pru, May will be expecting us."

She took her arm and led her out of the sitting room and whispered,

"I have a surprise for Roger. His lovely friend, and our Doctor, Alasdair is piping us into lunch tomorrow. It will be such fun! You know Roger complains about Willy, in fact they are, and have always been since small children, as thick as thieves!"

Whilst Sir Roger, Daphne and Pru sat down to gazpacho followed by curried chicken with spinach and lentils, Barty and Lionel were getting outside pies in The Swotter Arms. Anita had recommended the venison and red onion one with runner beans, which had come from the one-man market garden Jim, whose wife Mary ran the village stores next door. Anita was lucky to be supplied by Jim. She and her chef, Matt, had a delivery every morning. A cardboard box stuffed with Jim's vegetables which he exchanged for an empty one, to be used the next day, just like leaving empty bottles for the milkman. This routine was only broken every Saturday morning when he delivered in person. Then over a coffee they chatted about what vegetables would be at their best for the coming week. Anita liked to tell her customers that those who were lucky enough to get Jim's vegetables, enjoyed better, healthier, and even longer lives. As the waitress, Jess, brought out the pies, Anita ushered Barty and Lionel to a circular table next to a woodburning stove.

"Jess, two wine glasses please," instructed Anita, as she placed a bottle of Côtes du Rhône aboard. Anita poured just the right amount of wine, above the hip of the glass, and then filled their water glasses.

"I hope you like Matt's pies, and wave a napkin if you need me or Jess, as it will soon be standing room only. Friday nights get pretty busy here!"

When Anita and Jess were safely behind the bar Lionel raised his glass and said,

"To a true friend. Who has put himself in harm's way, helping me restore the b..... to Kooling Towers and preserve my trading name in our lovely home town of Hastings."

"I wouldn't have done it for anybody else but you. As without you, my life would be much poorer," responded Barty.

Chapter 46

Norfolk

The early creeping sunshine eased the village of Kooling in Norfolk into a new day. Whilst Barty and Lionel slept at The Swotter Arms, May, Cecil and Lou were ticking off jobs. If Cecil and Lou could do most of the jobs this morning they would be ahead when the public came for the cricket on Sunday. Cecil had already mowed the cricket square whilst Lou had cut the out field. May was making a coffee when Sir Roger came through the kitchen swing door.

"Happy birthday, Sir Roger."

"Many thanks, what a beautiful day."

As he spoke, May handed him a cup of coffee with birthday chocolate sprinkles on the top.

"Thank you May, that's very kind. Now are we all set for today?"

"Foodwise, we are prepped. Cecil is going to look after the waiting team who are scheduled to arrive at 10.30, and I will ensure that everything is ready in the kitchen. After coffee, Cecil and Lou are going to move the wine and ice into the tent. Do you want drinks in the Hall now that the weather is set fair?"

"Drinks outside, but better let Lady Daphne have the final word," he continued.

"Cecil, I have stacked those boxes of wine on the wooden pallet at the foot of the cellar steps. Have we got our trusty Croatian in your waiting team?"

"Darko, and his Omar Sharif moustache and bow tie will be on top-up duty," replied Cecil.

"Marvellous. No party is complete without that man. How is the cricket pitch?"

"All good. Lou has given it the final cut."

"Thank you."

Sir Roger made his farewells, and took his coffee to the conservatory. All seemed in order and it wasn't long before he was joined by Lady Daphne and Pru.

"Happy birthday Roger."

"Thank you Pru, aren't we lucky with the weather!"

"It's perfect," said Daphne serving the yoghurt and berries.

"I must tell May that drinks will be on the South Terrace, but before our guests arrive I would like to give you your birthday present."

"How exciting," said Roger as he held out his hands for a package.

"It's not that small, Roger!"

"All in good time, let's eat, I'm starving."

After breakfast, Daphne and Pru led Sir Roger through the hall and along the sitting room corridor. At the end, hung a large picture, covered in brown paper.

"Stay there and close your eyes Roger," instructed Daphne, as she and Pru continued walking towards the wrapped frame. They were a good 20 feet away when both the ladies turned to see Sampson sitting next to Sir Roger.

"Tear away," said Daphne to Pru. The brown paper wrapping

came off in large sheets, as Pru had lightly used, the masking tape. Once removed, both Daphne and Pru turned towards Sir Roger.

"You can open your eyes now."

As he looked up from stroking Sampson, ruffling the top of Sampson's broad head.

"It's my boy," he exclaimed.

"You are clever Pru, it looks just like him. Just bigger and better!"

Daphne and Pru walked back to rejoin Roger and the still seated Sampson.

"You haven't lost it," Daphne congratulated Pru, "You truly are very talented."

"It's marvellous. Thank you Pru, and to my lovely wife, what a fabulous present."

Sir Roger kissed Daphne and said,

"I'm so lucky to have you."

Then all three just stood and took in the abstract image of a bigger and better Sampson.

"You two are crafty, I had no idea you had even hung this."

"We have to thank May, Cecil and Lou. As stealth of this sort takes teamwork."

"Pru, I really am delighted. What a present."

"Well we must away and see that all's good with May, and check the tables in the tent. Remember, guests arrive at 12.30 and I have no doubt that Willy and Judith will be here before then!"

Daphne and Pru left a marvelling Sir Roger and Sampson. The picture only employed 4 colours that Sir Roger could see. Where his master stood, Sampson stood and where Roger was looking Sampson looked too. He could see Sampson's broad head, his chin and 'seen it all before' eyes. It was clever in it's thrift. Pru had caught his boy and conveyed his steady manner. As Sir Roger turned back towards the hall he exclaimed, 'Extraordinary!'

Elsewhere, Daphne led Pru to the kitchen.

"I know you like cooking Pru, you will love May's kitchen."

Daphne pushed the copper finger plate of the green baize kitchen door. Beyond, was a light-filled room centred on a large scrubbed pine table. May stood behind it, almost lost in its vastness, but her presence was established by her ceaseless work, and she was currently chopping great big bundles of parsley with a knife the size of her forearm.

"May, Pru is my foodie friend. Have you got the time to show her around your kitchen?"

"Of course."

"Show her your new friend."

A twinkle moved into May's eyes. Pru scanned the room looking for this new friend. There was a four-oven cooker below a stainless steel canopy which must have once housed a cast iron range. On the wall stood 2 large commercial stainless steel fridges quietly guarding a larder door. May put down her knife and pointed towards the wall behind Pru.

"Lady Daphne and Sir Roger bought me this last year."

Pru turned and came face to face with a glass-doored oven on a shelved stainless steel stand.

"Wow, I haven't seen a Rational oven outside a commercial kitchen before," said Pru.

"Well, after May fed 180 people at last year's cricket match, I said to Roger that she needs more help. We were thinking along the lines of an apprentice, but May said she would rather have 'somebody who didn't need instructions and worked the same hours as she did!'"

May paused to respectfully ensure Lady Daphne had finished

speaking before she scooted around to her oven and opened the door. At once it emitted a warm bright light, and its control panel became animated.

"Lady Daphne and Sir Roger were so kind. It just makes my life so much easier. Now, when the Hall is full of choral singers at Christmas, I can cook 200 sausage rolls, and when the dining room is full I can deliver perfectly cooked beef wellington for thirty."

"That's why Pru, nobody turns down an invitation to Kooling, do they May?"

Before May could answer, Lady Daphne said,

"You are a dream, May. Come on Pru let's check on the tent," she swept her towards the garden door with just enough time to mouth a 'thank you' to May. Outside, they were joined by Daphnes' dogs. All of them knew that they weren't welcome in May's kitchen, as she would not tolerate dogs with pleading eyes and dribbling mouths, watching her trimming meat. Even May's own dog, Punch, had never entered her workplace.

Once Daphne had inspected the tent she and Pru walked back to the South Terrace.

"I think we can say your picture was a success!"

"I hope so," said Pru.

"You know I really enjoyed doing it. It was like being back at Art School again, it felt fun."

"I bet you Roger drags Willy along to look at it. They will both stand there, with Sampson sitting behind and looking in silence until Willy will ruffle Sampson's head and say, 'She's got you boy,' and then in silence they will potter back to the party. I do believe that he and Roger use telepathy to talk. A lifetime of shared interests in the country seems to have given them both that extra sense."

Daphne and Pru suddenly became aware of a wild haired man wearing, what appeared to be, a sand-coloured tropical suit. Behind him was an animated floral printed curtain. Before he could be identified beyond reasonable doubt, the tropical explorer shouted,

"Judith, Daphne's here."

As the two neared Daphne, she turned to Pru and softly said, "into the fray!"

Chapter 47
Norfolk

Barty and Lionel finally got to Holt just before noon. They had had a slow start, probably due to the relief of their previous afternoon's activity. As they had only been there a week ago, no time was lost finding its antique shops. So far, Barty had bought two 19th century steel-bladed knives. The blades were large enough to be used as chef's knives, plus they had fat horn handles and easily sharpened soft steel blades. Lionel had bought an Ashford black marble desk thermometer. He had always been keen on Ashford marble, explaining to Barty that they were made of coloured limestone rich in bitumen, hence the colour, and not, as commonly thought, black slate. This particular limestone is found close to the Derbyshire village of Ashford-in-the-Water. The stone being quite soft, can be cut and inlaid with decorative stones and minerals, using a technique known as Pietra dura. Lionel's obelisk had a Mercury thermometer with silvered scale between two strings of the realistic flowers: one of Forget-me-Nots and one of Periwinkles.

"Barty you're a flower and vegetable man. What do forget-me-nots symbolise?"

"I haven't a clue."

"Apparently the month of May is the busiest time for witch activity. But fear not! If you wear a spray of forget-me-nots, this will protect you against spells and potions."

"What a font of knowledge you are."

"I haven't finished there. Periwinkles?"

"Again, not a clue."

"The plant is often given to newlyweds having a reputation as an aphrodisiac!"

"I'm impressed Lionel."

"Don't be, it's all written down on the sales tag!"

"You old fraud!"

"I need to eat. My blood sugar is dangerously low."

"Can you manage a short drive?" replied Barty.

"Yes, but on condition that we share a sausage roll from Byfords Deli."

"Of course. You retrieve the van, and I will meet you outside Byfords." Five minutes later both were re-united tucking into half a sausage roll each.

"Where to?" asked Lionel.

"To Wiveton Farm Café. It's 12 minutes away, north east towards the coast."

"I have heard of it. It's owned by the man with the eyebrows, but won't it be busy on a Saturday lunch?"

"I'm sure it will, but I believe it's always packed. Let's take our chances."

They were right, it was heaving.

"Isn't it beautiful amongst these marshes? I wonder how Pru is getting along. I do hope Sir Roger liked his painting."

"We will find out tomorrow," said Barty.

At Kooling Towers the lunch party had finished, and Willy

had finally been torn away from Pru. Roger, Daphne and Pru sat in a now empty tent and enjoyed the large canvas covered space.

"There is always something ethereal about canvas light," commented Roger.

"More memories of Cubs and Scouts," said Daphne, winking at Pru.

"That was a truly lovely lunch and to be piped in as well. May's samosas were very special. Was it spring onion with the lamb?"

"It was," said Roger.

"I had a couple in the kitchen with May yesterday. She made 150!"

"What did Willy make of the picture?" asked Daphne.

"He saw Sampson immediately."

Sunday couldn't come soon enough for Kevin Smythe, he liked cricket and he also liked Kooling Towers, plus, he had a hunch that a lead on the bronze might unfold. The match started at 11am, but Kevin wanted to get there for 9.30am. Experience had taught him that watching people arrive at events had unspoken signals. Where some are nervous, others are bold. Did they stroll purposefully towards the refreshments tent or did they stalk about? He would station himself opposite the tent and watch for people straying away.

In London, Mercy and her mother were boarding the 8am train from Liverpool Street to Sheringham. Mercy's father was to join them later in Norfolk but, in his absence, he had organised a taxi from Sheringham to Kooling Towers. He knew that his wife liked to travel by train, and understood the connnection it gave to her deceased parents.

"I like your job," said Mercy's mother, "so far it's taken us to Brighton, Hastings, and now Norfolk. Tell me about Kooling Towers and more importantly, its owners."

"I have only spoken to Sir Roger Swotter on the telephone. He is serious, like Daddy. I'm really looking forward to seeing the houseå. It sounds like a mythical castle. I know the Detective Inspector from Norfolk Police will be there too."

"How exciting, castles and drama. It sounds like something out of a Harry Potter of Agatha Christie novel."

Lionel and Barty were up and out of The Swotter Arms by first light, as Lionel knew that both Antique Markets and Car Boots are at their best right at the very beginning. Shortly after passing the road sign for Beccles town they started seeing parked white vans. Lionel parked his carefully keeping four inches from the kerb so as not to scuff the tyres. He knew Jack loved his Mercedes Sprinter, and he recognised the kindness in which Jack had freely loaned it. As they alighted and locked it, they headed in the direction of the church tower, knowing it to be the epicentre of this one-day market. Drawn in different directions, Lionel buying with vigour, recording each purchase with a photo. No point in lugging said purchases back to the van until the very end. So far, he had bought a folding purple baise covered bridge table for £45. It was not something he normally bought, but it had two differences to the norm: a manufacturers label and 4 concealed swing drinks wells. He knew it was the decorative and unusual that generally sold first. Barty was near the church, and he was now clutching a trug basket into which was squeezed a Le Creuset 2-handled saucepan with lid and a small but heavy, copper saucepan. He had bought the latter as the interior tinning was perfect. He was beginning to regret collecting his purchases, but he was of the old school; once bought, he needed possession. He did not have the easy-come-easy-go attitude of a dealer like Lionel. He looked at his watch after placing another purchase in his trug: a lovely circular sycamore bread board into which was carved the motto 'Waste not want not.' Normally the edges were crudely carved with ears of wheat. He had paid £30 for this one, he knew that Pru collected them, and felt sure that she didn't have this improving motto amongst her collection.

It was only 8am, but it felt like noon. He popped into a café and bought 2 cappuccinos to give them both a little lift. He rang Lionel to find out his whereabouts. Two minutes later he came across him negotiating with an angry looking man at the back door of a red Renault van.

"This man still wants £375 for 4 Lloyd Loom chairs and their matching circular table. He says that the Wimbledon dark green is an unusual colour, and I have reminded him that he has had it for sale since 5.30 this morning! Barty, he is just not having my offer of £220 being £30 for each chair and £100 for the table!"

Lionel would have carried on if it wasn't for the angry man suddenly saying,

"Piss off you old poof!"

"Now, there is no need for that," retorted Lionel taking a step away from the angry man, "£275 is my final offer."

"Done, and I bloody well have been!"

Lionel brought out the cash and paid the owner. As they moved away Barty handed Lionel his cappuccino.

"That was very close, I thought he was going to hit me for a moment."

"As an observer, that was my impression too!"

"I never thought this was a dangerous occupation before now. No doubt, in the future, we will only be allowed to enter the market in helmets and hi-vis," mused Lionel.

"I'm sure your trade is safe enough. Rather funny that Wimbledon furniture should bring out that man's inner McEnroe."

As Barty said this, Lionel's phone began to ring.

"Hello, Lionel speaking."

"It's Ollie Croyd from St James's, about your Chinese vases that your friend Norman dropped in last week. I do apologise for ringing you on a Sunday."

"No problem, I'm currently buying at a street market in Beccles," said Lionel.

Ollie Croyd pressed on, "The reason I'm calling today, is that I'm catching a flight to Hong Kong tomorrow, and I would like to take your vases with me as we have squeezed them in our current Oriental sale."

Lionel put his hand over the receiver, and whispered to Barty.

"My luck may just be about to turn!" Lionel removed his hand and continued,

"How exciting. Have you put an estimate on them?"

Ollie Croyd replied and it was only then that Lionel dropped his cappuccino!

Chapter 48

Norfolk

Detective Inspector Kevin Smythe, his wife Helen and their two children, were the first guests to arrive at Kooling Towers. Whilst Kevin established an observation spot by rearranging a table and two chairs to face the main tent, Helen and the children explored the garden and grounds. Once the observation spot met with his approval, Kevin made his way to the refreshment tent, where he found Cecil and Lou tapping two barrels of beer.

"Morning Mr Trowel"

"Good morning Sir," replied Cecil.

"All set for today's cricket?"

"The wicket has life and the boundary flags are in place, so just the beer to tap now, and then we will be ready."

"How many are you expecting?"

"Hopefully, around 200 plus the cricketers."

"Thank you Mr Trowel, and when you see Sir Roger, would you tell him that I am here?"

"Of course, Sir, I will be sure to tell him."

Kevin returned to his observation station feeling better that his presence was duly logged. It wasn't long before the players started arriving; all bags and bats. They made their way to a

Victorian white-painted cricket pavilion whose roof extended to cover a wooden floored verandah, enclosed by a rather attractive Chinese pattern trellis railing. It seemed a little exotic for a cricket pavilion: no doubt, another addition by the late Sir Noel Swotter. Sir Roger, Sampson, Lady Daphne, pugs and Pru, arrived at the pavilion shortly before the umpires and team captains walked out on to the wicket. After tossing a coin and numerous handshakes, the party of 3 returned to the pavillion. Within five minutes the game had begun. Kooling village had put Wiveton Hall into bat first. The first wicket fell within 2 overs. Kevin thought this could be all over quite shortly, but luckily batsman number 3, who had a very impressive pair of eyebrows, steadied the batting partnership. Then, Sir Roger's party who had been meeting the players, moved from the pavilion to the refreshment tent. Kevin thought that they made a graceful party: Lady Daphne in a large panama hat and boldly printed orange dress, was followed by Sir Roger chatting to another lady, with the honourable Sampson adding quiet gravitas to the walking party. Arriving at the tent, Lady Daphne checked on Cecil and Lou and enquired whether May was happy. Once they were settled with coffees, Kevin allowed his observations to wander to other people. It being only 11.30am, the ground was lightly peopled with wives and children of the two cricket teams. Nothing suspicious to report thus far, thought Kevin.

Mercy and her mother were met at Sheringham station by a charming man with a broad Norfolk accent. He was intrigued that two ladies should travel 3 hours from London to watch a cricket match but, as he said, or at best Mercy could make out, "Kooling was no ordinary village." Once the taxi turned into the drive past the pretty little lodge house, the smiles and the arm clutching started.

"It's magnificent and pretty too," said Mercy's mother. "Isn't it exciting?"

Just before they arrived at the house, the taxi followed a sign saying 'cricket visitors' which led them to a 200 metre avenue of tall lime trees, at the end of which, they found other cars before a perfect Victorian landscape of a cricket pavillion and ground.

"How charming," Mercy's mother said, as she paid the bearded owner of the Norfolk accent.

"Now, if you want collecting at anytime, mind you call me."

"Many thanks but we are hoping my husband will collect us later."

In search of coffees, Mercy led her mother towards the larger tent.The Detective Inspector's watchful eye locked on to what he assumed were an elegant mother and daughter team. The daughter wore a pink linen top with white flared linen trousers and white Gucci loafers, whereas her presumed mother, seemed to be teaming a nautical blue and white striped jersey with navy blue palazzo pants and an oversized light tan bag. As the two neared the tent, Sir Roger stood up and greeted the younger of the 2 women. He was then introduced to the older one. He observed that the greeting was business like, as one might adopt on a first meeting. He decided now was the time to make himself known to Sir Roger. As he approached the group, Sir Roger caught his eye.

"Ah, how fortuitous, Detective Inspector, may I introduce you to Mercy Penfold and her mother Rose."

"What a pleasure to, at last, finally meet you," said Kevin to Mercy, before quickly turning his attention to Sir Roger.

"What a lovely day, we are lucky with the weather."

"We are, but do we have any luck with my bronze?" replied Sir Roger.

"The investigation is ongoing, Sir."

"Mercy and her mother have been travelling since early this morning. May I suggest Detective Inspector that you have a coffee together, as Mercy has done a little digging of her own in Hastings."

"It would be my pleasure, Sir Roger."

"Marvellous. But before coffee why don't you show them the crime scene?"

"Come with me ladies," said Kevin as he guided mother and daughter towards the hornbeam walk.

"Sir Roger said you went to Hastings. Did you find this Mr Hix?"

"No. We first went to meet Sergeant Arnold in Brighton who in turn, introduced me to his very glamorous colleague WPC Helen Tredwell."

"How funny, my wife was also a WPC and is a Helen too!"

Both Mercy and her mother giggled at this revelation as they passed a small red poled tent. They turned into the high hedged walk, there right in front of them was a rather untidy stack of tables and crates.

"Here is where the bronze once stood," said Kevin.

"What a mess," Rose said beginning to straighten a crate that looked precariously balanced. As she fussed, she tried to straighten the other crates pushing them away from the edge, but something was in the way, so she slid the stack of crates to one side to identify the obstruction.

"Mercy, will you give me a hand, I believe that there is something larger behind these crates." She started removing them as Kevin manhandled the stacked trestle tables, and with a "one, two and three" Kevin and Mercy pulled away a heavy canvas cover.

There, on the plinth, in front of them all, stood a quarter sized bronze race horse with jockey up!

"Well I never. That definitely was not there three weeks ago," said an extremely baffled Detective Inspector.

"A miracle," gasped Rose.

Ten minutes later, there was a buzz about the place. Sir Roger was congratulating DI Kevin Smythe, Mercy and her mother.

"What a birthday weekend: a surprise portrait of Sampson, a lovely birthday lunch, a cricket match and, to cap it all, Nijinsky and Lester Piggott back where they belong. Order is restored."

At the end of the day it was an animated Sir Roger who drew the raffle prizes. The final and best item in the draw was a Magnum of South African Vondeling Rosé Wine.

"And the final prize goes to, pink 369."

Dective Inspector Kevin Smythe looked down at his strip of pink tickets numbered 365 to 370 and stood up beaming.

As D.I. Smythe walked towards the tent, Sir Roger read a card stuck to the bottle,

'Kindly donated by a...... Mr Barty Hix.'

The End